P9-CFV-952

Tess caught a glimpse of her father talking to someone.

She pushed closer. When she reached his back she started to say, "Dad, I made it. I—" She was interrupted by a popping sound. A champagne cork? Tess wondered. The crowd surged around her and she had to fight to keep her balance.

Lawrence turned then and saw her. Tess grinned. "It wasn't easy, but I—" The words froze on her lips. There was a strange expression on her father's face, one she'd never seen before. Shock, an awful blankness.

"Dad?" she breathed.

He stood there, utterly still, as if paralyzed; his eyes met hers. A hush fell over them, cutting off the noise and wild tumult. Time stopped, held still, and her father's gaze drilled into her, a gaze full of fear and relief and horror and love. And mute supplication, an awful kind of helplessness.

Tess didn't think. She didn't judge. Lawrence's mouth opened, closed. Tears sprang to his eyes.

Then a scream cut through the air like a chef's cleaver. The crowd surged. Everyone was moving, shoving, trying to run. A stampede. Shrieks and sobs and cries.

The canvas sides of the tent were pushed out, ripped, flung aside. Tess was swirled along, outside at last. Blessed air and sun. She took a deep breath and was hastening her steps to get away when she heard a voice cry, "Somebody shot Robbie Childress!"

Also available from MIRA Books and
LYNN ERICKSON

ASPEN
NIGHT WHISPERS
THE ELEVENTH HOUR

LYNN ERICKSON

THE RIPPLE EFFECT

MIRA

If you purchased this book without a cover you should be aware that this book is stolen property. It was reported as "unsold and destroyed" to the publisher, and neither the author nor the publisher has received any payment for this "stripped book."

ISBN 1-55166-498-4

THE RIPPLE EFFECT

Copyright © 1999 by Carla Peltonen and Molly Swanton.

All rights reserved. Except for use in any review, the reproduction or utilization of this work in whole or in part in any form by any electronic, mechanical or other means, now known or hereafter invented, including xerography, photocopying and recording, or in any information storage or retrieval system, is forbidden without the written permission of the publisher, MIRA Books, 225 Duncan Mill Road, Don Mills, Ontario, Canada M3B 3K9.

All characters in this book have no existence outside the imagination of the author and have no relation whatsoever to anyone bearing the same name or names. They are not even distantly inspired by any individual known or unknown to the author, and all incidents are pure invention.

MIRA and the Star Colophon are trademarks used under license and registered in Australia, New Zealand, Philippines, United States Patent and Trademark Office and in other countries.

Printed in U.S.A.

This book is dedicated to
Maureen Stonehouse,
editor and friend.

PROLOGUE

The Robbie Childress murder trial provided all the elements that make news directors salivate: celebrities, courtroom theatrics, extramarital sex, Hollywood, high-profile legal teams and a glamorous blond wife dead long before her time. It had become a peculiar and monumental obsession with the viewing public as it dragged on into its fifth month, the trial of the century. Everyone tuned into the television coverage and avidly watched the drama unfold. When court wasn't in session, they languished in a kind of withdrawal.

Long before the trial, Robbie Childress had made a name for himself as a baseball player, and when his body could no longer take the punishment, he turned to acting. People everywhere recognized him. But now, on trial for the murder of his wife, Andrea, he was known in the farthest reaches of the planet. No one before him had ever attained this particular status. Even his lawyers, the best money could buy, the presiding judge, the Los Angeles district attorney and assistants, were all famous now, each one signing lucrative book contracts and poised to enter the talk-show circuit.

The trial had gone on too long, all the pundits agreed, but it was over now; the jury had been deliberating for days, and late last night the judge had received word from the foreman that they'd reached a verdict. The news was a shot heard round the world: a verdict, at last.

Court convened at nine o'clock in the morning. There was much whispering and murmuring, and tension was high, as everyone speculated on the fate of Robbie Childress.

Theresa Bergen, Tess to her family, entered the courtroom with her parents, Carole and Lawrence. Andrea had been their older daughter, Tess's sister. The three of them had attended the trial every day. At intervals the TV cameras sought out the threesome in the packed courtroom to show viewers their reactions, the minute changes in their expressions, as the interminable stream of witnesses testified.

Commentators remarked endlessly on their dignity, their stoicism, the ordeal they'd undergone.

Tess hated every agonizing minute. She knew, her parents knew, that Robbie had murdered Andie. And they'd had to listen to his hotshot lawyers distract and prevaricate and obfuscate.

Now was the moment of truth. Now the jury would declare Robbie the murderer, reveal him for the egocentric, cold-blooded killer that he was. God, vindication would be sweet.

Tess sat there in her uncomfortable chair, holding her mother's hand, trying to control her expression. She knew the world was watching, but she didn't think about that; her mind was on Robbie and her dead sister, Andie. Now she waited, her heart beating slowly and heavily, her mother's grip on her hand almost painful.

The jury filed in, twelve men and women, their

faces as familiar to the viewing public as the rest of the actors in this show. They sat, their faces unreadable. Tess stared at them, willing them to mete out justice.

She saw Robbie trying to make eye contact with the jurors; his lawyers must have told him to do that, or was it just his incredible egotism? One of the female jurors smiled faintly at him, and he preened. Tess gritted her teeth.

Judge Kennedy's door opened and he entered, his countenance sober, fitting the momentous occasion, his black robe swishing audibly in the hushed courtroom.

Everyone rose, the clerk gave the traditional pronouncement, and then everyone was reseated, the rustle filling the air as if a rookery of birds were settling.

The clerk crossed to the foreman of the jury, who handed him a slip of paper. It was taking so long, so horribly long. Tess couldn't bear another minute, another second. Her father said something under his breath she couldn't hear.

The clerk passed the paper to the judge. The moments ticked by. The judge read it silently, handed it back to the clerk. Everything moved in slow motion, intolerably prolonged.

The clerk began to read the verdict aloud. The courtroom held its collective breath; not a throat was cleared, not a person shifted in his seat.

"In the case of the people of the State of California, County of Los Angeles, against Robert John Childress," the clerk intoned, "we the jury find the defendant Robert John Childress not guilty of murder."

Shock took Tess by the throat, stopping her breath. Her mind screamed *No!*

Her eyes flew to Robbie, and she saw the words hit,

sink home, saw realization coagulate. He bit his lower lip in apparent profound relief, and tears rolled down his cheeks. The head of his defense team clapped him on the shoulder in congratulation. And then she saw Robbie mouth an undoubtedly heartfelt thank-you to the jury. Tess could read them with utter clarity: "Thank you," Robbie had whispered.

No, Tess thought again. It couldn't be happening. Robbie innocent, free? The enormity bludgeoned her, and she felt cold as death.

She looked at the team of prosecutors. All of them with dour faces, tight-lipped disapproval, their hands aimlessly shuffling the useless papers in front of them. One was crying.

Tess heard her mother sobbing, saw her father's profile. He was gray-white, his lips quivering. He looked very old.

Tess leaned across her mother and reached out a hand to her father. Her face twisted in anguish, and she felt tears spring to her eyes. Lawrence put his arms around his wife and daughter, and they held one another tightly, an island of agony in a rapidly emptying courtroom.

Lawrence mumbled something then, and Tess had to strain to hear him. "It's not over," he said. "I swear, it's not over."

And Robbie Childress, surrounded by adoring fans, the frantic media and his high-priced attorneys, walked out of the court into the bright California sun, a free man.

ONE

Seven months later

In Aspen, Colorado, there's no such thing as a subtle change of seasons. The skiers exit the town by mid-April, despite the many inches of snow—sometimes feet—still to fall on the steep mountainsides that bracket the quaint Victorian enclave. April and May are not winter, but neither are they recognizable as spring.

The locals call this transition mud season, the time when winter grudgingly gives way to summer. There is no spring at eight thousand feet. One day the skies are steel gray and blustery, tree branches bare; the next day the leaves of aspen and cottonwood burst forth, snowfields give way to flower-strewn meadows, and the sky is a dazzling blue bowl overhead. It's June.

Tess Bergen was familiar with the cruel Rocky Mountains springtime. While in college and later in medical school, she'd often visited her sister, Andie, and brother-in-law, Robbie, at their second home in the mountains.

Early June, when Tess was done with classes, had been the ideal time for Andie and Robbie to open the Aspen house for the coming summer, and frequently Tess had helped. The perfect houseguest. She'd liked being in Aspen then. It was a peaceful time, the shops reopening after the quiet mud season, streets uncrowded, an air of expectancy hovering over the town. Would it be a long, warm summer? Would the monsoon season come early? Would the tourists invade in their sunburned masses and spread life-giving largesse among the town's merchants?

Several annual events ushered in the idyllic summer season: the world-renowned Aspen Music Festival opened, the International Design Conference convened, the Aspen Institute lured brilliant minds from around the world to its think-tank sessions, and the Bon Vin Festival—a weekend of indulgence in the best foods and wines from the four corners of the earth—kicked it all off.

It was the Bon Vin Festival that brought Tess Bergen and her mother and father to Aspen, Lawrence being the founder and editor in chief of *Bon Vin* magazine. They'd missed the past two years—Andie's murder and the trial of Robbie Childress had consumed them. And though it had been seven months since Robbie's not-guilty verdict was handed down, it was still hard to function in the real world. Tess had lost just about everything but her sanity. Lost her coveted residency spot at the UCLA Medical Center. Lost her friends and her boyfriend and almost lost her parents to the tragedy of Andie's murder and the media charade of Robbie's trial.

A month ago, when Lawrence had to make a decision whether or not to travel to Aspen for the festival, Tess had come unglued. "When are we going to live again?" she'd cried at their Monterey, California, house. "Mom mopes around all day on tranquilizers, afraid to even go grocery shopping, and you, Dad, it's like the weight of the world's on your shoulders. Do you think this would make Andie happy?"

"Please, Tess, don't..." Carole began, then she got up from the dinner table and went to her bedroom, which, ever since the death of her older child, was off-limits to even her husband.

"This isn't like you, Tess. You've upset your mother," Lawrence said.

"My mother? What about me? Dad—" Tess was trying to control herself "—I've missed the last two years of my life. My God, I even missed my thirtieth birthday. I blew my residency, I blew my relationship with Mark. I'm not saying I don't miss Andie. I think about her every second of every day. But I'm done ducking life. I really am. I thought it was all decided. We're going to Aspen for the festival. It's your deal, Dad, your magazine, your contacts. I want to be there with you. With Mom. Then I'm going to work on getting back my spot at the medical center."

"I didn't say we weren't going," Lawrence put in. "It's just that your mother may not be quite ready. There'll still be reporters and cameras, all that to deal with."

"So? Are you saying it's healthy for her to stay cooped up here? Dad, she needs to get back in the swing. She needs to face the fact that Andie's gone now. And I'm not going to be able to get up here to visit for months on end when I start at the hospital. You know how it is. Mom's going to have to deal with it sooner or later, and she's got to quit relying on anti-depressants."

Tess heard it again in her tone, the frustration, the need to take control where there seemed to be none left in her family. She'd donned the mantle of parent.

"Okay," her father finally said.

"Okay what?"

"We'll go to Aspen. I'll open the event this year."

"You will?"

"Yes, I will. You're right—it's time."

"And Mom will go?"

"We'll convince her to."

The next night Tess had taken her mother to dinner and a movie in Monterey, and they'd actually laughed, walked down the sidewalk with Tess's arm tucked into her mother's, and Carole had said, "I feel...good. Oh, Lord, Tess, I actually feel good tonight." After that things had gotten better. Day by day. The healing process had finally begun.

Tess stretched out in the back seat of the car as they drove the final few miles into Aspen, and she listened to her parents talk. Carole even pointed out the street where Andie and Robbie's house sat, and all she said was, "Andie really did love that place. I wonder if Robbie kept it." Then Carole went on to another subject, noting that the lilac bushes dotting the town were just past the prime of their bloom.

Tess said nothing about Robbie's house, though she did catch her father's eye in the rearview mirror. Robbie most certainly still owned it. But neither Tess nor her father wanted to belabor the subject; it only upset Carole, and they conspired constantly to keep Carole on an even keel.

When Lawrence pulled into the condominium complex and announced "Here we are," Tess promised herself that for now she'd think of nothing but the glorious mountain mecca of Aspen. Good times. Renewed friendships. And the best part was that in Aspen it was considered gauche to acknowledge celebrities. At last the Bergen family was going to have some peace.

"I'll get the bags," Lawrence said. "Tess, you and Carole go check us in. We should be in 107. It's a ground-level corner unit on the Ute Avenue side. Nice and quiet."

They'd rented condos at the Gant before, though usually Tess had stayed with Andie at her west end house, giving her parents more privacy. Besides, Andie and Robbie had been a whole lot more fun—in the beginning, anyway.

Tess tried to think only of the good times, but it was difficult. All the more so since she'd sat with Lawrence and Carole for more than four months in the Los Angeles courtroom trying not to look at the police photos of the crime scene. Of Andie.

She walked with her mother to the office and wondered if anything could ever be the same. Were they all just faking it, pretending normalcy was returning to their lives?

The condo unit was luxurious, done in the muted desert colors of the Southwest, right down to the lap blankets strategically placed on the couch and armchairs and the sun-bleached skull of a steer over the mantel. There were three bedrooms, one for Tess, one Lawrence would use as an office and the master suite, which Lawrence and Carole would share. It would be the first time in almost two years that they'd slept in the same bed. Tess unpacked and smiled. Good for them.

It was well after noon when they walked the few blocks to Aspen's downtown Wagner Park, where the huge tent had been set up for the next day's opening of the Bon Vin Festival. Along the route, several people noticed them, but, thank God, no one said a thing or even made eye contact. In a year or so, Tess hoped, people would no longer recognize them at all. She couldn't bear the gawking. Mostly she couldn't bear the pity she read on their faces.

It was a perfect day, a pellucid June sky arching over the town, white-capped peaks on Independence Pass, the air champagne-dry. On the downtown pedestrian malls near the park, the flowers were bursting with life, and café umbrellas sprouted like multicolored mushrooms. Tess loved the aspens. Their leaves always seemed to shiver, and in a rainstorm they defiantly turned silver undersides to the sky.

"It is a wonderful little Shangri-la, isn't it?" Carole said, voicing Tess's thoughts.

If there was a cloud on the horizon, it was the possible presence of Robbie in Aspen. Because of his second home here and because of the festival—where in past years he'd always been highly visible—he was bound to be in town. But surely, Tess thought, despite his addiction to media attention, he wouldn't attend this year. Even Robbie Childress wasn't that crass.

While Tess and Carole waited in the pedestrian mall outside the tent, Lawrence got them their VIP weekend passes. The festival was a very exclusive event. Either you paid to get in or you volunteered to work—but without that pass, worn around your neck on a chain, you wouldn't get past the security guards.

The scene in the big tent was chaotic when Tess and Carole walked in behind Lawrence, who was immediately recognized and besieged with warm welcomes by vintners and distributors and local politicians. No one said a thing about the ordeal the family had undergone for the past two years; they merely said how glad they were that Lawrence was there. It was refreshing, and Tess saw her father easily slip back into his role as the founder and chief dignitary of the event.

The atmosphere was intense yet orderly. Dozens

and dozens of display tables were being lined up, covered with white linen tablecloths, pyramids of sparkling wineglasses, hundreds of bottles of wine, displays of fresh fruits and gourmet foods. At both ends of the tent were grills and sauté stands where the participants could partake of the scrumptious delicacies. Volunteers in their distinctive red T-shirts were bustling everywhere, carrying vases of flowers, trays of glasses, wine spittoons, trash cans and cases of wines from around the world. The air was humming with the expectancy of tomorrow's first grand tasting, scheduled for one in the afternoon.

Tess finally led Carole outside after telling Lawrence they were in the way and were going shopping. Carole had balked at first.

"Oh, honey, I don't know," she'd said.

But Tess had prevailed. "Come on, Mom, it'll be fun. I'll keep the gawkers at bay. We'll meet Dad back at the condo later."

Shopping in Aspen was a unique experience. Aside from a few national chain stores—the Gap, Banana Republic, the Sharper Image—the shops were locally owned and operated. There were gift shops offering select items from countries all over the world. There were clothing and bedding boutiques where you coveted everything and could afford nothing. And art galleries. Loads and loads of galleries—Asian, European, American Southwestern—with price tags that boggled Tess's mind.

She stood in front of an original Remington etching and gaped. "My God. That costs more than four years of student loans. That anyone could just walk in here and lay out this kind of money..."

Tess was up to her eyeballs in debt with loans for medical school. Her parents had been helping her out—before Andie's murder, that is. But since then,

Lawrence's magazine distribution was flagging, and
Carole had given up her job at the Monterey aquarium, where she'd worked in the gift shop. A genteel
job. And Tess...other than putting in volunteer hours
at a nursing home—geriatrics was her field of
choice—she'd barely earned a dime in two years.
She'd deferred her school loans; she'd taken out
credit cards with low interest rates; she'd been careful
not to spend an unnecessary cent on anything. Still,
she was in debt, and everything hinged on getting her
residency. Once she was in practice, the debts would
get paid off. But right now that time seemed very far
in the future.

Carole and Tess stopped at an outdoor café and
had cappuccinos and croissants, turning their faces
up to the dazzling Colorado sun. "God, this feels
great," Tess sighed.

People strolled all around them. Tourists and wine-
festival attendees and music-school students freshly
arrived for the soon-to-open Aspen Music Festival.
Asians and Africans and Europeans here for the acclaimed International Design Conference. Academ-
ics, pale-skinned physicists in town for the meeting of
the minds at the Physics Institute, and would-be writers gathered for the Writers' Conference.

Of course, the streets were jammed with mountain
bikes and Harley-Davidsons. The local Harley own-
ers, Andie had once told Tess, were known as the Ro-
lex Riders. And Tess had giggled over the name with
her sister, who always saw the fun side of things. Almost always.

There were people in hiking gear, having just
trekked up Aspen Mountain. There were buses—
quaint little purple-and-yellow buses—with river
rafts stacked on top. There were pedestrian-mall gui-
tarists and a balloon-twisting clown. Tess laughed,

shaking her head. The old silver-mining town was like a carnival.

Tess was really enjoying herself. Despite the pain of losing her sister and the verdict at the murder trial, she realized she was truly coming back to life, ready to hit the books again, ready to work like a dog to complete her residency and begin a practice. It's what Andie would have wanted.

She looked at Carole, who seemed content to people-watch. Her mother still concerned her. The antidepressants. But maybe, with encouragement, Carole could begin to cut down and eventually not need the drugs. Tess didn't expect her mother—or her father or herself—to ever get over the loss of Andie or the injustice of the verdict. But she'd learned one thing from all this—life wasn't always fair. You had to go on, find the best way to survive.

That was what her father had done. She remembered her father's words moments after the verdict had been read, when he'd drawn Tess and Carole close: *It's not over. I swear, it's not over.*

Tess had thought a lot about what he'd meant, and she'd come to the conclusion that he believed firmly that someday, somehow, Robbie was going to have to account for his actions. In this life or the next, the piper would have to be paid.

For now, though, the family was just learning how to survive, going on with life, learning to accept what fate had so cruelly dealt. The Bergens were going to make it; they were survivors.

They dined at the elegant Hotel Jerome that evening with the president of the Aspen Resort Association, Jim Hinds, his wife and twenty-something son, Keith. The young man was tall and tanned and fit, a typical Aspen male specimen. Tess had to acknowledge his attractiveness even though he was at least five years her junior, but it was only an intellectual exercise.

The truth was, she was utterly off men. Andie's relationship with Robbie, the years of wild ups and downs, the abuse, the murder, had killed off any romantic yearnings Tess might have had. She felt sexless, without physical needs. So sitting next to this handsome and attentive young man was having no effect on her.

He was impeccably polite, even interested in her choice of career. "I admire you for going into geriatrics," he said at one point during the main course. "Old people make me a little nervous. I guess it's because no one wants to think about growing old."

Tess smiled. "I understand. But it's something we'll all have to face one day, and I'd like to think I can make a difference in people's lives, especially when they're afraid. And let's face it," she said, "most of us are afraid of growing old."

"Well, I'm one of them," he said. "But then, consider the alternative." He chuckled wryly.

He walked her home that night while their parents stopped at Bentley's for a nightcap. She felt pretty. Pretty with her shoulder-length brown hair held back in a silver clasp and her trim legs nicely shown off beneath the hem of her black dress. Tess was not exactly a knockout, but she did have an appealing old-fashioned look—soft, even features, round, dark-fringed eyes with high arched brows, a friendly smile. Whereas Andie had been sexy, pursuing life in the fast lane, Tess was more cerebral, though in college she'd had her moments: frat parties, a bout with cigarettes, a fling or two with a couple of movers and shakers. And then, three years ago, she'd met Mark. She'd had a bike accident, cut her forehead, and he'd been the new ER doctor at UCLA. He'd stitched her up and they'd gone to dinner. She'd thought Mark was the one. Down-to-earth, competent, directed. But he'd betrayed her. After Andie's murder and during all the media hullabaloo, he'd given a national magazine a terribly personal interview about his relationship with Tess and the Bergen family, and she'd been unable to forgive him. She'd already been predisposed to distrust men, she supposed, and she'd only needed an excuse.

She thought about Mark as she walked home beside Keith, and she wondered if she'd ever trust a man again.

"We could stop at the Little Nell Hotel for a drink," Keith suggested.

Tess declined. "Not tonight. I've got a dozen calls to make in the morning, and then there's the opening of the festival. Dad would never forgive me if I missed it."

And then, at the door to the Gant condo, she turned and said good-night. He made it very easy, simply giving her a peck on the cheek and leaving. She wondered about that. There was a time, not so long ago, when she might have kissed him. Was she giving off the wrong signals? Or perhaps they were the right ones. For her. For now.

Lawrence and Carole came in shortly after midnight. Tess was in bed, a textbook propped on her knees. She heard them in the hall, heard Carole giggle a little and Lawrence saying, "Shh, Tess is asleep." She smiled. Neither of them had been out past nine at night in so long she couldn't remember. In truth, she couldn't remember them going out at all since Andie's death. Now it was as if her father had come to a decision to begin living again, and he was taking Carole with him on the long-overdue ride.

Tess looked into the middle distance, thinking, tapping a pencil against her teeth. Only last week, when she'd begun making calls to the UCLA Medical Center, she'd felt guilty as hell for wanting to leave her parents, felt as if, after Andie's death, she was their only bulwark. But now, well, the guilt was easing. And that felt good.

It was after one when she finally snapped off the bedside lamp and pulled the covers up to her chin, to ward off the mountain chill from the open window. She fell asleep quickly, thoughts about the big day tomorrow carrying her off....

Then the hands were around her neck, big, strong hands, the fingers pressing into her flesh.

She couldn't breathe; her throat was collapsing under the pressure.

Air. She needed air. Her arms flailed as she tried to fight off her attacker, but he was so big, on top of her, grinding her down into the hard asphalt of the parking lot, the gravel digging into her skull, the fingers boring holes in her neck, no air, no air....

Tess screamed, a gargled, choking sound. She sat bolt upright, drenched and shaking. Her heart pounding a primitive drumbeat in her chest.

Oh, God, had anyone heard her scream?

But no. She'd had the nightmare before. Awakened before, soaked in sweat and terror. And the scream had only been in the dark territory of her mind.

It was a long time before she lay back down and closed her eyes. She was afraid of sleep again. Afraid of the dream. It was so real. It had been real. For Andie.

Someday, she lay there telling herself over and over, someday it had to end.

TWO

Robbie Childress was a big, good-looking guy. Six foot three in his stocking feet, with a baseball player's typically muscular butt and thighs. He had surprisingly small facial features, though, a perpetual naughty-little-boy expression, bright blue eyes and incongruous, thick black eyebrows. He was a hunk, and women had always adored him.

He'd been a good baseball player, just shy of great. A strong, southpaw slugger when up to bat and a quick-handed right fielder. He'd been with a Florida team for a long time, then he'd been traded around as his youth and talent had faded. But he'd lived in Los Angeles since his movie career had taken off and, of course, Aspen, when he could get away.

He took care of himself, knowing his career depended on his teddy-bear charm and his looks. If he let himself run to fat like so many ex-athletes, he'd lose out on the Hollywood roles he coveted.

He always set his alarm early, working out every morning in his gym in the Beverly Hills house and in the local muscle-man gym in Aspen. Ali didn't mind; he was back in time for breakfast, in time to make love to her or to turn off the television set and her interminable tell-all shows and watch her dress for the latest event—a fund-raiser or a baseball game or a lunch with a producer. Or an interview with someone in the endless stream of media people.

Robbie drew on his sweats and frowned. The stream had actually not been quite so endless lately; it seemed, in fact, to have dried up. Ever since the trial, in fact. Goddammit, he'd been found not guilty. What did they want from him?

He didn't admit to Ali that things had changed, and he wasn't sure how she'd react. He didn't tell her that he hadn't had a movie offer since, well, since his little problem began. But that was over, finished, taken care of. He was a free man.

He leaned over and kissed her on the cheek. She barely moved.

Moments later he backed his dark green Range Rover out of the garage and drove to the gym. It was going to be a beautiful day, clear and bright and fresh. No Los Angeles smog here.

The gym was close to empty at this hour. No one to give him surreptitious glances. The few hard-core lifters were encased in their own worlds, grunting and puffing and sweating. And no one in Aspen ever recognized him, anyway—or if they did, they pretended not to. He sort of missed the adulation, but what the heck.

This afternoon at the Bon Vin Festival he'd be noticed for sure. There'd be all sorts of media types there. He'd see his face on TV or in a magazine somewhere soon, and he'd feel better, not so left out of things, not so ignored. Robbie hated being ignored.

And Ali would be with him this afternoon. Cameras zoomed in on Ali like a magnet, so gorgeous she was, so young and pliable. She'd been in a couple of soft-porn films, then had a small part in a blockbuster

Right now she was counting on getting a role in an upcoming police thriller. He hoped she got it, although… Well, so she didn't have great talent; she didn't need it, not with her looks.

Yes, this afternoon would be good. It'd show the world Robbie Childress wasn't hiding, skulking around in the dark, ostracized. Hell, no. He'd walk right in that big tent, grin and say hello to everyone, including Mr. Big Shot Lawrence Bergen. Maybe he'd go up to him and say, "Hi, there, Larry, how're they hangin'?" Bergen hated being called Larry. Yeah, maybe he'd do that.

Robbie did the leg machine, grunting as he pushed. He added ten pounds, then ten more. His gaze drifted to a babe in skimpy shorts and sports bra next to him on the same kind of leg machine. Jesus, she was using almost as much weight as he was!

Robbie finished his workout and drove home, not showering. Ali liked him to smell sweaty; it turned her on. The west end of Aspen was still pretty quiet as he drove through, people out walking their dogs, a few joggers, a construction crew unloading equipment in front of a remodeling project. The century-old cottonwood trees shaded the streets in this part of town, and if he looked right out his front window, he saw Aspen Mountain, like a wave rising over the town, then frozen into stillness.

Ali was still asleep, but he woke her up and started kissing her. She moaned as if she didn't like being disturbed, but he knew that was only an act. She loved to play coy, and she loved Robbie to be overbearing. Big and strong and masterful. In control. Ali liked it that way and so did he. Never again would he make the mistake of marrying a woman who wanted to be independent. Independent women sucked.

Ali was making soft little whimpers in her throat

and reaching for him, and he put anything other than the sensations of the moment out of his mind. He only had time for a fleeting thought of how much he'd enjoy pissing Lawrence Bergen off that afternoon before Ali required all his concentration.

Lawrence got ready to leave for the tent at ten in the morning. "There's still a lot to do," he said, "and I want this to go off perfectly. The magazine needs a boost, and I think this'll help. I'm afraid the volunteers might have left that case of merlot reserve where it will get too warm. I may have to find some ice."

"Oh, no, warm merlot," Tess teased.

"Catastrophic," Lawrence replied mock-severely.

"Are you going to wear that jacket?" Carole asked.

Lawrence looked at her. "Why?"

"I like the linen tweed one better. It's so warm out today, and you know the tent gets stifling with all those people."

"This is fine," he said. "Will you be there later, Carole?"

"Oh, I don't think so. I'm feeling a little down today, dear. Do you mind?"

Tess said nothing, but she wanted to. She had a whole mouthful of things she wanted to say, but she'd said them all before, and they only upset her mother. Then her dad would get angry at her for upsetting her mother and on it went.

Lawrence patted his wife's hand, knowing better than to argue. He was distracted, probably worried about the tasting that afternoon.

"You'll be there, won't you?" he asked Tess.

"Sure, I'll be there. I may try to miss the mad stampede into the tent, though."

"Well, you know where my tables are set up."

"Come here, Lawrence," Carole said. "I want to

make sure you're presentable. There may be photographers."

Lawrence moved to stand in front of her, and Tess watched as her mother smoothed her husband's hair, straightened his lapels.

Sometimes Tess was jealous of their love for each other. This awful tragedy had not torn them apart, as it might have another couple. Lawrence had even accepted Carole's mental and emotional collapse. While Tess got irritated, her dad was patient, endlessly patient, with his wife, who had nearly lost her mind.

They'd always been a youthful, attractive, vibrant couple. Now Carole was faded, her spark gone. Lawrence had held up better, at least outwardly, a handsome man in his mid-fifties. He still had his hair, although it had turned quite gray in the past year. His dark eyes were like Tess's, but his features were bigger. A strong face. He'd been a knockout when he was young, according to Carole. He wore a mustache, still dark, neatly trimmed.

"There," Carole said, giving his shirt collar a last tug. And with that Lawrence kissed her cheek, smiled at Tess, waved a cheerful goodbye and let himself out of the condo.

"You sure you can't make it this afternoon?" Tess asked her mother.

"I really can't," Carole said. "Honestly. Your father understands."

Tess sighed and said nothing, then went into her own room to write a letter to the director of the residency program at the medical center. She was hoping to start in the fall. She'd written, it seemed, an endless stream of letters, made dozens of phone calls, had letters of recommendation copied and recopied, sent out, had her records transferred. She'd tried everything. But once you gave up a residency, you were considered unreliable, she guessed, and all she'd received so far were form letters and requests for more information. It was frustrating.

For a long time, after Andie's murder and during the trial, Tess hadn't been able to think of anything else, but now...now life was beginning to feel normal again, and she could look ahead, make plans, even think of leaving her mother alone.

She worked on the letter, made a call to the medical center, then stared out her window for a time, thinking. Ute Avenue was a the dead-end street tucked into a secluded corner of Aspen. It was only two blocks from downtown, but it could have been miles away. It was a quiet street, paralleled by a bike path.

Once past the Gant condos and the ritzy subdivision of tract mansions, there were only a few houses, the century-old Ute cemetery, unused and overgrown now, and a park where children played on occasion. Mostly the park was deserted, like the cemetery, with sunlight filtering through the aspen trees. It was a place where magpies patrolled and squirrels scolded from safe branches.

Maybe, Tess thought, she could take a walk along the bike path before lunch. Or sit in the sun at the Gant's pool. Or...

She glanced at her watch. No time. She had to shower and make herself presentable, eat lunch, make sure her mother ate, too, then walk across town to the tent. She'd put in an appearance for her father's sake, but she wasn't going to stay long. She knew the scene in the tent from past years.

It was insane. Hundreds of people waiting at the entrance until the security guards let them in, a surging sea of humanity pouring in through a narrow entrance, then spreading out inside the tent, rushing to their favorite vintner or restaurateur, successful, mature professionals, elbowing and shoving like cattle in a feedlot. Then drinking, rolling wine around in their mouths, spitting into the receptacles provided, tasting again and again, choosing vintages for their cellars. And the lines of well-dressed people waiting to taste chicken *cordon bleu* or shrimp scampi sautéed right in front of them or a delectable Southwestern specialty like pheasant enchiladas.

There was no place to sit in the tent, so everyone stood, shoulder to shoulder, drinking and eating from paper plates. A study in gluttony.

And her father would be there, smiling and conversing, remembering names, recommending a vintage that went particularly well with fowl or roast beef. Or a dessert wine. Extolling the virtues of a new vineyard he'd discovered in Oregon, another in California. The center of attention.

Actually, Lawrence adored the attention. That was one reason Tess had pressed him to come to Aspen this year. He thrived on it, and every time he made an appearance *Bon Vin* magazine saw its subscriptions multiply.

She dressed casually; even though today's event was a big deal, no one dressed formally in Aspen. A skirt, a V-neck T-shirt in a becoming shade of blue, flat shoes so she could walk to the tent in comfort and then stand about.

It was close to one by the time she was ready.

"Okay, Mom, I'm going," she said, then made one last attempt. "You sure you don't want to come with me? I'll wait."

Carole was still in her bathrobe. She smiled. "No, really. I'm going to lie down. I'll be ready to go out tonight, though."

"Okay. See you later." Tess rolled her eyes. "I may not stay long. That crowd."

"Yes, that crowd," her mother agreed.

Tess grabbed her bag, slung it over her shoulder, hung her festival pass around her neck and gave Carole a peck on the cheek.

The walk through Aspen took only a few minutes, across a little park with ducks swimming on a pond, past the gondola that took people up Aspen Mountain for skiing in the winter and for sightseeing in the summer, along Durant Avenue past the Chanel boutique and the Ralph Lauren Polo shop and art galleries and the central bus stop. The crowds grew more concentrated as Tess approached the huge tent in Wagner Park. The atmosphere was exciting, stimulating, crazy.

Tess could hear the people through the tent walls as she approached. Everyone was already inside for the grand tasting. Good. She'd timed her arrival perfectly. That initial wild crush to get in was too much for her.

The guard at the entrance saw her Bon Vin pass and waved her in. The noise hit her first, a sustained low roar of conversation, then the smells—a combination of garlic and oil frying and sharp spices and herbs. And wine, the pungent scent of burgundy and beaujolais and chardonnay, of champagne and port and merlot and pinot.

It was warm and humid in the tent, even though the flaps were tied back wherever possible. The volunteers scurried through the crowd, emptying spittoons, replacing bottles, casting off empties.

Tess could hardly move; it was mayhem between the linen-draped tables. A middle-aged woman draped in purple silk and hung with gold chains stepped on her toe.

"Excuse me," she said.

"That's okay," Tess replied, smiling. "Always happens in a crowd."

Next to her a sweating, red-cheeked man ate jumbo shrimp off a paper plate, then drank from his wineglass. Someone jostled his elbow, and wine splashed onto his shirt. He smiled and kept on chewing.

Tess dodged under a man's arm, slid past a couple arguing the merits of pinot gris versus riesling, bumped into a reporter taking notes. It was slow-going, shoving through the throng to where Lawrence's tables were set up. He had a prime position, taking up a whole corner, but it was as far from the entrance as you could get.

A smartly dressed woman behind a table offered her a glass of wine, but she declined and pressed on.

"Excuse me," she said again and again, slipping past people. There was her father's corner, everyone milling about, waiting for a turn at one of Lawrence Bergen's new California discoveries, a 1990 Freemark Abbey merlot.

My God, she'd never be able to reach him at this rate. She couldn't even see him yet, not behind all those people. Good thing she wasn't claustrophobic.

She got by a few more people. All around her men and women were talking, drinking, jammed together, eating, jostling, some yelling over the noise, a huge tentful of mouths and faces and the sharp bouquet of wine on the air.

Tess caught a glimpse of her father, recognizing his navy blue blazer, but she could only see his shoulders and head behind the cases of merlot on his table. His back was turned. The crowd ebbed and flowed around her, hiding him again. No sense trying to call out to him or wave—he couldn't see or hear her.

She pushed closer, scooted around the end of a table, but people were jammed against her, even behind her father's tables, which was supposed to be kept clear. She stubbed her toe on a case of wine, muttered "damn." There was her father at last, talking to someone, she couldn't see who. Slipping between two men, evading someone's elbow, Tess reached her dad's back.

She started to say "Dad, I made it. I—" She was interrupted by a popping sound. A champagne cork? Tess wondered. The crowd surged around her, and she had to fight to keep her balance.

Lawrence turned then and saw her. Tess grinned. "It wasn't easy, but I—" The words froze on her lips. There was a strange expression on her father's face, one she'd never seen before. Shock, an awful blankness.

"Dad?" she breathed.

He stood there, utterly still, as if paralyzed; his eyes met hers. He saw her, recognized her, and then a very odd thing happened, something Tess would forever remember but never comprehend.

A hush fell over them, the two of them, as if a glass dome had been lowered around them, cutting off the noise and wild tumult. Time stopped, held still, and her father's gaze drilled into her, a gaze full of fear and relief and horror and love. And mute supplication, an awful kind of helplessness. His gaze dropped then to his hand; hers followed, widened.

A gun, a small chrome pistol, dangled from her father's fingers. Oddly colored fingers, pale, like a corpse's. No, latex gloves, her mind registered. He wore latex gloves.

A gun.

Tess didn't think. She didn't judge. Something, some power, took over her mind. She reached out, snatched the gun from him, thrust it into her purse.

Lawrence's mouth opened, closed. Tears sprang to his eyes.

Time started again with a jolt like electricity. Noise, the babble of hundreds of voices, garlic frying, the tang of wine spilled.

Then a scream, a piercing scream, then another, cutting through the air like a chef's cleaver. The crowd surged, knocking Tess against her father. She tripped on something soft but solid, refused to look down, whirled and pushed her way out from behind the tables. Shoved, jammed against people. There were more screams. Her mind registered them, discounted them. Out, she had to get out.

Everyone was moving, shoving, trying to run, like a school of fish startled by a shark, a flock of sheep by a wolf. Spreading out, away, elbows jabbing, arms flailing, a living entity of screaming, thrusting bodies. In front of Tess someone fell, she tripped over him, propelled from behind, got knocked into a table, a sharp corner in her hip.

A stampede. Shrieks and sobs and cries. Bodies flung about, the stronger rushing. Tess was carried along like flotsam on a raging flood. She fell once, somehow lurched to her feet, panting, her heart pounding like a hammer, her mouth dry.

The canvas sides of the tent were pushed out, ripped, flung aside. People poured through, some cut by broken glasses and bottles, shoes lost, stained with spilled wine like blood.

Tess was swirled along, outside at last. Blessed air and sun. She took a deep breath and started to run to get away when she heard a voice cry, "Somebody shot Robbie Childress!"

And then Tess gathered herself and ran.

THREE

With great difficulty Dan Hadley opened one eye to see the alarm clock by his head.

Up at the crack of noon, he thought wryly, and then the pounding behind his eyes began. He buried his face in the pillow and groaned, flashes of last night's debauchery sparking in his brain. Had he really been drinking shots with his beer? Tequila, whiskey? He couldn't recall, but the thumping in his temples felt like tequila.

It was nearly twelve-thirty by the time he pushed aside the sheet and sat on the edge of the mattress in his boxer shorts and bare feet.

Goddamn, even his feet hurt.

How had he gotten so screwed up last night? He remembered the beginning, but not much else. He'd just finished up a case for the law firm that retained him as a private investigator. It was Thursday, and he'd thought, well, what the heck? He had three days off, why not call a couple of his old cop buddies and tip back a few beers?

He hadn't even taken a pack of cigarettes along to the Marina district bar. Of course, by the second beer he'd bought one. And by the fifth beer and the first shot—yes, definitely tequila—he'd smoked half the pack.

His lungs ached. On top of the brutal hangover, his goddamn chest felt as if cotton were wadded up inside it and no air could get through.

Suddenly he was struck by a wave of nausea. He lurched to his feet and just made it to the bathroom in time. After flushing the toilet, he braved a look in the mirror: sandy-blond hair stringy, too damn long, bags under red-rimmed blue eyes, his complexion pale as a corpse's and a two-day growth of beard on his flat cheeks.

Not a pretty picture.

He padded into the kitchen of his one-bedroom apartment on San Francisco's Powell Street and rinsed out the coffeepot, found a filter and the nearly empty can of coffee in the fridge. There was a pizza in there, too, his hazy brain registered. Untouched, still in the box. Had he ordered a pizza?

Dan made the coffee, then leaned over the sink, dizzy.

This had to stop. Even when he'd been a cop and hung out in the bars at night with the boys, he had never been a true carouser. But he was turning into one now.

Susan.

Holy shit. They were supposed to have had dinner last night. In North Beach. At her place.

He straightened and took a breath. He'd call her. Right now.

But he didn't, couldn't. He wasn't ready for the recriminations and a lecture.

He poured a mug of coffee before it was done brewing, making a mess. Hell, he'd clean it up later. Then, head still pounding, he sat down in his small but functional living room, found the TV controls and switched on the set.

The afternoon soaps were on. Forget that. He punched in the numbers for CNN "Headline News" and settled back on the couch, still in his boxer shorts, a strand of sandy hair falling in his eyes.

The report came on right after the commercials. "This just in..." Dan sat, sipped his coffee, only mildly interested. "CNN has learned that shortly after 1:00 p.m. mountain time, baseball star and movie actor Robert John Childress was shot and killed in Aspen, Colorado. There are no details on the shooting as yet...."

Dan sat up straight, his mind suddenly clear. Robbie shot. Killed. A wicked grin curved his thin lips. Whoever did Childress deserved a goddamn medal.

With keen interest, he clicked up the volume and waited for more news. Dan knew Childress, knew him well. After having left the San Francisco Police Department—lured away by a prominent legal firm—he'd been intimately involved with the Childress murder trial. It was Dan Hadley who'd uncovered police blunders, Dan who'd exposed the affair Andie Childress was having. It was Dan who'd delivered to the defense team the evidence that created reasonable doubt in the jurors' minds. Oh, yeah, he'd been partly responsible for getting the creep off even though there was never any doubt in Dan's mind that Childress had murdered his wife.

Robbie Childress—the sports world's blue-eyed boy—had been busted for physically knocking people around long before his marriage to Andie. More than one girlfriend, too, from Florida to California, had reported physical abuse. He'd lied his way out of the charges or simply bought off the girlfriend. He'd beaten Andie more than once, but like most abused wives, she'd covered for him, lied about her bruises.

When it came to his women Robbie was a power freak. He liked them docile and sexy and dumb, and Andie hadn't been like that. Dan had learned these things as the investigation progressed, and the D.A. had brought it out in the murder trial, but nothing had stuck. Robbie Childress was Teflon.

Yeah, Dan knew all about Childress. He'd completed his assignment, though, and he'd been paid handsomely. The trouble was, he sometimes felt bad—real bad—about the verdict.

Most of the time, however, his reasoning was an exercise in self-deception: hey, he'd only been doing his job, one that he was exceptionally good at. And every time he recalled the agony on Lawrence Bergen's face when the verdict had been read, he pushed it aside. Hell, it wasn't as if he'd created the system.

Only seldom did Dan allow himself to wonder why he'd been hitting the booze so hard lately—well, since the trial—but he guessed he was tense, just needed a vacation.

There was an update on TV, and Dan brushed aside the disquieting notions to listen. A camera was panning in on the redbrick facade of the Pitkin County Courthouse in Aspen, and a Western Slope reporter was talking into a mike. "We're here in Aspen, Colorado, at the county courthouse where local authorities have brought Lawrence Bergen in for questioning in connection with the murder of Robert Childress early this afternoon. CNN has learned that the shooting occurred at the Bon Vin Festival only three short blocks from here, where Lawrence Bergen, the publisher of *Bon Vin* magazine, was present for the opening wine-tasting ceremony."

Lawrence Bergen. The name beat at Dan's brain,

and he swore aloud, thinking this never would have happened if he, Dan, hadn't been so damn good at his job. Bergen was an honorable man, a likable man, always the gentleman, always on an even keel. During Robbie's trial, even in his agony, Bergen had kept his dignity. Still, Dan bet Bergen did the shooting. Hell, Dan might have done the same.

He got up from the couch, his face twisted, and found the crunched-up pack of cigarettes in a jacket pocket. He lit one, an eye still on the TV set.

The phone rang then, and he almost didn't answer it. He could imagine who it was—one of his cop pals, calling to laugh.

It wasn't a cop.

"Susan," Dan said. "I was going to call you this morning...."

"It's afternoon, you jerk."

"Well, I know, but I—"

"Never mind that," she cut in. "Have you got the TV on?"

"I'm watching it right now," he said.

"Can you believe it? Lawrence Bergen killing Robbie?"

Dan shrugged. "Allegedly killing Robbie."

"Oh, come on, Dan, of course Bergen did it."

Playing devil's advocate, Dan said, "Hey, Robbie's got more enemies than you could shake a stick at. Just because the cops are questioning Bergen doesn't mean he's guilty."

"Really, Dan, you don't believe that," she said. "Maybe you'd like to believe it, but... Oh, never mind."

And then there was a long pause. Uh-oh, Dan thought.

"About last night," Susan McPherson said. "What

makes you think you can stand me up like that and get away with it?"

"I'm sorry," he muttered. God, he hated this. "I got hung up. Unavoidable."

"Bull," she said. "The only thing you were hung up with was those creep cops you pal around with. They're a bunch of drunks, Dan, and you're getting to be just like them. Ever since—"

"Come on," he said, wounded, not wanting to hear the rest. "I said I was sorry. Maybe we could—"

"Forget it," Susan said. "I only called to see if you'd heard the news." And then she hung up.

Dan let out a breath. He'd go over to her place after work. When she'd simmered down.

He poured a second cup of coffee, opened the blinds and squinted out at the magnificent view of the bay and Alcatraz. He paid plenty for this view. It wasn't Nob Hill or Telegraph Hill, but close enough. And the view was worth every dime.

The TV station had more on the Childress murder, and Dan moved back to the couch. The cameras were now following two women, and Dan recognized them even before the reporter said, "Carole and Theresa Bergen are just entering the basement of the Pitkin County Courthouse where the Aspen Police Department is located...."

Dan grimaced as the camera closed in. Both women looked as if they were in shock, their faces white, eyes staring straight ahead. He switched the set off, heading into the shower, as if it could cleanse his soul. But as he picked up the bar of soap, everything came rushing back. It was as if he was in the L.A. courtroom all over again and the verdict had just been read.

On the charge of murder in the first degree, we the jury find the defendant Robert John Childress not guilty.

And Robbie's pathetically grateful boyish face, the tears in his eyes, and then the Bergens' faces: stricken, agonized, Lawrence pulling his wife and daughter close, whispering something to them. Maybe something like, "I'll get him, I'll kill him myself."

A few minutes later, when Dan had inadvertently come face-to-face with Tess outside the courtroom, she'd said, "You son of a bitch. How can you sleep at night knowing what you've done here?" He'd never forget it.

Dan stood with the soap bar in hand, hot water splashing on his back, and realized she'd been right. Without a bunch of alcohol in his blood, he couldn't sleep.

He pictured Tess Bergen. A pretty lady, thirty or so, with an air of quiet strength, soft brown hair, big dark eyes and smooth white skin. Kind of old-fashioned-looking in a way, and her arched eyebrows gave her a faintly surprised expression. It was common knowledge among the press corps that she'd stopped seeing her boyfriend and given up a coveted medical residency when her sister had been murdered.

And now this, Dan thought.

My fault. The words rang in his head. And he knew that one way or another he was going to pay for it.

Tess held her black woven purse in her lap with both hands. She could feel the hard outline of the gun inside it. Beside her wallet, wedged up against her makeup kit. Her palms were clammy. No, of course, the gun wasn't there. Not any longer. Oh, God, she thought, get yourself in control.

The detective, a sergeant with the Aspen Police Department, paced the small room then faced the two women again. "It would really help if you'd tell us what you know," he said. "We're all just after the truth here."

Tess reached over and held her mother's hand. "Don't say anything, Mom," she said, catching Detective Gray's eyes. "We don't have to say a thing." She could feel Carole trembling.

"There's no reason for this lack of cooperation," Gray began.

Tess sat up straight. "Why is my father being held, Detective?"

He said nothing.

"I insist you tell us what you're holding him for," she went on.

"That's police business, Miss Bergen."

"You can't just hold him like this."

"I'm afraid we can."

They found the gun, pounded through her mind, *they found it.* "Does my father have legal representation yet?" she tried.

"We're arranging for someone local to handle things."

"That won't do," Tess said.

Finally Carole spoke. "My husband deserves the best legal representation there is. This is so unfair. Lawrence couldn't have shot anyone."

"Mom," Tess said quickly, "don't say anything."

"But he couldn't have. Tess, you were there, you know he couldn't—"

"Mom."

Carole subsided, muttering only that she needed to see her husband, which the cops wouldn't allow.

It was a dreadful afternoon. Tess and her mother sat in the basement of the Pitkin County Courthouse, where both the Aspen Police Department and the Pitkin County Sheriff's Department were located. The murder had occurred within the city limits, so the police had jurisdiction, but the sheriff's office was cooperating, too.

No one would tell them a thing. Not why the police were holding Lawrence, not if there was any evidence against him, not even if legal counsel had arrived to represent him. Tess kept demanding to know why her father was being held, but no one would tell her.

Evidence, her mind kept coming back to. If they had the gun—the smoking gun—wouldn't the place be buzzing with the news? Wouldn't they arrest her, too? Or maybe Lawrence had broken down and confessed and... No. He'd never do that. Not now.

Her father, her *father*, had killed Robbie Childress. She couldn't fit her mind around that idea. He couldn't have. And yet she herself had taken the gun. Run with it. That made her...an accomplice. And now Lawrence would never confess and throw himself on the mercy of the court. To do so would bring charges down on her head, too.

Tess went to the ladies' room several times, scrubbing her hands compulsively, positive someone was going to figure out what had happened to the gun and make her undergo tests for powder residue. She scrubbed and scrubbed, sure that surveillance cameras were on her in the bathroom, sure that they knew everything she'd done.

What if they made her take a lie-detector test? But they couldn't force someone to do that, could they? And what about powder residue on her father's hands? His sport coat? But he'd been wearing gloves. Yes. All the servers wore latex gloves. She'd seen them. Or had she?

Robbie had been in the tent. Tess remembered, just yesterday, that she'd decided he wouldn't be so crass as to show his face at the festival. She'd been wrong. Dead wrong. But her father hadn't misjudged him.

Her father had known Robbie would show up. Probably to gloat. Lawrence had counted on it.

Tess's emotions lunged between hysteria and terror the whole afternoon. People, cops and God knew who else scurried up and down the hall in front of the room where she sat with Carole. The chief of police came in, spoke to them, then the detective again, with his usual line that they really could help by telling what they knew.

He even said, "Hey, if Lawrence Bergen did this, no one would blame him." But Tess wasn't buying that line one bit.

And then, finally, a lawyer stopped in and introduced himself. "I'm Steve Sutton," he said, shaking their hands, sitting down across from them.

"Are you going to represent my husband?" Carole asked, her voice breaking.

"For now," he told them. "But in the morning, I'm sure you'll want to contact someone with a lot more experience. I do criminal defense cases, but I've never handled a murder case."

"What evidence do they have against my father?" Tess demanded. "How can they hold him?"

Sutton gave a weary smile. "They've swabbed him for gunshot residue. They'll send the swabs and his jacket to the CBI lab— that's the Colorado Bureau of Investigation—in Montrose. The results will be back quickly, tomorrow at the latest. They do have the right to hold him without charges for twenty-four hours. There also seemed to be bloodstains on his jacket. Of course," the lawyer hastened to add, "Mr. Bergen was knocked down during the panic, and there are apparently glass fragments and wine stains on his clothes, too. I'm sure that will help in his defense. Contamination, you know."

Tess swallowed. "The gun?" she said in an even

voice. "Shouldn't there be a gun if my father really did do this?"

He looked at her for a long moment, then said, "The police haven't found the gun. There's talk that someone may have removed it from the scene. Your father's gone on record as saying he's never owned a gun and that someone put it in his hand, apparently the killer. He alleges that he doesn't have any recollection of what happened to the gun during the panic after the shooting."

"Oh," Tess said, and her heart raced. It was painfully obvious that Steve Sutton didn't believe a word of the story. But at least they hadn't found the gun. Yet.

"My father," Tess said then, looking up. "Is my father all right?"

"He's fine," Sutton said. "He's holding up just fine. He's a strong man."

"He's a good man," Carole put in.

"I'm sure he is, Mrs. Bergen," Sutton concurred.

When Tess and Carole emerged with a police escort from the courthouse late that afternoon, they were met by a jumble of satellite vans and cameramen, reporters talking into mikes. The press was awaiting the appearance of Lawrence, but the law allowed for him to be held for twenty-four hours without charging him with murder. And so when Tess and Carole appeared, the throng advanced on them. The cops tried to keep the press at bay, but there was pushing and shoving and dozens of questions being shouted.

"Is Lawrence Bergen being charged?" "Who's representing him?" "Mrs. Bergen, did your husband kill Robbie Childress?"

Tess held her mother's arm tightly, pulling her along within the shield of the police to an awaiting patrol car. The press followed until they reached Durant Avenue, where two Sheriff's Department cars had pitched in to help, forming a barricade. Only the car with Tess and Carole was allowed through.

"God, I hate this," Carole said in a harsh whisper. "It's just like Andie's trial. It's awful. Oh, Tess."

"I know," Tess said. "I know."

And then, when they got back to the condo, there were more cops. Only this crew wasn't there to protect them. They were there with a search warrant.

The gun.

Tess made her mother a cup of tea while the police tore the place apart. She tried to function normally, tried to ignore the tossed cushions, the rummaging in dresser drawers, the overturned mattresses. Oh, the officers put everything back, but she and Carole still felt physically violated. It was horrible. She sat with her mother, the teacup in her hands, and tried to appear unconcerned.

"Why are they doing this?" Carole sobbed.

But Tess couldn't find her voice. She was frozen in her place, wooden, a wooden statue with a furiously beating heart.

Finally the police left. But Tess couldn't rid herself of the panic. They hadn't found the gun yet. But they might. They very well might. They'd figure it out and search some more, and tonight or tomorrow or the next day they'd find it.

Later, Tess somehow made dinner. And somehow they ate. Afterward, Tess called the police department to see if they could speak to Lawrence, but the answer was still no. Perhaps if Tess called in the morning... She hung up, shook her head at her mother. "Dad's fine, Mom. I'm sure he's fine."

All evening Carole kept insisting there'd been a dreadful mistake and in the morning everything would be cleared up.

"That awful Robbie Childress had a million ene-mies," Carole said. "Anyone could have shot him. Why have they arrested Lawrence? Don't they realize he'd never do such a thing? Why don't they try to find who really did it?"

Tess was at an utter loss. What could she say to her mother? And the idea of Carole knowing that her daughter—her only surviving daughter—had aided and abetted in the killing would put her right over the edge.

Still, there was something she had to ask. "Mom," she said as she stacked dishes in the washer, "did Dad ever own a gun?"

Carole looked up sharply. "What sort of a question is that?"

"Mom, if Dad owned a gun, the police are going to want to know. What do you think they were in here looking for?"

Had her father purchased a gun recently? Was there a record of it? Or maybe he'd owned one for a long time and there was no record. She didn't know what to think or believe anymore. Maybe this was all just another one of her terrible nightmares. Maybe any minute, she'd awaken.

"A fox…" Carole was saying.

"A fox?"

"Oh, you remember. It was months ago. Kelly Free-man, down the road. His cat was killed by a fox, and your father was afraid it would get our cat, too. He talked about buying a gun."

"Did he?"

"Did he what?"

"Did Dad buy a gun, Mom?"

"Oh, gosh, I don't know."

"How could you not know something like that?"

"Tess, don't talk to me like that. I'm not an idiot. I

merely told your father I didn't want to know. I guess I told him to do what he had to and that was the end of it. I hate guns."

Tess leaned against the counter and tried to think. If Lawrence had bought a gun, he would have had to register it. All guns had to be registered, didn't they? And if that was true—and if the police found the gun—then it could be traced directly back to her father.

My God, she thought, what had her father done? What had *she* done?

FOUR

Even though it was Saturday morning Barbara McCleary was up early, showered, dressed and on her way to her office by nine. She'd reached her position of Pitkin County district attorney because she was smart and because she could put in a fifteen-hour workday without blinking an eye.

She was thirty-eight years old and the first to admit she had no life outside of her job. No husband, no kids, no ex-husband. Hell, she didn't even own a cat. Her job came first.

This bright June morning might be the highlight of her career. Murder and mayhem in Aspen. Celebrities. My God, this could make her. She'd have her pick of jobs in New York, Los Angeles, Miami, anywhere she goddamn pleased.

The courthouse annex that housed the district attorney's office was deserted, it being a weekend, although the courthouse next door was hopping. Celebrity murder sure brought the cockroaches out of the walls.

Barbara picked up her phone and dialed Tim Hendrickson, the police chief. She knew he'd be there today, even though he'd prefer to be out fishing. Not for a while, Tim, she thought.

He answered, sounding weary already. He'd probably been up all night.

"Okay," Barbara began, "so what have you got?"

"Results from the swabs show gunshot residue on the man's face, on his jacket, none on his hands."

"Yes!" Barbara crowed.

"None on his hands," Tim repeated.

"He wore those gloves," she said.

"You can't prove it."

"Surely there's a test, DNA or fingerprints, some high-tech thing I never heard of."

"No way to get prints off those gloves, Barbara. They were trampled in mud and wine. No DNA, nothing. Anybody in that tent could have worn them."

"Shit. Okay, then, the autopsy results."

"Hold on there, Barbara. It'll be a week, ten days."

"Preliminary, then. The bullet. They must have the bullet by now."

"The medical examiner is going to call about it any minute." There was a pause. "You realize the bullet doesn't mean a thing without the gun."

"We'll find the gun," she said tightly.

"Do you have enough to charge him?" Tim asked. "Without the gun, I mean?"

"The gunshot residue and a hundred eyewitnesses. Hell, yes."

"No one has said they actually saw the shooting, and Bergen says someone else did it, then handed him the gun."

"Right," Barbara said scathingly.

"You let me know when you've decided," Tim said.

"Don't worry. I will. Soon."

Barbara hung up and sat at her desk, thinking. It was up to her to decide if there was enough evidence to charge Lawrence Bergen, entirely up to her. If she let him go because she doubted the strength of her case, she could be releasing a murderer, never to see him again. If she charged him and the case fell apart, she'd be a laughingstock at best, unemployed at worst.

Her decision.

The phone rang then, and she hoped it was some new bit of evidence. The gun. Maybe they'd found the gun.

"McCleary," she said impatiently.

"Ms. McCleary, this is Brian Kreitner in Denver. I know it's Saturday, but I thought you might be in your office."

Brian Kreitner, state attorney general. Oh, God, they were sending some big shot in to steal her case! "What can I do for you, Mr. Kreitner?" she asked.

"The Bergen case, of course. Can you bring me up to speed on it?"

She told him everything she knew, emphasizing Lawrence Bergen's apparent guilt.

"Are you charging him?"

"I'm just making up my mind," Barbara said, "but I think I probably am."

"I see. Do you think he might submit to a polygraph test?"

"His local lawyer won't allow it."

"Mm. I suppose not. Well…"

She waited, not breathing. Now he'd tell her he was sending someone to Aspen to take over. Some famous prosecutor. Some man.

"It's going to be difficult, Ms. McCleary. The media coverage is going to be unrelenting."

"I can handle it."

"Bergen is going to hire a tough defense lawyer, and he'll go after you, you know."

"Fine, let him try."

There was silence on the phone for too long. Then, "How much more time do you have?"

"Till this afternoon. I only need to let Judge De-Carlo know what I decide, and he'll hold the arraignment hearing."

More silence. Her nerves shrieked, her fingers whitened on the receiver.

"Okay, Ms. McCleary, please let us know if you need any help, anything whatsoever. Our resources are at your disposal."

"Thank you, Mr. Kreitner, I'll keep that in mind. I appreciate your faith in me."

"Goodbye, Ms. McCleary."

"Goodbye, Mr. Kreitner."

Barbara leaned back in her chair, let out a long pent-up breath and grinned. Then she got up and did a little impromptu dance around her desk.

The Bergen case was hers.

She'd be on every TV set in the nation. My God, she'd write a book, host a TV show. Fame, fortune.

She couldn't lose this case. It was pretty straightforward. Motive, means, opportunity. Witnesses. A hundred people saw Bergen talking to Robbie. It was premeditated murder. First degree. Her mind whirled, raced. So much to do. She'd ask for the death penalty. No, too many emotional bombs, mitigating circumstances. The jury, the judges on the penalty-phase panel might be sympathetic. Okay, she would ask for life imprisonment without parole, and she'd get it.

The only problem she could foresee was the missing gun. Someone near Bergen could easily have taken it and hidden it, a friend of his or his daughter, Theresa, Tess she was called.

Barbara would find the gun, though, because no one had had time to get very far away with it. The cops had gone to Bergen's condo shortly after the shooting to bring Carole and Tess Bergen down to the police department for questioning. Both women had been there, and the gun had not been found later when the condo had been searched.

That gun was out there somewhere, thrown in a gutter or a Dumpster, tossed on a low rooftop. Aspen was a small town. They'd find it.

Okay, okay. Barbara paced her office, bent over to jot notes on a yellow legal pad. Things to do, calls to make.

She wanted to talk to Tim Hendrickson again to help her decide. And he'd be getting new evidence as it came in. She headed to his office.

Tim looked frazzled. His desk was piled with papers and he was on the phone, apparently with the CBI lab. He waved Barbara to a chair, said a few words into the receiver and hung up.

"Holy cow," he said, running a hand through his hair. "It's one thing after another."

"I know. The state attorney general just called me."

"Oh?"

"Don't worry, it's my case." She leveled her gaze on Tim. "Okay, now, what about the murder weapon?"

"No dice so far. I've had guys out looking all over. Every step of the way from the tent to the Bergens' place. Every garbage can, every patch of weeds, even that stream that runs down the middle of the mall. They're starting over this morning with metal detectors at the tent, and they'll go in circles, farther and farther out."

"I want that gun," Barbara said. "I can probably

get a conviction on the gunshot residue and the proximity, but the gun would make it open and shut."

"We're looking." Tim sighed.

"The autopsy results?"

"Not yet. But the medical examiner called in the bullet—.22-caliber, like we thought. A small handgun."

"I don't suppose Bergen has a gun like that registered to him?"

"Nope. CBI checked the national database."

"That would have been to much too hope for."

"He'd be really dumb to shoot someone with a gun registered to him, and Bergen isn't dumb."

"No, but he's guilty as hell."

"Maybe."

"Dammit, Tim!"

"Okay, probably." The police chief scrubbed his head. "I hate to see Lawrence Bergen go through this. I gotta tell you, I'll do my job, but that Childress is no loss to anyone."

"Your job is to uphold the law, not to make personal judgments."

"I know, I know."

Barbara cocked her head at the chief of police. "You wouldn't shirk your duty because you feel sorry for Lawrence Bergen, would you, Tim?"

"No, Barbara, I wouldn't, and I goddamn resent that question."

"Forget I asked it. Now, let's go over all this again, everything you've done, everything you're going to do. I'm going to charge Lawrence Bergen with first-degree murder, Tim, and I want nothing left to chance, no screwups, no excuses, no mistakes. I want only the best labs used, no contaminated evidence."

"We got a problem there, Barbara. Everything and everybody in that tent yesterday got contaminated.

Wine, food, dirt and grass from the ground under the tent. We have forty-three people in the hospital who bled all over everything, cut by broken wine bottles and glasses. It's a mess."

"What about the people close to Bergen? The eye-witnesses?"

"We tried. There were close to eight hundred people in that tent, and they all scattered in every direction. I've put out notices on the local radio stations, TV stations, in the papers, for anyone who was there to come in for an interview. I've got calls in to every volunteer department head for lists of volunteers. There're hundreds of them. We'll talk to them, but it'll take time."

"Keep working on it. Out of nearly a thousand people in that tent, someone saw the shooting. I don't know what's keeping them from coming forward, but we've got to find them and convince them, Tim. It's vital to the case." She paused and inclined her head. "What about Robbie's fiancée, Ali what's-her-name?"

"Ali Barnes. She was there. She says she saw it all, but to tell the truth, even I don't believe her."

"We'll prep her, don't worry."

"You can try."

"That bad?"

"Uh-huh."

"Anyone else see anything?"

Tim sighed. "A lot of people saw Robbie talking to Lawrence. Angrily, I guess. In the corner behind the tables. Then they all heard a pop. Half of 'em thought it was a champagne cork. Nobody saw Robbie fall, it was so damn crowded. It even took a minute before anyone saw him on the ground. By then the gun was nowhere to be seen, and Lawrence was over by the tent entrance."

"Hmm." Barbara thought, a finger on her lips. She

looked at him, frowning. "Have you questioned Tess Bergen?"

He shrugged. "She won't talk, won't let her mother talk."

"Okay, I'm going over to the tent right now. I'll be back for the arraignment. Keep looking for the gun."

"Yes, ma'am."

Barbara gave him a sidelong look. "No mistakes, right?"

"Right."

Barbara walked the few blocks to the tent. The whole thing was surrounded by yellow crime-scene tape. Policemen and sheriff's deputies stood at every entrance, but there were still people gawking and wandering around, and a familiar-looking anchorman stood in front of the tent, talking into a microphone, a video camera on him.

Barbara showed her ID, although she knew the cop on duty at the entrance.

"What a mess," the cop said to her, and when she entered the tent she saw why.

Nothing had been removed from the cavernous interior except the people and Robbie Childress's body. Everything remained as it had been after the mad stampede yesterday afternoon. The grassy ground trampled into mud, the white linen tablecloths torn and stained and dragged onto the ground, fresh flowers strewn everywhere, wilted and dying, broken bottles and glasses, toppled tables, fallen cases of priceless vintage wine, spilled food. The air reeked of vinegary wine and the cellar-stink of mud.

A mess.

She walked carefully, avoiding broken glass, to the corner where the shooting had occurred. There, behind a crazily listing table, was the chalked outline of Robbie's body. The blood was hard to see against the ground. Not like on a floor. She'd look at the crime-scene photographs later; first she wanted to see the real thing.

That was where Bergen had stood, and Robbie. Right there. But surrounded by people, all crammed together. Noise, commotion. No one had noticed the little gun or recognized the shot for what it really was. The body had fallen noiselessly underfoot.

Barbara walked around, seeing the scene in her mind's eye. Bergen must have planned for months, knowing how crowded and noisy it was in the tent, believing Robbie would come, knowing Robbie's arrogance and ego would bring him close to him sooner or later.

The gun, unregistered, bought somewhere—who knew where—and latex gloves. Bergen would have gotten Robbie to come close, perhaps said something to elicit a rise out of him, maybe Robbie blustered and threatened. In the crush, with their bodies nearly touching, over there in the corner. One shot. In the heart. A pop. Handing the gun off to some accomplice, a split-second job, then pulling off the latex gloves and throwing them on the ground to get stepped on. Running toward the entrance, falling, rolling in the mud and spilled wine, deliberately contaminating his skin and clothes. Cut all over with glass, bleeding.

Yes.

The accomplice. One very real possibility was Tess Bergen. His wife, Carole, was a basket case, everyone knew that, and she'd never left the condo, anyway. But Tess Bergen was right here.

If Bergen hid the gun in the tent, they'd find it. Barbara made a note to herself: check every case of wine, every box of glasses before they were removed from the tent. Every spittoon filled with spat-out wine.

Okay. Tess Bergen had to be brought in for questioning, no doubt about it. If she knew where the gun was, Barbara would get it out of her.

Even without the gun, the worst scenario, Barbara still had a case. Gunshot residue was convincing-enough evidence. The shooter got residue on himself, and the smaller the gun, the smaller the area the residue spread. The bullet that killed Childress came from a small gun, little more than a peashooter. And Bergen had residue.

Sure, people would sympathize with Lawrence Bergen, but in Aspen juries tended to be pretty damn sophisticated. They felt their responsibility, and they could mete out justice despite emotional ploys by the defense. She'd just have to make sure to seat a jury that could handle the emotional burden.

Barbara took a last look around the forlorn destruction of the tent and walked out.

"Thanks," she said to the cop on duty.

"You going to charge Bergen?" he asked.

"You bet your ass," she replied.

Back in her office she filed the formal charge against Bergen, wrote herself notes, phoned Tim Hendrickson and asked for the faxed reports from the CBI lab.

The arraignment was set for one. It was pretty unusual to do anything like this on a weekend, but no one wanted to keep Lawrence Bergen any longer than necessary. His defense lawyer would spit wooden nickels and demand a mistrial if there was any deviation from the letter of the law.

Barbara figured it would be quick. Bergen's lawyer would put in his not-guilty plea and waive any plea-bargaining sessions. She'd ask for bail—a million, she decided. The judge wouldn't keep Bergen in jail, but there would have to be a large bond. After all, this was a murder case, and Bergen wasn't a resident of Aspen or even of Colorado.

But Lawrence Bergen wouldn't run. No, he'd already gotten what he wanted.

The phone rang and Barbara picked it up. "McCleary."

"Hey, babes, it's me."

"How'd you know I was here?"

"Because you weren't home. Are you on this Bergen thing?"

"I certainly am."

"Christ, Barbara."

"Isn't it wonderful?"

"Just dandy."

"What's that supposed to mean?"

"It's a pretty nasty business."

"That's what I do, Eric. I clean up messes."

"I take it the weekend's off, then?"

"I'm sorry. Bergen's going to be arraigned in—" she looked at her watch "—two hours, and I have so much to do."

"How about tomorrow? Just a short ride on the Harley?"

"I can't. Oh, Eric, you know how I get. I'd just be worrying about the case."

"Well, tonight, then."

"Yes, okay, tonight. Can you come over?"

"I'll be there."

"Oh, God, Eric, could you do me a great big favor? Pick up something to eat? A pizza, anything. I don't have time to shop or cook or—"

"Okay, okay. I'll grab something."

"Thanks. I'm sorry about this, the timing, just when Maggie's away. I know you looked forward to it. So did I."

"Listen, Barbara, I knew the minute I heard about

the shooting yesterday that you'd be too busy to go. It's no big surprise."

"Are you mad?"

"No."

"Liar."

"A little. I'll get over it."

"Tonight, Eric."

"Yeah, tonight."

She hung up, feeling a little flutter in her belly. Eric, long and lean, that nice beard of his that made him look like a Viking. The blue eyes, the big strong hands. Yes, she loved the man's body, and she'd been looking forward to this weekend. His wife and the kids gone, two whole days and nights to themselves. Steamboat Springs or maybe Cripple Creek. Somewhere on the new Harley-Davidson motorcycle he was so proud of.

But this case was more important than Eric, more important than anything. She'd make him understand that tonight. She felt a sudden surge of power and wondered if Eric realized the changes her life was about to undergo. Would it turn him on if she got rich and famous? Would he leave his wife and share her fortune?

She felt excited, almost sexually, but more in control. It was her case.

Thank you, Lawrence Bergen, she thought.

Barbara McCleary watched the nationally televised "Judge's Advocate" program whenever she could, even in her office, where she had a small TV set perched on a shelf amid her law books.

Despite it being a weekend, she switched on the set, dying to know if the show's writers had stayed up all night to prepare a script for the nation's latest and hottest story: the murder of Robbie Childress. She wondered, as well, if her name would be mentioned this early in the game. She hoped so. Yes, that would be very nice, wouldn't hurt her career in the least.

The writers had indeed stayed up to air a special, live weekend edition, because when Gail Hollister appeared on the screen, she immediately announced that today's topic was vigilante justice.

Barbara sat back in her wooden swivel chair and listened intently. She'd always respected Gail—who was also a prosecution attorney—but Craig Kramer pissed Barbara off. A defense attorney, Craig always took the side of the accused. Hell, Barbara mused, ninety-nine percent of those charged with a crime were guilty. Craig Kramer often made it sound as if the accused were the victim. What a crock.

The two TV attorneys began their discussion about vigilante justice, and predictably Craig took on the role of devil's advocate, trying to defend Bergen. Gail Hollister, of course, was eminently reasonable, upholding the law of the land, laying aside emotional issues. Gail. A smart lady. But that Craig Kramer... He made Barbara as mad as a hornet.

"I simply don't believe in vigilante justice, Craig," Gail was saying firmly. "I don't believe in an eye for an eye unless the court dictates it. No man has the legal right to take justice into his own hands."

"Yes," Barbara hissed.

"What if the legal system failed him, Gail? Isn't there a higher moral issue here?" Craig said.

"Our system can't take into account every individual case—there'd be too many. The law, Craig, is the same for everyone. It has to be."

"Maybe that's what's wrong with it, Gail."

"You're assuming there's something wrong with it. I'm not convinced there is."

There's not a damn thing wrong with our system,

Barbara thought. Okay, maybe it isn't perfect, but how could it be? Nothing's perfect.

"It sure isn't perfect, Gail. My God, a patently guilty man got off scot-free. An innocent woman was murdered and no one paid for that crime."

"I should have been prosecuting that case," Barbara whispered. "I'd have nailed Childress."

"I'm trying to keep this discussion above specific, aberrant cases, Craig," said Gail. "The point I'm trying to make is that, as a civilized society, we can't condone vigilante justice. Lawrence Bergen must be punished if he's found guilty."

Absolutely, Barbara agreed. Well stated, Gail.

"If we can't occasionally forgive vigilante justice, Gail, then the application of the law must be more stringent. Mistakes, such as the acquittal of Robbie Childress, are lethal to our system," Craig said solemnly.

Lethal, Christ, Barbara thought off the TV set.

Tess sat stock-still next to her mother in the first row of benches, right behind the table where her father and Steve Sutton waited. Her heart beat a slow, heavy rhythm, and she felt slightly nauseated. Steve Sutton had assured Carole and her that Lawrence would be released on bail, but that he would be required to stay in Aspen until his trial. Or until the D.A. dropped the charges, which was unlikely.

Tess switched her attention to the other table where the D.A. was seated. Barbara McCleary, Tess had learned, was a hard-nosed prosecutor, no holds barred. Smart and ambitious. She was tall and thin, clear skin, a straight nose, very short, man-short, dark hair. Not that D.A. McCleary appeared mannish, not one bit. She was, in her way, quite beautiful.

Behind her, Tess heard the weeping begin again.

Ali Barnes, the bereaved girlfriend, was there, accompanied by Robbie Childress's family. Tess felt their eyes shooting daggers into her back. But how could she blame them? It didn't matter that Robbie had been a wife-abuser, a murderer; they'd lost a family member, and if anyone knew that pain, it was Tess. She closed her mind to their presence. To all the pain and loss. Even to Andie. Tess had to block it out or she'd go insane.

Aside from the Childresses and the Bergens—and Ali Barnes—the spectator seats were empty. No cameras, no media people, only the pertinent parties. Judge DeCarlo ran a tight ship.

The courtroom itself had stately old Victorian tall windows and lots of oak, but except for that Tess could have been back in that L.A. courtroom. She had the same feelings of anxiety, of awful tension, of wondering what would happen. But worse this time, much worse.

Lawrence turned in his chair and gave his wife and daughter a weary smile. He looked all right, Tess thought, just tired, with a few cuts on his face from broken glass and a bandage on one hand. Tess recalled the last time she'd seen her father, yesterday in the tent. His face, white, blank with shock, then dawning fear. The gun in his hand...

No, she wouldn't think about it. She would erase it from her mind; she had to. Maybe later, maybe, she could bring the memory out and examine it and understand what had happened. But now she could only sit there and try to smile back at her father, hold Carole's hand and forget about those few frenzied moments when she'd run and run, and her bag had banged against her hip, and she'd been able to feel the gun in it, hard and somehow very, very heavy.

There was a stirring in the courtroom. The door to

the judge's chambers opened, the clerk emerged, and everyone rose like puppets on strings. Judge DeCarlo entered, dressed casually in a polo shirt and khakis under his open black robe. A slim blond man with horn-rimmed glasses, he held himself so straight he looked taller than he was. And this afternoon, very stern.

The clerk intoned his lines—"Criminal case 24-356"—and Tess felt her heart constrict. Criminal case.

Steve Sutton rose, put his hand on Lawrence's arm to draw him along. They walked up to the tall oak bench along with D.A. McCleary.

Tess listened hard, straining to hear every word. The judge asked counsel to identify themselves for the record. McCleary replied in a clear, confident voice. "Your Honor, District Attorney Barbara McCleary, on behalf of the people of Pitkin County."

"Steven Sutton, Your Honor, of Sutton, Kemp and Kern, on behalf of the defendant, filing our appearance."

There was some more talk, legalese. The only thing Tess really understood was that her father pleaded not guilty and waived pretrial conference.

"Plea of not guilty," Judge DeCarlo repeated. "Bail is set by agreement as a seven-hundred-fifty-thousand-dollar signature bond. Defendant is released, but must not leave Pitkin County. The trial date will be set when I consult my calendar. Questions, counsel?"

Sutton and McCleary both replied, "No, Your Honor."

Bang went DeCarlo's gavel; he rose, walked swiftly out of the courtroom, and his door shut behind him.

It was over.

Lawrence walked up to the oak barricade and

leaned over it to hug his wife. Then he turned to Tess and hugged her.

"You okay, Dad?" she asked quietly.

"Yes, I'm okay," he said, but when she tried to meet his eyes, gauge his expression, he turned away, to thank Steve Sutton.

"It was a pleasure, Lawrence," Sutton said. "And I'll put a call into Mr. Morris as soon as I get to my office."

"Morris?" Carole asked.

"Cody Morris. He's a top defense attorney, Mrs. Bergen. Your husband requested him to take his case. I have great hopes that he will."

Tess looked at her father, puzzled. How did her father know about this Cody Morris? But everyone was moving toward the door of the courtroom, and Carole was looking very done-in. This was not the time to ask.

Steve Sutton was going on about Morris. "He'll provide the best defense you can get. His team is extraordinary. He's an excellent choice."

"Where does he live?" Tess asked, thinking New York or L.A. Some big-city firm.

"Warm River, Idaho," Steve Sutton replied.

"Idaho," Tess repeated.

She tried to meet her father's eyes again, but he was looking straight ahead. His arm was around his wife and he was moving out of the courtroom, down the backstairs and toward the waiting car Sutton had ready to avoid the media. They crowded into the car, Sutton driving. No one said much.

Tess sat in front, her parents in back. She didn't have the courage to turn around and see the silent torment on her father's face. It wasn't because of the cost of his defense—thank God he could afford it—it wasn't because of Robbie Childress; it wasn't even because of Andie anymore. It was because of her. He'd never meant to involve her. He couldn't bear the thought that he had, that he'd caused his daughter to be as guilty as he was in the eyes of the law.

Tess turned to look out the passenger window. She wanted to comfort her father, to tell him she wasn't sorry she'd helped him. She owed Andie that. She'd only helped him mete out true justice.

Oh, but she was afraid of being found out. Terrified, in fact. Terrified also of her father being convicted of murder, her mother losing her mind, her family destroyed.

Was she worried about the morality of what she'd done? she asked herself. Yes. No. God, she didn't know. She was absolutely sure of one thing, though—she was plagued constantly with the fear that the police would find the gun.

FIVE

Along with millions of other viewers, Cody Morris tuned into Craig and Gail on "The Judge's Advocate" and thought about vigilante justice. As one of the country's top criminal defense attorneys, nicknamed the Miracle Worker, Cody had given the issue a lot of consideration during his thirty years in practice. Naturally he didn't as yet have many details on the shooting of Robbie Childress, but he'd watched the Childress murder trial and listened to the verdict, and he had his personal opinion about whether justice had been served.

He sat in the living room of his comfortable log home just outside Warm River. His snakeskin-booted feet were propped up on the glass-slab coffee table that was supported by entwined elk antlers. He thought about what Lawrence Bergen had done—had *allegedly* done—and hoped the man retained defense counsel just as good as Robbie Childress had gotten himself.

He had to assume that Lawrence Bergen was innocent until proved guilty, and that he deserved the very best defense he could procure. Every citizen of the U.S. deserved this kind of protection, and to

Cody's mind very few got it. Except of course those with money. A lot of money.

Cody turned off the TV, walked to the huge plate-glass window with the multimillion-dollar view of the Grand Tetons and felt a familiar hankering—he'd like the Bergen case. If anyone could get Bergen off, he could.

That afternoon, running his Saturday errands in town at the post office and hardware store, at least a dozen locals stopped him on the streets. "Hey, Cody, Bergen ought to hire you," they all said.

And Cody, in his good ol' boy Western drawl, replied, "Well, maybe I'll be gettin' a call. Never know."

Cody Morris, born and raised in Idaho, had always cut quite the figure around town. With his thick silver hair, a boiled felt Stetson, the fringed cowhide jacket, the Native American silver-and-turquoise jewelry, he was hard to miss. Three U.S. presidents had vacationed at his ranch retreat within sight of the majestic Tetons on the outskirts of Yellowstone National Park. He'd had his own TV show a few years back, broadcast nationwide by satellite from his living room—Cody on the leather couch, the huge antler chandelier above him, Navajo rugs and Western art adorning the log walls—in which he extolled the virtues of criminal defense law. He was canny, an expert interrogator, using his soft-spoken Western drawl to manipulate and befriend. To destroy.

He'd defended the best of them and the worst, and was the repository of more celebrity secrets than any columnist.

When Cody got home from his errands, he saddled up his favorite quarter horse mare and went for a ride in the sage-dotted valley he owned. It was a glorious June afternoon, the sky cloudless, the peaks of the Teton and the Sawtooth Mountains still capped by snow.

The phone rang that afternoon. "Mr. Morris? This is Steve Sutton. I'm an attorney from Aspen, Colorado, and I wonder if I might have a minute of your time...."

"Uh-huh," Cody said, repressing a self-satisfied grin. "And just what can I do for you, son?"

"I'm making this call, sir, on behalf of Lawrence Bergen."

"Uh-huh," Cody said.

Private investigator Dan Hadley parked his car three blocks from Susan's North Beach condo—on a Saturday in the middle of the tourist season, he was lucky to get even that close—and wondered why he was bothering with this relationship at all. He'd never been much good at relationships and, at forty-two, he doubted he'd ever develop the knack.

He sat in his car for a long time thinking about his history with women. Not much to think about. He'd hoped to change all that with Susan. He was willing. The thing was, Susan was hedging. Okay, so he'd blown it Thursday night—and she'd been busy last night—but he was here now, wasn't he?

He thought about the ticket in his pocket. It was to tonight's Giants-Braves game at Candlestick Park, a seat right behind home plate, just high enough up so that the foul-ball net didn't obstruct the view. He could be at the game. Instead, he was doing the right thing, trying to make it up to Susan, who had tickets to the theater.

"You mess Saturday night up, Hadley," she'd said, "and I'm calling it quits."

Susan didn't need him. She tolerated him, and they were good in bed together. But over the three years they'd been dating, she'd kept a measure of distance between them, almost as if she sensed she needed to protect herself from the inevitable moment that he'd self-destruct. And she'd had other men in those three years, too. There'd been George and Hank, both investment bankers, the same field as hers. He couldn't believe she'd waste her time on two of the most boring individuals on earth—especially when she could have been with him. But she had. Every time Dan had screwed up a date she'd thrown him out on his ear and gone searching for someone who was, in her words, reliable, stable. Her coldness at those times, her abandonment of him, had hurt like hell. And yet…Dan had to admit he'd enjoyed the freedom. If only for a few weeks, it had felt safe, normal. Can't get hurt too badly if you're alone.

He finally got out of the car and walked up the hill to Susan's condo complex. When she let him in, he took one look at the strapless, calf-length dark green dress she was wearing and felt like a heel. A lovely woman like Susan deserved better. And he'd been a mess lately.

"You look beautiful," he told her.

"Flattery will get you everywhere," she quipped, and she did that thing that always turned him on— she raked her fingers unconsciously through her long, curling chestnut hair.

Dan kissed her, and Susan responded, even laughing a little as she whispered against his mouth, "I don't know why I put up with you." Then he drew his fingers across her naked back, felt the satin-smoothness of her skin and the way she responded to his touch. If nothing else they had that effect on each other.

She made dinner for them before the theater, lobster in some sort of tomato pink, creamy sauce, and asparagus. Dan would rather have played around in the bedroom, but the dinner was excellent, and God only knew when he'd last had a decent meal. Certainly not Thursday night, or even last night, when he'd done a repeat performance with his buddies.

He helped carry the dishes into the kitchen, stacking them while Susan freshened her makeup. "We have only about thirty minutes to get to the theater," she called from the bathroom, and his first thought was that the Giants game would be in the fourth, maybe fifth inning.

Dan walked back into the white-on-white living room and switched on the TV. Wouldn't hurt just to know the score.

"What are you doing?" Susan asked behind him, and he winced.

"Checking the score."

"The baseball game?"

"Uh, yeah, I'll turn it off."

"Do that," she said.

They took her car, and Dan drove. Later he'd wonder why he admitted it, but at the time he told himself it never hurt to tell the truth.

"I have a ticket for the game," he said.

"Oh? Where did you get it?"

"One of the guys. You know."

"Last night, I suppose."

"Well, yes. You had that bankers' dinner, and I was just hanging out with the stray cat...." Oops, Dan thought, Susan hated the stray he fed. Said the cat had fleas and bad breath. "Anyway," he went on quickly, "Lonny had this extra ticket. It's no big deal."

"But you took it even though you knew we had a date."

"Well, I... It didn't mean anything, Susan."

"And you were out again. What time did you get in? Two in the morning? Three?"

"Oh, not that late. I'm sure it wasn't much past ten."

"Uh-huh."

Out of the corner of his eye, he saw her fold her arms over her chest. Bad sign. "I know I've been going out too much lately," he offered.

"It isn't going out, Dan. We're going out right now. It's that you're hanging around with that bunch of losers. You're drinking too much and you're smoking again. You're a wreck. It was that trial, Robbie Childress's trial."

"Come on, Susan, the trial wasn't that big of a deal." Liar, he thought, and then Tess Bergen's words smacked him in the brain again. *How can you sleep at night knowing what you've done here?*

"You are such a bad liar," Susan was saying. "You're beating yourself up because of that Childress thing. Because you did your job. And now you'll beat yourself up because Lawrence Bergen did what the jury should have done in the first place."

"That's bullshit," Dan muttered.

"No, it's not. You blame yourself for uncovering all that stuff about police screwups and Andie Bergen's fast-lane friends. Oh, Dan, you're such a blind fool." She fell silent for a moment, then said, "Take me home."

"Ah, no, Susan, let's not do this."

"Take me home, Dan. Go to your game. Go out with the boys. Get drunk. Get lung cancer. I don't care anymore."

"We're going to the show."

"Turn this car around, Dan Hadley," she said.

So he did.

He walked her to her door, the silence between

them pulsing in the chill night breeze from the bay. Then, when she'd managed the key in the lock, he let out a low breath. "Look," he said, "I'm reforming. I really am."

Susan turned and glared at him. "Wait a minute," she said, and she disappeared inside. When she returned she plunked the razor he kept in her bathroom into his hand. "Here," she said, "you need a shave. Now get out of my life, please," and she closed the door in his face.

He made the game by the bottom of the seventh inning.

Barbara McCleary unzipped the side zipper on her linen skirt, did a little wiggle—as thin as she was it didn't take much—and let the skirt drop to the bedroom floor.

"A garter belt?" Eric Pedersen said from where he was stretched out in bed, hands behind his head. "Now, that I like."

"Thought you would." She slid out of her jacket, carefully tugged the silk shell over her head and raised a playful brow at her lover as she slowly ran her hands over her hips. She closed her eyes for a moment. "Oh, God, I feel so good tonight," she whispered.

"I bet you do." Eric sat up then and caught her hand, pulling her close. He turned her around and patted her fanny, then ran a finger inside her garter belt, snapping it lightly against the back of her leg.

"Mm," she said, and she felt his lips on her, the scratch of his Viking beard on the small of her back, and shivers of pure, raw delight ran up her spine and along her hip. "What are you doing back there?" she asked.

He turned her around then and kissed her belly,

running his hand up beneath her bra to cup a small, firm breast. And then she lowered herself to him, straddling him on the side of the bed while his mouth found hers and he undid her bra, slipping it off her shoulders, dropping it to the floor.

Eric kneaded her breasts with his big hands and she arched her back. He moved a hand lower then, pushing aside her panties beneath the lacy garter belt until he found her warmth.

"Oh," Barbara moaned, "you're torturing me."

"Good," he said.

They came together like that, still sitting, Barbara above him, on the side of her bed. Eric moved in and out of her, asking, "Do you like it? Is it good?" but she shook her head and silenced him with her lips, lost in a world of her own sensations, riding the waves as they flowed and ebbed and flowed stronger yet.

When it was over, Barbara in a sweatshirt and cut-off jeans, Eric dressed, they heated the Chinese food he'd brought from nearby Aspen. They sat in the tiny alcove of the kitchen in her Pan-Abode—a poor man's log home. It was on the river, though, and not all crowded in with the neighbors' like the mega-homes in Aspen. Woody Creek was only six miles from Aspen. It could have been sixty.

"I take it you had a good day in court," he said, holding a forkful of chicken in midair.

"Excellent."

"And Bergen's here in jail?"

Barbara looked up. "Not in jail, Eric. He's been released on bond. He can't leave the county, though."

"When's the trial?"

"DeCarlo won't set a date till early in the week, but I'm guessing it won't happen till after Christmas."

"You mean Bergen's got to stay here for seven months more?"

"Uh-huh."

"Wow. And what if he's innocent? Isn't that unfair?"

"He's guilty as sin."

Eric shook his head. "I thought you were innocent till proved guilty."

Barbara leaned close over the table. "Eric, sweetie, that's just for the public. It sounds good. I can assure you there's not a prosecutor in the world who believes it."

"That's pretty cynical."

Barbara shrugged.

"So you must have a lot on him."

"Enough."

"The gun? I heard on the radio today that the cops haven't found the gun yet."

"The gun's a problem," she admitted. "But I can get a conviction without it, no prob, though it sure would be easier if we can find it. If I can just get Tess Bergen in for an interview…"

"You think she's got it?"

"My gut instinct tells me she had it. And I don't think there're too many places she could have stashed it, either. Too little time."

Eric gazed over her shoulder for a moment, then refocused. "I feel sorry for that family," he said.

"The Bergens?"

"Look what they've already been through. I've got kids. If anything ever happened to one of them… well, I don't know what Maggie and I would do."

Barbara couldn't help her cool reaction to Maggie's name. It wasn't that she disliked Eric's wife. It was just that she didn't like any reminders of her. And Eric had a bad habit of doing that. Sometimes men were so dumb.

She shook her mind clear. "Are you saying you'd kill someone who hurt one of your kids?"

"I don't know. I just know that if anything happened to either of them, it would be the end of my life. I guess, yeah, I'd want the guy that hurt them dead. Especially if he was found not guilty. I could kill him."

Barbara pushed aside her plate and sat back, staring at her lover. "You're saying you'd take the law into your own hands and commit murder?"

"It wouldn't be murder."

"What the hell else would it be?" she demanded.

"Justifiable homicide."

"In a case such as this there's no such animal, Eric. Justifiable homicide would only work if, say, someone broke into your house, threatened you with a gun or something, and you were forced to defend yourself. Bergen shot Childress in cold blood. Nothing on earth can justify that."

They dropped the subject, but the mood between them had soured. And then Eric, who'd been prepared to spend the night because Maggie and the kids were out of town, said he had to ride his motorcycle home and let the dog out.

"The dog?" Barbara asked.

"Yeah. The dog freaks out. But I could drive on back and then we could go for a midnight ride...."

"Never mind," Barbara said.

"You're mad."

"No, I'm not. I'm just tired. Coming down from a big high today."

"Are you sure?"

"I'm sure," she said, but when Eric was gone, she leaned against the door and let out a breath. Was everyone going to think she was the villain here? It wasn't fair. For God's sake, Bergen killed Childress and he should damn well have to pay for it. He was lucky she hadn't asked for the death penalty.

SIX

On Monday morning, before the press got wind of his arrival, Cody Morris landed in Aspen in his private jet. He leased a black Ford Expedition at the airport for the duration of his stay and drove into town directly to the Little Nell Hotel at the base of Aspen Mountain. It was a small hotel, but luxurious, and he'd reserved a two-bedroom suite for himself and two more rooms for his team members, who would join him shortly.

He called the concierge and gave him a list of requirements: extra telephone lines for his fax and computer, a large coffeepot and small refrigerator—not the already stocked minifridge, either. He wanted snack-type groceries, a full bar, the works. Then he said, "Oh, and you can let the press corps know I've arrived. I'll speak to them in an hour out on that nice patio below my windows. You got all that, son?"

By midmorning he was on the phone to Steve Sutton, arranging a meeting in his suite for that afternoon—all three Bergen family members were to attend—and then he informed Sutton that he was going to speak to the press shortly.

"Do you think that's wise, sir?" Sutton asked.

Cody laughed. "My dear boy, the media can be either friend or foe. I think I'll make myself a few new best friends this morning."

"Should I be there, sir?"

"You just let me handle it, son. Alrighty?"

"Yes, sir," Sutton said.

After speaking to the local attorney, Cody stood at the window of the suite looking up the slope of Aspen Mountain and the *Silver Queen* gondola running up and up and disappearing over a rise. The gondola cars were full of tourists and hikers and mountain bikers. Under the gondola people walked up the road that switchbacked across the face of the mountain, many with dogs romping beside them.

Idyllic, scenic. But that wasn't what Cody was in Aspen for. No, sir. He'd see little of the mountain scenery, but what did he care? He could go home to enjoy the scenery.

He considered putting in a call to the district attorney on the case. Sutton had provided Cody with her name and number: Barbara McCleary. Sutton had said she was tough.

Excellent. Cody liked a good fight. In the end he decided not to talk to her yet; he wanted to find out more about her first. Be Prepared was his motto, just like the Boy Scouts. He hated surprises.

At eleven he walked down the four flights of stairs to the lobby and made his way out to the patio, where crisply uniformed waiters and waitresses were setting tables for lunch by the pool. The media had gathered, he saw, near a long stone planter graced with petunias, pansies and geraniums. A nice bucolic setting for the interview.

"Hello, boys and girls," Cody began when they gathered before him, no one pressing or yelling out questions. They all knew better than to harass Cody

Morris. "Nice of you to come over on such short notice." He got a few laughs on that one. "I just want to say a few words this morning, and then I'll take a couple questions." He smiled a winning smile, relaxed, easy with them. The truth was he adored the attention and knew that viewers all over the world would listen in.

For his media pals, Cody put on his very best Western drawl. "I wanna first thank all you newsfolk for comin' over this morning," he said as the cameras were switched on and videotapes rolled. "And I wanna say how much it means to me to be on this important case."

"Have you met Lawrence Bergen yet?" one young reporter interrupted.

Cody allowed for the boy's rookie status. "No, son, not yet, but I'm looking forward to it." Then he went on, his cadence slow and easy, intimate, as he asked for some privacy for the poor, beleaguered Bergen family who were, as he put it, "still deep in their grief over the loss of Andie. The torment to their souls is more than any of us can imagine," he said solemnly, taking on the role of preacher now, mustering sympathy for the Bergens.

He finally fielded a few questions to keep everyone happy.

"On what basis are you going to defend Lawrence Bergen, when the entire world already believes he shot Robbie Childress?"

"Oh, my goodness," Cody said, smiling, "the whole world? That's a lot of folks, ma'am. But we hardly know the facts yet. I, for one, am gonna wait and see."

"Any word on the missing gun, Cody?" came another question.

"No one's told me a thing, son."

"How about Lawrence Bergen? Will he plead temporary insanity?"

"Now why would the man do a thing like that? You're making the assumption Mr. Bergen committed a crime. Far as I see, the man's innocent till he's proved guilty."

"Cody," one of the veteran reporters said, "how are you going to defend a man who had motive and opportunity and gunshot residue all over him?"

"Now, who told you that?" Cody asked smoothly. "I never reveal my sources. The question stands, though. There's not a man, woman or child who doesn't think he's guilty. How are you going to mount a defense?"

"First," Cody said, letting out a whistling breath, "don't go believin' everything you read in the papers." He got a good laugh on that one. "And second, son, if what you say is true, I guess I better get to work, hadn't I?" And with that he turned, gave a friendly wave over his shoulder and disappeared back inside the hotel.

Satisfied with his performance, Cody returned to his room and ordered lunch to be brought up from the restaurant. Not bad. Fresh trout and saffron rice and a salad with an original vinaigrette. Then he checked himself in the mirror, passed a hand over his longish silver hair and waited for his client to arrive.

Steve Sutton ushered the Bergens in precisely on time. There were introductions all around, a bit awkward on Lawrence Bergen's part. Cody had them all seated in short order, comfortable on the pale leather furniture. He offered them coffee or bottled water or juice, but there were no takers. Too nervous.

"All right," he said, seating himself on a chair that he pulled over, "I'd like Steve here to give me a rundown on what's happened up to now. Just in case I've missed something." He didn't really need this re-capping of the case, but he did need the time to study the people gathered in front of him.

Sutton began, and Cody nodded and made appropriate remarks, but he was watching the Bergens very carefully all the time.

Lawrence. A nice-looking man, kept himself in shape, tired now. Some scratches and cuts—the tent scene, of course. He gave the impression of being much the gentleman, calm and in control. His eyes were not exactly afraid but anxious. Very anxious. Who wouldn't be in this situation? Guilty or innocent? Hm. Not that it mattered, not yet. It could, though.

Carole. Her eyes were a little glazed, out of focus. He recognized that look—drugs. Tranquilizers? Anti-depressants? She'd been a lovely woman, but now she was diminished. The death of a child did that to you.

Theresa. Tess. Pretty. Circles under her eyes, trying for composure but not quite making it. She kept glancing at her parents, one, then the other, as if worried, as if she was responsible for them. Interesting.

"So," Steve Sutton was saying, "this is how it stands now. The D.A. will go ahead with the prosecution on the basis of the gunshot residue."

"Trial date set?" Cody asked.

"Uh, yes, Judge DeCarlo set it this morning. January 4."

"We have seven months. Okay."

"You don't want a delay?" Sutton asked, surprised.

"Heck, no. I'll be ready by then. I can only hope the D.A. isn't. Let's get this thing over with."

"January," Lawrence repeated.

"Now, I'm going to need—" Cody checked himself. "Anyone locate the murder weapon yet?"

"No," Steve replied.

"Fine, good. Anyone come forward with a new story, anyone from the tent, eyewitnesses?"

Steve shook his head. "The police are still asking people to come in, sending their clothes to the lab when they can."

"Uh-huh. Now, are there any particular problems, any pressure being put on anyone by the cops or D.A.?"

"McCleary wanted Lawrence to take a polygraph."

Cody laughed. "Well, now, I take it you refused on behalf of your client?"

"Yes, sir."

"Good. Anything else?"

Steve cleared his throat. "Barbara McCleary has also requested an interview with Tess. A strongly worded request."

"I'm not surprised. And you're worried it'll make Tess look uncooperative if she doesn't comply quickly."

"Yes."

"No problem. I'll accompany Ms. Bergen to the interview. Tell McCleary we can be there whenever she wants. Tomorrow."

"But—" Tess began.

"Don't you worry about it, young lady. I'll be there. I'll control the questioning. Watch me and you'll do fine. I'm very, very good at this sort of thing."

Tess Bergen took a deep breath. "I really have to do this?"

"Yep, I'm afraid so. Unpleasant but necessary. Don't worry about it, you hear?"

Cody stood up and faced the four people in front of him. "I want to spell out some of my rules. There are a few things I will not budge on. One, except for myself, no talking to the press. No statements, no interviews, no off-the-record remarks. Not a word. Two, I have complete discretion on the members of my team. Now, I have a staff in Idaho, and some will stay there, but I'll need a couple of them down here for the duration. I'll also need a top-notch psychiatrist, but that can wait. I'll put out feelers. I'll certainly want Steve here to be my local liaison—that okay with you, son?"

"Yes, sir, Mr. Morris."

"Heck, call me Cody. We're going to be real good pals before this is over." He paused in thought. "One more thing. I'm going to need an investigator. The best there is. We're going to run down every lead no matter how small, follow every suggestion of impropriety on the other side, dig up God knows what. I know who I want, and I hope I can get him. You folks know the name Dan Hadley?"

Lawrence and Carole looked at each other.

"Hadley?" Carole said. "Isn't he the one…?"

"The one on the Childress trial, that's him," Cody said. "Hadley's already intimately familiar with Robbie Childress, his friends, enemies, habits, the whole nine yards. With Dan Hadley on the case we'll save months of digging. I want him."

Abruptly Tess Bergen stood up, her hands on her hips. Her face was white. "Not that son of a bitch," she blurted.

Cody regarded her, his head tilted, one eye half-closed. "Well now, miss, I don't know about his mama, but he is one hotshot investigator. You want your daddy to beat this rap?"

"Of course, but…"

Carole was tugging at Tess' hand. The girl's cheeks were showing red splotches now. She was a fighter, it seemed. Well, good, Cody thought. Before this was over, she'd need to be.

"I only use the best. No arguments. It's Hadley or I'm outta here."

The appointment with the D.A. was set for ten in the morning. Tess had been given the option of putting it off till later, but she'd decided she'd rather get it over with.

She met Cody in the lobby in the Little Nell Hotel, and they walked across town toward the D.A.'s office, the press on their heels. Cody said only one thing to the followers, that Ms. Tess Bergen was complying with a request that she talk to the D.A. And then they walked on, Cody reassuring her this was the right thing to do.

"Don't you worry about the D.A., honey," Cody told her. "I won't let her get into anything touchy. I know you were there in the tent, and I know you were close to your father. That's fine. Everyone knows that. Beyond that nobody needs to be told anything. People are just jumping to conclusions. I'll stop you if you seem to be treading on thin ice, okay?"

"Okay," Tess said, "but…do you, I mean, should I…?"

He patted her hand. "Do I want a confession? Not on your life, little lady. And I'm not rehearsing you, either. I want you to act perfectly natural. Upset, scared, nervous, whatever. Anyone would be."

Confession, Tess thought. Even Cody assumes I took the gun, which makes me an accessory.

"I'm sorry you have to do this," Cody was saying, "but if you refuse to talk, it can backfire on us. We want to appear cooperative. Nothing to hide, that's our motto."

They went into the building, up an elevator. Tess was terrified that the truth would show in her eyes, that the D.A. would read her mind. She told herself it wasn't possible, but her hands shook and her heart pounded and her chest felt constricted.

"Cody Morris to see Barbara McCleary," Cody said to the receptionist, and Tess took a deep breath.

Barbara McCleary came out of her office and introduced herself. She was stunning, Tess thought, feeling dowdy in her denim skirt and sleeveless blouse. Barbara wore an impeccably tailored pantsuit in beige. She was so tall and so reed-thin, with short, short hair only very attractive women could pull off. A patrician beauty with incredible self-confidence. Tess tried to smile as they shook hands. Barbara's grip was firm and warm; hers was clammy and trembling.

"Please, let's go into my office," the D.A. said. "I really appreciate you coming in so quickly. I know we all want to get to the bottom of this case as expeditiously as possible."

"Of course we do," Cody said, his eyes locked on Barbara's.

"I'm going to record this interview. Any objections, Mr. Morris?"

"Call me Cody," he said. "Save Mr. Morris for court. No objections to a recording."

"Okay, let's start." She turned on a tape recorder, established the participants, the date and location, then consulted her notes.

"Ms. Bergen, please describe your arrival at the tent the afternoon of Friday, June 20."

Tess started to speak but had to clear her throat, then begin again. "Well, I walked from the condo where we're staying, the Gant. It took maybe, uh, ten minutes." She swallowed. "I got there a little after one, because I didn't want to get caught in that awful crush."

"What time did you arrive at the tent?"

"Oh, I don't know exactly. I didn't check my watch."

"Approximately."

"Say one-twenty."

"You're doing fine, honey," Cody said encouragingly.

"I showed my pass at the entrance and went in. It was very crowded. I knew where Dad's tables were located, so I headed in that direction. It took a while because of all the people."

"How long?" Barbara asked.

"Ten minutes maybe?"

"And you saw your father there?"

"Well, at first people were in the way, but then I could see him. His back was to me, and he was in the corner behind his tables, talking to someone."

"Did you recognize who he was talking to?"

She shook her head. "No, no, I couldn't see who it was." She realized her hands were locked together, her knuckles white. She forced her fingers to relax. "Then...then I heard something. I know now it was the gun going off."

"Did you see Robbie Childress at any time?"

"No, I didn't. The crowds—"

"Did you see who shot Mr. Childress?"

"She said she didn't see him, Ms. McCleary," Cody Morris cut in, "and any questions beyond that are immaterial as far as I'm concerned."

"I'd like to know. I'm trying to establish if she saw the murder weapon, Mr. Morris."

"I think she's answered all the questions she needs to, don't you? If she never saw Childress, then how could she have witnessed the crime or seen the gun?"

"It's possible that—" Barbara began.

"I don't believe so," Cody interrupted. "I think we're done here. Tess?"

Grateful tears burned behind Tess's eyes. She nodded.

Angrily Barbara turned off the recorder. "This is what you call cooperation, Morris?" she snapped.

"I certainly do. Ms. Bergen here came in of her own free will, told her story without any reluctance. Heck, you want more than that?"

"I sure as hell do."

"Well, that's all there is," he said, hands wide, palms up. "We've cooperated and we're done." He leveled a suddenly hard gaze on the district attorney, and Tess noticed that he lost his drawl. "Barbara, if you think Ms. Bergen here is in any way culpable, in any way a suspect, then you charge her. That's your choice—you charge her or we walk outta here. Ms. Bergen doesn't have to say another word to you or anyone else."

Tess held her breath. This was it, this was when she got arrested, charged, put in jail. Oh, my God.

Barbara McCleary crossed her arms over her chest and tapped a foot, studying Cody. Finally she said, "She'll need to be deposed."

"Fine." He nodded, his thick silver hair glinting in the overhead light. "A pleasure to meet with you, Barbara. A real pleasure. Shall we go, Tess?"

Outside, Cody turned to her and grinned. "You did fine, Tess, just fine. You tell your story like that and your daddy hasn't a worry in the world."

"Unless they find the gun," Tess whispered, then was appalled at what she'd said.

"You think they'll find it, honey?" Cody asked, cocking his head.

"I...I don't know. How would I know? I just meant..."

"Sure, I know what you meant, but I bet you that gun's long gone, don't you?"

She looked at him, yearning to tell him, to answer his question, craving the release of confession, but her tongue froze in her mouth. She was afraid. Her secret was taking on a life of its own, becoming a living entity that whispered constantly inside her head. *Don't tell, don't say anything, don't let anyone know, don't trust anyone.* And every day that went by the voice grew, the secret became more irrevocable, more powerful, more dangerous. No one had found the gun, not even with metal detectors. No one.

Maybe they never would.

"Sure," she finally said, trying to smile. "Whoever shot Robbie is probably in Mexico now, and the gun's probably in the ocean somewhere."

Cody looked at her, one of his eyes half shut. "Most likely you're right, honey. You heading home now?"

"Um, no, I don't think so. I think I'll take a walk. Would you mind calling my father and telling him what went on?"

"Sure, I'll tell him."

"Thanks, Mr. Morris."

He turned away, and Tess waited till he was gone before drawing in a deep breath and hurrying down the hill away from the reporters who were approaching Cody. She spotted the bike path along the Roaring Fork River then, right behind the courthouse. She walked fast, gulping huge breaths of air, warm, dry high-altitude air.

The secret weighed on her heavily, like something horrible growing inside her. If only she could tell someone. If only... Her father? Her mind recoiled instantly from the thought, knowing the subject was taboo between them. Cody? But if he had information about the murder weapon, wouldn't he be legally obligated to turn the evidence over to the police? After all, this wasn't lawyer-client privilege, because she wasn't his client.

No, there wasn't a soul on earth she could confide in. She was absolutely, uncompromisingly alone.

Cody Morris got back to his hotel room in time to catch the tail end of "The Judge's Advocate." Gail Hollister and Craig Kramer were going at it, discussing the responsibility of defense attorneys in the American legal system.

Cody took his hat off and sat down to watch; he enjoyed their sparring immensely.

"The defendant has the benefit of the doubt," Craig was saying. "He's innocent until proven guilty. That's the cornerstone of our system, Gail."

"Fine, I'll give you that, but too many guilty criminals get off on technicalities or high-powered legal sleights of hand."

"You mean," Craig said slyly, "like Robbie Childress?"

Yes, Cody thought, ain't *that* the truth.

"I'm not going to get into that, Craig. It's beside the point."

"It is the point, Gail. Without that miscarriage of justice, we would not be sitting here discussing this sad affair."

"Well, since we are," Gail said in a deft change of subject Cody had to admire, "how about you explain to our viewers how a defense attorney can defend a client he knows is guilty?"

Cody listened carefully. He got tired of defense lawyers being portrayed as sleazebags. Maybe Craig could shed some light on the subject.

Craig faced the cameras. "Our legal system, as I said, gives the person charged with a crime the benefit of the doubt. Without that, we're no different from an authoritarian regime, where people are imprisoned for no reason and without recourse. China, the old Soviet Union, Nazi Germany. Okay. Defense lawyers are charged with upholding this rule. Every one of our clients has the constitutional right to a fair and speedy trial by a jury of his peers, and to the best defense possible."

"Words, Craig, just words. What really happens when you have to defend an ax murderer, a vicious cold-blooded killer?"

Well, Craig? Cody thought. We've all had to do it.

"A defense lawyer does not ask a defendant if he is innocent or guilty. Of necessity, he goes into a mindset in which he looks at the facts, the evidence, and tries the case on its merits. His client is entitled to this."

Gail leaned forward. "What if your guilty client confesses to you?"

"That's different. Ethically, if a lawyer has knowledge, specific evidence of a client's guilt, he has to go to the court with it. Or at the very least he should resign from the case."

"And I suppose," Gail said sarcastically, "every defense lawyer adheres rigorously to these ethics?"

Craig shot back, "And, Gail, every prosecutor is above reproach, tries every case on its merits? Come on."

Cody smiled and clicked the TV set off. The legal profession was becoming a circus. All the hype got in the way sometimes, but it really was fun most of the time. For Cody, not for the defendant. Not for Lawrence Bergen.

Oh, yes, there was a sad man. What he must be going through. And Tess, she was going through hell, too. Poor, poor people. Well, Cody thought as he went to his desk to start working, he'd do his best for them all. And for that dead girl, Lawrence's daughter Andie, the man's flesh and blood. The most innocent victim of them all.

Dan Hadley crushed out his last butt, dumped a half-empty bottle of vodka down the sink and packed his bag. The call from Cody Morris had come two days ago, and it had been a godsend. Not only was it a good job with good pay, but he'd be able to leave San Francisco, leave the temptation to party with the guys, leave the dead-end life he was living, leave the relationship hassles with Susan. Just leave.

Work had been slow at the law firm in any case; he hadn't been able to charge many hours lately, and the attorneys were quite amenable to his taking a leave.

Yeah, he needed the work, but more than that he needed this particular job to even the score, to help get Lawrence Bergen off. Between Dan and Cody Morris, they could find some small, overlooked detail that no one else could find, cast doubt on the prosecution's case. Just like he'd done for Robbie Childress's defense team.

He walked down the steep front steps of the building he lived in, took one last look around at the view, at Alcatraz and the Golden Gate Bridge, which was hidden by its usual morning veil of fog, and threw his bag into his car. He leaned over and pulled a road map out of the glove compartment, then zeroed in on Aspen, Colorado, with his finger. About forty miles south of I-70, an easy two-day drive. It seemed kind of a vacation to Dan, two days of nothing to do but drive. Time out.

As he crossed the Bay Bridge in his gray sedan, he considered the irony of this new job. Dan knew he'd aided in the subversion of justice in the Childress trial. Hell, he'd known that all along. Even as he'd dug out facts about screwups in lab procedure, about nasty, well-kept secrets of prosecution witnesses, he'd known Robbie Childress was guilty of murder. He'd done his job, that was all. So, it'd be easier this time, far easier, because he'd be balancing the scales. If the system didn't work the way it was supposed to, he could give it a little shove to even things up.

He didn't analyze the morality of his actions as he drove down off the Bay Bridge, the cool, salty air of San Francisco Bay coming in the open window, blowing his hair onto his forehead. Dan was a pragmatic sort; he did what allowed him to escape his guilt.

He'd left California by lunchtime, picked up Route 50 across Nevada, a two-lane highway that reached nearly to Colorado, with nothing to see but jackrabbits and tumbleweed and squat ugly mountains where nothing grew. He got on I-70 the second day, marveled at how much dry, sagebrush-dotted land there was in the West, and figured he'd make it into Aspen by four in the afternoon.

He'd felt his strength and his will returning as the miles fled under his tires. He felt focused, and his craving for cigarettes seemed a bizarre eccentricity. His radio was tuned to various country-and-western stations, but every hour he paid attention to the news and listened carefully to every word on the Bergen case, even though most of it was probably crap. Still, he listened.

Signs announcing the Pitkin County Airport, Sardy Field, appeared. There it was, the air-traffic control tower, the tarmac. And there, also, were dozens and dozens of private jets parked wing to wing. Dozens. Jesus.

Then a golf course dotted with people, then another golf course on the other side of the highway.

As he drove past the city-limits sign that read Aspen: Altitude 7,980 Feet, he started looking around carefully. He was on the wide central artery, Main Street. Victorian mansions converted to lodges lined the street, and old-fashioned streetlights, like gaslights, stood at intervals. There were green lawns and wrought-iron fences and potted flowers and big old graceful cottonwoods along the sidewalks, with a hundred-foot-tall blue spruce every once in a while.

Three stoplights in a row, and he was at the corner of Mill and Main, with the elegant brick Hotel Jerome on his left, and a zillion tourists crossing every which way. Then he was in real city traffic, even though it was a small town, Range Rovers everywhere, his low sedan lost among the mostly four-wheel-drive utility vehicles and pickup trucks. People swarming, toting shopping bags with expensive logos.

Aspen. Hmm. He reserved judgment. Turning down a side street toward Aspen Mountain, Dan saw shops, bars, restaurants. Mezzaluna, Boogies, the Hard Rock Café. Beautifully restored Victorian brick buildings with the dates they were built carved on them, malls, brick-paved pedestrian malls. Goddamn, there was a magician in the mall doing tricks for a crowd of spectators.

The ski mountain on one side of town, with a gondola running up it, another mountain across from it, with houses built up its side, huge houses he could see from downtown.

Aspen. Busy place.

The mountains were green and glorious, and way beyond the town there were even taller, more jagged peaks still white with snow. In June.

Women with long legs and short shorts, hair-tossing gorgeous women, prosperous men in pastel polo shirts. Bicycles everywhere. And gleaming motorcycles—Hogs—parked in a glittering row in front of Mezzaluna.

Dan turned again and saw a grocery store. So these people ate regular food, maybe cooked at home sometimes. Goddamn.

It was beautiful, but it felt artificial to Dan, like Disneyland, a mini Magic Kingdom, no dirty little corners, no garbage cans, no cigarette butts on the sidewalks. But then, it *was* a resort. It was supposed to be like that.

He drove around some, getting the feel of the place. He passed the Little Nell Hotel where Cody Morris was staying. Too ritzy for Dan, even if Cody *was* paying the bills. It'd make him nervous.

Back to Main Street. Ah, there was the Pitkin County Courthouse, where the trial would be held. He'd get to know that place real well, he supposed. A big old squat building of redbrick trimmed with granite, quite prepossessing.

Aspen. He hated it; it was too full of tourists, too gorgeous, too perfect. Like the place was trying too hard to be what it used to be a hundred years ago. But it missed the mark. And then he noticed the satellite vans parked alongside the courthouse, people milling around carrying video cameras on their shoulders or microphones. Shit.

The media was here. Well, what did he expect? He turned his car up a street away from them. He'd like to stay incognito as long as he could, which probably wouldn't be very long, not with a high-profile case like this. Some of the newspeople here would have covered the Childress trial, and they'd recognize him. Oh, well, he'd deal with it when it happened.

The afternoon was hot, the Southwestern sun glaring through the moisture-free air. He hated it, already missed San Francisco's cool, damp air and fog.

Get over it, Hadley, he told himself. You're here for the duration.

He wondered what Morris had planned for him. The gun, probably, and no doubt some red herrings to distract the jury from Bergen.

The gun. Interesting that it hadn't been found. Did Morris know where it was?

He drove toward the east end of Aspen, following the dogleg Main Street made, and saw a nice unpretentious ski lodge. It felt right to Dan, so he pulled in and got himself a room. "For a week," he said to the desk clerk. "And then maybe for longer."

"You're lucky," the clerk told him. "This is our last room. The town's full up."

"Don't tell me," Dan said dryly. "The media."

He unpacked in the small, neat room with a view of Aspen Mountain over the treetops, took a shower and set out to walk around the town, get his bearings. He'd told Cody he'd call after dinner, because he hadn't known exactly when he'd get in, so he had time. It was what Dan always did in a strange town to get the feel—he walked around, hit a few bars, struck up conversations.

In Aspen, though, he'd have to seek out the joints where the locals hung out. Tourists were less than useless to him.

He asked the desk clerk.

"A cheap place to eat, let's see," the young guy said. "Try La Cocina or the Cantina, they're Mexican. Or the Chinese place. Locals' bars? Eric's Bar, the Red Onion, Cooper Street Pier."

"Thanks," Dan said.

He ordered a beer at the bar of the Red Onion, deliberately sitting next to a guy in dusty overalls. Definitely not a tourist.

"Where's that tent," he asked the guy, "you know, where that celebrity got shot last week?"

"Half a block that way," the man said, pointing.

"That must have been something," Dan said.

"Hey, I just went to work the next day like usual. The only thing that bothers me about it is the damn traffic's backed up because of all the newspeople coming into town."

Traffic, that seemed to be a big thing to locals. As for Robbie Childress or Lawrence Bergen, they were not Aspenites, they were celebrity visitors, and although Aspen residents seemed curious about how the case would turn out, they hadn't much real interest in these people's lives—or deaths.

He couldn't get any of them to open up about how they viewed the shooting or the parties involved or what they'd do if they got summoned for jury duty for this trial.

At La Cocina he ordered a beer, sat at the bar and talked to the very tall blond bartender. "So, who do you think did it?" Dan asked.

The bartender shrugged, his hands busy mixing margarites. "I'd bet on Bergen, but who knows? You can't believe a damn thing you read in the paper or see on TV. Maybe the butler did it." And he laughed.

Dan ate a plate of chicken enchiladas that were tasty, left a big tip and tried a couple of other places. At the Cantina a gorgeous woman with the longest, reddest nails he'd ever seen told him that the defense team would do well not to ask for a change of venue for the trial, because Aspen juries were known to like the concept of justice. "Very sophisticated," she said, drinking her beer and winking at him.

She knew her stuff, he figured.

At Eric's Bar no one gave a damn about the shooting, the trial or anything besides one another; it was a young crowd.

At Cooper Street Pier, the crowd was older, but no one had much to say about the case. The traffic, though, they sure bitched about that.

It was dark by then, and Dan wandered around the brick-paved malls. Thousands of people, it seemed, were wandering with him. The sun sank behind the mountains in a spectacular array of color. The air grew cool. Lights came on. Quartets of music students from the summer festival played chamber music here and there on the malls, a hat on the ground in front of them for tips.

Dan stopped near one, hands in his pockets, and listened. Beautiful music, something that sounded familiar, something that Susan had dragged him to hear at the opera house.

Susan. She seemed a million miles away.

He was revising his opinion of the town. This was okay, the music, the cool air, and there were real people here. You just had to search for them.

He walked back to his lodge, savoring the evening air, looking at the young girls. You're too old for that crap, he told himself, but he looked, anyway.

Back in his room, he kicked off his shoes and propped himself against the headboard of his bed, pulled the phone close and dialed Cody Morris's number.

"Glad you made it," Cody said in that easy drawl Dan had heard on television so many times before. "Welcome to Aspen. Quite a place, isn't it? Where you staying, son?"

Dan told him.

"I've got a block of rooms here at the Little Nell. The room service ain't bad," Cody said.

"I'll stay here for the time being. It suits me fine."

They talked some more, Cody catching Dan up on some things—the trial date, the still-missing gun, the way the shooting appeared to have gone down.

"Lawrence Bergen isn't breaking and neither is his daughter."

"Tess," Dan recalled.

"That's the one. Cute, nice girl. Looks mild, but there's something there inside that's pretty damn tough."

Dan replied with a noncommittal comment. Cody was right, though.

"So, ready to go to work?" Cody asked.

"I sure am," Dan said.

After he hung up, Dan put his hands behind his head and sat there like that, looking out the window, watching the moon bulge up over the shoulder of the mountain. He wondered how the Bergens would react to him. They were well aware by now that Morris had hired him, and they sure as hell knew what he'd done in the Childress trial.

And Tess. She hated his guts. Told him so, too, right to his face. Hey, he didn't blame her then, and he wouldn't blame her now.

But he would have to face her and work with her, closely, for months, probably.

And, from what Cody hinted at on the phone, Tess Bergen would have to face him with her own secrets, because if the rumors were true, she sure as hell couldn't tell those secrets to Cody.

SEVEN

Tess was having a memorable morning, and not a particularly pleasant one.

It began when she left the condo early to hike up Aspen Mountain and was followed by a young cameraman, followed until he gave up on the third switchback of the summer road below Ruthie's Run, one of the popular ski slopes on the face of the mountain.

She hiked on, though at a slower pace, trying to forget her fears, trying to forget the nebulous wedge that seemed to have been driven between herself and her father ever since the moment she'd pried the gun from his fingers.

She hiked, breathing deeply and evenly, and concentrated on medical textbook data, percentages of oxygen flow to the blood, normal diastolic and systolic pressure, borderline hypertension levels, blood-sugar-level ranges—numbers and norms. It was calming, at least, and she felt as if she was getting back in the swing, although in reality that was quite impossible. It would be at least seven months before she could think about residency, and then, depending on what happened at her father's trial, she might not even be accepted into the hospital of her choice, if any hospital at all would accept her.

Her mind shut down then. What was she doing, thinking about the future? Her future? Was she crazy, pretending her family wasn't in the midst of a nightmare? And what if the police found the gun and matched it to the bullet that killed Robbie? They had ballistics tests that could do that. And then, what if they found her fingerprints on it? She'd wiped it, desperately wiped it over and over. Still…

She stopped, leaning over and breathing heavily, then turned and looked down into the valley, into Aspen, which lay like a colorful jeweled collage of trees and square city blocks below. Could she see the spot where the gun was hidden? No. It was around the shoulder of the mountain from her, over that ridge and far below. But she could see it in her mind's eye. Oh, you bet she could.

At the top of the mountain, where the gondola stopped at the Sundeck restaurant, she rested for a while, sitting at a picnic table that overlooked the backside of Aspen Mountain, down into Little Annie Basin and beyond, to the peaks of Mount Hayden and Pyramid and the Maroon Bells. It was spectacular scenery. Fourteen-thousand-foot peaks, rocky, snow-capped tops that pierced the azure sky. All above timberline. And below, on the gentler mountain slopes, forests of midnight-green pines, huge open meadows, thickets of aspen and buck brush, and hawks wheeling in the valleys where the Castle Creek River twisted sharply, cutting the green earth.

It was magnificent country. Yet Tess could barely appreciate its beauty. She wondered if she ever would again.

And then, just as she was getting onto the gondola to ride back down to town, she saw Robbie's sister and brother-in-law right behind her.

Oh, God.

From behind her sunglasses she made eye contact for the briefest of time, uncomfortable as hell, realizing that of course Robbie's family would still be in Aspen. Because of the shooting, yes. But also because of his estate: the bank accounts, the Aspen house, his beautiful furnishings. All of which Andie had selected.

She turned and got in the six-person gondola car as it made its circuit in the roundhouse. Her legs felt watery and her skin prickled. Robbie's family. Awful, she thought. How could she have run into them like that?

By the time she reached the Gant condo her hiking shorts and T-shirt were sweat-soaked. Her cheeks were red from heavy exertion and from the close encounter with Robbie's family.

And she was late. There'd been a ten o'clock meeting with Cody and his defense team at the condo, and her presence was required. It was ten-twenty.

In the dark entranceway she kicked off her hiking shoes, yanked off her damp socks and straightened, running her fingers through her limp, dark hair. No help for it.

"Tess? Is that you, honey?" Her mother.

"Uh, yes. I'll be right there, I've just got to change."

"Come on in, we're all friends here." Cody.

Darn it.

Tess walked into the living room. "Sorry," she began, "I was hiking...." And then she saw him sitting there. Dan Hadley.

The men all rose politely. Her father. Cody. Brad

and Patrick, from Cody's Idaho office. Steve Sutton. And Hadley.

"Come, come, sit down," Cody said, and he patted the spot next to him on the long couch.

Tess sat obediently, but she was stiff, and she knew her face was growing even splotchier. Hadley. No one had told her he was in town.

"Did you have a nice walk?" Cody was asking.

"Yes…" she began, then, "well, not really. A reporter followed me, and then I ran smack into Robbie's sister and brother-in-law at the top of Aspen Mountain."

"Oh, my," Carole said.

"You didn't have a problem or anything?" Patrick, the youngest member of the team, asked.

"No, nothing like that. It was…awkward." She spoke to the group as a whole, and yet it was Hadley she was most aware of.

She glared at him malevolently, looked away, looked back again. He was the same fortyish man who'd sat on the witness stand for the defense and coolly destroyed Andie's reputation. It was him, all right. But back then, in the L.A. courtroom, he'd been groomed to the nth degree: expensive tweed jacket, conservative shirt, slacks, shoes, razor-cut sandy blond hair, insolent blue, heavy-lidded eyes, that deep, gravelly voice. The women jurors—five of them—had loved it. But now he looked different. Still handsome, yes—Tess grudgingly gave him that. But older somehow, leaner. He wore a blue button-down shirt, a little frayed, and a loose-fitting summer-weight tan sport coat that had also seen better days. The Levi's, too. And instead of the spiffy tasseled loafers, he had on scuffed cowboy boots.

The sharp blue eyes, Tess couldn't help noting,

seemed a little less clear, and she'd bet he hadn't shaved since yesterday. The arrogance was still there, though. It oozed from him. Shove it, she wanted to tell him, but instead, she looked over at Cody, who was speaking.

"Our own results from firing a .22-caliber handgun at a firing range... I think we can prove on the witness stand that it's possible to have gunshot residue on your clothes and skin if you're within a foot of the shooter. Brad," Cody said, "see if you can't talk the CBI into running a firing-range test. If you can't get their cooperation, we'll use a team from the Idaho Falls Police Force. I know they'll do it for me. It would be better if the local Colorado cops would, but..."

Tess listened, as did Dan Hadley, who had yet to say a word. Even when Cody spoke to him directly, Hadley merely nodded or voiced his agreement with "Uh-huh."

"What about witnesses at the tent?" Carole said. "Surely someone saw something. I know it was crowded, but someone must have seen who shot Robbie."

There was a heartbeat of silence in the room before Cody turned and replied, "Dan Hadley here will be checking on all that, ma'am. He'll interview hundreds of folks who were in the tent before we're done."

"But maybe they're afraid to speak up. Oh, I don't know." Carole subsided. But not before Tess caught her father's eye for a long moment. Her mother really didn't know.

Everyone else did, though. Everyone else in that room assumed her father was guilty.

Finally Hadley spoke. He leaned forward in his chair and said to Carole, "It's my job to get the truth out of those people, Mrs. Bergen." Then he smiled faintly, a slight uplifting of the corner of his mouth. Carole smiled back tentatively.

Dear God, Tess thought.

Steve Sutton mentioned a man by the name of Bob Winthrop. It seemed he was a private detective who had been retained by the Aspen district attorney's office.

"You know the man?" Cody asked Dan.

"Uh-huh," Dan said. "He's out of L.A. Winthrop's been in the business a long time."

"He any good?"

"Yeah, he's good. And don't let his looks deceive you. He's fat."

"Mm," Cody said. "I imagine he'll be looking for the gun."

"Uh-huh," Dan concurred. "We can take that to the bank."

Oh, my God, Tess thought, a private detective looking for the gun. A cold hand squeezed her heart.

"Enemies of Robbie's..." Cody was saying. "We need a list and we need to get on it, especially anyone local who had an ax to grind."

Patrick grinned. "I suppose it would be too much to hope that Childress had an enemy here in town who was also at the tent."

Everyone nodded. Cody even laughed. "That'd be my kind of defense, all right."

The meeting broke at noon when the fire whistle downtown sounded. "Gotta be on my way," Cody said, rising. "Briefs to file down at the courthouse. Now, you all know your assignments, so let's get on the ball. Time's money."

The group moved toward the front hallway, Carole politely saying there was more coffee made if anyone wanted a last cup. Lawrence hung back with his wife, an arm around her waist. *Tell her the truth,* Tess wanted to cry, but then she shut off the thought. What good would it do for Carole to know?

She wished, futilely, that she didn't know what her father had done. But still, she did not find that knowledge and her complicity reprehensible.

A second before her father had pulled the trigger, Tess couldn't have said how she'd felt about the act of final retribution. She knew now, though. She could never explain it, never expect anyone to comprehend who hadn't been through the ordeal of Andie's murder and the not-guilty verdict. But there it was. The truth. Her father had meted out justice when the system had failed to. She could never, would never, fault him. Nor would Andie, wherever Andie was.

She followed the group to the door, where Cody took his Stetson off a peg and placed it on his head.

It was Carole who, in her guilelessness, put her hand out to Dan Hadley. That was to be expected. But when Lawrence did the same, Tess drew herself up.

Then Hadley said, "Mr. Bergen, I hope there're no hard feelings. I'll do my best for you."

Lawrence nodded graciously.

Tess snapped. "Sure," she said. "You'll do your best. Anything for money, right, Mr. Hadley?"

He was several feet away, moving toward the door. He stopped, though, and stepped back to her. He leveled his steely blue gaze on hers and said, "I'm not sure an adversarial relationship is going to be productive, Ms. Bergen," and then he nodded to her parents and left.

The next few days were a whirlwind of defense brainstorming sessions. Sometimes everyone gathered at the condo, sometimes at Cody's Little Nell

Hotel suite. Tess preferred it when they met at the hotel. Because she was seldom included in the strategy meetings, she could avoid running into Hadley there. But at the condo...

It had been nearly a week since Hadley had arrived in town when Tess, who was in her bedroom, overheard Cody and his team in the living room.

"Dennis Wilson" came Hadley's distinctive, gruff voice.

"And who's Dennis Wilson?" Lawrence asked.

Hadley again. "I got his name from one of the wine-festival volunteers. Wilson was a volunteer, too, some sort of local wine expert who works at a fancy dinner theater here in Aspen, does all the wine buying for the owner. Anyway," Hadley went on, "apparently this Wilson used to be a caretaker for Robbie at his Aspen home. Wilson and his wife, who was pregnant at the time, lived in the caretaker unit."

Tess remembered the couple. Yes. Dennis was a good-looking, thirty-something guy Robbie and Andie had met at the Crystal Palace dinner theater. They'd talked about wine at the bar, Andie, of course, telling Dennis about her father's magazine. One thing had led to another, and Dennis and his wife—six months pregnant—had moved into the caretaker unit at Robbie's. Tess had met the couple that Christmas in Aspen, when she'd visited Andie and Robbie on semester break. Must have been four, five years ago, Tess thought, and she remembered the bruise on Andie's cheek. One of many Andie had gotten over the years.

"Robbie fired Wilson and his pregnant wife right in the middle of the winter ski season," Hadley was telling the team. "Word is the Wilsons couldn't find a place to live in town and had to move clear down the valley. The volunteer told me that Wilson and Robbie had a huge blowup and Wilson told everyone who'd listen that he was going to pay Childress back."

"Good stuff," said Cody.

"There's more. About a week after this big fight, the windshield of Robbie's Range Rover was smashed by a rock. Robbie reported it to the police, but no one could prove who did it."

"Wilson did it?"

"Robbie thought so."

"Excellent," Cody said. "Now tell me that this Dennis Wilson was in the tent at the time of the murder."

"I've got a meeting with the head of the volunteers tomorrow morning," Hadley said. "I want to talk to her before I interview Wilson. I'm also checking to see if Wilson has any guns registered in his name—although I'm learning that just about every male in this whole valley has at least one registered gun. Big hunting area around here. People own plenty of .22-calibers, for small game, grouse, even rabbit."

"Let's hope Wilson owns an arsenal," someone said.

Poor Dennis Wilson, Tess thought, but, after all, that was what Dan Hadley had been hired for. He dug up anything and everything that a defense team could use to point a finger in a direction other than her father's. Dennis was the perfect foil. In Andie's murder trial it had been Andie's fast-lane friends, the affair she was having and police blunders that had sidetracked the jury. Wilson would no doubt be just one in a line of witnesses that Cody Morris would put on the stand to prove to the jury that others had motive and opportunity to murder Robbie. The gun, though. That was the key. If the police found it...

As if reading her thoughts, she heard Hadley say, "I'm real concerned about the gun, Cody. You know what the speculation is."

Everyone knew, Tess thought. Even respectable papers were writing that the Aspen police and the D.A. were betting Tess Bergen was involved in the disappearance of the gun.

"Anyway," Hadley went on, "I think it might be a good idea if Tess left town."

"Oh." Carole's voice, anxious.

But Lawrence spoke up. "You're right, Dan. There's no reason for Tess to be stuck in Aspen for six months while I await trial. My daughter needs to work on her residency, which she can't do from here."

"Uh-huh." Cody. "And if Tess is in Monterey, which I assume she will be, our very sharp D.A. Barbara McCleary won't be able to ask for another interview."

"Exactly," Dan Hadley said.

"I'll miss her," Carole put in.

"I know. I will, too." Lawrence.

So, Tess thought, her life was not her own. Dan Hadley was deciding where she should go and when. She bristled at the idea, and yet she knew in her heart he was right. The farther away they got her from Aspen, the better.

Her parents. Carole, anyway, was going to miss her. They'd been together for so long now, ever since Tess's graduation from med school and Andie's murder, which had happened only a few months later. Tess had barely left their sides. She'd parented them, missed starting her residency, put her career on hold. Now, well, she didn't know what to expect. She'd like to leave Aspen, go home to Monterey and have the time and the freedom to get her life back on some sort of track. But could she? With the murder trial looming, could she concentrate on anything?

"I'll talk to Tess," Lawrence was saying. "It wouldn't hurt for her to have a little breathing room."

"I guess she could take care of the house," Carole said dully. "My flowers. They're probably all dead by now."

Fine, Tess thought, whatever. And she'd be rid of Dan Hadley. She could talk to her parents every day on the phone, and of course, she'd come back for Thanksgiving and Christmas....

Now Tess heard Cody finally broach the subject of whether or not Lawrence had ever owned a handgun. Her father told the story about the fox. He said he'd purchased a cheap gun.

"Where?" Hadley asked.

But Lawrence said he couldn't recall.

There was a heavy silence, pulsing right through Tess's wall. No one believed him. How could they?

"You've got to understand," Lawrence finally said, "I was consumed with Andie's murder and the trial. I couldn't tell you where or when I did a thing during that time. I know how it sounds," he said. "All I can tell you is that when you lose a child, it's as if you're on autopilot. Nothing matters. Not what you eat or where. Not where you sleep or if you sleep. Which you don't."

"He's telling the truth," Carole said quietly.

Then Hadley spoke. "Do you know where the handgun is now, Lawrence?"

"You're not going to believe this," her father said, "but it was missing from the garage. At the time, a few months ago, I thought maybe the garbage collector or the gardener's crew took it. I just don't know."

Someone uttered, "Jesus."

Tess sat cross-legged on her bed and thought, You're right, Dad. I don't believe it. There wasn't a person in that room who didn't know that Lawrence Bergen had planned and carried out a cold-blooded murder. And that she'd helped.

"Well," she heard Cody say, "if you do recall, Lawrence, where you bought that gun or if you find it, you tell Dan here. Not me, you understand? I don't do the investigating, and frankly, I don't want to know more than I have to. I'd be walking a fine line if I had hard evidence in my hands, and I don't want to do that. But Dan isn't bound by the same rules. And the information could be very significant."

"I know, I know," her father said, his voice tortured.

In her room, Tess buried her face in her hands.

She took the evening flight out of Aspen on the Fourth of July. Hugged her parents and cried. Dan Hadley was there. Cody had asked him to drive them to the airport to keep at bay any press that might catch wind of their whereabouts. She told her mother and father she'd call every day and for them not to worry. She felt Dan's shrewd blue eyes on her the whole time, eyes that gave no secrets away.

The plane took off over Shale Bluffs, circling, and through her tears Tess could see the annual July Fourth fireworks exploding over Aspen Mountain in huge, glorious-colored blossoms of fire, shooting up into the night sky, lighting up the valley in strobe flashes. The plane rose over Woody Creek, and she watched the valley below diminish, silent bombs bursting into red, blue, green and white over the town. Then it was dark and the night-shadowed white peaks of the Continental Divide appeared in the windows.

She was crying. Couldn't stop. She felt like a lost child. Alone. The future so uncertain. But by the time the plane reached the Denver airport, where she'd change planes and fly west, she was in control again, glad she was leaving Aspen and Dan Hadley behind. Exceedingly glad, too, that she was putting distance between herself and the gun. That damn gun, hidden right under their noses. How long before someone figured it out?

EIGHT

≈≈◆≈≈

Dan Hadley walked from his lodge to the Little Nell Hotel, where he was meeting Cody for breakfast. It was becoming routine, this breakfast conference. Cody always had a list of things he wanted Dan to do—interviews, background checks. It had been tedious work, talking to dozens and dozens of people who'd been in the tent that June afternoon. For Dan the questions had become rote, and he listened to the same answers over and over.

"No, I didn't see a thing. It was too crowded and noisy." Or, "I was at the other end of the tent, didn't see anything." As for Robbie's fiancée, Ali Barnes, and a few others who'd been close to the shooting, it was obvious no one had seen the shooting itself, although a couple of them, Ali included, had convinced themselves they had.

Cody had hung a chart on the wall in his suite, with circles locating every person they could accurately place. Amazing how crammed together everyone had been, and still there wasn't one reliable eyewitness. Yet. Of course, Barbara McCleary could come up with one any minute. Then Dan would go to work on that individual's background.

The police were still in hot pursuit of the murder weapon. The possibility remained that someone could stumble across it. For Lawrence Bergen that would be disastrous. For Tess, if she was really involved, locating the gun would be equally disastrous. She'd end up in prison, charged as an accessory after the fact and with obstruction of justice. She could get life.

The thought of Tess Bergen in prison was very discomfiting. Dan examined the feeling and wondered why. He didn't necessarily feel that way about Lawrence, and the man could easily end up in prison, too.

But Tess... It was because she was a woman, a young woman. Her life had hardly started.

Dan walked up to the hotel, where a gaggle of handsome young doormen stood; they recognized him now and always said hello. Nice kids.

He wondered about Tess's involvement, couldn't stop himself from wondering. Had she been in on the plot to murder Robbie all along? Had Lawrence gone to her for help? Or had it been an accident that she'd been there at the right place and the right time? Dan couldn't see Lawrence deliberately involving his surviving daughter, but you never knew about people.

There were Dan and Cody, Steve Sutton, Patrick and Brad at breakfast that morning. The main topic was Dan's meeting that day with Dennis Wilson. It had taken quite a while to get Wilson pinned down to a date; he kept canceling.

"Guess he doesn't want to talk to you," Cody said dryly.

"Do you blame him?" Dan asked. "He probably figures he's the next suspect."

"You will explain to him that as a member of the

defense team, you don't charge or arrest anybody, won't you?"

"Sure. That doesn't mean he'll buy it, though."

"Well, heck, tell him that the cops are one hundred percent positive they've got their man, and they aren't looking any further for suspects," Cody said.

"I'll do that."

"What about the gun angle?" Brad asked. "The police checked, and there's no .22-caliber handgun registered to Lawrence, but we all sat at the Gant condo and listened to the fox story." Brad shook his head. "If the cops find out he bought one, registered or not..."

"I'm on it," Dan said. "But it's going to take some legwork in California."

"Soon," Cody said. "First this Dennis Wilson and his grudge against Robbie. We need it."

Dan nodded. "I've got Wilson today. If he doesn't duck out on me, that is."

Dennis Wilson was really nervous. He'd tried to avoid talking to Dan Hadley as long as he could, but the investigator had been quietly persistent and had finally threatened to show up at Dennis's home, so this time he'd had to keep the appointment. He'd told Hadley to meet him in the office above the restaurant. He'd deliberately piled the old oak desk with invoices and menus and bills, so he'd having something to do while he awaited his inquisitor.

Hadley turned out to be a good-looking guy with a casual way about him. He held out his hand and said, "Nice to meet you."

Wilson took the hand, but he grimaced, not agreeing with Hadley's statement.

They sat facing each other, Dennis in the oak captain's chair and Dan on a rickety restaurant chair.

"I didn't shoot Robbie" was the first thing Wilson said.

"Nobody says you did. I just have some questions, that's all. I've talked to five hundred other people who were in the tent that day, too."

"Okay, what do you want to talk about?" Dennis tried to sound cooperative.

"We know about your history with Childress, the fight you had. We know he evicted you in the middle of the high season while your wife was pregnant."

"The bastard," Dennis couldn't help uttering.

"Uh-huh. There's also a police report Childress made about his smashed windshield."

"No one ever proved I did that," Wilson said too quickly.

"No, they didn't, but the facts form a pattern."

"What pattern?"

"Revenge?" Hadley suggested.

"Bullshit," Dennis said heatedly.

"Relax, Mr. Wilson. You don't notice the cops pulling you in for interrogation, do you? They figure Bergen did it. You're safe."

"You think so?"

Hadley shrugged.

"God, I hope so. I've got a kid now. I—"

"Do you own a .22-caliber handgun?"

"No."

"Any guns?"

"A hunting rifle and a shotgun, that's all."

"Are they registered?"

"Well, I got them years ago from my father. I don't think he ever registered them."

"Any unregistered handguns?"

"I said no."

"I heard you." The investigator leaned forward.

"Look, I'm not here to trip you up. I'd just like information."

"I gave it to you."

"Where were you in the tent when Childress was shot?"

"I was at the other end. I never saw anything."

Hadley sighed. "I have statements from two wine sellers that you were tasting their wines right around the time of the shooting."

"Okay, I guess I did move around some. I had to. I was ordering wine. It's my job."

"How close were you to Lawrence Bergen's display?"

"Not very close. Twenty yards away, maybe. And only for a few minutes. I was going around, tasting."

"Did you hear the shot?"

Dennis shifted his gaze to the side, then back. "No."

"Wilson, come on. I have people way across the tent who heard the shot."

"I thought it was a champagne cork."

"Uh-huh. What were you doing at the time you heard the shot?"

"I was tasting a zinfandel. I spilled it all over myself. My wife had a fit."

"Where's the shirt?"

"Oh, God, thrown out. It was stained and ripped when I ran. I fell. I even got a cut on my elbow." He showed Hadley a new pink scar.

"Can you remember exactly who was serving you at the time?"

"Hell, no. Someone from Spain." Dennis looked at him. "You want an alibi."

"Actually, it's the D.A. who would prefer your alibi, Dennis," Hadley said mildly.

Dan left the meeting, feeling he'd made progress.

Wilson had motive and opportunity and no real alibi. He'd be good on the stand. Good for Bergen.

That afternoon there was the usual gathering in the Bergens' living room. Dan reported on his interview with Wilson, checking the notes he'd written up after the meeting.

"Heck, that's a great piece of information. I like it, Dan," Cody said.

"Why haven't the police arrested that man?" Carole asked. "Or at least questioned him?"

Lawrence put a hand on her arm. "Because they've got me, and they aren't looking for anyone else."

"That's so unfair," Carole said.

"Okay, folks, anything else new?" Cody said.

"I've got us a short list of psychiatrists, Cody," Steve said. "I thought you'd want to talk to each one."

"Yes, I do, son. Very good."

"I thought of something," Lawrence put in. "Someone, that is." He looked directly at Dan then. "His name is Frank Ferrara."

Dan nodded. He remembered Ferrara, all right. The man had had an affair with Andie Childress. Dan had been the one to bring the affair to light, and although the judge in the Childress murder trial had not allowed testimony on it, the defense team had leaked the story to the press, creating sympathy for Robbie. It had been one of the smoke-and-mirror techniques the defense had used to distract the jurors from the real facts of the case.

Carole Bergen was sitting in the living room with her head down, and Lawrence had a hand over hers.

"As Dan probably remembers," Lawrence went on, "Frank Ferrara lived in Aspen. He may still live here. He certainly had a grudge against Robbie."

Yeah, Dan thought, a big grudge. Robbie had

found Ferrara in bed with Andie and he'd threatened the man's life. They'd come to blows.

"I wonder if he was in town during the festival?" Cody reflected aloud.

"That would be nice," Patrick said, grinning.

"I'll certainly check," Dan said.

"Tess knew him a little," Lawrence said.

"I'll call her—" Dan began.

But Cody was shaking his head. "Call her? No, son, you can ask her in person, because you're going to Monterey."

"I am?"

"Yes, you are. There's some evidence stored at the Bergen home. Mail, tons of mail Lawrence received since his daughter's murder and the trial. There are sympathy letters, but a lot of hate mail, too—from cranks and nutcases. Advice, schemes, diatribes on the evil of Andie or Robbie or…well, you get the idea. We figure there might be a lead among that mess of letters. Someone who looked like he hated Childress so much he followed him and when the opportunity arose, he popped him."

Lawrence sighed. "I'm sorry I didn't remember the mail sooner."

"Hate mail," Dan repeated.

"Yes, son, you're going to go to Monterey, and Ms. Bergen is going to let you in, and you're going to read every damn letter Lawrence got."

"Does Tess know?" Dan asked.

"Not yet, but she will," Cody said.

"Huh," Dan said thoughtfully.

When they left the Bergen condo, Cody drew Dan aside and walked with him, waving the other lawyers on.

"Now, look," Cody said, "when you're in Monterey you've got the perfect opportunity not only to talk to Tess about the gun, but maybe you could nose around, see if there was ever a receipt for its purchase. I know Lawrence says he can't remember where he bought it—" Cody rolled his eyes "—but maybe there's some paperwork. Now, son, I don't want to know any details. You understand?"

Dan nodded. He sure did. Cody was an officer of the court, legally bound to turn over evidence.

"So you'll look?"

Again Dan nodded. "If Tess will let me in. The truth is, she hates my guts."

Cody waved his words aside. "Son, I've been married four times. They all hate our guts. Just use your charm. You're a good-looking fella."

Dan laughed out loud. "You want me to seduce Tess Bergen?"

"No, no, perish the thought. What I want is for you to become her friend, her father's savior, someone safe she can talk to."

"Safe?"

"I mean I want you to pump that girl about where she hid that damn gun. Get the information, then do what you have to."

"I'm telling you, I'm the last person she'll talk to."

"Look, be nice. She's alone, scared, a lost little girl. She's gone through hell. Be nice to her. Pump her, but do it gently. She'll tell you."

"And if she doesn't?"

"She will. Sooner or later she will. Make sure she trusts you."

"Do I get a bonus for this, Cody?"

Cody cocked his head, one eye closed and smiled. "Maybe so, my boy, maybe so."

Later, when Dan was at the police station checking on the statements of volunteers at the Bon Vin Festival, he caught sight of a familiar form coming out of the police chief's office.

There was no mistaking this particular individual; he was fat, although he moved with surprising lightness for his size. In his shapeless, rumpled off-white summer suit, he looked like a shrewd-eyed puck. Pink cheeks, small features sunken in fat, a head of curly brown hair.

Bob Winthrop.

They passed in the hallway of the police department. Dan nodded. Bob nodded. They knew each other, all right. Once they'd worked together on a case, back when Dan had been a San Francisco cop. Winthrop was smart, relentless and, as Dan had warned Cody, not to be underestimated just because he looked like a clown. Dan didn't like the man, never had. There was something distinctly unsavory about Bob Winthrop, private investigator.

Dan got copies of the statements, left a set for Cody at the desk of the Little Nell Hotel, kept a set for himself and returned to his room to pack. He loaded his car and drove out of Aspen. It was good to be on the move again, doing something more than asking frightened, innocent people the same questions over and over.

Hate mail, the possibility of a receipt on the gun and Frank Ferrara. Interesting leads, challenging. He drove along the Roaring Fork Valley away from Aspen and wondered how Tess Bergen would receive him.

Grudgingly at best. He pictured her face, abruptly realizing he'd never seen her smile. Whenever he was around she didn't have much to smile about, he guessed. He wondered how she'd look if she was happy. Her lips would curve, her big dark eyes would light up. Yeah, he'd like to see her smile, but it wasn't going to be him that made her do it.

First thing in the morning Barbara McCleary held a meeting with the Childress family, Ali Barnes and Bob Winthrop.

Robbie Childress's brother had come from California, his sister and brother-in-law from New York. His parents were too old and ill to make the trip. And there was his fiancée, Ali, who still wore the very large diamond ring Robbie had given her on a chain around her neck. She cried a lot.

"I want that man to get the death penalty," Ryan Childress said.

"I've already explained why I can't ask for that," Barbara answered.

"I don't understand," his sister, Lisa, put in. "It's premeditated murder."

"His case doesn't call for the death penalty," Barbara tried again. "There are too many mitigating circumstances."

"What mitigating circumstances?" Ryan asked.

"There is a widely held perception that Lawrence Bergen was avenging his daughter's death. There would be too much sympathy for him. We'd never get the death penalty. This is simply not a capital case," Barbara said with more patience than she felt.

"I don't understand," Lisa said. "Robbie was found not guilty. He didn't kill Andie. So why—"

"Oh, shush, Lisa," her husband said. Barbara smiled at him.

"I wanted you all to meet Bob Winthrop. He's come from Los Angeles at the request of my office. He's a private investigator. He'll be working with my office very closely."

"What's he going to investigate?" Ali asked, a

catch in her voice. "We know who did it. I saw it happen. I was there. You said I'd be your star witness and everything."

"That's right, Ali, but we also need more hard evidence. The better prepared I am when I step into that courtroom, the more likely I'll be able to convince a jury that Lawrence Bergen is guilty." Barbara paused and smiled at everyone. "The first thing he's going to look for is the murder weapon. It would be the single best piece of evidence we could get."

"But can you win without it?" Lisa wanted to know.

"Yes, I can win without it. It'd be insurance, though."

"What'll I tell Mom and Dad?" Lisa cried. "This has just about killed them."

"You tell them that the system is working, that I will prosecute this case with every resource I have, and that Lawrence Bergen will go to prison for life. Justice will be done," Barbara said.

"It damn well better be," Ryan Childress muttered.

When they left, Barbara sighed and sagged in her chair. "Idiots," she said to Bob Winthrop.

"Ignore them," he suggested.

"Mm. Hard to sometimes."

"The righteously indignant," Winthrop said, "the salt of the earth."

Barbara met his gaze, and she knew precisely what he was thinking: the Childress family was out for Bergen's blood, totally ignoring the widespread belief that their brother had murdered the man's daughter, then gotten off scot-free. She was almost going to say something about it, but she lowered her gaze and kept her own counsel. Never give anything away.

"So," she said, "you've started on the gun?"

"Yes, I have. I've got some ideas. If we can't find it

here, then the next step is to locate where he got it from. A sales record, a friend he bought it from. I'll start here, but I'll probably have to go to Monterey and check around there. People almost always buy guns close to home. It's just one of those little facts of life." He grinned, his mouth a perforation in his face.

"Okay, I'll get your expenses covered one way or another. If you need to go, fine." She paused, then asked, "Did you know Cody Morris hired Dan Hadley?"

"Yes. I saw him in the police department."

"How good is he?"

"Damn good."

Barbara got up and stalked around her office. "I need the gun. I need the goddamn smoking gun."

"Or, if she's involved, Tess Bergen's confession," Bob said.

"They won't let me near her," Barbara growled.

"She has to give a deposition, and she has to go on the stand," Bob reminded her.

"The deposition is only...hell, it's like foreplay."

"Ah, but when she's on the stand, it'll be an orgasm, my dear."

Barbara watched Bob Winthrop leave, his bulk disappearing through her door. God he was an unattractive man, but he was smart. He'd do the job. After all, this race went to the clever and devious, not to the swift. She was confident he'd trace that gun for her.

She sat down to read the detailed reports on the lab findings and the autopsy. She leaned back in her chair and went through the papers carefully: lividity and trajectory and ventricles; near contact wound and massive trauma to the heart.

The ballistic report on the bullet retrieved from Robbie's body was very specific—a surprisingly well-preserved .22-caliber bullet, which could easily be matched. If she had the gun. Damn.

The gunshot residue test reports contained nothing new. Lawrence Bergen had residue on his face, none on his hands. His jacket had some residue, also, mostly on the right side. Because he was right-handed, Barbara supposed. The bloodstains were all from cuts he'd received in the ensuing melee. The latex gloves had residue on them, also, but couldn't be tied to Bergen. Dead end there.

Of course, Cody Morris would argue that the shooter had been standing next to Bergen, and that some of the residue from the shot had gotten on him. Even though it was a small-caliber pistol and the range of gunshot residue wasn't very great, Cody would argue that it was possible, hence reasonable doubt that Bergen pulled the trigger. Cody would do firing-range tests, have experts testify as to the possibility, the whole nine yards. He'd be convincing as hell.

Okay, okay. Barbara put down the reports and chewed on the end of a pen, thinking. She still had another ace in the hole. Lawrence Bergen had been interviewed on television dozens of times. And in how many of those interviews had he stated that Robbie Childress deserved to be punished for killing his daughter Andie? How many times? And hadn't he even said, more than once, that he believed in the death penalty and that Robbie deserved to die for taking Andrea's life?

She had to get copies of those interviews: TV stations, CNN, "The Harry Bingham Show."

All during the trial and even after the innocent verdict, everyone in the world must have watched and heard Lawrence Bergen, in his gentlemanly, calm way, state that Robbie was guilty as sin and deserved to die.

And witnesses, people who'd heard him talk that way. Live witnesses. She'd get Winthrop on it. More motivation. Yes.

She couldn't miss getting a conviction.

Barbara met Eric at the Ute City Bank restaurant at six. Locals called it the Wax Museum, because so many celebrities sat in the big plate-glass windows to be seen in all their well-preserved glory. It had been a long day, and she'd had to deal with the Childress family, among other irritations. All her days had been long lately. If Barbara had one failing, it was her inability to delegate work. She felt as if she had to oversee everything that was done on this case, even though she had a competent assistant D.A., Paul Howard, and her faithful secretary, Melanie Smith. Not to mention a law clerk from C.U. Law School for the summer. Still, Barbara held staff meetings every morning and went over every detail.

She waited for Eric in a booth in the back corner of the bar. They'd chosen this particular one because locals rarely went into it, so it was unlikely they'd see anyone they knew. Eric always told Maggie he worked late, and she always believed him. So far.

Barbara loved watching Eric move through the crowd toward her, tall and lean, so self-possessed. And he was there to meet her. Illicitly. Which made it even better.

He got to her table, leaned down and kissed her. "I can't stay long," he said, sliding into the booth opposite her. "Maggie's home."

"I know."

"You look beat," he said, leaning across the table and holding her hand.

"I am beat. This case…"

"Isn't there some way you could get off it?"

"Get off it?" she asked. "I'm busting my ass to stay *on* it!"

"Everyone says the state should pin a medal on Bergen, not prosecute the poor son of a bitch."

"The law is above all that, Eric. It has to be."

"Why do you want to be on this? It's making you pretty damn unpopular, spending the taxpayers' money this way."

"Is that what you believe, Eric? Is it?"

"I don't know. I see you working your butt off to try to convict this poor guy, when nobody really wants him convicted."

"The Childress family wants him convicted. So do I. The law has to be respected or society will degenerate into chaos. There have to be laws, Eric."

A waitress came by. Barbara ordered a gin and tonic, Eric a Coke. "If Maggie smells booze on me, I'm done for," he said.

"The hell with Maggie. Tell her you had a drink with the guys. Tell her you had a drink with me. Tell her the truth for a change."

"I will. I told you. Give me some time."

"Time," Barbara muttered.

He gave her hand a pat. "You know I'm crazy about you."

"Love me, love what I do," Barbara said.

"Not necessarily."

"Dammit, Eric."

"I think you've gone overboard on this case. You're obsessed with it. What if Lawrence Bergen didn't do it? What if his story's true and someone else did it?"

"That is utter crap, and everybody knows it. Who is this mystery killer who was standing next to Bergen? Come on, Eric." She upended her drink and waved an arm at the waitress, pointing at her glass, mouthing "The same." The waitress nodded.

"Do you really think you can get a jury to convict Bergen?" Eric asked.

"Damn right I can." The drink came, and Barbara took a long swallow.

"Don't summon me," he said, shaking his head.

"I don't summon anybody. Your name gets spit out by the computer."

"I know that, Barbara."

She swallowed the rest of her drink. It hit her suddenly in the pit of her stomach and in her joints. She leaned toward Eric. "I want you to leave Maggie. It's time, Eric. You're playing with both of us."

"Whoa there, Barbara. Who's the one who isn't interested in commitment? And I've got two kids to consider."

"Chicken."

"Yeah, maybe."

"We could live together, see how it works for us."

"We wouldn't last a month living together," he stated flatly.

"You're just pissed off because I've been spending so much time on this case. Well, I can't help that."

"You could. You could decide you didn't have a strong enough case and let Bergen go. You could plea bargain or something."

"Fat chance."

"Like I said, you're obsessed."

"And you're a jerk."

"I guess this is where I say my wife's expecting me home," Eric said coolly.

"I guess it is."

"I'll call you when you're in a better mood, Barbara."

"You do that."

He left and she ordered another drink, sat there alone and drank it down. Men. Now she realized why she'd never married. They always wanted something you weren't prepared to give them. Selfish little boys. If they didn't get it, they went home sulking. The hell with them. The hell with them all.

Barbara drove the six miles to her home very carefully. Of course, she figured, if she got stopped, she could talk her way out of it. She was the D.A. of this county, after all.

At home she played the messages on her answering machine. Routine stuff, then one that she had to back up and repeat. "This is Kay Esterhazy at Cronos Books in New York. We're interested in talking to you about a possible book contract on the Bergen case. We have ghost writers available, in the event that aspect worries you, Ms. McCleary. I'd appreciate it if you would call me." She left a phone number and a thank-you.

A book deal. Yes. That was what Barbara wanted, hoped for. Fame, fortune. How much would they pay? A hundred thousand? More? A million?

She grinned, kicked off her shoes and did a little soft-shoe step. This was what Eric was forgetting. When it was all over, the trial, the convictions, she'd have it made. He could come along for the ride if he wanted to. And a wild ride it was going to be.

NINE

Private investigator Bob Winthrop's feet were killing him. For a man his size, pushing three hundred pounds, he had tiny feet, delicate, except for the roll of fat at his ankles. But worse than the ache were the blisters he was getting from retracing the terrain between the park where the Bon Vin Festival tent had been and the Gant condominiums.

He knew that the gun was somewhere in between. Had to be. The cops had searched the tent and the Bergen condo with a fine-tooth comb. No gun. They'd gone over and over the ground in between with no results. But Bob was still convinced the gun was there, and doubly convinced Tess Bergen must have taken it, heaved it into the summer growth along the undeveloped areas on Ute Avenue. Tossed into a garden at one of the luxury homes. How far could she have thrown it?

The cops had drained the pond in the only park on the route. No luck. They'd held up trash pickups at every hotel, business, condo and apartment complex on Durant Avenue, which Tess would have taken. They'd searched the malls, the alleys, even low rooftops. Bob was relatively certain Tess hadn't had time to plan her course of action, unless she'd been in on the murder plot the whole time. But first, Lawrence Bergen's profile precluded involving his surviving child. Second, neither Bergen nor his daughter could have known where or if Childress was going to be in the tent or that he was going to approach Bergen. No one could have planned the murder to an exact time and place. But obviously, Bergen had the gun on him and was prepared. He had three days of the festival to await Robbie Childress.

Bob lumbered along Ute Avenue, thinking, trying to get inside Tess Bergen's head. His feet were sore, aching, sweaty, and his head and back were baking under the hot mountain sun. He wasn't used to the altitude, either, much less the uphill incline he was trudging.

Ahead was the Gant, where the Bergens were staying. To Bob's left was the bike path and the little park with the pond. To his right were three relatively new homes, nicely landscaped. He walked into the yards, checked the juniper bushes and flower gardens, though the cops had already been over this ground a dozen times.

He moved on when a big German shepherd appeared from behind the third house—gumshoes and dogs didn't mix.

Then he looked up the road toward where it dead-ended a quarter mile past the ritzy health club located between the Roaring Fork River and the steep forested slopes of Aspen Mountain.

Could Tess have gone past the Gant toward the club? Bob had driven the route in his rental car. Nothing but woods and more woods, the bike path winding through them. There were a couple of homes nestled in the stands of aspen and an old, overgrown cemetery of some sort, obviously unused now, mon-

uments toppled, wrought-iron fencing rusted or lean-
ing askew. All overgrown, retreating into the earth.
The cops had been up there, too, with metal detectors.
Found some old tin cans and a hunting knife. No gun.
But with this much area it would be a miracle if they
found it.

He crossed the road to the left side and walked
along the bike path beneath the aspens, the sweat
streaming off his face. He mopped at it with a hand-
kerchief and felt dizzy.

There was the condo, number 107. He crossed a
patch of lawn toward it, stopped at a nicely planted
garden, snooped around, looking for any sign of disturbed earth. The cops had checked all this, too, and
all around the condo complex. Zip. It was possible,
Bob conceded, that Tess Bergen had not taken the
gun, but the odds of that were astronomical. She took
it. And she hid it. Quickly. There'd been a tail on her,
too, ever since that same afternoon, and she hadn't retrieved the gun. Now she was in California. She
couldn't have gotten through airport security with it,
so it was still here.

There was another way to find out where the damn
thing was. Bob sat on a bench in front of the condo
complex and caught his breath, thinking. He could
head back to California and pay Tess Bergen a visit.
There were ways of making a person talk. He wasn't
thinking of physical means—not that he hadn't used
those before. Rather, he was considering psychological pressure, implied threats. Trouble was, the
woman wasn't dumb. She was a doctor, after all, and
she'd probably squeal to the cops and the media and
he'd end up on the hot seat. He'd have to consider
that, too.

He finally rose, his feet protesting his weight, and
began the slow trek back toward town, searching,

moving back and forth on the road, thirty yards in and out, in and out. The gun was here. Close. He could smell it.

"Come here, little gun," he said under his breath. "Come to Papa."

The past couple of weeks since Tess had arrived home in Monterey had been like a breath of fresh air. There were minutes, even hours, when she was almost able to forget her troubles. She put in a lot of time at the local nursing home as a volunteer, and she took long walks in the rolling hills or tended her mother's gardens. She cracked her textbooks and put her mind in neutral. But always, inevitably, the peace was shattered: When it was time to talk to her mother on the phone, which she did every day at dinnertime. Or when, for no accountable reason, the image of the gun would crash into her head and her heartbeat would quicken and her palms grow damp, as if she could feel the damn thing right in her hands.

The media, for the most part, had backed off. She knew, of course, from her experience during Andie's trial, that when the time for her father's ordeal neared, the press would start in on her again: the constant phone calls despite changing the phone number every week, the cars tailing her, reporters showing up at her door at all hours. It was just a matter of time. But for now she'd revel in the sweet quiet.

And in Monterey, where she'd been born and raised, she still had friends. Paula Appleton was her best friend. They'd grown up together, gone to medical school together and almost begun their residencies at the same time. But then Andie had been murdered and Tess's life had ground to a halt.

Now Paula was back home and in her first year with a local health clinic. The sign in front of the clinic read Dr. Paula Appleton, Pediatrics, and Tess couldn't help burning with envy.

It was Paula's idea to have dinner on Friday night in the nearby quaint town of Carmel. "Time you got out and about, Bergen," she said on the phone.

Tess protested. "I don't know. I feel like a freak. I know everyone's been supportive, but still—"

"Forget it. We're having dinner. We'll go to Clint Eastwood's place and sit outside and drink. Neil can drive—he gave up booze."

Neil was Paula's fiancé, a great guy who worked at the Pebble Beach Resort outside Carmel. Tess had met him several times, and he was a lot of fun and a good conversationalist.

"Okay," Tess said, "but just the three of us."

"Of course," Paula said.

But when the three of them arrived at the Bear's Head Inn, a friend of Neil's was waiting. Tess's heart sank, and she shot Paula a murderous look.

Neil introduced them. "Tess, this is Alan Knight... Alan, Tess Bergen."

Tess shook his hand. He was a nice-looking man, mid-thirties, with receding blond hair. As the meal went on, Tess realized how uninterested she was despite Alan's being both pleasant and intelligent, someone she once would have taken an interest in.

What was wrong with her? She was only thirty-two, yet she was dried up inside. Yes, her reaction to men after Andie's abusive marriage and the murder could perhaps been expected. Now the awful ordeal her father was going through colored her whole life. But couldn't she, if only for a few minutes, feel something for the opposite sex? Even just a twinge?

But she didn't. Sure, she ate her meal, drank her wine, carried on a conversation. But she was only pretending at life, not living it.

Paula dragged her into the ladies' room of the Carmel restaurant and chewed her out. "Hey, Bergen," Paula said from inside a stall, "what gives?"

"What do you mean?" Tess stood in front of the mirror eyeing her reflection, head cocked. Was it possible to barely recognize yourself?

"You're only going through the motions. Okay, I can forgive that for a time. But don't you realize everyone's on your side? Don't you read the papers? Your dad's becoming a hero, for God's sake. And you're right up there with him. You should feel good. That bastard Robbie finally got what he deserved."

Someone came into the ladies' room then, and Paula and Tess fell silent.

When the woman left, Tess said, "I appreciate what you're saying. But you can't imagine what it's like. Not for me, but for my parents."

"What do you mean, not for you?" Paula came out of the stall and went to work on her short strawberry blond hair and makeup. "You're a mess. I know you. Is it the gun thing?"

That was the first time anyone, anyone except Barbara McCleary, that is, had directly confronted Tess about the gun. She drew in a breath.

Paula sighed. "It's not as if it's some big secret, Bergen."

"I...I don't know what you mean."

"God. Did you take it?"

"Paula."

"Well? I'm your best friend on earth. You can tell me. Just nod or something."

Tess couldn't help a smile. "I'm not giving you a nod or anything else."

"Why not?"

"Because, if I had taken the gun, and this is all just

hypothetical, but say I did, then if I told you, it would make you an accessory after the fact."

"Whoa, now there's some legal jargon."

"With as much time as I spend around courtrooms, I should've become a lawyer myself."

"You still aren't answering me."

"And I'm not going to."

"That means you did it. If you didn't take it, you'd tell me right away."

Again, Tess smiled and shook her head. "You're a piece of work. Now, can we drop it, Appleton?"

"No," Paula said as they left the ladies' room, "we'll put it on hold."

Paula would never know how close Tess had come to telling her, how desperately she needed to tell someone the truth. It was a weight that seemed to be growing by the day, that awful thing inside her she needed to purge.

She fixed everyone a nightcap back at her house, everyone but Neil, who was on the wagon. And then when they left, after Alan asked if he could call Tess sometime, she sat down alone on a kitchen stool, fist under her chin, elbow on the counter, and she wondered what kind of man it was going to take to attract her. Maybe there was no such animal. Maybe...

Mark, she remembered. Her former boyfriend. Handsome, caring, smart. But he'd given that interview to the magazine and, well, Tess thought, that was history. Ancient history. He'd called, though, just the other day. He'd gotten her unlisted number from a mutual friend and called and said how sorry he was about everything and how glad he was that Robbie had paid for murdering Andie and could he see her sometime?

She hadn't wanted to see him. It was over. It had been over for a long time. Now there was Alan. She'd told him it would be better if he waited till after her father's trial in January before calling and—

Tess's thoughts screeched to a halt. What was she doing thinking about her troubles with men? Was she nuts? But then, she was so tired of it all, worn out, talking to her mother every day, walking on eggshells when her father took the phone to say hello. She'd have thought the secret between her and her father would have drawn them closer together, but instead, it had driven a wedge between them. Oh, God, she was sick to death of her questions about morality and justice. She was tired of the ever-present dread that someone was going to find that gun. Was she so wrong to want it all to end, to have a life of her own?

Tess brushed her teeth, washed her face and sat on the edge of her bed, frowning. When she'd talked to her parents yesterday evening, her father had told her someone was going to come by the Monterey house and go through the mail he'd received over the past two years. He told her where the boxes storing the mail were. She thought about that—records. Her father kept records of everything. She got up, padded down the hall and opened the kitchen door that led to the garage, where he kept two file cabinets crammed with receipts and invoices and every last slip of paper he'd ever received. He'd been audited several years back by the IRS, and since then, he hadn't thrown out a thing.

She switched on the lights and stared at the file cabinets, still frowning. And then she walked around her old Subaru and opened the top drawer to the first cabinet. She felt foolish. Paranoid. But she started searching, wondering, fearing that when Lawrence purchased that gun he'd kept some sort of a receipt. She knew what he'd told Cody Morris. And it was very possible her father had no real memory of where he'd gotten it. Still, he'd bought the damn thing someplace. And if someone found out where...

She searched the jammed drawers, thinking about the absurdity of his having told Cody—and everyone else—that he'd bought a gun, an unregistered one at that, then put it in the garage and it had disappeared. Cody must have laughed himself silly over that one.

On the third drawer, disgusted, Tess slammed it shut and went back inside. The whole thing was crazy. The cops were going to find out that he'd bought a gun, a .22. They'd find out when and where he bought it, and then, in the courtroom, D.A. Mc-Cleary would get Lawrence's "missing" gun story put on the record. The jurors would have a heyday with the story. They'd know he'd bought a gun. They'd know he'd bought an unregistered gun. And they'd hear how that gun had been supposedly lost or stolen. Her father was doomed.

She turned out her bedroom light and stared into the darkness. She was going to drive herself stark raving mad before this was over.

Dan drove south out of San Francisco toward Monterey and wondered if he wasn't making a mistake not calling Tess before showing up at her door. Of course, if he did stop and telephone her, she might tell him to forget it. Yeah, he thought, he could hear Tess telling him to drop dead despite his orders to go into that house and search Lawrence's mail. The gun was an even bigger issue.

Cody wanted him to get Tess to confide in him. Lots of luck. Of all the people on earth, he'd be the last person she'd consider blabbing her deepest, darkest secret to. Still, maybe he could find some sort of paperwork on it, something that could tell him where Bergen had purchased the damn thing. And then what would he do with that knowledge? He knew what Cody wanted him to do. Make it disappear.

Okay, fine, Dan thought. He'd cross that bridge when he got to it. The bigger problem was still the gun itself. And only one person had that answer. "And she ain't talkin'," he said out loud.

He drove Route 1, the coastal road, avoiding the heavy weekend traffic around San Jose. Down through Half Moon Bay and south along the rocky shoreline. It was a beautiful summer morning, fog lying in soft folds in the valleys to the east, the Pacific Ocean sparkling deep blue in the sun, waves crashing on the rocks.

It took only a little more than an hour at that time of morning, and then he was driving along the bay, directly through downtown and toward Pacific Grove on the Monterey Peninsula. The Bergens lived in an upscale neighborhood off Ocean Highway. Just to the south of them on California's famous Seventeen Mile Drive were the world-renowned golf courses of Pebble Beach, Spyglass Hill and Cypress Point, some of the most exclusive addresses in the country.

He found the Bergens' house with little trouble. Nice-looking place. Spanish Mission-style with its off-white stucco facade and red-tiled roof, graceful archways. It sat on a private road in a cypress grove on an acre of land. Nothing cheap about it. He parked at the bottom of the drive, noticed that there was no car outside the garage. Maybe she wasn't there. Or maybe she parked in the garage. He walked up the drive, noticed a big old tabby sharpening its claws on a tree trunk. The cat that Bergen was afraid was going to get killed by a fox?

Dan rang the bell and thought again what a bad idea this was. Tess Bergen hated his guts, and Lawrence had asked that Dan not remove any of the mail from the house. Dan could understand that. But how was Tess going to react to his working there?

She answered the doorbell in a bathrobe, mug of coffee in hand. Her expression went from surprise to anger.

"I should have known it would be you," she said.

"Your parents told you, then."

"Only that someone was coming to go through the mail. Couldn't someone else do this?"

Her dark eyes bored into his; he felt her hostility and it made his back go up. He was only doing his goddamn job, and he didn't need her to make it any harder. He was trying to help her, for God's sake.

"If you'll just show me where the mail's stored," he said coldly, "I'll get to work."

But when Tess dug out the storage boxes, they both stared at the volume of mail. "Jesus," Tess said. "This is going to take forever. I had no idea."

Dan let out a low whistle, then turned to Tess. "Look, you're right. This is going to take a while. You might consider dropping the indignant act."

"It isn't an act, Mr. Hadley," she said. "I don't like anything about you or what you do for a living. I won't apologize for that."

"What I do for a living, Ms. Bergen, is going to keep your father out of jail."

She faced him, not backing down an inch, her eyes blazing. He admired her for that, but she also pissed him off—he had work to do.

"I don't have to like it," she finally snapped, "and I'm not very good at pretending."

He narrowed his gaze at her. "Neither am I, and you know what? I'm going to have to ask you where your father's gun is. No pretending, Ms. Bergen, okay?"

He saw the flash of fear on her face, saw her body

shrink with it, and he felt a slight stab of guilt for doing it like that. Not at all the way Cody had envisioned, was it?

She turned around then and walked out of the room, her back stiff and unforgiving.

He used Lawrence's desk and began sorting through the first layer of envelopes. He was astounded at the number of people who'd taken an interest in the plight of the Bergen family. Of course, if Andie hadn't been married to a celebrity, it would have been just another murder. As it was, people from around the world had written to Lawrence, everything from letters of sympathy and well-wishing to letters delivering hate and venom. Some of them were real weirdos, and it was no wonder Lawrence had kept the volume of mail practically a secret from his wife and daughter.

Dan read through a hundred letters that morning, sorting them by the degree of interest—support and hate—making pile after pile on the desktop till he ran out of space.

The whole time he sat there, he was aware of Tess in the house. He heard her padding around. Doing dishes. Running a load of laundry. In the shower. He tried hard not to think about her in the shower, but he knew she had white skin and slender arms and legs and a small, firm backside. Small breasts. He was just thinking she was a bit too thin when he caught himself. First of all, she despised him. Second, he was ten years older, and third, there was Susan. At least he thought there was Susan. He'd been home in San Francisco last night, but he hadn't called her.

Tess appeared in the door to the office shortly before noon. She was wearing a sleeveless print dress and low heels, her dark hair held back in a barrette, makeup. She was wearing perfume.

A date, he thought.

But she wasn't going out on a date. "I'm putting a few hours in at the nursing home today," she told him matter-of-factly. He guessed she'd declared a truce. "If you're hungry, there's stuff in the kitchen."

"Thanks," he said.

"I'll be home before five."

"Uh-huh."

"Will you, ah, still be here?"

"Oh, yeah," he said.

"Mm."

"I'll probably get a room in town."

"Mm," she said again.

"Or I could stay right here on the pullout." He nodded toward the couch. "It'll save your father the expense." What he didn't say was that it would also give him time to snoop around and look for paperwork on the gun. She didn't need to know that.

"The pullout," Tess was saying. "I'll think about it." And then she was gone.

He read letters for another hour, did a little snooping and then made himself a ham sandwich and wandered into the living room. Spacious. Lots of heavy, dark Spanish-style furniture mixed in with white couches and richly covered pillows. Then there were the family pictures, mostly on one wall. Lawrence and Carole in happier days—Lawrence holding up the cover for the first issue of *Bon Vin* magazine. Carole and a girlfriend at the gift shop at the Monterey aquarium where, Dan recalled, Carole used to work.

And Andie and Tess. As toddlers and little girls. As teens. At graduations. There was even one of Andie in her wedding dress—no Robbie in this one. And Tess in a white doctor's coat somewhere, a stethoscope around her neck. Smiling. Very, very pretty.

He munched on his sandwich and walked back to

the office still thinking about the Bergens and their closeness. A real family. They'd stuck together through thick and thin, right down to Tess's having hidden the gun for her father. It was hard to conjure that up, such total loyalty. Especially for Dan, who'd had no family since age four, when he'd been orphaned.

Tess returned home shortly before five. She stuck her head in the office and merely said, "You can stay here, I guess," and he couldn't miss the resentment in her tone.

Oh, yeah, he knew all about being resented. After his folks were killed in a car accident, his grandmother had taken him in. But it hadn't gone well, and within a year she'd farmed him out, literally pawned him off on the state of California, and then she'd moved. Dan had realized, when he'd grown up, that it wasn't because his grandmother hadn't loved him. It was because she hadn't been able to bear the constant reminder of the death of her only child. So she'd run from it.

He'd lived in at least eight foster homes after that. With families that hadn't wanted him but had needed the extra support money the state paid them for keeping him. He'd always felt resented. Unloved. And very lonely.

He'd become a cop right out of San Francisco State, and thinking back on it now, Dan guessed he'd chosen the police force because he believed they'd be like a big family, there for him. But it hadn't worked quite the way he'd imagined. The paperwork was hell, and to make it as a cop was tough. You were either dead broke, never able to afford a meal over ten bucks, or you went on the take. Neither choice appealed, and he'd gotten out when the law firm had offered him a retainer that was almost double his annual salary. Economics.

Dan figured that he'd lived his life with the expectation that something good was coming. It was right around the bend, over that hill. In his gut he desperately wanted it to be true. His brain told him that this was all there was. He felt as if he'd been waiting forty years for that something to arrive, and there was an emptiness inside him from the waiting.

He worked on into the evening and then drove into Monterey and ate dinner. Back at the house, he found Tess sitting in the living room in blue jeans, legs crossed under her while she read a textbook.

"Studying?" he asked, just to say something.

She glanced at him. "It really doesn't concern you," she said, and then she went back to her reading. He'd wanted to talk to her about Frank Ferrara, but as he stood there feeling unwelcome, experiencing that godawful familiar sense of being an outsider in someone's home, he figured it could wait till tomorrow.

He shrugged and started back toward the office, and the phone rang. He noticed that Tess let the answering machine pick up. Then he heard the message. It was a reporter from the *Global Star* asking for an interview, offering money. He heard Tess swear.

He walked back into the living room. "Don't you have an unlisted number?" he asked. His tone might have been a little belligerent. Not his intention.

"Yes," she said. "We change it every week, it seems. They get it, anyway." And she was, naturally, defensive.

"Have you checked other options with the phone company?"

"Dad has. At least I think he has."

"Do you want me to handle it? I can make damn good and sure your number stays unlisted."

"It's not your problem," she said in a hard voice.

"Okay, fine." He held up a hand to show her the subject was finished. Let her suffer.

Back in the office, opening more letters as the sun splashed onto the Pacific and a rose light settled in the room, Dan realized Cody had it all wrong. There was no way in hell he was going to gain her confidence. She didn't like him. She never would.

So he was surprised when an hour or so later, Tess appeared in the door, her arms full of sheets and blankets, a pillow on top.

"You'll need these," she said.

He got up, came around the desk and took the linens from her. "Thanks."

"I can help make up the bed." She nodded toward the couch.

"I'll get it later."

"Mm." Then she took a breath. Something was on her mind. "Look," she began, "I guess it would be...well, it would be nice if you could fix the phone thing."

He studied her for a moment, then decided she'd fallen far enough on her sword. "Done," he said.

"Thanks." She didn't meet his eyes. She hesitated, still standing there. There was something else on her mind. Finally she lifted her gaze to his. "I'm having a lot of trouble getting over what you did to my sister, to Andie. It was so ugly, so...and she was already dead."

"I was doing my job."

"That's what Eichmann and Mengele said."

"Oh, shit, don't pull that crap on me. I'm doing the same thing now, can't you see that? I'm working my ass off trying to find someone who looks as guilty as your father, so that Cody can get him off."

She turned her face as if slapped. The thought hung between them: Lawrence was guilty.

"We're on the same side," he said.

"Next time you could be on the other side, working just as hard for Barbara McCleary," Tess replied.

"Maybe. Maybe not. I didn't like what I had to do, what I had to find out about your sister."

"Oh, they twisted your arm," she said.

"It was my job. If I hadn't done it, somebody else would have."

"That's a lousy excuse."

He shrugged. Then he tried another tack. "You could help your father's case a lot."

"I don't see how."

"Oh, I think you do," he stated, and he saw her expression close.

"I'm going to bed." She turned to leave.

Dammit, Dan thought. "Sit down for a minute," he said.

"I really don't—"

"Just sit. These questions aren't going to go away."

She hesitated, then finally sat in a corner chair, her arms folded tightly across her chest.

"Okay." He sat down, too. "Let's start with your sister's...friend, Frank Ferrara. I believe you knew him."

Tess nodded.

"What can you tell me about him?"

"Andie met him in Aspen. He managed a restaurant there."

"And your sister started to see him?"

Tess lowered her eyes. "It was during a rough time in her marriage. Robbie was having an affair and, well, I'm not making excuses for Andie, but she was miserable. Lonely."

"Uh-huh," Dan said. "And?"

"She saw him a few times. Hey, you know all this from the murder trial," she said, looking up sharply.

"Yeah, I do," he admitted, "but you may know something, some small detail I don't. Forget about the trial. Tell me all you know about Ferrara."

"I don't know anything about him."

"You have no idea where he was originally from? Nothing?"

Tess shook her head. Then her eyes widened. "Florida. He was from Florida."

"Good," Dan said. "You wouldn't happen to know where in Florida?"

"No. I don't." She sighed and shifted in the chair. "Is this leading where I think it is?" she asked.

"I don't know. Where do you think it's leading?"

"Well, thanks to you, everyone knows Robbie discovered Andie in bed with Frank and there was a fight. I have to assume you want to find out if Frank was in Aspen the day Robbie was shot. You'd like to point a finger in Frank's direction. But you can't locate him. Am I close?"

Dan allowed a thin smile. "Very good," he said.

"It's the same tactics you used to get Robbie off." She studied him. "I guess leopards don't change their spots."

"They don't need to. They hunt real well with those spots." And then he held her gaze for a heartbeat too long before he said, "You'll try to remember everything you can about Ferrara?"

"Yes." She got up, ready to go, her back turned to him.

And Dan stood, too. But it wasn't over. "We've got to talk about the gun," he said in a level voice, and he saw her go stiff. "It's the single most important piece of evidence. It's missing, okay. But if it ever turns up...if it can be linked to your father..."

Tess whirled. "Whose side are you on, Dan Hadley?"

"Your father's. Yours."

"Bull."

"Talk to me, Tess."

"No. There's nothing to talk about."

"But there is."

She shook her head violently, and he had the unaccountable urge to shake the truth out of her, to shake and shake, his fingers digging into her shoulders, and then when she stopped struggling she'd sag against him, and...

"Everyone assumes my father's guilty," she said in a strangled voice. "Everyone. But what if...what if somehow he didn't do it and—"

"Hey," Dan said. "Look. It doesn't matter to Cody or to me or to anyone on the defense team. Our job is to help Lawrence in every way we can. It's what the system allows for. It's the way it works."

She said nothing.

Hell, he thought. "Tess," he tried again, "you've got to trust someone. I need to know about the gun. Cody can't be in on it. So it's me. Do you understand what I'm saying? Tess?"

"There's nothing to know," she said. "Nothing." And with that she spun out of the room, leaving him standing there, spitting mad.

Damn. He'd warned Cody.

TEN

Dan couldn't resist turning on "The Judge's Advocate" that morning when Tess wasn't around. Bad habit, he thought. But he might, just might, pick up a tidbit of information that could help his investigation. Besides, he was curious to hear what the pundits were saying about the case.

Gail Hollister was her usual hard-nosed self. Attractive, but far too tough for Dan. Although, he had to admit, she got some good licks in.

"So, Craig, you're saying Lawrence Bergen is a hero?" she asked, her eyebrows raised dramatically. "He shot a man in cold blood and he's a hero?"

"Give it a rest, Gail. I wouldn't recommend Bergen's action as a general rule, but you've got to try to understand where the man was coming from."

"He wanted revenge."

"No, he wanted justice."

Dan frowned. That was the question, wasn't it? And Dan sure knew how Lawrence felt—Andrea Childress had been treated shabbily by the media and the courts. And by him. And she deserved the justice Lawrence had meted out for her. No question.

"Justice doesn't come in the form of a .22 bullet at a

crowded social event, Craig. It comes through the legal system."

"Not always, Gail," Craig reminded her.

They talked and talked, but they always came back to the same point, Dan thought. Either you felt in your gut that Lawrence did the right thing or you didn't. All the TV shows on earth couldn't change that.

"The polls show that a vast majority think Bergen was right," Craig Kramer was saying.

"And a great majority of the populace think WCC professional wrestling is real," Gail retorted. "That doesn't make them right."

Right. Wrong. Dan didn't deal in those kinds of nebulous concepts. He dealt in practicalities: Where was the gun? How could he get Tess to disclose its location to him? He got up and turned the program off. He hadn't learned a damn thing from it today.

Carole Bergen was fifty-five years old. She'd always been considered quietly beautiful, with brown hair and expressive dark eyes and a graceful, ladylike demeanor. She'd been pampered all her life, an only child of loving parents, graduate of an excellent college. After that, a job in an elegant woman's shop, and then, as a matter of course, marriage.

The turbulent sixties had passed her by; she'd never done drugs, marched in Washington or been in the Peace Corps. She'd been raised to be a loving, intelligent and informed wife and mother, and she'd excelled at the role. It was all she'd ever desired.

She'd met Lawrence at a party given by one of her school friends in San Francisco. He'd been an up-and-coming wine connoisseur at the time, writing for both newspapers and magazines. A freelance writer. Carole had found that very daring—Lawrence didn't have a job in a stuffy law firm or corporation like most of the young men she knew.

And Lawrence had big plans. He came from an ordinary middle-class Sacramento family, not poor, but not wealthy like Carole's folks, and he was very ambitious. She admired that, a self-made man, not a drone who'd inherited everything.

She'd married Lawrence in a big society wedding, loved him and supported him, waited to have children until *Bon Vin* magazine was established and bringing in a decent income, and borne him two gorgeous, loving daughters.

Carole Bergen had had everything she'd ever wanted or expected. When her children were grown, she'd taken the job in the Monterey aquarium nature gift shop, a genteel sort of job.

Life had been wonderful.

Then her oldest daughter, her bright, beautiful, vivacious child, had been murdered. Not dead from disease or an accident. Murdered. And Carole hadn't even known about the years of abuse Andie had suffered. Oh, God, why hadn't Andie told her?

Carole hated very few people in her existence, but she hated Robbie Childress. Her life was over, anyway, so she allowed herself the luxury of hating him. She hadn't wanted him to get the death penalty; she'd wanted him to suffer in prison for the rest of his life.

Then he'd been found not guilty.

Carole's doctor had prescribed tranquilizers and antidepressants eighteen months ago, and they'd helped her go through the motions of living. She owed it to her husband and her remaining daughter, she knew, and she tried to cope.

Aspen had been a milestone. She'd actually smiled, and she'd forgotten Andie's death for a few minutes here and there. Not that she'd ever really forget; a mother never would, never could, get over a child's death. It was unnatural for a child to die before a parent; it was unthinkable.

But life went on.

Then another blow. Were they never to end, the bludgeons of fate?

Robbie Childress shot to death, and Lawrence arrested. If he was found guilty and sent to jail, what would she do? Alone, married to a convicted felon. She couldn't think about it, she simply couldn't.

Carole, still in her bathrobe, was doing the breakfast dishes while Lawrence sat at the kitchen table, finishing a cup of coffee and reading the paper.

Without turning around, she brought up the subject. She couldn't have done it face-to-face. Just when had she become afraid of her own husband?

"Uh, Lawrence, I heard something on the news last night."

"I thought you weren't going to watch the news," he said.

"Well, I did this once. They said that the police think Tess took the...the gun from you and hid it. Lawrence—"

"Good God, Carole!" he interrupted. "Do you believe everything you hear on TV?"

"No, but why do they think that? How could they—"

"Because Tess was there in the tent. No other reason."

"Why didn't you tell me?" she asked. She leaned forward on the sink, feeling dizzy. "No one tells me anything."

"Why upset you?"

She turned around then, a spark igniting inside her, unfamiliar, scary. "Upset me? What could you possibly tell me that would upset me more than I already am?"

Lawrence got up then and put his arms around her. Carole pressed against him, trying not to cry. Once she started, it was so hard to stop.

"There, there," he said, stroking her hair.

"Is it true? Did Tess do that? Is there...?" she asked, her voice muffled against his chest.

"Carole, darling, if you think Tess took the gun, then you'd have to believe I shot Robbie. Of course it's not true."

"I'm so afraid," she whispered.

"I know, I know."

"Aren't you afraid?"

"Yes."

"How can you stand it?"

"Well," Lawrence said, "one thing that really helps is that I know Robbie is dead. That makes it easier. Terrible of me, isn't it?"

"No, it's not terrible, it's okay," Carole said, holding on to him. "It's perfectly natural."

Carole decided that she and her husband were going on a picnic that day. They were going to get out of the condo and take the gondola up Aspen Mountain, and at the top, at the Sundeck restaurant, they'd get a bite to eat and sit outside on the deck and watch the scenery. Maybe walk the nature trail. Just the two of them.

"Okay," Lawrence said when he heard the plan. He didn't have much to do aside from the conference calls he made every day to *Bon Vin* magazine headquarters in Monterey and the faxed-in articles he had to approve.

"It's a beautiful day," Carole said, "but don't forget it's bound to be chilly up there. Take a sweater."

Without consulting each other, they both wore hats

and sunglasses, ridiculous disguises, but they felt too vulnerable without them. They slipped out a back door to avoid the media and walked the two blocks to the gondola, bought tickets and sat in the gondola watching Aspen recede below them.

It was twenty degrees cooler at the 11,300-foot summit, and they needed their sweaters.

"Look at the view," Lawrence said. "It amazes me every time."

On one side was a long green valley leading up to immense snow-capped peaks; on the other side was the Roaring Fork Valley, winding its way up to Independence Pass and the Continental Divide and more snow-capped peaks.

Tourists stood around, oohing and aahing. Off to the west, beyond the peaks, clouds were building, towering cumulus clouds that so often formed from the mountain thermals in the afternoon.

"Breathtaking," Carole said.

"This was a great idea," Lawrence commented. "A change of scenery."

They got their lunches in the cafeteria-style restaurant and carried their trays out to the deck.

"Did you take a look at the wine selection?" Lawrence asked.

"Not really."

"Not bad for a place like this."

They ate, enjoyed the fact that no one recognized them and took in the fresh air and the scenery.

"Nice," Lawrence said once, smiling, and Carole smiled back, trying hard to act normally.

After lunch they walked along the ridge of the mountain, just a short walk, but soon they were out of sight of the Sundeck. There were a few tourists and the occasional pair of mountain bikers or backpackers, but mostly they were alone among the stands of spruce and the miniature alpine flowers that grew under their feet.

Carole got up her nerve to ask after they'd turned around to return to the Sundeck.

"Lawrence?"

"Yes, darling?"

"Would you...would you tell me the truth about that day in the tent? The whole truth, no matter what it is? Please, Lawrence, I need to know."

He stopped and faced her, his expression pained. "You know the truth, Carole."

"Lawrence, please." An image flew into her mind then, a scene from *The Godfather II*, Al Pacino's wife asking him if he was behind the murder of his brother. And his answer. A lie. He met her eyes and smoothly, convincingly lied. But that was a movie. This was her beloved husband, Lawrence.

"After all these years together, don't you know the answer?" he said.

"I need to hear it, Lawrence."

"Of course I didn't do it, Carole."

"And Tess?" Oh, God, she thought.

There was the slightest trace of hesitation. No one on earth would have noticed it but Carole. "Tess did nothing. She wasn't involved."

"Lawrence."

"You believe me, don't you?" he asked.

"Yes," Carole whispered, but only because she had no real alternative.

They walked back to the gondola without speaking; Carole didn't notice the scenery. Not even her pills could take away the traitorous notion that her husband was deceiving her.

"You don't have a case and you know it," Cody Morris said.

"Oh, I have a case all right," Barbara shot back from behind her desk.

"Drop the charges, and there'll be no hard feelings, Barbara."

She laughed. "I haven't noticed you filing a motion for a summary judgment, Cody," she said with heavy irony.

"It's going in next week."

"It'll get turned down."

"Maybe. It doesn't matter. Without a gun you don't have a case."

"You're beginning to sound monotonous."

"I speak the truth, my girl. The pure, unadorned truth."

"Oh, quit the John Wayne act, Cody. It turns my stomach."

"And a very nice stomach it is," Cody said with a smile. "Well, I imagine it's a very nice stomach."

Barbara gave him a look, which he translated as surprise, enjoyment and offended dignity.

"That's disgracefully politically incorrect," she finally said.

He looked at her, eyebrows raised. "Consider me chastised, Barbara."

"You are a piece of work," she declared.

"So are you, Barbara."

"Look, I'm going to put Tess Bergen on the stand, and she'll have to answer my questions. She's not the type to lie without giving herself away. I'll break her, Cody, you know I will." Barbara got up and came around her desk to face him.

"Do I look worried?"

"You can't fool me. You're worried. Tess is your weak link."

"The girl has nothing to tell you."

"Bullshit, Cody." She smiled at him, leaning back

against her desk, her long, slender legs stretched out, her arms folded across her chest.

Very attractive lady, Cody thought. Even her use of profanity comes out sexy.

"I want her deposed soon," Barbara said.

"Sure, we'll set it up. In Monterey, though."

"I'll send Paul Howard," Barbara said.

"Okay, fine." He studied the district attorney a bit too long, deliberately trying to rattle her. He usually liked real feminine women, buxom, long-haired. His four ex-wives were all that type, but this woman—skinny, half-inch-long hair, close to his height, definitely not buxom—was damn fine-looking. Tough, and smart, too.

"What're you looking at?" she said, her eyes narrowed suspiciously.

"Nice suit," he said. "Armani?"

"No," she replied.

"Woulda fooled me." He'd heard some stories about Barbara, mostly from Steve Sutton. She was known to be a hot number around town. Thirty-eight years old, single, never married, but she liked men.

He'd love to toss out some tidbits of gossip, push her a little, but it could wait. He'd save that ploy till he really needed it; she didn't rattle easily.

"You'll let me know, Barbara, won't you, when you find the murder weapon? And, oh yes, I'd like a list of your witnesses, complete disclosure."

"It's not complete yet."

"You can send me the additions as they come up."

"I want yours, too. Quid pro quo."

"It'll be faxed over this afternoon."

"Is that it, then?"

"That's it. I wouldn't want to take up any more of your valuable time, Barbara."

"Cut the crap, Cody."

"I love it when you talk dirty," he said, grinning, then he turned and left her office.

On the way back across town to the hotel, Cody thought about Barbara's words. She was right in one respect—Tess was his weak link. He'd prep the girl until he was blue in the face, and by then she might even have confessed to Dan about the gun, but Cody suspected Barbara could still break her on the stand.

He wasn't worried about Lawrence; the man would protest his innocence forever. Convincingly, too. Besides, there was no way Lawrence was ever going on the stand. He didn't have to. But Tess could be subpoenaed, and she was different, clearly more fragile, and he worried about how much pressure she could withstand. On the other hand, there was a core of strength in Tess, remarkable strength, and her instinct to protect her father was powerful.

Cody got back to the hotel for a quick meeting with the boys.

"Dan called in. He's there. He's looking at the letters," Patrick reported. "He says it'll take a few days. There're more than he thought."

"Did he say how he was getting along with Tess?" Cody asked.

"As well as could be expected," Patrick answered.

"They must be at each other's throats, then," Cody said.

"He didn't say that."

"Didn't have to, son," Cody replied, shaking his head lugubriously.

ELEVEN

Tess enjoyed the hours she put in at the Colonnades Advanced Care Facility. For one, she was working within her field, caring for the sick and elderly, tending to their most basic needs. But she was also their friend. And no one, not a single resident or staff member, had said a word to her about her father's predicament or even her own troubles, which had been splashed all over tabloid front pages, pictures and all. Tess figured the people at the nursing facility had more important things to worry about. Such as life and death.

Mornings were busy getting everyone bathed and dressed, fed, their medications delivered, paperwork filled out, appointments made with doctors and dentists, more paperwork and then lunch. But after lunch, when volunteers often showed up to entertain everyone—a piano player, a school choir, a local artist who helped with crafts—the nursing home quieted down. Tess had time to sit and chat with the patients or play a few hands of bridge or visit with family members and answer their questions.

Tess had her favorite patients. There was Edith Cutter, once a renowned California artist, and Jane

Sloan, an Alzheimer's patient who'd been a history professor at Stanford University. Jane could remember all her history down to the tiniest detail, but often she had no memory of yesterday or even an hour ago. It was frustrating and sad, and yet Tess had been at the facility long enough to have seen Jane's progress with the latest Alzheimer's treatments. That was gratifying. That was why Tess had wanted to become a doctor in the first place.

On this particular afternoon, two days after Dan Hadley had arrived in Monterey, Tess was playing a few hands of bridge with three of the residents, two women and a man, Gilbert Raines, a retired civil engineer. Gilbert could be a sweetheart, but he also had an attitude at times, and the women referred to him as the grumpy old man.

Tess was his partner. When her turn to bid came around, she eyed her cards and said, "Pass."

Gilbert grumbled.

The woman to Tess's left bid one heart and Gilbert toyed with his cards, then said, "Three spades." He looked up and glared at Tess as if she could miraculously turn the cards in her hand into spades.

They lost the hand, badly; the woman to Tess's right had all the spades. Gilbert fumed and fussed and blamed Tess, who said merely, "Alrighty, I think I better drop out and visit Mrs. Cutter now. See ya."

She was thinking about Gilbert as she walked down the corridor toward Edith Cutter's room. Men. She'd never figured them out. A woman wouldn't have risked that three-spade bid, especially after her partner had passed. But Gilbert, and a lot of men, would do it. It was a male thing, taking risks, wanting to win so badly they'd stick their necks out.

Hadley, she thought. He was that kind of man.

Couldn't stand not to get the last word in, even when she hadn't pushed his buttons.

Tess knew she could get under his skin. And he sure got under hers. She still couldn't believe Cody had sent him. She'd tried to be civil, she really had, but it was so hard around that arrogant jerk.

She entered Edith's room and found the woman dozing in an easy chair, her TV tuned to a soap. Tess adjusted the blanket around her knees, then went out quietly onto the tiny porch and watered the pots of geraniums and pansies Edith lovingly kept.

Hadley. Tess couldn't even stay in her own home in peace. He was there. Morning, noon and night. Mostly opening letters, marking them, stacking them, sorting. Sitting behind her father's desk in his frayed blue cotton shirt and faded jeans, a day's growth of beard on his jaw. Looking cool. Macho.

She pictured him as clearly as if he was there with her, the way his sharp blue eyes narrowed to slits when he was angry, the grooves from nose to mouth deepening. He often had a grim expression when he was concentrating. World-weary, as if disappointed by life.

She wondered about that. Somewhere she'd heard he'd been a cop. Tess didn't know a thing about cops except what she read in novels or saw on TV. She knew they could be mean. She knew a lot of them got a high from the power they held over people. She also knew the suicide and divorce rate among cops was well above average.

But Dan had quit. She wondered why. Disillusionment? Money? Had he ever been married, divorced? Had he—

"Oh, Tess" came Mrs. Cutter's frail voice, "there you are."

Tess shook the thoughts off, turned and smiled at

Edith. "Just watering your plants." She went back into the apartment and sat down to visit, but Hadley's face kept popping unbidden into her mind. It was the gun, of course, she told herself all afternoon. She was afraid he was going to keep pressing and pressing until she broke. And she couldn't give in. For all she knew, Hadley might turn the information over to the D.A.

It was on the drive home that afternoon that Tess remembered something else about Frank Ferrara. It wasn't much, but maybe it would help.

She found Dan in the office, reading letters, making his notes.

He looked up and said nothing.

"I've remembered something about Ferrara," she said, tossing her purse and car keys onto a chair.

"Go on," he said.

"He's definitely from Florida."

"I already know that."

"I think he lived with a relative or something in a trailer."

"Yeah?"

"I know. There must be a million trailer parks in Florida." She shrugged. "I just thought you'd want to know. Any progress on the mail?" There, she thought, she was at least trying to be civil.

"Some," he said in that low, husky voice.

"Is it a state secret?"

Dan studied her for a moment, then said, "No. There're a couple of real crazies who took an unusual interest in your sister's murder and Robbie's getting off. They wrote to your father more than once."

"And you think…?"

"I don't think anything yet, Tess. I'm doing homework."

"Then let me ask you this," she tried. "Where do you go from here with the letters?"

"Wherever they take me," he said, and she turned on her heel and left, smarting.

She talked to her mother at six, but all Carole said was not to be upset about the media fuss over the missing gun.

"I'm not upset," Tess said.

"It just seems to be in the papers or on TV every day."

"I'm not reading the papers or watching TV, Mom. And I thought you weren't, either."

"I'm trying not to."

Tess was longing to ask Carole about her state of mind, about how many pills a day she was relying on now. But Carole put Lawrence on the phone then, and the opportunity was lost.

She talked to her dad for several minutes, telling him that Dan Hadley appeared to be making progress with the mail.

Lawrence said, "Good, good," but very little else, except what was the weather like and how was the cat. It was stilted conversation. What Tess really wanted to discuss was their relationship. She wanted to blurt out that he wasn't responsible for her actions. She'd taken the gun and hidden it on her own.

Tears burned behind her eyes as she told him about the cat and the heavy rain they had on the coast last night. God, how she wished Andie was still alive. Andie would know how to handle everything.

Tess hung up shortly after that, and she sat on the kitchen stool and bit her lip. "Oh, Andie," she said. "Did I do the right thing?"

That night Tess had a terrible dream. Usually it was Andie's murder that filled her nightmares. But tonight she dreamed she was running along Ute Avenue, running, her breath coming in short, painful gasps. Her purse was slung over her shoulder, heavy as a rock, the gun banging, banging, against her. Then she was on her knees, her brain whirling. She was digging furiously, her nails breaking, her breath ragged.

She heard something behind her, a crack of a twig underfoot. Panic exploded in her chest and she spun around. So afraid. Fear knifing through her. It was the cops.

She looked up, panicked. The cop's face took form and shape and it was Dan's face looming above her. He was grinning. Ferociously.

It was Tess's idea to spend Saturday with Paula. She needed to get out. She was sick to death of hiding and cowering and feeling like a leper. She was sick of the fear. She'd wear a hat and sunglasses, and if anyone recognized her, so what?

Paula arrived at the house at ten in the morning to pick her up. But Tess was on the phone with her mother. She opened the door, mouthed "Come in, it's Mom," then left Paula in the living room while she finished talking to her mother from the back patio.

Her friend was not in the living room when Tess returned. Paula had found Dan in the office, and Tess caught them in the middle of a conversation.

"God, I just loved that show," Paula was saying. "I get into the city whenever I can and do the theater. You're so lucky to live there. I can't afford it. Yet." She laughed.

And Dan. "Yeah, it's expensive, but I've pretty much lived in Frisco all my life, so it's not that bad. Not if you know the ropes, anyway."

"When did you leave the police?"

"Um, four, almost five years ago."

"And you like being an investigator?"

"It's a good living."

"Probably exciting."

Dan laughed. A genuine laugh. "Not really. Mostly I dig through records. Like this." He nodded at the piles of letters stacked everywhere.

"But you travel a lot? I mean, you were just in Aspen." Then Paula noticed Tess behind her. "Oh," she said, "be right with you. Dan and I were just chatting."

"I see that," Tess said.

"I travel some," he replied, his gaze sliding from Tess back to Paula. "Frankly, I prefer to stay home. In the city."

"You have a family there? A wife? Parents?"

Dan shook his head. "No one. Never was."

"Never?"

"I'm an orphan." He shrugged.

Tess stared.

"I lived with a grandmother for a year or so," Dan was saying, "but it didn't work."

"How awful," Paula said. "I mean, God, foster homes and all that. I've got a couple of kids I see at the clinic who're foster children. They're always so...wounded. You know what I mean?"

"Oh, yeah," Dan said, "I know."

Tess listened in utter disbelief. Here was Paula, who'd known Dan Hadley for less than ten minutes, getting him to tell her his life story. And Tess...she'd known him for weeks and couldn't even have said if he was married. What amazed her more, virtually stunned her, was that if she didn't know better, seeing him like this with Paula, she'd have said what a nice person he was. A sad, awful upbringing, but an open, friendly guy.

In Paula's car, heading down the coast past Carmel, Tess couldn't help offering her opinion of Dan. "He's a real ass," she said. "Honestly, Paula. I don't know what came over him back there. Maybe he was possessed by some sort of a nice-guy ghost or something, but trust me, he's a number one dickhead."

Paula gave her a sidelong glance. "He seemed so pleasant. I mean, I just poked my head in while you were on the phone, and he introduced himself and said he was from San Francisco. We got to talking."

"I saw that."

"Anyway, he seemed so friendly. Sort of like Neil, you know, a good talker."

"Dan Hadley," Tess muttered.

"Yes. I mean, didn't your heart break when he told us he was an orphan?"

"No," Tess said, "it didn't."

"Liar."

"No, seriously. All I could think was that no wonder he was so cold and nasty."

"And you didn't feel sorry for him?"

"God, no. Not then and not now."

Paula looked askance. "Well, if nothing else, he's quite a hunk."

"You must be joking."

"Come on," Paula said, "you're full of it. He's gorgeous."

"I don't see that at all."

"You are such a liar, Bergen."

They had a wonderfully expensive lunch at a cliffside restaurant just north of Big Sur then drove back up the coast, crossed the coastal range and ended up in Gilroy, the town famous for its summer garlic festival.

Tess had a peaceful day despite being recognized as she and Paula shopped in a Gilroy mall. It kept coming back to her, all afternoon, the conversation Paula had had with Dan—the orphan, the bachelor, the loner. Alone by choice? Or was he incapable of sustaining a relationship? Surely he had a girlfriend. Or at least, upon occasion, he slept with someone, screwed someone, she thought, just like he'd screwed her family.

"He's a real user," Tess said as they descended into Monterey from the hills later that day.

"Excuse me?" Paula said.

"Hadley. He's a real user."

"Are we still on him?"

"You know what he did to my family. For money. Pure and simple."

"So? He's obviously trying to make amends."

"Oh, my God, Paula," Tess breathed, "you are so naive."

"Well? What do you think he's doing, then?"

"Getting paid a fortune again. He's in it for the bucks."

"Come on. He could make money some other way."

"Let's just drop it," Tess said, and she turned and stared out the window.

"You're the one who brought it up," Paula growled.

They met Neil at a fern bar in Monterey, a locals' spot that Tess and Paula had frequented during college breaks. Paula and Neil had shrimp cocktails and greasy stacks of fried onion rings, but Tess stuck with red wine. Three of them. She'd never been that big a drinker—a cheap drunk, her friends had always said. And when she'd visited the rest room she realized she was smashed.

Good, she thought, swaying when she returned to the table.

She didn't care. Didn't care about anything at that moment. Not Hadley. Not her parents and not the gun. Let them find it, she thought, and she giggled. They'd never know she was the one who buried it. There were no prints on it. She'd wiped them off. Rubbed and rubbed. And so what if she hadn't gotten them all? She giggled again. She'd just say...well, she'd say they were planted there. Sure. And that dickhead Hadley could go out and find some poor sap to frame for planting her fingerprints on the gun. Hadley would do it. For money. She hiccoughed.

"That's it, Bergen," Paula said, "we're outta here. You're going to feel like hell tomorrow."

"I want another wine," Tess slurred.

Paula and Neil drove her home. By then her head was beginning to pound and she felt sick to her stomach. She still giggled, though. "Great example of a doctor," she said from the back seat.

"About typical," Paula said.

Dan was still up when Tess let herself in. Bumping into the back of an armchair, she made her way into the kitchen and saw him at the counter, reading a newspaper.

"God," she said, teetering, tossing her sunglasses on the counter but missing, "you're still here." She opened the fridge and took out a bottle of wine from the back and sat it on the counter with a heavy thunk, almost spilling it.

Dan stared at her.

"I'd offer you some, but you can buy your own." She walked over to a glass-front cabinet and found a wineglass, but had to steady herself for a moment with both hands on the counter.

With her back to him, she said, "You really snowed my friend. Oh, you're good, Dan Hadley, really good. I'll give you that."

"You've had enough," she heard from behind, and

she turned. He was standing right there, right in front of her.

"Go to hell," she said, looking up.

"I said, you've had enough." Then he tried to reach around her and take the bottle.

"Don't you dare."

"I'm trying to help," he said. "You'll thank me in the morning."

"Thank you?" She stumbled backward a little, coming up against the counter. "I suppose you'll want a bonus for helping the poor drunken woman. I can see it now."

"Go to bed," he said.

"No. It's my house."

"Fine. It's your house. Now go to bed."

Tess drew herself up. "Why are you doing this?"

"Because you're going to feel like sh…hell in the morning."

Tess looked up and tried to focus on his face with one eye. "No," she said. "Why are you doing this? Working for my father?"

"Let's just say I owe him."

"Bull. Are you telling me it's guilt?"

"Call it what you want. Now go to bed."

"Y'know," she said, "I really want to hit you. I've never—" it came out *neffer* "—wanted to hit anyone in my life before."

Dan just stared at her, a slight twist on his thin lips. He finally said, "Take your best shot."

And she did. She closed her fist and swung at him. But he caught it in midair and held her wrist until it hurt, and then he let go.

"You bastard," she said, tears spilling from her eyes. "I hate you." And she tore away from him, around the counter and into the living room. She thought she heard him say "I know you do," but it didn't matter. Marshaling her dignity, she groped her way down the hall, opened her bedroom door, slammed it shut and fell onto her bed fully clothed.

It was the last thing she remembered.

Dan finished with a pile of letters, stood and yawned, then stretched to get the kinks out. He'd been sitting there for two solid hours, and he felt a quiet sense of satisfaction; he'd found two letter writers who fit the profile Cody was seeking, fit it to a T.

Nutty as fruitcakes, full of undisguised rage, much too interested in Andie Childress and her murder and the trial. Obsessed by it. One guy was in prison in California. Dan would have to find out if he'd been in prison at the time of Robbie's shooting. The other, though, lived in Seattle and worked for Boeing Aircraft. His name was Roger Pearl and he was absolutely perfect. Hell, from the sound of his letters—there were lots of them—he could easily have shot Robbie.

Dan rubbed his eyes. It was late and he was tired. But he was still going to drive back to San Francisco tonight and sleep in his own bed. Tess would be happy as a lark to find him gone in the morning. Even with a hangover she'd be thrilled. She couldn't stand him. So much for Cody's big ideas.

He stood there in the dim, silent house and smiled to himself at the memory of her taking a swing at him. He'd been a little rough—too rough?—but she'd asked for it. Well, she probably wouldn't remember in the morning, anyway.

The house was quiet. Even the Bergens' cat was out cold on the living-room couch—he'd put in a rough day chasing birds outside. Dan eyed the cat, then took the opportunity to snoop around Bergen's files out in the garage. He still couldn't believe Bergen would have been dumb enough to have kept any sort of paperwork on the gun. Still, he looked. Nothing. He went back inside through the kitchen, then glanced at the dark hallway leading to the bedrooms. He wondered if she'd even made it into bed. For all he knew, she'd passed out on the floor. He thought about that for a second and then shrugged. Hell, he'd better take a look before he split for the city.

He walked down the hall and found her bedroom door ajar. He considered knocking, but that was ridiculous—wherever she was, she'd been passed out for hours now.

Pushing the door open silently, he went in, stopped to let his eyes adjust to the dark. He could smell her, a particular scent, perfume and women's clothes and something else he couldn't put his finger on.

He saw her then, lying fully clothed on her bed, her hair spilled across the pastel cover. His feet took him closer, he couldn't stop them, and he stood over her, watching her chest rise and fall gently. One hand lay by her cheek, curled like a child's, and her lashes lay on her cheeks like miniature fans.

He leaned down and examined her face in the dimness. It was a study in black and white, an old photograph, a charcoal sketch. White skin, black brows, shadows of nose and lips and brow in every shade of gray. He leaned closer, so close he could feel her warm breath, in and out, in and out.

He stood there like that for a time, then whispered, "Yeah, it is guilt," and he touched her lips with his. She was soft and warm and she smelled of woman and liquor.

She made an unconscious restless movement, and Dan drew back quickly, but she subsided into stillness again. He watched her for another moment, backed away and left her room.

Walking down the hall to the office, Dan drew a hand across his face and thought, What in hell am I doing? He threw his few things in his bag, took the bundle of letters wrapped in a rubber band, glanced around the office to see if he'd left anything there. He let himself out of the Bergens' house noiselessly, got into his car and drove away, turning north on the highway to San Francisco, alone in the night with his thoughts.

TWELVE

Dan woke up late, the sun cutting a swath across his bed, streaming through his own familiar window. He lay there for a few minutes, feeling good; he was home. It was just a studio apartment, but it was big and airy, and it was his.

Finally he got up, padding around on the hard-wood floor in his bare feet, scratching his flat belly, yawning. One errant thought flashed through his mind—he bet he felt better this morning than Tess Bergen did—then he promptly put her out of his head.

He fixed coffee, showered, ate a stale piece of toast. The familiar scratching started at the fire-escape window and he went to let Cleopatra in. She snaked around his ankles, rubbing and purring, a black cat, a stray. No one knew where she lived, and she came and went as she pleased, like the queen that she was.

He stroked her back. "Hey, how's it going? Catch any mice, Cleo, old girl? Got any boyfriends?"

She looked up at him, green eyes unblinking. He figured she thought he was big and clumsy and stupid, but she put up with him because he fed her.

"Milk," Dan said, "right?"

Her answer, though unspoken, was clear as a bell. Yes, you fool, and hurry.

While Cleopatra lapped at a bowl of milk, Dan phoned Cody in Aspen.

"Where you calling from, son?" Cody asked.

"I'm back in San Francisco."

"Hm, no great luck with the young lady?" he asked.

"No." Should he tell Cody Tess had taken a swing at him last night? No, he didn't think so. "She wants to tell someone, though. She'd dying to tell someone."

"Just not you, I take it."

"Or anyone else. I figure she's afraid of what someone would do with the info."

Cody said nothing. He couldn't. Dan knew that and Cody knew Dan knew. Cody was just praying Dan would get the information out of her and do what had to be done. The most Dan could ever tell him was that everything was okay.

Dan switched to a safe subject. "I've got a couple of prospects from Bergen's letters. Promising ones. One is a guy in prison right here in California, sounds like domestic abuse. The guy definitely wrote to Bergen from prison, but he could have gotten out on parole. Name's Lester Ostrander."

"You'll check him out?"

"Right away. But our best prospect is a pen pal named Roger Pearl. I know the man works, or at least he did work, for Boeing. He bragged about it in a letter. Must have wanted to impress Bergen. But there was never a return address on any of the letters, only Seattle postmarks. I'll tell you, Cody, this one's good. He even wrote a detailed scenario of how Bergen could kill Childress, and it's pretty damn close to what actually went down."

"No foolin'."

"I knew you'd like that."

"I don't suppose this Roger Pearl wrote back to congratulate Lawrence for using his plan?" Cody asked.

"No such luck," Dan said. "Must have chickened out."

"I take it you're going to Seattle? Don't spare the expense. We're going to need all the smoke and mirrors we can get."

"I'll try to leave tomorrow. Day after at the latest."

"Excellent."

"How's everything else going?" Dan asked.

"Well, now, we've lucked out in a lot of areas. The bloodstains on Lawrence's coat are his. DNA came back. I've been talking to the psychiatrists, and I think I have one lined up. He understands what's at stake. The D.A. has a forensic psychologist ready to interview Lawrence, a well-known one, worked for the FBI. He'll say Lawrence is a natural-born killer, I have no doubt, but our boy will say he's an angel. They cancel each other out." Cody paused. "I see only one serious problem, Dan."

"I know."

"Get her to tell you."

"I tried."

"Apparently not hard enough, son," Cody said.

Cody sat at his desk reviewing motions and depositions, all the paper detritus created by a trial. He kept an eye on the television screen at the same time, checking in on "The Judge's Advocate."

The topic they were discussing that day was anarchy. A pithy subject, Cody thought. Had a bite to it. The word frightened people, brought to mind a crazed, topcoated man lurking in dark alleyways, ready to set off an explosion in a crowded public place. Great subject, but how much relevance would the watchers attribute to it?

"All we have is the law, Craig. It's been honed to perfection for centuries by the greatest minds on earth."

"I beg to differ, Gail. The law is not perfect in any way."

"All right, not perfect. But the best humankind has come up with so far."

"Sometimes it's not good enough, though. Then where does that leave us?"

"The greater good prevails, Craig. Individuals sometimes lose out. If a man's guilty of murder, he must be punished for the good of society."

"Quite a sermon, Gail, but remember that's what the prosecutor told the jury in the Robbie Childress trial, and look what happened. He was acquitted."

Gail sighed dramatically. "Like it or not, the law is what holds society together. It may be imperfect, but without it we would sink into anarchy. Remember Bosnia? Rwanda? Or how about the Russian Revolution?"

Craig grinned. "Oh, Gail, are you getting historical on me?" he said.

Cody shook his head. One justified shooting did not anarchy make. Gail was really stretching it. If she wanted to talk anarchy, she should look to the inner cities. There was real anarchy. Anarchy was irrational, undeserved, mayhem, every man in equal danger. The shooting of Childress was rational, deserved, totally controlled, and had not put another human being in danger.

Dan knew he had to do it. He hadn't been home in weeks and he hadn't called Susan once. Hell, he hadn't even thought about her much, to tell the truth.

But he was back in San Francisco now, and she was not very far away. He owed her a call.

Dialing her work number, he braced himself. He got her company's automated service and punched in her extension, walking with his cordless phone to the window while he waited for her. The bridge was beautiful in the sunlight, and the bay was dark sapphire blue, the sun catching the tops of the rippling waves. No mountains, no theme-park buses, a real city.

"Susan McPherson," she answered.

"It's Dan," he said.

"Well, well. Welcome home, stranger."

"How've you been?"

"Fine. And you?"

"I've been working hard, real hard."

"Which is, naturally, why you didn't have time to call me," she said coldly.

"Well, you did tell me to get out of your life." Of course Dan knew even as he said this that such words from her were spoken only in the heat of the moment. She always expected him to call again, and he always did.

"You bastard."

"Now, Susan—"

"I have to get back to work, Dan."

"Hang on. Just give me a minute. Look, I want to see you. Meet me after work. I'm only in town for a night or two."

"Drop dead."

"Susan, come on. We're old friends. I...I've missed you."

"And cows fly."

"Susan, this case, it's a tough one. Morris is a slave driver. Honest. Tonight, Ben's at the Marina, okay?

Just a drink for old times' sake." He was groveling and he hated it, but he owed it to her.

She didn't answer right away. Then again, she didn't hang up.

"Okay," she said reluctantly. "Ben's at six."

"Thanks, Susan. See you."

She hung up without another word.

He put the phone down, relieved. One chore completed.

Well, he *had* missed Susan, he told himself, gathering laundry together to drop off at Sun Lee's. But as he moved around the apartment, ignoring a monster pile of mail, it was Tess Bergen's face that came to mind. Asleep, the shadows lying gently on her skin, delineating, caressing, her hair spread out around her face like an untidy halo, her breasts rising and falling.

Whoa, he thought, surprised. She despised him; what was he thinking?

Yet he couldn't get out of his head the feel of her, the scent of her skin, the whisper of her breath, the texture of her lips.

He looked at the pile of mail on his kitchen counter, looked away and smiled to himself, contemplating Tess's reaction if she knew he'd kissed her while she slept. Maybe he'd tell her someday.

He thought about her and about what Cody wanted. What Cody wanted was for Dan to do the job he was hired for, to see that there were no surprises between now and the trial, no gun turning up and no paper trail to a .22 purchased by Bergen. He'd tried to get Tess to tell him what she knew, but she wouldn't. He almost didn't blame her, yet at the same time he wanted to take the burden from her.

And her father—that nonsense about the fox and losing the gun. Bergen just hadn't decided to tell anyone the truth yet. And when he did, it would be Dan he'd have to tell.

Dan finally got to his mail, paid some bills, then sat on his couch and made several calls to Seattle, trying to locate Roger Pearl. Then he phoned a hacker friend of his in San Francisco, gave him Roger Pearl's name and asked him to get ready to do a thorough search when he located the man.

"Usual money?" the man asked.

"The usual," Dan said. "And if you come up with something juicy, there'll be a bonus."

"Great. I love it."

Dan then phoned the California Department of Corrections and found out that Lester Ostrander was still in jail. So, he was out of the picture as a suspect. That left Dennis Wilson, Roger Pearl and Frank Ferrara, address unknown on the last two, each a strong possibility of being Robbie Childress's murderer. Motive galore. Opportunity was the problem. And means.

At five-thirty he dressed in khaki slacks and an open-neck blue oxford shirt with a tweed sport coat over it, and drove down to the Marina to meet Susan.

She was late and entered the trendy waterfront bar looking slightly harassed but very beautiful. Her suit was navy blue and cut to show off her figure to perfection. Her heels made her calf muscles bunch up and relax as she walked. He loved her calves, curved and muscular.

He stood and greeted her and gave her a big kiss. "God, you smell great," he said.

"You're looking healthy," she said, sitting across from him, dumping her briefcase on an empty chair.

"I told you I was reforming."

"Uh-huh."

"You didn't believe me."

"No."

They ordered drinks. Dan drank his slowly. No sense antagonizing Susan. He asked her about work, and she warmed slowly, relaxing as her drink took hold.

"I missed you," he offered again.

"You're so full of it, Dan," Susan said, but she smiled. Then she leaned her elbows on the table and asked, "Is all the stuff about the Bergen case true? It's on TV incessantly."

"What stuff?"

"That there are no other suspects? That they think his daughter took the gun and hid it?"

Dan felt a sudden strong spurt of irritation. "Don't believe everything you hear," he said gruffly.

"So it isn't true, then."

"Susan, I can't discuss the case with you."

"What are the Bergens like?"

"They're nice people. Nice, ordinary people who had something bad happen to them."

"So, do you think he didn't do it?"

"Ah, hell, Susan…"

"I know, you can't talk about it. Party pooper."

"Can we talk about something else?"

She pouted, but it was a mild pout.

"Have you been going out with anyone special?" Dan asked. Carefully.

"Well, I wasn't about to sit home alone. Sure, I've gone out. None of them is as cute as you, though."

"I'm not cute."

"Sure you are. Not that it helps your total lack of commitment to a relationship."

"Hey, that's unfair," he said.

"It's true, though."

They ended up walking down the wharf to a seafood restaurant for dinner. The fresh abalone was terrific.

"There's no abalone in Aspen," Dan mused, eating a morsel of the firm mild flesh.

"What's Aspen like?"

"A resort. Big mountains, pretty old Victorian buildings, lots of tourists. Not my cup of tea."

"You like San Francisco better?"

"Definitely. I like the dirty alleyways and the bad neighborhoods. There're no bad neighborhoods in Aspen, like it's not real."

"I'd like to go there sometime."

He shrugged.

They ate dinner, then walked along the Marina, looking in shop windows, buying ice-cream cones. The sea air cooled the city, stroked the skin, tingled in the nostrils. Dan was full of good food, and a pretty lady was walking next to him.

When he drove Susan home, she was oddly quiet. He wondered if she was deciding whether to ask him in or not. He'd go, of course.

He parked on the steep street and walked with Susan to her door.

"Thanks for dinner," she said softly.

He bent his head and kissed her as he had so many times before.

"You want to come in?" she asked.

"Yeah, I'd like that," he said, his hand on her arm.

She poured them snifters of cognac, sank onto her couch next to him, wiggled her feet out of her heels and sighed blissfully.

Dan pulled her close and kissed her thoroughly, feeling her respond to him. He'd thought he would be horny as hell, not having slept with a woman in so long, but the foreplay seemed rote.

He pulled back and looked at her, at her half-open

mouth and pert nose and avid expression, at the erect nipples showing through her silk blouse.

"Yes?" she purred.

"You know what, Susan," he said, "you look tired and it's late, and I've got some real important calls coming in, maybe tonight. I think I better go home."

"What?"

"Yeah, I think I better," he repeated, rising.

"You're kidding."

"Susan, it's this case, and I know you're beat. You need a good night's sleep."

"You *are* a bastard," she said furiously. "You probably met some goddamn bimbo in Aspen, and you're saving yourself for her!"

"I did not. Don't be ridiculous. I just think—"

"Get out!"

"Susan—"

"Get the hell out, Dan!"

Dan walked back down the hill toward his car, hands jammed in his pockets. What had just happened in there? He'd gone to Susan's, ready and willing when she'd asked him in for the nightcap. He'd kissed her, and then...what? Was she right? Was he that afraid to make a commitment, so afraid he couldn't even make love to her? Or was it something else?

Ah hell, he thought. It didn't matter. He knew one thing, though. Where Susan was concerned, he'd better shit or get off the pot.

THIRTEEN

Tess wasn't sure if she was indignant or pleased that Dan had disappeared without a word. She kept expecting at any moment he'd drive up, that he'd use the spare key she'd given him to let himself in, then saunter in as if no time had passed.

She cringed with humiliation whenever she thought of the other night. She never drank like that. Her memories were foggy, but she knew she'd made an ass of herself, and she distinctly recalled taking a swing at Dan. God, she'd actually tried to hit him. She had bruises where he'd held her arm in self-defense.

It occurred to Tess that she owed him an apology. Maybe he really did believe he was leveling the playing field. Maybe he was capable of feeling guilt. Maybe Dan Hadley had a conscience.

Dammit, he was on her mind far too much.

It was a foggy day, the house surrounded by a cloud of mist, the sun's glare trying to break through. Sound was muffled, the air pressed still and heavy on everything, leaving droplets of moisture on every surface.

Tess decided to make another call to the director of

residency at UCLA. She'd been waiting for a return call for more than a week, but it had never come.

After an interminable wait she was put through to the man, the first time she'd ever actually been able to speak to him.

"Ms. Bergen?" He sounded as if he was in a hurry.

"Ah, yes, Mr. Hanson, I was wondering how my application to renew my residency was coming along."

"Well, I'm going to be frank with you, Ms. Bergen. Your credentials are still excellent, your recommendations are first rate. None of that has changed."

Tess felt her spirits rise.

"But we're aware of the situation you're in... I should say, your family is in at this time. And we'd really rather not draw the kind of media attention that might result from your presence here."

"But I'm sure—"

"Yes, this...situation will be resolved sooner or later, no doubt. Perhaps you might reapply at that time, Ms. Bergen."

"I can't believe you'd be so concerned about the media," she couldn't help saying.

"It's not only that. Your, ah, name comes up often. Speculation, I know, but it would cast a shadow on you, and we really feel it wouldn't be productive for either you or the hospital."

They all think I'm guilty, she thought as she hung up. And they're right. I am guilty. I hid the gun, and no one knows where it is, and I'm an accessory after the fact in a first-degree murder case. My own father's case.

Her career was down the tubes.

She fought back tears. No self-pity, she thought. She'd done the deed with full knowledge; there was no one else to blame. And maybe when this was all over, she'd accept her role with better grace. She'd done the right thing, she knew she had, but it was so very hard to keep her own counsel.

Paula had asked and asked. But could she tell her best friend? God, it was tempting. Yes, she could. She could trust Paula. But Tess knew she could never lay that responsibility on her.

It was a slow, dull day. She didn't even have to go to work. Wandering around the big house alone, Tess almost wished Dan would walk in. At least she'd have company in her misery.

But Dan would badger her about the gun.

She thought about Dan Hadley too much. The scene of him talking to Paula kept returning to her mind, the pleasant way he'd chatted with her friend, the things he'd told her.

He'd said he was an orphan. Said it unselfconsciously. No family. Completely alone. Tess couldn't imagine that. No parents, no close, loving family, no one to go to when you needed help, no one who knew you from the day you were born, who fed you and brought you up and knew your past and your birthday and the time you crayoned on your aunt's new wallpaper when you were three.

How did a child survive in that emotional wasteland? Yet Dan seemed so sure of himself. Where had that air of competence come from? Who had been his role model? How had he found the strength inside himself to become the man that he was?

So many questions she could never ask. Despite herself, Tess felt a tiny spark of admiration for Dan, overcoming such a background. She knew what she'd said to Paula that day in the car, that she had no sympathy for the man. But that wasn't entirely true.

That afternoon she found herself searching through her father's files again. Searching for a receipt, a sales slip, a bill, anything that would link him to the gun. Maybe there really was a receipt and Lawrence wanted it destroyed, but he couldn't leave Aspen to do it, and he couldn't bring himself to ask her to do it.

Or maybe she was just paranoid, and there was no record whatsoever. Still, she searched all afternoon, the fog smothering the Monterey Peninsula, her heart pounding slowly and heavily in her chest. It was awful going through her father's private records, awful, but she couldn't stop.

She went through files and files of papers, then his desk drawers, then the boxes stored in the garage. Old yellowed stuff that smelled of mildew. Ripped and folded, tattered.

Finally Tess sat on the cold garage floor, papers strewn around her, papers dangling from her fingers, and she wept. She wept with frustration and fear and loneliness, she wept for her lost ambitions, her father's plight. She wept for Andie.

Then she got angry. Why had Andie put up with Robbie's abuse? Why hadn't she left him earlier? If she hadn't stayed with him, none of this would have happened. Andie would be alive. Goddamn her sister. And goddamn Robbie.

She drew in a quavering breath. No, it wasn't Andie's fault. Andie had married a handsome, rich, famous athlete whom the world idolized. She'd done her best. She'd been hit by Robbie so many times. No one had really known the extent of it. Hit and smacked and humiliated and verbally abused.

And then…and then Andie and Robbie must have had a terrible fight. Tess would bet that Andie gave him an ultimatum of some sort that night, such as wanting a divorce. Then Andie left, went for a ride in the Mercedes convertible Robbie had bought her and ended up at a movie theater in the Santa Monica hills.

Tess could imagine the scene as if she'd been there. Andie felt free as a bird—she'd made a decision, finally, that she knew was right. She was going to divorce Robbie, leave him, never again put up with beatings, with having to give excuses for bumps and bruises, never again have to wear sunglasses to cover a black eye.

Andie watched the whole movie, not wanting to go home until Robbie cooled down. And if he was still too angry, she'd simply pack a bag and stay in a motel. She could even drive up to Monterey tomorrow and go home. But she felt good, having at last made a decision.

After the show she went outside into the cool California spring night and drew in a deep breath. She could see the city's lights spread out below her to the sea, that special Los Angeles view. She felt as if a burden was lifted from her shoulders; she felt young again.

Andie walked toward her car, rummaging in her bag for her keys. She was reaching for the door handle when she realized someone was behind her. She turned. It was Robbie. He'd followed her.

Tess saw it all. Saw it over and over in her nightmare.

Everyone had left the parking lot, and it was night, and Robbie was strong. He was screaming at her: "Whore, slut, you met him here, didn't you?" He grabbed Andie, yanking her along, a hand over her mouth. He pulled her into the darkness under the trees that ringed the empty parking lot. She was terrified; she knew his temper, his rage, his strength.

He hit her then, so hard she lost consciousness for a few seconds, and when she came to he hit her again, so that her head snapped around and she was on the ground, pressed into the asphalt, and he was kneeling on her stomach and his hands encircled her throat, those big, strong hands. They closed around her throat, and she couldn't breathe, and he was so heavy, and the world was receding, turning dark, and there was only the awful choking, her lungs crying out for air and his hands squeezing and squeezing.

Tess sat there on the cold garage floor, rocking back and forth, and she wept for Andie. Why was it that even in death so many things were left unresolved in a relationship? Now Tess would never be able to ask her sister why she'd put up with the years of abuse. And in her heart she knew that this whole awful, sordid mess was Robbie Childress's fault. His alone. And, God help her, she really did believe he'd gotten exactly what he deserved—true justice.

Dan arrived back that afternoon around five. He let himself in the front door, giving her nothing more than a casual nod as he went into the office.

She followed him. "Where were you?" she asked. "You might have called to let me know when you were coming back. This isn't a hotel, you know."

He gave her a slightly bemused look, his eyes narrowed in a catlike way. Narrowed as if for the hunt. "Sorry" was all he said.

"Where were you?" she repeated.

"San Francisco. Home."

"Oh." She didn't want to drop it, though. "Well, next time please have the decency to let me know."

"You weren't in any condition to listen to my plans when I left," he said.

She felt herself flush.

"Hey, never mind. I won't be here much longer, anyway. I've got what I need." He held up some letters.

"Are those...?"

"Uh-huh," he said.

"Can I see one?"

Dan studied her face for a long time before he nodded. "I don't see why not." And then he handed her the one on the top of the pile. "You'll find this particularly interesting."

Tess took the envelope and sat down, turning it over in her hands. There was no return address. She did notice the postmark: Seattle.

She looked up. "It's anonymous."

A semblance of a smile crossed his lips. "Yeah, well," he said, "this one is. But the guy wrote your father a dozen letters over an eight-month period and signed the first few. Handwriting's identical and they're all from Seattle."

"You must have had to go through a ton of mail to sort this out," she said.

"It's my job. No big deal."

She opened the letter and pulled out a single sheet of paper that had been folded four times to fit into the small envelope. She started to read.

Dear Mr. Bergen,

I have written and written and you don't seem to be listening. Last week that scum was in Mexico with that woman. I saw it in the tabloids.

I don't know why you let him get away with this. Maybe I was wrong about you and you didn't love your daughter.

The time has come. You must face up to it. Robbie Childress must be killed. I know how. He loves crowds because he thinks they love him.

He's always in the public eye. You must buy a gun and be sure it isn't registered. There are gun shops that sell them for the right price and people do, too. Or you could go to a pawn shop or borrow one from a close friend who knows Childress is the scourge of the earth.

You take this gun to a place where he's sure to turn up. Make sure there's a crowd around him. You wear gloves. Then you shoot him. Make sure it's a heart shot. Head is no good. He could live. Then you throw down the gun and gloves and walk away. The crowd will be in a panic and no one will notice.

Get rid of your clothes. The police may arrest you, but there won't be enough evidence to hold you. Even if there were, no jury on earth will convict you.

Everyone wants him dead.

Buy the gun, Mr. Bergen.

A Friend

Tess let out a long breath she'd been holding the whole time, and then she looked back up at Dan. "Wow," she said.

"My sentiments exactly. His name's Roger Pearl, by the way. And, as I'm sure you can tell, he's one sick puppy."

"It's...it's so much like what really happened," she said in a whisper. "You don't think...I mean, this Pearl couldn't have..." And then she shut up. My God, she thought, she'd taken the gun from her own father's hand. She closed her eyes and bit her lip, afraid to look at Dan, afraid of what she'd see in his expression.

Was he laughing at her? Was he thinking she was naive and stupid? He knew who'd really shot Robbie; he knew she'd taken the gun. This business about Roger Pearl was a game, a sleight of hand. Cody Morris would use it to show a jury that Lawrence wasn't the only one who had a motive to kill Robbie. And Dan would find something, no matter how insignificant, to connect Pearl to the murder. It was what Dan Hadley did for a living.

She opened her eyes and looked up. "Is this ethical? I mean, to implicate a man, an innocent man..."

But Dan's face hardened. "Roger Pearl, whoever the hell he is, implicated himself when he wrote this letter. And he wrote a lot more of them, too. This one just happens to be the closest to what actually went down."

"Still," she said, and she dropped her head onto the back of the chair and sighed. It wasn't right. Nothing was right anymore. Not her sister's murder or the innocent verdict or her father being forced to take the law into his own hands or her ending up with the gun and having to hide it and lie and be so damn afraid....

"Tess?"

"What?" she said woodenly.

"Are you all right?"

"No. No, I'm not all right. I hate this. I hate it."

He didn't say a word, but she could feel the weight of his gaze on her, pinning her like an insect to the chair. She knew what he wanted. What they all wanted. The goddamn gun.

"You look as if you could use a friend," she heard him say, and she wanted to laugh hysterically.

"You?" she said.

"Well, someone."

"Right," she said.

"I'm going to courier this stuff to Cody, then I'm off to Seattle."

Tess looked up.

"Tomorrow. But I could use a favor."

"From me?"

"It would save me weeks of digging. If you could call a few of Andie's old friends, ask about Frank Ferrara."

"Of course."

"Ask if anyone has any idea where in Florida he's from. Okay?"

"Is he another one of your suspects, Dan?"

"Let's just say he was in Aspen during the festival."

"I see."

"Hey," Dan said, "all I'm doing is covering the bases."

"Like you did in Robbie's trial."

"That's right."

"Fine."

"Goddammit," he said, "you want to see your father go to prison?"

"No."

"Well, neither do I."

"Oh, really."

"Yeah, really. So make the calls. Okay?"

"Yes, I'll make them," she said coolly. "And you stay in touch this time."

"Fine." He started to leave the room, then stopped. "You got anything else you want to tell me before I go?" he asked.

She swallowed and stood. "No, what could I have to tell you? You're the investigator," she said with false bravado.

"Cut the crap, Tess. You know exactly what I mean."

She felt tears sting behind her eyes. She wouldn't start crying again, though, she wouldn't. She turned her back to Dan and took a deep breath. She wanted to tell him so badly it hurt; it was an actual ache inside her, like labor pains.

"Come on, Tess."

She shook her head and walked past him out of the room.

* * *

Cody Morris didn't mince words. He asked his newly hired psychiatrist, Dr. Sandy Martinez, straight out, "Well, what did you think of the letters? Is Roger Pearl crazy enough to have committed murder?"

"In my professional opinion, and naturally this can't be construed as an exact science because I haven't interviewed the man—"

"Come on, Sandy, cut to the chase," Cody said.

"He could be, yes, he might be. There are signs of psychosis, or at least very strong signs of antisocial tendencies," he replied.

"Excellent. You'll write a report, with all those fancy Freudian terms?"

"Of course."

"Good. And you'll testify to that at the trial?"

Dr. Martinez shrugged. "You're paying me."

Cody nodded, thinking ahead. Now all Dan had to do was locate this Pearl character.

Carole heard about the letters at the daily strategy meeting in the condo. They wouldn't let her read them—"too upsetting," Lawrence said—but she got the idea. This Roger Pearl was a bona fide nutcase; he hated Robbie Childress, had even concocted a murder scenario.

While Cody and his boys talked motions and discovery and Dan Hadley's traveling to Seattle and lines of questioning, Carole sat there swamped with relief. She was sure Roger Pearl was the guilty man, and Dan would track him down and bring him in for questioning.

Then Carole felt guilty herself. How could she have doubted her husband's innocence? She felt all twisted inside, betraying more than thirty years of life together, of love and caring. How could she have done that?

When everyone was gone, she went to Lawrence and confessed. "I'm sorry. I don't know how I could have doubted you. I know you're not a murderer, Lawrence. I know you couldn't have done it. Do you forgive me?"

Her husband looked at her with love and sorrow in his expression. "Carole, I know how it looks. Believe me, I know. It was only natural. Don't worry about it, sweetheart."

Carole put her arms around him, laid her head on his chest, feeling the familiar warm strength of her husband, and she wept for her treachery.

Tess had spoken to at least six of Andie's old friends. And to each of them she'd posed the same questions: Where did Frank Ferrara live? Where did he hang out? She also asked for the names of other friends of theirs, mutual acquaintances of Andie's who might be able to tell her something.

She'd left several messages, too, when she couldn't get hold of people, hoping they'd call back so that she wouldn't have to phone them again, bugging them.

So far no one had been much help. Two told her Frank was from Florida. That, of course, she already knew. Another thought he worked in Beverly Hills, but that may have been the year before. They all knew about his relationship with Andie, and they all knew about his fight with Robbie and how after that he'd told everyone he was scared that Childress would kill him, so he'd left Aspen. Several of Andie's friends made some shrewd guesses as to why Tess wanted to locate him.

"You think *he* did it?" Andie's old tennis partner

asked. "I mean, no one's mentioned his name, not the police or anyone like that."

"I'm only trying to find out where he is. My father's lawyer just wants to ask him some questions."

"Right."

Another friend of Andie's called back and told Tess that she thought she remembered Frank talking about the Tampa Bay football team.

"So, he could be from that area?"

"Got me."

"Well, thanks a lot. I appreciate your calling back."

Tess had to leave then, because she was scheduled at the nursing home that afternoon. She arrived to the news that Gilbert Raines had died, and she went about her duties with a heavy heart. She helped Mrs. Marks shampoo her hair, and she gave simple tests to a couple of Alzheimer's patients, tests she did once every few weeks to mark their progress on their new medication.

Mrs. Lowell seemed improved, so much so that she was well aware of Mr. Raines's death.

"You know I never liked him," the elderly woman said. "He was nothing but an old grump."

"Mm," Tess said. That wasn't the first time today she'd heard that sentiment. It was funny how the residents reacted to death. For the most part they seemed to go into a state of denial. A few were terribly upset. Others immediately found fault with the deceased. Tess supposed it was all a way of coping.

She herself needed to believe that death among the elderly was as natural as birth. It completed the cycle of life; all living things died. As a geriatrics specialist, she knew she would have to come to terms with the concept and with the reality, and she already felt strongly that life should not be artificially prolonged when patients were suffering or drugged to the point of being unaware of their surroundings.

But the death of young, vibrant people was unacceptable. Like Andie. She could have divorced Robbie, remarried, had children. Been happy. She'd only been thirty-three when she'd died. Not like Gilbert, who'd lived a full life and died in his sleep at eighty-eight.

God, poor Andie.

She helped one woman decide whether to wear her pink dress or her blue pantsuit, led a wheelchair exercise class and helped calm an Alzheimer's patient who kept trying to leave the facility because he had to pick up his wife at the grocery store. His wife had been dead for seven years.

It was a tough afternoon. Tough but rewarding, and Tess felt better as she pulled into the driveway at home. At least she was doing something constructive.

She checked her machine for messages, anxious for Dan to call and leave a number where he could be reached in Seattle. She didn't know what he could do with the information about Ferrara and Tampa Bay, but then, that wasn't her problem.

He hadn't called, though.

And he didn't call the next day or the next.

It was making her crazy.

She did speak to her mother, however, as she'd done every day. The conversations were strained—at least on Tess's end—because her mother kept talking about Dan Hadley locating Pearl in Seattle and wouldn't that be a relief?

"This Roger Pearl is a terrible person," Carole said. "Did you read the letters? I understand one even gives the details of the murder plot. Oh, I hope Dan finds him soon."

In another conversation Carole had more news.

"Oh, Tess, this is wonderful. You recall I told you about this man here in Aspen named Dennis Wilson?"

"Uh-huh," Tess said. Wilson was the one Robbie had evicted from the caretaker's unit, the one with the pregnant wife. Oh, yes, Tess remembered.

"Well, this Wilson has apparently hired a lawyer. Cody's been on his case, and all I can think is why would Wilson hire a lawyer if he was innocent?"

"That's good news," Tess said, feeling as if she were on autopilot. Wilson, Pearl, Ferrara. They were all merely defense devices. How could her mother be so naive?

"Here," Carole said, "I'll put your father on for a minute. He's dying to talk to you."

Sure he is, Tess thought.

The truth was they still didn't really talk, and when they did, they discussed the mundane. She wanted to scream out her frustration, scream at him to get over the guilt he felt at her taking the gun. She'd done it, and that was that. She wasn't sorry, and it was time he accepted the facts. Instead, they discussed the weather.

The third day since Dan had left came and went, and she found herself beginning to obsess about him calling. She even telephoned Steve Sutton in Aspen, but he didn't have a number for Dan, either.

"Stay in touch this time," she'd said to Hadley, and he'd promised he would. Sure.

She went to work, weeded the garden, had dinner with Paula on the fourth day. But Tess wasn't fit company.

"What's with you, Bergen?" Paula asked.

But all Tess could tell her friend was that she was getting anxious. "Dad's trial is only five months away," she said. "I guess I'm starting to freak out."

She was beginning to think about Dan constantly, wondering if he'd found Pearl, unable to put Dan out of her mind, and resenting his mental presence as much as she'd resented his physical one. He was like a sore tooth she couldn't help probing. She kept hearing his voice, seeing him in the office or in the kitchen, remembering the way his blue shirt matched his eyes, the insolent tone he used with her, the way he moved, lithely and easily. Had he ever known his mother?

He was a ghost in the house, always present but untouchable.

Damn him.

Five days, six. No word, nothing, yet he was there with her every moment. She dreamed of him at night, and in her dreams he asked her where the gun was. He followed her. She kept dreaming of the place she'd hidden it, and Dan was always there, watching.

She heard from several more of Andie's friends. One said Frank had definitely moved from Aspen to L.A. Another was sure he'd gone back to Florida, Miami or maybe Fort Myers. Nothing definitive.

The news from Aspen was good and bad. The defense team's psychiatrist examined Lawrence and determined that he was unable to murder anyone, anytime, under any provocation. Barbara McCleary had a forensic psychologist ready to interview Lawrence for her side. Things moved along slowly, or so it seemed to Tess, but Carole said the case was shaping up quickly, according to Cody.

One night Tess fell asleep early, exhausted. She dreamed of Dan again. They were in the place she'd hidden the gun. It was nighttime, and it was cold. Dan didn't just watch in this dream. He took the gun from her shaking fingers, and he crushed it in his hand until it was only a crumpled piece of metal. Then he put a hand on Tess's arm and pulled her to him. She could feel his hand in her dream, the way she'd felt it that night he'd stopped her from hitting him.

He bent his head and his face came closer and closer, and he touched her lips with his, lightly at first, then harder. He kissed her in the dream, there in the dark cold of the hiding place. And the bizarre thing was, she didn't try to stop him.

She kissed him back.

The following morning she finally had a call from Seattle. But it wasn't Dan. It was her father's sister, Aunt Sis, who lived on Bainbridge Island. She asked Tess about Monterey and what was going on in Aspen. And then she said, "I'd love it if you could get away for a few days and visit me. It's such a beautiful time of year here. Almost no rain. I know it's probably impossible for you right now, but—"

"I'll come."

"What?"

"I said I'll come. I'll call you back with the flight info."

"This is marvelous!"

"I don't know about that," Tess said, "but I'll be there as soon as I can."

FOURTEEN

Barbara McCleary had a headache. She took two aspirin, splashed cold water on her face in the rest room at the courthouse annex and fixed her makeup.

She should have felt great. She'd just finished a four-hour session with the nation's number one forensic psychologist, Dick Lambert, and the news about yesterday's examination of Lawrence Bergen had been good beyond her wildest dreams.

So why were her temples pounding?

She looked at herself in the mirror, ran her fingers through her short-cropped hair and analyzed the situation.

It was Cody Morris who bothered her. Not Cody himself—she actually liked and respected the man—but what he might do to her expert psychologist on the witness stand. She could never, not for an instant, allow herself to underestimate Cody. He hadn't attained his lofty position as the number one criminal defense attorney in America, the Miracle Worker, by getting ambushed in a courtroom.

Cody had Dr. Sandy Martinez to counteract Lambert's testimony. Was there a way she could tear Martinez down? Did he have an Achilles heel, perhaps have testified in too many trials, always for the defense?

No, Barbara thought, Cody wouldn't be that careless. If he'd chosen Martinez, it was because the man was beyond reproach. And did Barbara have the resources to delve into Martinez's past and find a chink in his armor?

She left the rest room, feeling uncharacteristically nervous. She turned her mind to the session she'd just had with Lambert, which put her in a better mood; his report couldn't have been more perfect for her case.

He'd said, "Lawrence Bergen exactly fits the profile of a man who was dealt a lethal blow and would never rest until the score was evened. Bergen's a man who climbed a business and social ladder entirely on his own merits. He came from a middle-class family, none of whom had ever achieved a college education. He's a man who sets goals and knows how to reach them. There is no way Lawrence Bergen would allow the murderer of his child to walk away unpunished."

Lambert had taken off his thick glasses, rubbed his eyes and put them back on. He'd smiled at Barbara. "Oh, Bergen is perfectly capable of planning and executing the murder of Robbie Childress. And he was patient. He knew that eventually he'd run into Childress somewhere, and there was always a crowd around Robbie due to his celebrity status, hence he could count on panic and confusion. Note the convenience of his wife's fear of flying. Bergen drove everywhere, and he could carry the .22 revolver with him at all times without having to worry about airport security. And look how perfectly the wine festival worked for Bergen. He knew Robbie always attended it, and he knew all the vintners wore gloves. He counted on Robbie showing his face, and he counted on the ensuing panic.

"So, my dear district attorney," the forensic psychologist had concluded, "Lawrence Bergen planned and executed the murder down to the last tiny detail. The only thing I question after my session with Bergen is the apparent involvement of his surviving daughter."

"Go on," Barbara had said, frowning.

"He would not have solicited her help."

"So she was there in the tent by accident and took the gun?"

"Most likely. If she was the one who took it, that is."

"I'm positive she was."

"Perhaps," he'd said. "Be that as it may, I'm still quite convinced Tess Bergen was not in on the plan. Not initially."

Barbara sat behind her desk now and contemplated Lambert's conclusions. He was, of course, the expert, but that did not mean he was always correct. The business about Tess Bergen's involvement...well, it didn't matter whether Tess had been involved from the beginning. Barbara's job was to find the gun. Failing that, her job was to show, beyond a reasonable doubt, that Tess had both the opportunity and the motive to have taken and disposed of the murder weapon. Barbara would paint a picture down to the last detail for the jury, amid a zillion objections from the defense, and let the jurors draw their own conclusions. If Tess broke on the stand, all the better. And there were ways of breaking her. If she held up, okay. The twelve men and women would still have to conclude she was an accomplice.

Hell. Everyone knew Bergen did it. Cody could put on that good ol' Wyoming country-boy act all he wanted and charm the jurors till kingdom come, but it wasn't going to get Lawrence Bergen an acquittal.

Barbara stopped at the hairdresser after work for a quick trim. The local women in the beauty salon recognized her immediately and wanted to chat about her future prospects. No one asked direct questions about the case, but everyone wanted to know about book and movie deals.

"You're going to be so famous. Do you think you'll even stay in law?" one woman asked.

It was a good question. Barbara could go on the TV talk-show circuit. Stay in that loop for years on cable TV. Make a fortune. Or she could do consulting work. Or lecture at the nation's top law schools: Harvard, Tulane, Yale, Vanderbilt, NYU. God, it was exciting. She was at the very top of her game.

Her hair trimmed, she drove down Mill Street, stopped at the post office, where again she was the center of attention, then dashed into Clark's Market and picked up two salmon steaks and a medley of fresh vegetables. Then she drove home, changed into jeans and a cropped T-shirt and awaited Eric. It was his wife's volunteer night at the lemonade stand at the music tent, and Barbara would have Eric all to herself till at least ten. She quivered with delight at the thought of the evening.

He arrived on his Harley at six, his long dark-blond hair pulled back in a ponytail, still shower-damp. He took off his small round sunglasses at her door and smiled, and her heart banged against her ribs. "Mm, you look good enough to eat," she breathed.

He glanced past her to where the salmon was prepped and ready to go under the broiler. "Will the food keep?" he asked.

"For a while," she whispered.

They came together as if starved for human contact,

Eric hurriedly tugging her T-shirt over her head, un-snapping her bra, dragging the straps down her arms while his mouth found her small breasts. Her hands, meanwhile, tore at his belt buckle and the metal buttons on his jeans, until she could feel his hardness. She squeezed him and he groaned, and then they fell together, Barbara on top, onto the living-room couch, the front door still wide open.

Barbara liked him to be rough with her, liked the ease with which he lifted her into a straddling position and pressed himself upward until he entered her, her thighs grinding against the sharpness of his hip-bones. His hands were still on her breasts, and she let her head fall back and arched her spine. He squeezed her nipples, and she rose and fell against him, moaning, quicker and quicker, desperate to find that pinnacle, sliding backward, climbing again, further and further each time until she cried out in wonder and surprise, as she always did. Then he, too, was reaching that height, saying, "Don't stop, don't stop. Oh God, Barbara..."

They dressed there in the living room, giggling like two teenagers. Then she turned on the broiler and slid the salmon steaks into the oven.

They pulled the curtains against the strong evening sun and lit candles, sated from their lovemaking but hungry. Barbara felt terribly alive, her headache long gone, her senses acute as they often were after sex. She finished lighting the candles and turned to Eric, who was watching her, and she rubbed her cheek against the blond stubble on his chin. "I want to look like I just made love," she purred.

The meal was good. Between forkfuls of fish and vegetables, Barbara studied her lover, adoring him. She'd never been married. Never found the man whom she felt could satisfy her for a lifetime. She wondered about Eric, though. He was everything she wanted. And she wondered if he appreciated her as much. If only he truly realized the impact this murder trial was going to have on her life.

She put her fork down, folded her arms on the tabletop and cocked her head. "You haven't asked me about the trial lately," she said softly.

Eric was looking at his plate. He shrugged. "What's to ask? The *Daily News* is full of reports."

"So are all the national papers," she said. "But I'm wondering what *you* think."

"What do you mean? What I think doesn't matter."

"Oh, Eric," she said, "I don't mean about the murder or Bergen or anything like that. I mean about my role in it. I'm getting terrific press."

"Mm," he said.

"Come on. I'm a celebrity now. How does that make you feel?"

"How should I feel?"

"Well...excited. Turned on."

"Come on, Barbara."

"I'm serious. You must think about it. A little, anyway."

"I guess."

"Don't be coy. Tell me. I'm a big girl and I can take it. There's something bothering you."

"You'll be pissed off."

"No, I won't." But already she was feeling an itch of irritation.

He hesitated, then finally said, "I think this whole media thing, all the write-ups and stuff, is going to your head."

"Oh," she said.

"I told you you'd be pissed off."

"I'm not. Really."

"Bull."

Barbara waved a dismissive hand. "I realize I'm liking it. I know I'm on a roll. If I'm being an ass, I'm sorry."

He made some sort of throaty sound, unintelligible.

"But it is exciting. Put yourself in my shoes."

He looked up. "I honestly wouldn't want to be in your shoes."

"Why not?"

"It's all at Bergen's expense."

"Eric, he's the one who committed murder. I don't know why everyone in the goddamn world keeps forgetting that little point."

"In my opinion," he said pensively, "Bergen did society a favor."

"Maybe he did. Okay. I'll grant you that, if it makes you so blasted happy. But this is a legal issue. And I guarantee the jury will do its duty."

Eric laughed. "You'll never seat a jury that doesn't sympathize with him. Get real."

"Well, you're dead wrong about that."

"Am I?" he said.

The evening didn't improve. They dropped the subject, but it hung there between them as Barbara cleaned up the kitchen and they switched on the TV. They put their feet up and sat close together, Barbara's head on his shoulder, and they entwined fingers. She tried not to think about what he'd said. Hell, every newspaper, magazine and TV news show said the same thing: how could Aspen's district attorney seat an impartial jury? She would, though.

And then she wondered about Eric and his wife. Did they talk about the trial? Everyone else did, all the time. Did Maggie voice an opinion at breakfast? Barbara could imagine it. "That Barbara McCleary's a real bitch." And what would Eric say? What could he say? "She sure is."

Ah, screw it, Barbara thought, and she turned her face up to Eric's and kissed him on the neck. But when he was gone, his Harley roaring to life in front of her house, Barbara reached for the phone despite the late hour.

She dialed the county manager at home. "Charles," she said, "did I wake you? It's Barbara McCleary." And then she went on to tell him she was going to petition the state attorney general's office for funds to hire a jury consultant. "And I'm not talking about some hack. I want the best. That woman. What's her name? Fran something. And if I can't get the bucks out of the state fund, I want you to petition the county commissioners for it."

"Well…Barbara, I, uh—"

"No waffling, Charles. You get it out of the emergency fund or wherever you damn well please."

"You don't have to take that tone, Barbara."

"I'm sorry. It's been a long day."

"I'm sure."

"But you'll get it for me."

"Surely the state can—"

"I know, I know," she cut in. "But I want to call this woman first thing tomorrow and I don't want to promise something I can't deliver."

"How much will a…jury consultant, this Fran person, cost?"

"I have no idea, Charles," Barbara snapped. "Just back me up. And if I need it, get me the money. That's all," she said, and hung up.

Barbara kept an eye on "The Judge's Advocate" while she sat on hold, waiting for the court clerk to schedule a motion hearing. Today Gail and Craig were discussing how the Bergen family relationships were affected by the case.

"You know, Gail," Craig said, "when a family

member is accused of a crime, it has repercussions on the entire family unit. Anger, guilt, helplessness, depression, the whole gamut of emotions is felt. Can you imagine what the Bergens must be going through?"

That's what you get for committing murder, Barbara thought. You pay the consequences.

"Well, I'm sure it's a terrible thing, but the guilty party should consider that before committing the crime," Gail was quick to say.

"But, Gail, what if the accused is not guilty?"

"They're all guilty," Barbara said to the TV screen.

"And what if Tess Bergen was in on the murder plot and spirited the gun away to help her father?" Gail said.

"That's an unfounded rumor, Gail. I'm surprised you give it any credence at all."

"It's sure to come out in the trial, Craig. Barbara McCleary will put Tess Bergen on the stand and grill her."

I sure as hell will, Barbara thought, smirking.

"That poor girl. What a terrible dilemma for her," Craig said. "But shouldn't families stick together no matter what? Isn't that the ground zero of human relationships?"

"One could make the argument that family members who break the law should be considered the same as anyone else."

"Oh, come on, Gail. Be realistic. Family members don't rat on one another. Period."

"That doesn't make it right," Gail retorted.

"Sure, it's right. It's the first rule of human behavior. It was probably the first rule of survival for the cavemen. Protect your own family."

Baloney, Barbara thought, and then the court clerk came on the line and she turned off the TV.

* * *

Dan had located Pearl in Seattle on the first day. It had been a cinch. He'd driven his rental car out to the huge Boeing plant complex on I-5 and asked at the main gate. The guard had told him Roger Pearl was there at work, but Dan wasn't on the visitors' list. Dan had fussed a little, then driven away, grinning.

That afternoon he'd made calls to every Pearl in the book, asking for Roger who worked at Boeing, and bingo, on the third call an older woman had said her son Roger wouldn't be home till after five. Dan wrote down the address from the telephone book. He had Pearl.

His next step had taken a little more planning and stealth. Dan had located a co-worker of Pearl's by calling Pearl at work—when Dan knew Pearl was out to lunch—and asking the co-worker, a woman, to give Pearl a message. Then Dan had asked her, "Oh, and who am I speaking to? I like to keep records."

He found the co-worker that evening in the phone book—she lived in nearby Bellevue. Dan tailed her the next evening. She was obviously single and had a favorite hangout with her girlfriends, a nice upscale bar.

He'd struck up a conversation with her at the bar, saying he was visiting town, maybe going to move to the area. He knew a couple of people, one being a worker at Boeing.

"I work at Boeing," she'd said.

"Really?"

And so it had gone. He'd learned what he needed to know about Pearl as the evening wore on and the woman had downed her fair share of gin and tonics. And Dan had tucked the information away in his brain—couldn't take notes right there. His major coup was the information that Roger had a friend in

Salt Lake City, a man who used to work in his department at Boeing. His name was Teddy Delaney.

"Teddy," Roger's co-worker had said, and she'd snickered, shaking her head.

"What?" Dan had pried.

"Oh, well, let's just say Roger and Teddy are really good friends."

"Oh," Dan had said meaningfully.

It was just this morning, a Saturday, that he'd received a fax report from his hacker friend down in San Francisco. He was pleased.

He lay on his bed in the hotel room, pillows propped under his head, feet crossed on the paisley bedspread, and leafed through the report on Mr. Pearl.

Dan's friend had accessed Pearl's entire credit history, including all purchases—hotels, airlines, restaurants, gas stations, clothing, sporting-event tickets, grocery stores, superstores, medical clinics. The hacker had even downloaded info on Pearl's exact purchases at several one-stop superstores: fax paper, rubber bands, shampoo, plant food, kitty litter, a greeting card, a paperback novel—and women's underwear.

Pearl lived with his widowed mother on Mercer Street above Lake Union. Busy area. Lots of traffic and a shabby house. Two-story clapboard probably built in the late forties. Dan had checked it out.

Okay. The guy was a saint, taking care of an aging, arthritic mother. Fine. But Dan would bet his last dime that the woman's underwear was not for Mom.

Dan flipped through the pages of credit card history, studying the purchases, getting a feel for Pearl's life-style, the man's tastes and habits, collating this new information with what he'd learned last night.

Pearl was a homosexual. It was no secret from his

co-workers. He worked in the aerospace industry, which was huge in Seattle. Worked as an electronics engineer. Pearl made a good living and had a decent pension plan. He'd been with the aerospace industry for twenty-five years and never been laid off. A feat unto itself.

He liked books. Thrillers. Clancy, Harris, Sanford, Le Carré, Grisham. Which told Dan that Pearl was up on his courtroom-police procedurals. And Dan had to ask himself if Pearl hadn't gotten a few ideas from the books.

Okay. But Pearl had Teddy Delaney in Salt Lake City—a short day's drive from Aspen—and he'd been visiting his friend the week that Childress had bitten the dust. It was all there in front of Dan. The purchase of an airline ticket to Salt Lake City, the restaurants they'd eaten in, the lack of hotel reservations or related bills. Obviously Pearl had stayed at his friend's.

There was no record of Pearl flying into Aspen, so he had to have driven.

But there was a problem. There was no rental-car history. In order for Pearl to appear—*appear* was the key word—to have driven to Aspen and done Childress, it had to be shown that he had access to a car. He could have used Teddy Delaney's car, though. Hell, yes. Guess Dan would have to talk to Teddy.

To add to the appearance of guilt, the fact remained that Pearl had written those letters. Sick stuff. Maybe after a stint on the witness stand with Cody grilling him, Pearl would think twice about writing another letter to anyone. Even a postcard.

Dan stood and stretched, then turned on the evening sports news. The Seahawks were playing at home tonight at the Kingdome. Preseason against the San Diego Chargers.

Maybe he'd go. Heck, he could walk to the dome on the far side of Pioneer Square. Catch a cab back to the hotel.

He checked his watch. Plenty of time.

And then he looked at the phone. Which he'd looked at a hundred times since he'd arrived in Seattle last Sunday.

Tess. He'd promised he'd stay in touch and let her know what was happening with Pearl. He owed her that. And even though he wasn't going to see Pearl in the flesh until tomorrow, it had still been a week. Tess was going to be angry. At the very least, she was going to be anxious.

He didn't call her, though. He phoned Cody in Aspen, instead, and filled him in on the fax report and the background search he'd done on Pearl.

"He was in Salt Lake City the weekend of the Bon Vin Festival," Dan said.

"Oh, I do like that," Cody remarked.

"Yeah, well," Dan said, "no rental car from the airport there. That isn't to say Pearl couldn't have rented a car, using a credit card to guarantee payment, and then have paid it off in cash so there's no record."

Cody was silent for a moment, obviously mulling that over. "Why hide a rental car?"

"Well, maybe he didn't rent one. He could have used his friend's car."

"His friend's car?"

"They're really close friends," Dan said.

They discussed Pearl at some length, Cody reminding Dan to ask the man tomorrow exactly how he felt about Robbie Childress, why he felt that way, gauge his reactions.

"Of course," Dan said. Hell, he knew his job.

"Now, what about Tess," Cody said then. "Any progress?"

"I haven't spoken to her since I left Monterey."

"A whole week?"

"Uh-huh," Dan said, and he blew out a breath. "I told you before, she's shut down as far as I'm concerned."

"Damn, son," Cody said.

"I know, I know."

"Call her. Be nice and concerned and sweet-talk her. You've got to get her trust. Hang up and call her."

"I, ah—"

"Just goddamn do it, son," Cody said, and the line went dead.

Dan did not call Tess. He stared at the phone and just didn't do it. Instead, he took up his sport coat, jammed his keys and wallet and change into the pockets, and headed out into 6th Avenue, needing to walk with his thoughts.

He strode up the Pine Street hill, cut onto 4th and then down Pike to the Pike Place Public Market, which was still full of shoppers.

He'd always liked the market. It was huge and old and ran for three city blocks, rambling all the way down the steep hill to the waterfront. Flower vendors and vegetable markets and fish hawkers who tossed salmon into the air in a game that delighted the crowds of onlookers. Clothing shops and rare bookstores and collectors galleries. Art shops, selling everything from modern oils and glass to cut, quarried stones. Shops with Asian treasures and old sixties-hippie-type paraphernalia. It was a maze of stores, dug into the hill. Dan liked the feeling of being anonymous in this crazy jigsaw puzzle of exotic wares.

Then he was on the waterfront, breathing in the salty air, so fresh after the incense-scented air of the maze. Before him lay Elliott Bay, an appendage of Puget Sound. He strolled along Alaskan Way, listening to the mournful song of foghorns as the ferries crisscrossed the bay. Seattle did not have the cosmopolitan flair of San Francisco, but there was the dark water and the loading docks, the steep hills, excellent restaurants and streets that bustled at night. The place was alive.

He ate fish chowder and prawns at a waterfront restaurant that opened to the bay, and then he meandered along the edge of Pioneer Square until he saw the Kingdome, only two blocks up from the waterfront. He'd passed a thousand pay phones, and each time he remembered Cody telling him—no, ordering him—to call Tess. But then there was a row of guys standing along South King Street scalping their preseason tickets to the game. He picked up a ticket for ten dollars less than its face value.

What the heck, he thought, there were phones in the Kingdome.

The game started off badly for the Seahawks. Two fumbles and fourteen points down by the end of the first quarter. Dan checked his watch. Tess would probably be home. By the end of the first half, it was Seattle three, the Chargers seventeen. He bought a beer and some nachos and stood at the top of a ramp eyeing a bank of phones.

Why hadn't he telephoned?

He knew, though. He knew in his gut that the night she'd taken the swing at him, the night she'd passed out and he'd kissed her, something inside him had shifted. He'd never known anything quite like it and that frightened him. He needed to examine his feelings, but he couldn't. Somewhere in a dark corner of his mind, a small voice whispered from the gloom: watch out, man, this is uncharted territory.

But Cody had ordered him to call. Did it matter if it

was tonight, tomorrow, the next day? It wasn't going to get any easier.

Dan reached into his jacket pocket and took out a quarter. Then he stood there eyeing it like a damn fool. Finally he strode to the phones, slid in the quarter and dialed her number, using his credit card. By now, he mused, she was most likely out with her friend Paula. It was Saturday night, after all. Well, he'd leave a message on her machine. Sure.

"Hello?" Her voice. Live.

"Tess?" A dumb thing to say, he realized, and he fumbled for something else.

"Dammit, I thought you were going to call me, Dan," she replied. "It's been a week. Why didn't you call?"

"Well, I'm calling now."

There was a long pause, and he could picture her standing in her kitchen by the wall phone, elbow on the counter, drumming her fingers. "Is there any news on Roger Pearl?" she finally asked, and her tone was still tight.

"Yes," he said, "I've been making headway."

"Is it good? I mean... Oh, never mind," she said. "Listen, my aunt Sis invited me to Seattle. She lives out on Bainbridge Island. I'm going to take her up on it. I need a change."

"Oh," he said.

"Can you jot down her number and call me there?"

"Uh, sure." Tess. Coming here? "I don't have a pen."

"I'll wait."

"No," he said. "I mean, I'm at the stadium."

"The stadium?"

"Kingdome. Seahawks game."

"Oh. What's the score?"

"Seattle's down by fourteen. I didn't know you were a football fan," he said.

"You don't know the first thing about me," she replied coolly.

But he did. He knew how she tasted, the scent of her, the texture of her lips. "What's your aunt's name?" he asked.

"We call her Sis. She's Cecily Wasson. *W-A-S-S-O-N*. Can you remember that?"

"Of course I can."

"Sorry. I just want to make sure, you know."

"Uh-huh."

"So, you will call?"

"Yes, I'll call."

"And not a week from now, Dan. I want to hear everything, and I've got some news about Frank Ferrara."

"You do?"

"I'll tell you when you call me at my aunt's."

"Tess—"

"No, that way you'll have to get in touch."

"Blackmail."

"Sure. Now, don't forget, Cecily Wasson."

"Uh-huh. Got it."

"Aren't you forgetting something?" she asked next.

"What?"

"Where are you staying, in case I need to get in touch?"

"I'm at the Dominion Hotel on 6th Avenue."

"Okay, well, goodbye then."

"Uh, goodbye," he muttered, and hung up, his palms damp.

He watched the rest of the game, which Seattle ended up winning. It was hard to concentrate on it, though, because he kept thinking about her, trying to analyze why she was coming to Seattle. To visit Cecily Wasson? Or maybe to check up on him. He wouldn't put that past Tess. Or just maybe she wanted to talk. Pour her guts out to him. Right.

He left the Kingdome with the horde and then headed into Pioneer Square, which was pretty quiet this time of night, all but shut down except for a couple of bars and restaurants.

The gun was on his mind. That damn unregistered gun that Lawrence Bergen claimed had been taken from his garage.

There was no doubt Bergen had cooked up the story about the fox and the lost gun. He couldn't recall where he'd bought it—Dan loved that one—but, regardless, the story bothered Dan. The more it sat in his mind, the more he wondered. If Bergen had bought an unregistered gun to kill Childress, then why cook up a cover story to tell Cody Morris? Why tell Cody anything at all?

Dan walked, hands in pockets, collar turned up to ward off the damp night chill coming off the water. The only thing that made any sense was that Bergen had to have been worried someone would turn up a record of the gun purchase. So he'd covered all the bases. Maybe there really was a record of the gun sale somewhere. God help them all if Bob Winthrop got hold of it.

Tess was the key.

Dan climbed the hill on 5th Avenue, making his way back toward his hotel. He had to ask himself why all his thoughts kept circling around that woman. If he wasn't thinking about her straight out, she hovered on the edge of his consciousness. Right there, ready to come to light. Her face, the softness of her hair, the slight tilt of her chin when she was concentrating.

Okay. So she was a nice-looking woman. Pretty. And she was devoted to her family, and that intrigued Dan, who had no family. She was smart, a doctor. And she was quick on her feet. But so were a million others.

He walked and pondered that, and he wondered all the more why he was so goddamned obsessed with her. It was because of the gun, he told himself.

The gun. Right.

FIFTEEN

They met in Barbara's courthouse-annex office, Bob Winthrop, police chief Tim Hendrickson, assistant D.A. Paul Howard and Barbara. They discussed Fran Rosen, the jury consultant Barbara had contacted a few days before, but mostly they discussed the gun.

"Not a sign of it," Hendrickson said, shaking his head. "Almost two months now, and not a sign of it."

Bob Winthrop sat with one fat thigh crossed over the other, casually examining his fingernails. "It's out there," he said, "but it could be so well hidden we'll never find it."

"Goddamn it, Bob!" Barbara said. "I want that gun."

"I was just going to say," he said calmly, "that we have to go to plan B now, trace it from the other end. Where Bergen bought it."

"Which could have been in a dark alley somewhere," the police chief observed.

"Near where Bergen lives, though," Paul Howard put in.

Winthrop shrugged his round shoulders. "I'm striking out on this end here. I need to go to California. I'll start the search in Monterey, and if I don't find anything, I'll widen it."

"Gun stores, sporting-equipment shops?" the police chief asked.

"Yes, and pawn shops. They're always full of guns. Less likely to register them, too."

"Okay," Barbara said. "And, Bob, the taxpayers of Pitkin County better get their money's worth."

"I can't give you a written guarantee," Bob said, unperturbed, "but chances are good I'll get a line on it."

"If I can prove Lawrence Bergen bought an unregistered .22-caliber pistol, I'm home free," Barbara said. "It'd be almost as good as the gun itself."

"And we'll keep looking here, too," Hendrickson said. "We're concentrating on the river right now."

"Okay, boys, keep up the pressure," Barbara said. "No slacking. I want Bergen. And I want his daughter. I want them so bad I can taste it."

"Amen to that," Winthrop said.

Tess arrived at Seatac International Airport in the afternoon. She was tense, wondering what the hell she was doing running away to Seattle in the middle of everything. It was an impulsive thing to do, and she wasn't generally an impulsive person, but the idea of getting away had been too tempting to resist.

And then there was the fact that Dan Hadley was in Seattle. Tess examined her motives and wondered whether she wanted to be near him to keep an eye on him. But that meant she didn't trust him to do a good job, and she knew that wasn't true. He was a dogged pursuer of his prey.

You want to tell Dan your dirty dark secret, her mind whispered to her. She'd come to Seattle ready to tell him, to trust him, to confide in him.

Her heart gave a sick leap at the thought. It was scary to even consider confessing to Dan. How would she start? How would she say it? And what would Dan do?

As she left the plane and moved down the jetway, she was already framing her words. The Dominion Hotel, he'd said.

But when she saw her aunt in the terminal she forgot her doubts and her questions and flew into her arms.

"How are you, honey?" Aunt Sis asked.

"Better now," Tess answered.

"It must be hell," Aunt Sis said.

"It is." Tess put on her sunglasses. People were staring.

"How's Lawrence doing?"

"Okay, better than you'd think."

"And your mother?"

"Okay, not great."

"Poor Carole. Is that all you have?" she asked, indicating Tess' carry-on bag.

"Yes."

"Fine, let's go. I'd like to get the two o'clock ferry."

Aunt Sis was younger than her brother, Lawrence. She was thin and a bit stooped, but had porcelain-smooth skin, lovely features and prematurely gray hair. She was a widow, and her children were grown and gone. She and Tess had always been close.

She drove from the airport into the city center where the ferry terminal was located. Tess just sat, feeling tired and relaxed, relinquishing decisions to Cecily. It was a beautiful, sunny August day, Puget Sound sparkling, the ferries slicing through the water, leaving behind creamy wakes on their routes to the outlying islands. The sea breeze was salty and refreshing, and Seattle throbbed with energy.

On the ferry, they got out of the car and strolled along the upper deck, the wind blowing Tess's hair, her aunt tying on a scarf. Seagulls swooped and flapped above them.

"Damn pests," Sis said. She got a bag of crackers out of her pocket and tossed crumbs in the air. Tourists watched, fascinated, as the gulls caught pieces in midflight.

"It's so beautiful," Tess said, sighing. "I always forget."

"Mm, it is nice." Sis turned and gave Tess an assessing look. "Okay, now I want to hear all about it. Your father hasn't exactly been forthcoming. He just keeps saying he didn't do it when I talk to him."

Tess was grateful that she was looking out over the rail toward the islands. "I'm sick of talking about it or thinking about it," she said.

"You're not getting off the hook so easily, Tess. Spill the beans."

"There's nothing to tell."

Sis laughed. "Come on, this is your old aunt you're talking to. Listen, I've known Lawrence a lot longer than you have, and I'd say he was perfectly capable of plotting and executing a murder. I know how Andie's death affected him. Believe me, I know. And I sympathize, Tess. I'd never blame him."

"Well, then, what's left for me to say?" Tess made her tone light.

"Not much, I guess." Sis paused. "The gun, though, what happened to the gun?"

"Oh, God," Tess said, turning her face into the wind.

"If you took it, like they're all saying, so much the better," Aunt Sis said with feeling. "I hope they never find it."

"Me, too," Tess muttered, the wind tearing the words away.

Sis put Tess in her oldest daughter's room. "It's got a nicer view than the guest room," she said.

The view *was* impressive. The house sat on a rocky promontory, surrounded by Douglas firs, and looked out over the sound.

"It's gorgeous," Tess said, standing at the window.

"That's why we built here," Sis said. "Now, you just take it easy, honey. I'll put dinner on. I want you to relax. You look pale and skinny."

"Compliments will get you nowhere," Tess said.

When her aunt was gone, Tess unpacked her few things, then sat on the edge of the bed and looked at the phone.

He was so close. Just across the bay in Seattle, half an hour by ferry. The Dominion Hotel.

Finally she picked up the receiver and dialed Information, jotting down the number. Then she looked at the phone number scribbled on the pad, tempted, so very tempted. And if she did get hold of him, what would he say? "Well, Tess, since you're here, how about we go out for some seafood? I'll meet you at the ferry terminal. And don't worry, I won't bug you about the gun. You can tell me when you're ready."

Right.

Oh, God, she thought, just pick up the phone, call, tell him and get it over with. *Do it.*

Suddenly Tess remembered the dream—Dan kissing her. It was crazy. The only thing she could come up with was that she desperately needed to trust him, and that was why she'd dreamed he'd kissed her and she'd kissed him back.

Or was that just her logical mind making up an excuse?

She didn't know. She didn't know anything anymore except that the burden of what she'd done with the murder weapon was unbearable.

She picked up the phone and dialed the number, and when the front desk of the hotel answered she asked for his room. Her mouth was dry, her chest tight. The phone rang once, twice, three times. Twice more, and then a recording came on. She could leave a message.

Tess hung up.

She felt frustrated and relieved in equal measure. Frustrated because she'd been all set to tell him, relieved because she had a reprieve. One more day without having to make the fatal confession. It occurred to her that he might call her tonight. She could tell him then. No, not over the phone. It had to be in person, face-to-face. She had to see his expression, judge his reaction.

Where was he? Out looking for Roger Pearl, of course. Working hard to implicate an innocent man.

She finally went out onto the redwood deck of her aunt's house, taking a magazine with her. She sat on a lounge, half in the sun and half in the shade of a huge fir tree, and gazed out over the water.

"You okay out there, Tess?" Her aunt's voice.

"Yes, I'm great, Aunt Sis. Don't worry about me."

"Take a nap, honey."

And Tess did, reading half of an article, then dozing in the sun, sleeping, forgetting about Dan and the gun and the trial, forgetting about it all for a few precious minutes.

Aunt Sis shook her awake for dinner when the shadows had grown long and the water had turned to dark sapphire.

"Oh, wow, I guess I slept," Tess said groggily.

"I should say so," Sis replied proudly.

"I'll be in in a minute," Tess said. And then, as she

rose from the lounge, she suddenly remembered something important about Frank Ferrara. Something she'd had no idea that she knew.

Cody could not have been more surprised when he answered the knock at his door and found Lawrence Bergen standing in the hall. Bergen had not once sought Cody out in all these weeks. Cody believed the man was in a state of complete denial over the murder, over his wife's obvious drug dependency, over his surviving daughter's involvement. For self-protection. Lawrence Bergen, as far as Cody could tell, was living in a world of impossible fantasy.

"I know it's late," Lawrence said, "but I wanted to talk to you in private."

Cody swung the door wide and smiled. "Never too late for me. Come in, come in."

He offered his client a drink, which Lawrence took absently. Then he set it down and began to pace the room, stopping at the window overlooking the Little Nell patio.

"Wouldn't you like to sit awhile?" Cody asked.

But Lawrence didn't sit. Clearly he was too agitated for social niceties.

"Well, then," Cody tried again, "what can I do for you this evening?"

Lawrence turned, and Cody was taken aback; the man's face was ravaged, and for the first time Cody felt that Lawrence was showing him what was in his soul. "I'm going out of my mind," Lawrence said raggedly, "and there's no one I can talk to."

"You can talk to me."

"Yes, I know. Lawyer-client privilege."

"That's right," Cody said.

Lawrence sat down abruptly, as if the strength had

gone out of his legs. "It's Tess," he said. "I can't stand what they're doing to her."

"Who?"

"The press."

"Ah."

"I can't stand it. And she'll have to testify. Barbara McCleary will torture her." He looked at Cody. "Can you...can we somehow get her out of the country? Make sure no one can find her?"

Cody took a chair across from his client and studied him for a time. "It could be done, Lawrence, but I don't think you'd like the results. First, Tess could never come home again. She'd be an exile. And second, she'd never go for it. You know her. She'd never leave you and Carole to go through the trial alone."

"If I ask her. Or you..."

Cody shook his head. "No, no. Your daughter, God bless her, Lawrence, will be there in the courtroom, and you know it."

Lawrence sagged visibly. He put his face in his hands, and his shoulders heaved convulsively.

Cody leaned forward and placed a hand on his back. "Now, now, it's not that bad. We're gonna win this one. Tess will have to testify, but she'll do fine. She'll do just fine."

It took Lawrence a few minutes to regain a semblance of composure, but Cody was used to distraught clients. Heck, that was the only kind of client he had. So he sat there and patted the man's back.

Finally Lawrence looked up. "I'm sorry," he said, his voice still choked.

"It's all right, don't worry about it. You're entitled."

Lawrence looked down and took a deep breath. "There's something else."

"Go on."

"The gun..."

Warning bells sounded in Cody's head. Careful. "The one you bought to protect your cat from a fox?"

"Yes, yes, that one." Lawrence looked up, then closed his eyes. "What if...what if there's a receipt lying around in a store?" He opened his eyes and looked at Cody, fear making him appear much older. "If there is a receipt, and if the D.A. finds it and traces it, then it ties me to a gun. Case solved. No one will believe I bought it to protect my cat. I'm guilty." He paused and licked his lips. "And so is Tess."

"That would constitute a serious drawback to the case," Cody said, nodding.

"Even though it wasn't the same gun—the murder weapon—it makes me look guilty."

"Yes, that's true."

"What do we do, Cody?"

"Well, now, you're gonna have to try real hard to remember where you got that gun." Cody studied his client. Oh, yes, Bergen hadn't forgotten at all. He was desperately afraid to tell, though.

Cody smiled reassuringly. "And when you do remember, tell Dan Hadley. Not me, you understand? You tell Dan. He's the one who needs to know."

"Dan Hadley."

"That's the man."

"But... You're sure, Cody?"

"Listen, Lawrence," Cody said gently, leaning forward, "you can trust Dan with your life." He paused dramatically. "And with your daughter's life."

"I'll...I'll think about it." Then Lawrence's face screwed up, as if he were going to break down again, but he got himself in control with apparent great effort. "And Tess, you'll try to protect her?"

"As much as I can."

"Thank you," Lawrence whispered.

* * *

Cody stayed up past his usual bedtime to watch the late-night repeat of "The Judge's Advocate." The topic was interesting and pertinent: miracle defense teams bought by wealthy defendants. For once, Craig and Gail were in complete agreement.

"We all know the saying that rich men never end up on death row," Craig said. "And as much as I stand behind Lawrence Bergen, I have to admit it bothers me that he's got Cody Morris to defend him."

"I couldn't agree more," Gail said into the camera. "Morris isn't known as the Miracle Worker for nothing. On the plus side, Barbara McCleary is extremely capable."

"She doesn't make a fifth of what Morris does."

"Her salary notwithstanding, Craig, all she had to do is find the gun or at least prove Bergen owned one."

"That could be easier said than done. No one's found the gun. That is, of course, if you believe Lawrence Bergen ever had a gun. Cody Morris will surely point out that an unknown assailant shot Robbie Childress and that he took the gun with him when he ran out of the tent in the crowd."

"I certainly will," Cody said to the screen. And it doesn't take a high-priced attorney to point that out.

"I'm sure Cody will do just that," Gail said. "It's the only other possible scenario, isn't it? But will anyone believe it? No one saw this mystery person."

"Cody Morris can be very persuasive, Gail. He'll set forth a plausible theory. He'll create reasonable doubt in the jurors' minds."

I'll sure as heck try, Cody thought, admiring the way Craig Kramer's mind worked.

"That's what he's paid for," Gail said.

"Sure he is, and you know I stand behind the right of every accused person to a fair trial and the best defense he or she can get. But, I have to admit, if Lawrence Bergen had a rookie public defender just out of law school, I'd be very worried about his receiving decent representation."

"You're right, Craig, and that's the crux of the matter. A defendant who can afford an experienced hotshot has a much better chance of acquittal than a poor defendant."

"Sad but true, Gail. It's certainly not what the men who framed our Constitution had in mind."

Hotshot, Cody thought. I like that. And you're right, you two, a poor man with an iffy case hasn't got a snowball's chance in hell.

SIXTEEN

Roger Pearl knew something was wrong when he arrived home from work and noticed a car parked across the street with a stranger in it, a man, who was staring hard at him.

"Is that you, Roger?" his mother called when he let himself in. "Is that you, dear?"

"Yes, Mother," he said absently, and he pulled aside the blind in the front window. Panic roiled in him. The man was getting out of the car, crossing the street. And Roger knew. He'd been expecting this for months, ever since he'd stupidly written to Bergen and outlined the murder, almost exactly the way it had gone down.

"Stupid, stupid," he moaned. And now they'd traced him.

His mother, he immediately thought. This was going to kill her. She'd find out everything.

Roger Pearl was one of those men who'd discovered his homosexuality at a very young age. He'd come out of the closet to a certain extent but lived in constant fear that his mother, whom he adored, would find out.

His appearance was ordinary, pleasant. He was

five foot eleven, trim, his light brown hair just beginning to thin, and he wore round wire-rimmed glasses. His clothes were ordinary: khaki slacks, short-sleeved Madras shirts in the summer, hand-knit sweaters in winter, with tennis shoes or loafers. He had a friendly smile.

He lived with his mother, who fretted that her son was never going to get married. She wanted grandchildren—although, even she admitted, at her age it was unlikely she'd ever see them.

"You should find a nice young lady and settle down, dear" was her stock phrase.

Well, Roger didn't want to settle down with a nice young lady. He wanted to settle down with Teddy, but he had to wait for his mother to... He hated to think about it, but he had to wait till she was gone. His mother was in her eighties. She wasn't going to live that much longer. And she certainly wasn't going to have grandchildren.

What would kill her outright, though, would be to learn that her one and only son was gay. Roger was really afraid that this cop, or whoever he was, the one walking up the steps right now, had found out and would tell his mother. It would break her heart.

Think, Roger ordered himself. He felt sick, hot sweat oozing from every pore.

The doorbell rang.

"Would you get that, dear?" his mother called. "I'm fixing pork chops. Your favorite."

"I'll get it, Mother," Roger called back. *Think.*

Roger hesitated, then opened the door. The man standing there looked like a cop, all right, or what Roger thought a cop should look like.

He was tallish. Six foot, anyway. And he wore casual street clothes—a pastel golf shirt under a tan summer sport coat and blue jeans—like a vice detective might. He had sandy blond hair and a sort of mean look to him, tough-guy, with sharp, heavy-lidded blue eyes and a thin-lipped, unsmiling mouth. Roger knew two things at once: his visitor was all male and he was in control.

"You Pearl? Roger Pearl?" the man asked, and Roger nodded, swallowing. Why in hell had he written those letters?

"Name's Dan Hadley," the man said. "I'm a private investigator with Lawrence Bergen's defense team. I imagine you know why I'm here." Then he smiled, but it never reached those cool blue eyes. "Can we talk?"

Roger didn't know what to say. He stood staring at the P.I. Just staring, his insides bunched up in knots. Finally he said, "My mother...my mother's very old and I—"

But Mrs. Pearl appeared as if on cue from the kitchen in the rear of the house. "Oh, company. You didn't tell me, dear." She walked in her slow, aged way up to Dan Hadley, wiped her hands on her flowered apron, craned her neck up to him and shook his hand. "Are you staying for dinner, young man?"

Roger spoke up. "No, Mother, he can't. We were, ah, just going to talk. Ah, out in the yard."

"Oh," she said, disappointed, and then she ambled back into the kitchen.

Roger took Hadley outside and out of earshot, and they sat in the small, tidy square of lawn on two plastic chairs. He was aware of the closeness of the neighboring houses, the open windows. The nosy neighbors. He was also aware of something else. He'd seen Dan Hadley before. On TV. Testifying at Robbie Childress's murder trial. And now the man was on Bergen's defense team?

"Like I said—" Hadley began, but Roger cut him off.

"Can you keep it down? Please. The neighbors, you know."

"Sure," Hadley replied, and then he went on, but in a low voice. "As I was saying, I'm sure you know why I'm here." Then he pulled a bundle of letters out of an inside pocket of his sport coat. He held them up. "As you know," he said, "you signed some of these."

Roger stared at the letters. Stupid. Why had he been so stupid?

"Of course, I'll be taking these to a handwriting analyst."

"I wrote them," Roger blurted, and he felt as if his throat were constricted. "Do I need a lawyer? I'm not an idiot. I'm not going to sit here and say anything..."

"I don't know," Hadley said, pinning him with a hard look. "Do you need a lawyer?"

Roger put a hand on the back of his neck. It was wringing wet. "Of course I don't. I just... The letters, you know. I shouldn't have written them."

"Why did you?"

"Childress. He was vile, evil. He said things, made horrible remarks...."

"About gays?"

"Yes, he was vicious. He's the kind of person who makes our lives a misery. The worst kind of bigot. And not only that. Murdering that poor sweet girl, his wife. And getting away with it. You were a part of it, too. I remember you, Mr. Hadley. You helped get that...that...creature an acquittal."

"Yes, I did. But that's not the issue here."

"So I wrote some letters to Bergen. That's not a crime."

"No, it's not," Hadley was saying. "But you did

write down the murder plot, and in pretty good detail."

Roger felt the blood drain from his face.

"You want to discuss that?"

"There's…there's nothing to discuss. It was obvious. Big deal. Everyone in the universe knew Childress liked big crowds. He was a show-off. An egomaniac. Anyone could have figured it out. Bergen figured it out."

"Uh-huh," Hadley said. "But you hated Childress, too. Those letters drip with venom, Roger."

"So? I told you why I hated him. He said those things—called us perverts, wimps." Roger dropped his voice. "We all hated him. And plenty of people hated him for what he did to his wife. I can't have been the only one who wrote to Bergen to sympathize."

"No, you weren't. But you're the only one who wrote down how to murder him."

"I told you already," Roger said in a rush, "any fourth-grader could have figured it out."

Hadley eyed him. "Do you own a gun?"

"What?"

"You heard me."

"No. I mean, yes. I own a shotgun."

"No handguns? Never?"

Roger shook his head vehemently.

"Okay. I'll check on that."

"Go ahead."

"And how about where you were on the Friday Childress was murdered?"

Roger thought fast. "I was fishing," he said.

"Fishing."

"Up in the north Cascades. A place called Mazama."

"Uh-huh. And I suppose you were with someone, someone who could alibi you?"

"I went alone."

"Uh-huh. But you have a fishing license, something to prove where you were?"

"I...uh, yes. Sure. I bought one in, let's see, I think it was a town called Twisp. But I'll be damned if I know exactly where."

"Still have it?"

"What?"

"The license."

"Uh...I don't know."

"I could check with Fish and Wildlife."

"Go ahead." Roger felt his chest tighten. "But I don't know why you're bothering with me. Everyone knows Bergen did it."

"If you say so," Hadley said.

And then Roger's eyes widened. "Oh, shit," he said. "You're...you're thinking about using me as a scapegoat! Like you did with those people at the Childress trial!"

Hadley stood up. "No one said that."

"But that's the plan, isn't it? You want to destroy me. I'll...I'll lose my job. And my mother. Mother will find out about me. It'll kill her! You can't do this to me."

Not a flicker of emotion showed on Hadley's face.

"Please," Roger begged.

"You should have thought about that when you wrote those letters, Pearl."

"Please," Roger whispered.

"I'm sorry, pal," Hadley said, then got up and walked away.

Carole bit her bottom lip and let the forensic psychologist's report drop to her lap.

She couldn't think. She never should have sneaked it from her husband's papers and read it. Now she couldn't think and was feeling the onset of an anxiety attack. A pill. She needed a pill. But hadn't she taken one this morning?

The report was totally damning. Carole couldn't understand why Lawrence and Cody and the entire defense team weren't tearing their hair out after that awful district attorney sent it over this morning. They called it discovery. Each side had to show the other what it had.

But this. This was terrible. It said that her husband fit the profile of a man who'd been wronged and who'd subsequently sought revenge.

It said Lawrence could have committed murder.

If only Tess was here, Carole thought frantically. Tess was a doctor—well, only just—and she'd know better how to decipher all that medical, psychological mumbo jumbo in the report. She'd read it for what it was—trash. Yes, it was lies and trash. But what was the jury going to think?

She telephoned Cody. Hands shaking, she punched in the numbers to the Little Nell Hotel and asked for his room. But he wasn't there.

"Is he in the hotel?" Carole inquired.

"I'll be happy to leave him a message for you, ma'am," the front desk operator said.

But Carole couldn't wait. "This is an emergency. Is Cody Morris in the hotel?"

"Just one moment, please," the operator said, and she was placed on hold, some local radio station blasting in her ear.

The next voice she heard was Cody's. "Thank God," she whispered.

"Carole?"

"Yes, yes, it's me, Cody. Did I...did I get you at dinner? I'm so sorry, but—"

"I was at the bar," he said, "holding court with some of the boys from the fourth estate. Necessary duty. Now, what's the trouble?"

"I...I know I shouldn't have, but I read the report from Barbara McCleary's doctor and, well, Cody, it's horrible. Have you seen it? But of course you have. I'm sorry. It's just that... Oh, God, Cody, how are you going to keep this out of court?"

She heard his gentle, soothing laughter. "I'm not. I'm simply going to counter it with testimony from our own man who'll say it was impossible for Lawrence to have committed the crime."

"But, Cody—"

"Now, now, Carole, this is normal pretrial maneuvering. Barbara was chomping at the bit, I'm sure, for me to read the report and break out in a real sweat. Well, I'm not. I fully expected it."

"And you think you can counter it?"

"Of course I can, dear."

"Oh, Cody, does my husband...does Lawrence stand a chance of being acquitted? Please, I have to know. I can take it. I really can. Oh, Cody—"

"Carole, Carole," he said in a tone that a lover might use, "we'll win this one. You just keep in mind that it isn't only in fairy tales that good wins out over evil."

Carole was silent for a moment, and she wiped at the tears she hadn't known she was shedding. Then she said, "Thank you, Cody, thank you."

When she was off the phone, sitting alone in the bedroom, she looked at the prescription bottle of tranquilizers on the nightstand. She stared at it. And then she reached out, opened it, dropped a single pill in the palm of her hand. Don't, a part of her said. Be strong, if not for yourself, then for Lawrence and Tess. She stared at it a minute longer and then finally dropped it back into the bottle. She got up, shook off her fears and left the room.

But ten minutes later she was back, and this time she took the pill.

Dan didn't recognize Tess at first as he strode into the hotel lobby. He noticed an attractive female sitting there in a Greta Garbo-type outfit—big round sunglasses and a straw hat with a floppy brim—but when she looked at him and reached a hand up to take off the glasses, recognition hit him like a sucker punch.

She stood up as he approached, giving him a tentative smile.

"How long have you been waiting here?" he asked. "If I'd known you were going to be here, I'd—"

"Not long," she said.

Liar. "So you're staying out on Bainbridge Island? With your aunt?"

"That's right. But I wanted to catch you, so I took the ferry in and here I am. Can we talk?" She got up from her seat then and looked around the lobby. "Someplace private?"

"Uh, sure. How about—"

"We could go to your room. I don't want to sit in a bar or anything."

"Well, sure, okay," he said.

They took the elevator, and neither spoke a word. Dan leaned a shoulder against the wall of the elevator and stared at her. She was wearing sensible open-toed walking shoes, oatmeal-colored linen slacks that matched her hat, a teal-colored silk top with short sleeves and a scoop neck. Very feminine. The rich color of the silk made her skin seem incredibly pale and milky, fragile. And he couldn't help noticing that the single, thin gold chain around her neck lay delicately off center in the hollow of her throat. The sight of that had a profound effect on him, and the walls of the elevator seemed to close in. He swallowed.

The ding sounded when they reached his floor and the doors clunked open, cool air rushing in. "After you," he said, standing aside. "It's to the right."

He followed her down the dim hall, aware of the slight sway of her trim hips and the way her dark hair swung against her neck when she pulled off the hat and shook her hair free. She was thin, thinner than he normally liked in a woman, and he remembered her from the Childress trial, when she'd been a few pounds heavier, a little more rounded. The past year had evidently taken its toll.

Dan used his key card to let them in, and although the maid had been there earlier, his boxer shorts were still thrown on the dresser. He strode over, picked them up, grinned lamely at Tess, then tossed them in his suitcase, slamming it shut.

"You want a cold soda?" he asked. "I could get one down the—"

"No. No, thanks." And she went to the window and sat in the upholstered chair, then crossed her legs. He noticed that she carefully avoided glancing at the bed. "I've got that news about Frank Ferrara," she said.

Dan half leaned, half sat against the dresser and folded his arms. "I'm listening."

"I think he's from the Tampa Bay area. A friend of a friend, you know, returned a call I made and told me Frank was a Tampa Bay Buccaneers fan. I figure if he lived on the east coast of Florida, he'd either be a Jacksonville Jaguars or a Miami Dolphins fan."

"You do know your teams," Dan observed.

"Yes, I do," she said. "Anyway, I woke up from a nap at my aunt's, and I suddenly remembered something else. It's really silly, and it may not mean a thing...."

"Let me be the judge of that," he said more harshly than he'd intended. She did that to him, dammit, made him feel ill at ease, and it was his way of keeping her at a safe distance.

Tess looked down at her lap, then back up at him, as if to say she understood why he was always so curt with her. But that couldn't be. He was misreading her. She didn't have any idea what really went on in his head. If she did, she'd take a swing at him again.

"Anyway," she began anew, "when I woke up I remembered something Frank said to me. It was when Andie had first met him in Aspen. You know, Frank kind of floated back and forth between Aspen and L.A., working at seasonal jobs, rubbing shoulders with the beautiful people. I remember Andie telling me she was thinking about dating him. Andie was going to leave Robbie. Oh, I'd heard all this before, but this was the first time Andie had actually thought about someone specific." Tess met Dan's gaze and held it. "I know how you made it look at Robbie's trial. You made it seem as if Andie ran around on Robbie. But she didn't. Until Frank she was faithful. And she was going to get a divorce."

Dan said nothing for a long moment, and then finally he let out a low whistle. "If I told you I was sorry about that stuff at the trial, you wouldn't believe me."

"Try me, Dan," she said.

"Okay. I'm sorry. I knew it wasn't true. I never lied about it, though. The perception that Andie moved in the fast lane just took hold and stuck. I'm not making excuses. And divorce plans notwithstanding, your sister did have an affair with Frank. He testified to it. He also testified that Robbie threatened to kill him. These are the plain facts, Tess. I can't change them, and I'm sorry if it's painful to you. Now Frank's going to end up on the hot seat, too. It's the way it is."

Tess seemed to digest that, and then, apparently, she let it go. "Anyhow," she said, "at lunch that day he made some comment about living in a trailer. Then he said a strange thing. He said it was right down the road from the Ringling Brothers Circus. I remember thinking, how could that be? A circus moves around, and—"

"Sarasota."

"What?"

"John Ringling built a huge estate on the bay in Sarasota. There's a college on the grounds now and a museum. A real hot tourist attraction. And it's just south of Tampa Bay. Sarasota," he said pensively. "Good work, Tess."

"That doesn't mean he's there, Dan."

"No, but it's a starting point. If he has family still there, then maybe he's in touch."

"You'll go to Florida?"

"Uh-huh," Dan said. "But first things first. I need to go to Salt Lake City. Has to do with Roger Pearl. And then there's the gun, Tess."

The word fell between them like a rock hitting the smooth surface of a lake, and a million ripples floated outward, unending.

Tess glanced out the window and then down at her clasped hands. Dan looked at her.

Finally she spoke. But it wasn't about the gun. "Roger Pearl," she said. "Tell me how that went."

"About as expected."

"And? Is he a good suspect?"

"Yes."

"Can you tell me? My father's case hinges on this."

"And on other things, Tess," he said pointedly. But she wasn't buying it. "Okay," he went on, "Pearl's pretty much what I expected. A bright guy, a little eccentric. And he's a homosexual. Also, he lied about where he was the day Robbie was murdered."

"Why would he do that?"

"Because he doesn't want his mother to know he's got a boyfriend in Salt Lake City."

"How did you find that out?"

"I've got my ways. Anyway," Dan said, his eyes on her, "Robbie Childress once made a really nasty statement to the press about gays. He said they were all sicko wimps and ought to get a life. You know how Robbie's mouth was."

"Yes." Tess nodded. "He always had a foot in it."

"Well, the media had a heyday with his statements, and he never did apologize. A lot of people followed the story. Including Roger Pearl."

"Did he admit that?"

Dan grinned. "Oh, yeah. He admitted hating Robbie and writing to your father. He even admitted writing down a murder plot. He claimed any fool could have figured it out."

"Why would he have lied about where he was?"

"I told you. He's got a secret life with his boyfriend in Salt Lake City. Doesn't want his mother to find out."

"Mm. But he must know what you plan to do. You said he was smart."

"Oh, he's definitely wise to it."

"And?"

"And he's upset."

"Is it fair?"

"You've asked me that before."

"Is it?"

"Yes, goddamn it, Tess, it's fair. I didn't make Pearl what he is, and I didn't write those sick letters."

"He's worried about his mother, Dan. Can't you see that?"

"Well, he goddamn wasn't worried about her when he tried to be your father's pen pal. Things happen, Tess. They just happen. Life isn't always fair. Pearl's exactly what Cody Morris is looking for. He'll put him on the stand and show motive and means and opportunity, and he'll bring out the lie about the alibi, and Pearl will get the jury thinking. Reasonable doubt. That's what this is all about."

Tess just stared at him. And finally she drew in a breath and let it slowly out. "I'm tired of arguing with you, Dan," she said. "I'm all worn out."

"Then let's not argue. You want to call a truce?"

"A truce," she whispered.

"Yeah," he said. "Maybe we could try it out for an hour or so and see how it fits. Well?" he asked. "I'm willing. Are you?"

SEVENTEEN

Tess didn't know how to answer Dan's question. So she tried to fill the awkward void with the most inane thing she could come up with. "Beautiful evening, isn't it? It stays light so late here. I—"

"Would you like to have dinner with me?" she heard him ask.

"Dinner," she repeated, as if it were a foreign word.

"You have other plans?"

"No, not really."

"Okay, then." He paused, and he actually smiled. It made him look boyish and very handsome. "It's too nice an evening to waste. And besides," he said, "we've got an hour before the truce is over."

"This is nice of you. I mean, you don't have to drag me around with you. I didn't come here to force you into some social situation," she said.

He looked at her. "Tess, will you just shut up?"

"Fine," she said. "Sure."

"I'm starved," he said, and he reached for her hand, pulled her up and steered her toward the door. "You mind walking? It's a great city to wander around in."

"I like walking." She could barely get the words out, because now his hand was on her elbow, and she couldn't think. She put on her sunglasses, her hat—he didn't move his hand away—and mumbled, "My disguise."

They strolled through the city, still crowded at this hour, full of summer tourists. A newer, rawer city than San Francisco or Chicago or New York, but an exciting, growing metropolis. There was every type of shop imaginable: jewelry, T-shirts, bookstores, microbreweries, coffee bars everywhere. And restaurants, seafood restaurants, with glorious aromas wafting out of them. Lined up on the waterfront, they all sported marine decors: fishnets and ship's lanterns and old wooden life preservers. Quaint, scenic, romantic.

"Do you like seafood?" he asked.

"I love it."

"Good. Which one of these places appeals to you?"

"Oh, gosh, I don't know. Any of them, I guess. You choose."

They walked side by side. He'd dropped his grasp of her arm finally, and she could think again. It amazed her that she was strolling along the Seattle waterfront with Dan Hadley, the man she'd considered her family's worst enemy. The man who'd attacked her dead sister's reputation and gotten her murderer released.

And now, apparently, he was seeking some sort of redemption. Or was he just buttering her up?

She risked a sidelong glance at him, at his profile. A good profile. Strong chin, jutting nose. Blond hair flopping over his forehead. A good-looking man.

So what? she thought. The question was, could she trust him?

She'd come to see him with the clear intent of confessing, but the words stuck in her throat now that she was faced with doing it. Would he keep her secret?

They walked past half a dozen restaurants, then turned and walked back. Dan stopped in front of one that was right next to the aquarium. "What do you say to this one?" he asked.

"Yes, it looks great."

They sat on the deck overlooking the bay. Tess studied the menu as if it contained vital information.

"Have the chowder," Dan suggested. "And the new potatoes. They're a specialty here."

"Okay," she said, glad for his recommendation, because she'd been studying the menu but hadn't really read a word of it.

When the waiter arrived, Dan ordered for them, then he turned to her and asked, "Wine?"

"Oh, just a glass," she said.

"Two glasses of house white," Dan told the waiter, and when the man was gone, he explained to Tess that he limited himself to a single glass. "I was drinking pretty heavily for a while there," he said. "Before Cody called me."

"Do you, uh...do you have a problem with alcohol?"

He shrugged. "Only when my head's not straight. I'm okay now."

"You're very good at what you do," she found herself saying.

"Yeah, that's what you hold against me," he replied dryly.

She looked away, out over the water, not answering. He was right.

"I'm glad you're not quite so mad at me anymore," he said.

"Mm."

"But you still don't trust me a hundred percent."

She looked at him directly for the first time. "It's hard."

"Trusting is hard, sure, I know that. But you've got to go with your instincts, Tess. You're a smart lady. You know in your heart what's going on."

"Do I? I wonder. This whole thing is so awful. I don't think I've been able to see things properly since Andie was killed."

He leaned across the table and touched her hand lightly. "Did I ever tell you I was sorry about your sister? About her death?"

"No."

"I am. I was back then, too. She didn't deserve that." His tone was sober.

"Don't—"

"Okay, forget it. It's over."

"It's never over."

"Listen, Tess, if there's one thing I've learned in my life, it's that you've got to leave things behind. I had to do it, or I wouldn't have made it. So do you."

Their wine arrived, and Tess was grateful to have something to do, to pick up the glass and sip, to set it down and twirl the stem. She finally looked up and asked, "How do you do that, let go of the past, put it away?"

"I don't know. I had to do it. I did it."

"How convenient."

He frowned. "It wasn't convenient. It was necessary. I didn't exactly have a 'Leave It to Beaver' childhood."

"So you told Paula."

"Nice lady, Dr. Paula."

"Yes, she is." Tess couldn't help her curiosity. "So how did you do it? How did you survive?"

"Oh, Christ, what're you—Dr. Freud?"

"Forget I asked. It's none of my business." She took another sip of wine.

"Sorry," he said.

"For what? I'm not doing my residency in psychiatry, you're right."

Their food came, a welcome diversion—steaming, fragrant chowder, warm sourdough bread and tiny new red potatoes.

"This looks wonderful," Tess said.

"It is. I've had it just about every night since I've been here. Either this or the giant prawns they have around here."

They ate without speaking for a time. What was this awful discomfort between them? Tess wondered. She never felt this way with other men. Was it because she still resented him from the Childress trial? Or was it because she didn't know whether she could trust him?

She could do it right now, put her spoon down and lean forward and tell him. She could. But she didn't. Instead, she asked him why he'd quit being a San Francisco policeman.

He narrowed his eyes and looked off into the distance. "Several reasons," he said. "I joined the force, you know, looking for a family. But it wasn't like that. And the money was lousy. But mostly, I guess, it was because they wouldn't let me do what I was good at. All the bureaucratic bullshit drove me nuts. Paperwork, reports, more paperwork. And office politics."

"So you found your niche."

He glanced at her and held her gaze. "Yeah, I'm an investigator. I ferret things out. That's what I do."

"Yes," she said quietly, and went back to her chowder.

He tore off a piece of sourdough bread, buttered it liberally and took a bite. Then he said, "Look, I didn't mean to be rude before, I mean about my past. It's not really very interesting."

"Please, don't talk about it if you don't want to," Tess said.

"I don't," he said.

Then she looked up. "You told Paula."

"What? Oh," he said, "yeah, sure. But not the gory details."

"So tell me."

"Why?"

"I'm curious."

"You want everything? The brand of shaving cream, all that?"

"No. But I would like to hear about how you were orphaned. It's...different."

"Different?"

"I have a family. A close one."

"Yes, you do," he said. Then he shook his head, as if relenting. "Okay," he began, "my parents were killed when I was really young. Car crash. I don't remember them. My grandmother took me in for a year, but then she got sick and moved away. I barely remember her."

"She couldn't keep you?"

"You know, after all these years, I think the reason she left was simply that she couldn't stand me reminding her of her dead daughter."

"No," Tess said, appalled.

"Yeah, I think so. Anyway, then I was in an orphanage for a while. Then foster homes. Lots of them. I was too old by then. No one wanted to adopt me, so I went from one foster home to another. Until I finished high school and got a scholarship for San Francisco State." He shrugged.

She ducked her head, afraid to say a word. Her childhood—birthday and slumber parties and riding lessons and ballet and trips to New York to see the Thanksgiving Day parade...

"You think it made me some kind of weirdo," he said.

"No, not at all. You seem...perfectly normal. I mean—"

He laughed.

"I'm sorry, I didn't mean it as an insult. You've done very well."

"I've survived."

They ate the rest of the meal, and Tess still kept wondering how he'd done it. How had he come through that kind of aloneness? He spoke about his past matter-of-factly, but she saw something in him now, something she'd never noticed before. A weariness, as if he was waiting for something good to happen, waiting a lifetime, and it still hadn't come. She wondered if he'd given up or if he held on to a shred of hope.

And it surprised Tess that she felt a stab of sadness that Dan might have given up hoping. And what *had* he been hoping for all this time?

But he was saying something, and she had to let go of her thoughts and answer him. "Your father... You know, I really like him. He's a nice man," Dan said.

"Yes, he is." How could he be a murderer? would be Dan's next question.

"I saw him every day at Robbie's trial. He never lost his dignity. It must have been hell."

"It was."

"I saw you, too. Every day."

"Oh." She looked up. "Do you think... Oh, God, do you really think Cody can get him off?"

"If anyone can, Cody can. But a jury trial is always a crapshoot. Any lawyer will tell you that."

"But he has a chance?"

Dan shrugged. "He'd have a better chance if I knew where the gun was."

She drew back as if he'd hit her, but he didn't pursue it. He just let his statement hang there between them like a body swinging from a noose.

Tess thought again: I could tell him now. Right this moment. Just blurt it out.

Instead, she changed the subject. Coward, she thought.

After dinner he walked her to the ferry terminal. The light was dusky now, the sun setting behind the horizon in bands of coral and pink and purple. The next ferry wasn't scheduled for twenty minutes.

"You can leave me here, really," Tess said. "You don't have to wait."

"I'll wait."

"Dan, really."

"Hey, I have nothing better to do."

She tried to lighten the tension between them. "That's not much of a compliment."

"Sorry." He looked at her, the shadows stark on his nose and eyes and jaw. "I guess I didn't have a mother to tell me how to treat a lady."

She searched his face. "You've never been married?"

"No."

"Why not?"

"No one ever suited me."

People were boarding the ferry now. Cars were lined up to drive into its huge maw.

"Why don't I get on?" Tess asked. "Then you can go."

Dan did a strange thing then. He took her by the shoulders, gently, and turned her to face him. "You've got to tell me," he said. "Tess, it's time to come clean." And he held her, stared into her eyes and wouldn't let her go.

She felt herself flush, then grow cold. Gooseflesh rose on her skin. She opened her mouth to say something, but nothing came out. She was strangled with fear. *Tell him*, a voice inside shrilled. *No*, rasped another.

"Tess," he urged.

"No," she finally whispered, breaking the spell, tearing herself from his grasp. She was trembling.

"Tess," he said again. "I won't hurt you. I'd never betray you."

She shook her head, denying his words, denying her culpability, denying what she knew she had to do.

"God, Tess," he said, almost a groan.

Then she turned away from him and ran onto the ferry, found a seat in a dark corner and sat there, hugging herself.

She watched the lights of Seattle diminish, and she gradually grew calm. She'd made a fool of herself again, she realized. She was always doing that with him. She got up and walked out onto the deck, the salt breeze ruffling her hair, cooling her skin. She closed her eyes and let it wash over her.

She pictured Dan's face, felt where he'd held her, and she shuddered. He looked so different to her now than he had at Robbie's trial last year. Now that she knew him.

I won't hurt you, he'd said, and his voice had been low and intense and intimate. She believed him. He wouldn't hurt her—if he could help it. He wanted to save her father from prison, and he needed her secret to do it. What was wrong with her?

Aunt Sis was waiting up in her bathrobe. "You found him, I guess," she said.

"Yes," Tess replied.

"And?"

"We had dinner."

"Aha."

"What's that supposed to mean?"

"What does he look like? How old is he? Come on, Tess. Why would you go out to dinner with the investigator for your father's defense team?"

"He was hungry."

Her aunt put her hands on her hips and shook her head.

"Good night, Aunt Sis," Tess said.

A sigh. "Good night, Tess."

She lay in bed, the window open to the fresh air, listening to the murmur and swish of the tide against the rocky coast. Her stomach quivered with her memories: Dan's hand on her arm, at the small of her back, on her shoulders. His blue eyes on her, his mouth hard when he asked her about the gun. Scary and exciting. Unbearable tension between them that meant something, something she didn't want to think about.

Tess woke up in the morning, the decision made. She would call Dan and tell him; she was through playing games.

She got a mug of coffee and took the cordless phone out onto the deck for privacy. She dialed his hotel and asked for his room. She was already awash in relief.

"Mr. Hadley just checked out, ma'am," the desk clerk said.

"He did?" Tess said stupidly. "Do you know where he went?"

"I don't know, ma'am."

"Thank you," Tess said dully, and she hung up.

EIGHTEEN

Maggie Pedersen was having a lousy morning. She marched into Aspen's only affordable grocery store, tugged on a shopping cart to free it from a row, pinched her fingers and swore out loud.

Damn that son of hers. Well, he was Eric's, too, but Eric was so busy at work he was never around for the bad news. Typical male, Maggie mused.

She headed up the produce aisle, nodded to the produce stocker—everyone in Aspen knew everyone—and thought about how pissed off she was at her son, Luke.

He'd put another dent in their car, and she was going to have to tell Eric. Well, what did you expect from a sixteen-year-old kid who'd just gotten his license?

She ran into several people she knew in the cookie aisle and then turned up the next one. Then she saw Holly Swenson. Oh, no. She and Holly had worked together eons ago at the ski company and had had a falling-out. Maggie still didn't like the woman. She plastered a smile on her face as they passed.

Holly paused. "Oh, Maggie," she said, "I want to

tell you how awfully sorry I am about the divorce. I just couldn't believe it when I heard."

"The divorce?" Maggie cocked her head.

"Well, yes, you and Eric. I mean, everyone's talking about it. And that horrible woman. God, I'd murder her if I were you."

"Woman?"

"Barbara McCleary. You know."

"The D.A.?"

Holly drew back, puzzled. "Of course. How could Eric see anything in her? She's such a climber. And that butch hair of hers. Jesus."

Holly went on and on, but it was as if Maggie had been poleaxed and the world had narrowed down to a small, dark hole from which not even light could escape. Eric? Barbara McCleary? Eric, having an affair? It wasn't possible. This was all wrong.

She must have mumbled something to Holly, voiced aloud her disbelief and confusion, because she heard Holly's voice as if at a great distance, saying, "I'm so sorry. I thought you knew. Everyone knows and I swear I thought..."

But Maggie had moved down the aisle, slowly, one step at a time, like an automaton. By the next aisle her mind was beginning to awaken. The times she'd called the house at night when she was in New England visiting her father and there'd been no answer. The nights—so many of them—that Eric had worked late or taken an evening ride on his Harley. Always showering first. She'd wondered about that.

The next aisle. How long had it been since he'd turned to her in bed and given the usual signals with his hands that he wanted to make love? And last week, when she'd had lunch with her two best friends in town... She'd come home with the distinct feeling something had not been quite right.

Could Eric be having an affair?

By the time Maggie got through the checkout stand—God only knew what she'd put in her cart—she felt sick to her stomach, her head light, her thoughts dashing around her brain. She drove home in a fog, not even remembering the trip. It was as if one minute she was in the grocery-store parking lot downtown and the next she was sitting in her driveway at the top of Mountain Valley, the dog jumping up on the car door.

Was it true?

Still in a fog, scared and confused, Maggie called her best friend. She was torn apart inside, humiliated beyond words, but she had to know.

Oh God, oh God, oh God, she kept thinking as Bonnie's phone rang. What was she going to say? How was she going to ask? Did Bonnie even know what the truth was?

Maggie never remembered what she said to her friend that morning, how she ever led into the conversation. She did, however, remember Bonnie's hesitation and then her exact words. Maggie would never forget them.

"I wanted to tell you," Bonnie said in a pained voice. "Oh, Maggie honey, I wanted to tell you a thousand times. I just couldn't."

"So it's true," Maggie whispered, devastated.

"I think so."

"Barbara McCleary."

"That's the rumor."

"And everyone knows."

There was silence.

Maggie choked back tears. "Well, I guess that answers that."

"Oh, Maggie, is there anything I can do?"

Maggie gave a strained laugh.

"What are you going to do?"

"I don't know, Bonnie. I honest to God don't have a clue. Kill myself. Kill him."

"Don't talk like that."

"I'm joking. If I kill anyone, it'll be Barbara McCleary."

Maggie sat on the deck of her house, which overlooked the Upper Roaring Fork Valley. She sat, the groceries not put away, the bed not made, phone calls unanswered, and stared out across the valley for hours.

She was in pain, worse pain than when her mother had died prematurely ten years ago. She had never known anything could hurt so damn much.

The hurt stayed. But finally the fog began to clear and she could think again. With her thoughts came anger and then rage. How could he have done this to her?

And then she knew what she had to do.

Eric was in Grand Junction at a seminar. But McCleary was here. No doubt flashing that toothy smile of hers for more cameras. Well, Maggie thought, the bitch might win the Bergen case, but she sure as hell wasn't going to win Eric.

Maggie got up, her face sunburned, walked inside and opened the phone book. There she was, McCleary, B., listed right there. And her street address. Woody Creek.

Maggie closed the phone book and felt the rage rise in her again. She looked at the wall clock. McCleary would probably be home in a few hours. And Maggie would be waiting.

Dan arrived in Salt Lake City in the afternoon. It was breathtakingly hot, and dry as dust in the Mormon city. He rented a car, checked the air-conditioning to make sure it worked, and got a good map of the area.

He ate lunch in a coffee shop, spreading the map out on the table, and located Teddy Delaney's address behind the Mormon Tabernacle near the downtown area.

As he drove to the place, he thought again about Tess's concern over implicating Roger Pearl and his friend Teddy. They were both, after all, innocent of any wrongdoing. But those letters, though. They were scary. There was something, some kind of resentment, buried deep inside Mr. Pearl to make him write stuff like that. And once Roger Pearl had set pen to paper to write those letters, he'd involved himself, like it or not.

Dan found Teddy's house, a nice, tree-shaded place, a duplex it looked like, on a steep hill. You could see the tabernacle from his front walk. He knocked, hoping the man was home so he could get this over with. God, was it hot.

Yes, someone was home—he heard footsteps, the doorknob turning.

"Theodore Delaney?" he asked in his best official voice, flipping his wallet to his P.I. license, closing it just as quickly.

"Yes?"

The man was older than Dan had imagined, around sixty, tall and thin, with a long face that drooped and a gentle manner.

"My name is Dan Hadley, Mr. Delaney. I'm a government investigator doing a security clearance check on Mr. Roger Pearl."

"Roger?" he said. "Why?"

"Boeing requires routine updates on employees' security clearances."

"Oh." He hesitated. "Do you want to come in?"

"Well, sir, I wouldn't mind. It's hot out."

His house was cluttered and a little fussy. Dan tried to picture Pearl with this man, and he wondered what their relationship was, what they saw in each other.

"This won't take long, Mr. Delaney. It's just that Roger is going to be involved in a top-secret government program, so we have to talk to friends and neighbors and so on."

"Okay, well, I don't know how I can help you, but ask away."

Dan posed a few questions about Pearl, inane stuff, things he already knew. Then he got down to brass tacks.

"I understand Roger was here in June," Dan said nonchalantly.

"Yes, for a long weekend."

"Does he visit Salt Lake City often?"

"Not as often as he'd like. There's his mother, you know. He has to get someone to watch her."

Dan nodded soberly. "And what did he do here? Did he rent a car, for instance? Did he go sightseeing?"

"Well, he did go to Canyonlands for a quick overnight trip. I wanted to go, but I'd started a new job and couldn't. I think it was a Friday, and I asked him to wait for the weekend, but he had to get back to Seattle because of his mother."

"That would have been Friday and Saturday the twentieth and twenty-first of June?" Dan asked carefully.

The man thought. "That was the weekend, but he got here Thursday night and went to Canyonlands real early Friday morning. He was back by Saturday."

"And did he go in a rental car?"

"Oh, no," Teddy said. "He used mine."

Well, well, Dan thought. How very convenient, and how perfect for Cody. Pearl had lied about where he was—fishing in the Cascades—when he was on the road in Teddy's car at precisely the right time to have reached Aspen to shoot Robbie Childress. This was too good to be true.

No wonder Pearl had lied. He wasn't dumb, and he knew how his trip to Canyonlands that weekend would look. Cody would be in seventh heaven over this.

Dan smiled at Teddy. "Oh, by the way," he said, "do you own a gun?"

Delaney looked a bit taken aback.

Careful, Dan thought. "I have to ask these questions, you understand."

Of course Teddy Delaney didn't. But he told Dan that when he'd first moved to Salt Lake City, Roger had insisted he buy a gun and keep it at the house. "For security," Delaney said. "There is crime here."

"So did you buy a gun?" Dan asked.

"Oh, goodness no. They scare me to death," Teddy replied, but Dan knew that Cody could still get Pearl to admit on the witness stand that he'd asked his friend to purchase a gun. It wasn't going to look good for Pearl.

He asked a few more questions of Teddy Delaney, even though he already had what he wanted, then thanked the man and left.

He stayed at a chain motel near the Salt Lake City airport that night, writing up his notes. He also called Cody.

"Goddamn, son, that's good stuff!" Cody said, chuckling.

"I'm flying back to San Francisco tomorrow morning. Probably have to go to Florida soon to check on Ferrara. But before I do, I'd like to talk to Lawrence again, see if he recalls anything about where he might have purchased the—" Dan hesitated "—item."

"Tell you what," Cody said. "I'll phone Lawrence and let him know you'll be back in the Bay Area tomorrow, make sure he has your home number. Maybe a little gentle pressure wouldn't hurt. At any rate, I'll try to get Lawrence to contact you. I think it's time."

"It's past the time Bergen should have come forward with this stuff. Hell," Dan said, "the whole damn family could use a lesson in trust."

"Amen to that," Cody said.

Dan hung up, yawned and stretched, then considered calling Tess at her aunt's. He decided against it. What could he say? What could *she* say? It was all pretty useless and uncomfortable, and a pain in the ass. And he'd thought for a minute there, at dinner last night, that they'd been getting along. Wrong again, Hadley.

He turned the TV set on to the late-night replay of "The Judge's Advocate." The topic under discussion was the media and pretrial publicity.

"There are countries where this kind of media frenzy over a high-profile trial is not allowed. England, Canada. You know, Craig, the civilized nations of the earth."

"We've always had a very open society, Gail. The First Amendment. Americans are proud of their rights to free speech and press."

"Yes, I know, but don't you think the media has gone overboard in recent years? The coverage really makes it hard to seat a jury. People know all the details of the case before it even goes to trial. It's patently unfair."

Damn right, Dan thought. It's a disgrace. Look

what the media did to Andie Bergen, even after she was dead. And I helped them do it. Deliberately.

"I have a feeling that the media is sometimes as disgusted with itself as we are disgusted with it," Craig was saying.

"Except for certain unscrupulous individuals, some of whom we could name. And, of course, there's the almighty dollar. Publishers want to sell books and papers. Producers want their shows watched. Network CEOs vie for the largest audiences. Money, Craig."

"It all comes down to that, doesn't it, Gail?" He looked straight at the camera. "Is there someone out there who still has morals? Gosh, I hope so."

"Yeah," Dan said quietly. "I'm trying. I'm trying to right one goddamn big wrong."

Then he went back to work. He picked up the phone and called Sarasota, Florida, information. There were six Ferraras listed in the city, and he wrote down their names and addresses in his notebook. He'd checked each one out; he was sure one or more of them was related to Fugitive Frank and could give him a lead on the guy.

Dan lay in bed, listening to the hum of the air conditioner in the window, the drone of the TV and the muted roar of airplanes taking off and landing. As he lay there in another strange bed in a strange city, he once again thought about Tess. He had really believed they were getting along. She'd actually smiled a few times, and she looked so good when she smiled. Pretty. He couldn't get out of his head the image of that gold chain lying on her collarbone, in that delicate hollow. He'd wanted to put his lips to that hollow, to trace the contours of her neck. But she'd run from him. It hurt, dammit. Why didn't she trust him? She had to tell somebody. She had to tell him.

Dan flew to San Francisco the next morning. He grimaced at the pile of mail that had accumulated and checked his messages—nothing that couldn't wait. As if on cue, Cleo showed up at the window that led to the fire escape, meowing to get in. How did she always know when he was home? He raised the window and she hopped in, and Dan noticed suddenly that she was fat as a pig. He felt her belly and groaned. Pregnant. Cleo was pregnant. Bad kitty.

He took care of his bills, jotted down a few ideas for Cody, and thought obsessively about Tess. He saw her in his hotel room in Seattle, trying so hard not to look at the bed. He saw her at dinner, talking earnestly, listening to him, listening to the story of his childhood. Dan had told very few people about his past, and he wondered why he'd told Tess. She hadn't grown distant or expressed pity—those were the most common reactions to his past. Thank God she hadn't. Pity was the worst.

He remembered how Tess had looked at the ferry terminal—torn, tortured, trembling under his hands. Had he frightened her?

Damn, if only she'd confide in him. He'd keep her secret if she told him, keep it till the day he died. He'd protect her.

Guilt. Sure, it was guilt over what he'd done to get Robbie Childress off. He owed the Bergens that much.

After a lunch that consisted of stale crackers and a can of tuna he found in a cupboard, Dan realized he had one more chore before he left for Florida. Once he'd made up his mind he picked up the phone and punched in her number before he had second thoughts.

"Susan McPherson," she answered.

"Hey, it's me," he said.

"Well, what do you know."

"Got some time after work?"

"Today?"

"Today," he said. "I'm going to hit the road again here."

"Busy boy."

"Yeah. Susan, today, okay? I'll pick you up at your office."

"My goodness, curb service."

"Just give me a time."

"Five-thirty."

"I'll be there."

"You know what, Dan? You're an ass."

"Yeah, I know," he said, and he hung up. Done.

Susan wore a gray pin-striped suit that day. Her auburn hair was pulled back into a French twist, and her calves were curved and muscular and lovely. She gave Dan a peck on the cheek. "Where to?" she asked.

"Can we just walk?"

"Sure, not too far, though. I'm wearing heels."

He'd been rehearsing what he had to tell her all afternoon.

"Uh, Susan, you know, I've been thinking about us, our relationship?"

"Is that what it is, a relationship?" she asked.

He looked down at her as they walked. "Uh, sure. It is. It was. Susan…"

"Oh, for God's sake, Dan, are you trying to break up with me?" she asked with exasperation.

"Well, yes, I guess so."

She stopped in the middle of the sidewalk and faced him, hitching up the shoulder strap of her bag. "Dan, I hate to break it to you, but it's been over between us for a long time."

Unexpected relief swept him. "I guess you're right, Susan." Then he added, "I'm sorry."

"Sorry for what? Don't be silly. We had a nice thing, and now it's over. If you think you're leaving me broken-hearted…"

"No, I didn't mean that. I still think you're a great lady."

She studied him for a moment. "So, Dan, who is she?"

"Huh?"

"It's so obvious it's laughable. Who is she?"

"What in hell are you talking about?"

"You're in love, Dan."

"Bullshit."

"Go on, deny it. You've met someone."

"I don't know what you're talking about."

But Susan only laughed, a tinkling, silvery sound.

They parted at the corner of Broadway and Pacific, and Susan kissed him once on the lips.

"Goodbye, Dan," she said. "Good luck with the new lady."

And Dan walked all the way back to his apartment, stymied, wondering what in hell Susan had seen in him, or thought she'd seen, to ask him such a dumb question.

In love. Sure. As if it showed, like sunburn or a bruise or something. Women.

There was a message on his machine from Lawrence Bergen: "Please call me. Cody gave me your number. I'll be in the condo most of the evening."

Interesting. Maybe the pressure Cody had applied had worked. Or maybe Bergen knew all along where he'd bought the gun and had been afraid to tell him. Dan opted for the latter.

He looked up the Bergens' number in his notebook and dialed it.

Carole answered. "Lawrence? Oh yes, Dan, he's right here."

There was a short wait, then Lawrence came on. "I wanted to take it in the bedroom extension," he explained. "Carole doesn't need to... Well, you know. She gets upset."

"I understand."

"I remembered something about the gun," Lawrence said.

"Uh-huh." Dan waited patiently.

"Where I bought it." Lawrence paused. "I would have told Cody, but he said he'd prefer I talk to you. I realize he doesn't want to know everything. I...I know how it looks. I mean, it's such a stupid thing, a gun I bought to shoot a fox, and then I didn't have the nerve to anyway, and then it was missing. I know how it looks."

"Look, Lawrence, don't worry about that, just tell me what you remembered."

"It was a pawnshop in Salinas. I was just walking by one day, and out of my mind about Andie. I wasn't thinking. I bought it, and then I never used it."

"The name of the pawnshop?"

"Nate's Pawn, or something like that."

Dan jotted it down. "Okay, thanks, Lawrence."

"What will you do now?"

"I'm not sure."

"Oh, I almost forgot. Cody said to tell you Bob Winthrop left for California recently."

"Is that right?"

"Does that mean he's looking for the same thing you are?" Lawrence asked cautiously.

"Probably."

"I see." There was a note of defeat in his tone.

"Does anyone else know about this?" Dan asked.

"I told Tess. I just called her."

"Tess?"

"I thought... Maybe I shouldn't have," Lawrence said.

"She's in Seattle. She can't do anything about it anyway."

"No, Dan, she's back in Monterey. I just spoke to her."

"Shit."

"You don't think...?"

"No, of course not. Don't worry about it. I'll call Tess right now."

"Thank you, Dan. Don't let her do anything... hasty."

"I'll take care of it."

"Keep in touch."

"Sure, no problem."

He hung up and dialed the Bergens' Monterey house instantly. It rang once, twice, three times. It rang and rang, and then the machine picked up. He left a message for Tess to call him immediately.

Where was she? He paced his living-room floor, then went to his window to stare out at the view. He didn't see the Golden Gate Bridge, though, or Alcatraz in the middle of the bay. Where in hell was she?

At work, probably, at that nursing home. Sure. Or out with her friend Paula. Why not? Or maybe she had a date this evening, or went to a movie. She could be anywhere.

He paced some more, tempted to phone her again, but he knew she wouldn't be there. She'd return his call when she got his message; he knew she would.

He paced, then he bent over to absentmindedly stroke Cleopatra's fat belly. She purred.

Tess. Where was she? He pictured her dressed in black, a cat burglar, breaking into Nate's Pawn, trying to find the bill or receipt or cash register tape that would prove her father had bought a .22-caliber pistol there.

She wouldn't. She had more sense than that, didn't she? Shit.

p.268 move her to her that her plea got there and
they
One column. See her story about the fifth door.

NINETEEN

When Barbara McCleary drove home from work that afternoon, she noticed a strange car parked in front of her house. Then she noticed that someone, a woman, was waiting on her front deck. She pulled into her driveway, got out of her car and gave the woman a questioning look, started to ask something, then froze.

It was Maggie Pedersen.

"I want to talk to you," the woman said angrily, moving toward her. Maggie wasn't a particularly big woman, but she had a look about her that scared the hell out of Barbara.

Barbara covered it well, though. She moved briskly past Maggie, deliberately turning her back to her, and unlocked her front door. "Actually," she said, "I'm kind of in a hurry. Someone's coming over in a minute, so you'll—"

"I don't give a rat's ass whose husband you're screwing today, Barbara, you'll listen to me." Maggie came around to stand in front of her.

"I don't know what in hell you think you're doing, Mrs. Pedersen, but you better leave," Barbara said coolly.

"I'll make it quick," Maggie shot back. "You end your affair with my husband immediately."

"What on earth makes you think I'm having an affair with your husband?"

"Cut the innocent crap, Barb. Just end it."

"Don't you think you should talk to your husband about this?"

"I will. Don't you worry, I will."

"Well, in that case, I don't see how I can help you."

"End it or I'll tell Cody Morris about it. You think he'll like that information?" Maggie said in a cold voice.

Barbara felt her stomach drop to her feet. She wouldn't, she couldn't.

"Well?" Maggie asked. "Is Eric worth it?"

Barbara gathered herself and glared at the woman. "You're bluffing."

"Try me," Maggie said with unbridled ferocity.

It was three in the morning when Dan drove along the main drag in Salinas and spotted the pawnshop. He parked, looked up and down the street, then got out of the car. If a cop came by, stopped, tried to roust him, he'd come up with some lame story.

But no cops were in sight.

He walked into the alley next to Nate's, eyed a side door, saw the security alarm. No good. The front, of course, was protected by a grill.

Around back. Another door. More security. But that window up there...

It wasn't easy getting in, especially as Dan was no spring chicken anymore and the window was six feet off the ground. The security was poor, though—an iron grill rusted out at its base. Loose as hell.

He got the grill out with a few huffs and puffs and set it on the ground in the back alley. Had anyone heard? But no one was around. Good. Then he hoisted himself up and slipped through—no easy feat at that height. He tore his jacket once, too.

Damn.

The place was typical. Shop up front. Office in the back. A tiny bathroom that reeked of urine.

Using his flashlight, he started with the desk, then went to the file cabinets, leafing through files by months, the flashlight held in his teeth.

July, June, May, April, March, February...and there it was, right around the time Bergen said he'd bought it, four months before the Childress shooting. Bergen had planned ahead.

Dan held the sales invoice up and studied it. Miscellaneous merchandise, sold to L. Bergen, a hundred and ten dollars. Big bucks, Dan thought, for a peashooter. On the other hand, it was unregistered. No wonder the proprietor had written miscellaneous. It was a miracle that he kept records at all. Probably the cops and IRS paid visits. Not to mention the Bureau of Alcohol, Tobacco and Firearms.

Dan closed the file and went toward the window. Then he paused, the invoice in his hand. Did he really want to do this? It wasn't too late to put it back. But then a slow grin spread across his lips. Yeah, you bet he did. Childress had murdered his wife, come away clean. Crime number one. The shop owner was dealing in illegal gun sales. Crime number two. And Dan was covering up. Crime number three. But not nearly as bad as one and two.

He paused another moment.

Or was he doing this for Tess?

He searched his gut. Yes. He was. And for Lawrence and even for himself. But mostly he was doing it for Andie. He glanced up. "Okay, kid," he whispered, "this is for you. I hope you'll forgive me now."

And then, satisfied, he moved toward the window.

Tess looked at her watch and then back at the entrance to the pawnshop. It was four in the afternoon. The sign said it closed at six.

She put her hands on the steering wheel of her old Subaru and drummed her fingers. She'd been here, in front of the shop, no less than four times in the past twenty-four hours. Last night. This morning. At noon again. And now. Then she'd driven off, driven around and around, and returned. But each time she was no closer to a plan than the last time.

She'd thought of arson, but that was abhorrent. She'd thought of a rock through the window late at night. But the police would be there in minutes. She'd thought of going in just before closing and somehow hiding and then breaking out later. But she wasn't a criminal. She'd thought a dozen times about calling Dan. But if Dan found the receipt, would he destroy it? She thought he would. Then again, maybe that was only what she wanted him to do.

She held on to the steering wheel of her car, her knuckles white, and stared at the door of the shop, thinking, thinking. Everything in her was fixed on that dingy door, that door—

The rap at her car window made adrenaline spurt through her like a flame through tinder. Her whole body jerked.

She heard a voice as if from a great distance, weak over the galloping of her heart. "Tess, roll down the window" came the voice. "Tess."

She swallowed, paralyzed, and then finally, slowly, her heart still beating like a mad thing, she turned her head and looked up through the glass.

It was Dan.

"Roll it down," he said again, and somehow she managed to find the window handle. "Goddammit," he said, and he leaned down close, "what the hell do you think you're doing?"

Tess licked her dry lips. "I...I don't know what—"

"Oh, save it," he snapped. "I want you to get out of here. Do it before someone recognizes you. Go home."

"I...I can't."

"It's done," he said in that gravelly voice.

"What?"

"I said, Tess, it's done. Now go."

"I don't understand."

"Well, then, think about it on the way home. I'm sure you'll figure it out."

Tess just stared at him. Finally she said, "I don't know if I can drive. I...I feel like I'm going to pass out."

"Wait till you get home," he said, but his voice had softened.

"Dan, how did you...?" she began, but he cut her off with a look. She couldn't ask. Not now. Not ever. He'd done it. That was all she needed to know.

She put the car in gear, her hands shaking. She glanced up at him, bit her lip and managed a tentative smile. He'd done it.

"Go on," he said. "I'll follow. Then, if you wouldn't mind, could I catch a bite to eat? I've been trying to find you for a whole day and I haven't eaten."

"Eaten?"

"Yes, Tess, food. You know. That stuff you put in your mouth and swallow."

"Food," she whispered, and she drove off, leaving him standing there on the street. Food.

An hour later she was pulling into her drive, Dan

right behind her. She could barely fit her mind around what he'd done.

She parked inside the garage, and they went in through the garage door to the kitchen. She still felt weak, as if all her energy had drained right out of her onto the floorboards of the car.

She found a container of frozen spaghetti sauce in the freezer and put it in the microwave. Then she placed a pot of water on the range top. The whole time Dan had said nothing, merely sat on a counter stool, watching. She was still weak as a kitten, a little nauseated—low blood sugar, she realized, no food in her. And her skin felt tingly, as if tiny little feet were marching up and down her limbs. She found some crackers in a cupboard and put the box on the counter, reached in and took a few, munching on them. Dan took a handful, too.

"I didn't realize," she said. "I was—"

"Forget it," he said, chewing. "Forget all about it. Forget you were ever there."

She busied herself getting lettuce and tomatoes out of the refrigerator.

"You want some help?" she heard Dan ask behind her.

"No, no, that's okay."

She boiled the spaghetti, poured sauce on it, set out two salad bowls right on the counter. Nothing fancy. She just needed to eat.

"Looks good," Dan said.

"My father would have a fit if he saw us eating like this. No linens, sauce out of the freezer."

"We won't tell him," Dan replied, starting to eat.

"Wait." She found Parmesan cheese in the refrigerator, and there was a half-empty bottle of wine on the top shelf. "Here, some of my father's newest discovery."

"Are we celebrating?" Dan asked.

"No...yes. Yes, we're celebrating. Why not?" She felt light-headed already, and she hadn't even taken a sip.

They ate, not saying much. She was starving, she realized, really hungry. And the wine was perfect.

"I feel human again," Dan finally said, putting his fork down.

It was odd, Tess thought, to be sitting at the counter and eating with Dan Hadley, as if they were normal acquaintances. Somehow—maybe it was the relief for what he'd done—she could no longer conjure up the animosity she'd felt toward him.

She took another sip of wine, her gaze lowered, not meeting his, and she knew something had altered between them. Something terribly significant, and it frightened her.

She looked up. "I called your hotel the morning after we, um, had dinner in Seattle," she said.

"You did?"

"You were gone. I wondered why you hadn't said anything that night."

"I wasn't sure when I was leaving." He studied her. "You called. Was there anything...?"

"Oh, no, no," she said, embarrassed. "I wanted to apologize. I was...I acted silly. It's just that I've been so stressed out lately."

"And I was already gone. Too bad."

"Uh-huh."

"So, did you have a nice visit with your aunt?"

"Oh, yes, fine."

"But you're still stressed out," he said.

"Well, my father..."

"Yeah."

She stood and piled the plates up, moving to the sink. She rinsed them, put them in the dishwasher,

her back to Dan. She knew, she could tell, he hadn't moved; he was still sitting at the counter, and she could feel his eyes on her, walking on her skin. She was glad she didn't have to face him.

She reached for a pot on the stove, touched the metal side of it by mistake, felt the heat sear her skin and couldn't help crying out.

He was at her side in a moment. "What'd you do?" he asked gruffly. "Let me see."

"It's nothing," she said, holding her hand to her lips.

"Let me see." He took it and opened her fingers. His eyes lifted to her. "It's red. It might blister."

"Oh, for goodness' sake," she said, trying to withdraw her hand.

"Here," he said, and he turned on the cold water and held her fingers under it.

"Dan—"

"Shush. Let the water run on it for a while."

"I can do it myself."

But he didn't let go, and he was so close, their arms touching, his hands holding hers under the faucet. She felt light-headed again, and the cold water raised gooseflesh all over her.

"Stop," she said faintly.

"What?" He turned, still holding her fingers, and they were chest to chest, face-to-face, his hand holding hers between them.

"Stop," she said again.

"Tess..." His eyes held hers, and very slowly he brought her hand up to his mouth. He touched his lips to her fingers. "Does it hurt?"

"No," she whispered.

He kissed them, one at a time, and Tess closed her eyes, melting inside, leaning toward him. Then suddenly she stiffened. "Don't," she said. "This is insane."

Dan paused, her fingertips at his mouth, a surprisingly soft mouth. "Do you really want me to stop?"

"Yes," she said. Then, "No. I mean—"

"Don't talk," he said, and his voice was hoarse. He turned her hand over and kissed the palm.

"Oh, God," she breathed, and she knew she wanted this. It was right, it was good, it was necessary in a way she'd never felt before.

His mouth came down on hers, and her heart gave a great thump, then settled into a rhythm. She kissed him back, her mouth moving under his, their tongues mingling, and her arms went up around his neck and drew him close.

"Tess?" he asked against her lips.

"Yes," she whispered.

And then he lifted her up into his arms and carried her down the hall to her bedroom. She felt safe, utterly secure, for the first time in so long. The past was erased. Nothing remained but this man who made her feel so good, beautiful and safe.

He set her down on her bed and sat beside her. It was nearly dark in her room, and his eyes were shadowed. She reached a hand out to trace the strong line of his nose, his jaw. He closed his eyes and groaned.

He unbuttoned her blouse, one button at a time. Their eyes were locked together. Then her skirt. She pulled his shirt out of his pants, undid it, her fingers fumbling, then reaching inside to touch his skin. It was warm and smooth. She lay with her head on his shoulder, her hands on his bare back, feeling him greedily.

He pulled the straps of her bra off her shoulders, one then the other, unhooked it, gently raised her head so he could see her.

"You're so lovely," he said.

She shook her head, but she was smiling.

They came together with a need so great, so long withheld, that was sweeter for the waiting. He was lean and hard, and he rose over her and entered her swiftly—neither had the patience to wait another moment.

She felt him fill her, and the joy of it washed over her, and she knew that he was what she'd needed all this time. He rested on his arms over her and asked, "Is it all right?" and she said, "Yes," and her insides were pulsing and a voice in her wanted to scream.

Then he rolled over, pulling her on top, and she gasped with the sheer pleasure of it.

They stared at each other, holding still, their flesh joined, and Dan gasped as she had. She moved on him, and he groaned, and her movements became faster and faster, and he heaved under her and breathed hard. Then she felt the tide rise inside her, the bursting glorious molten tide that drowned her and tossed her up on the strand, out of breath and exhausted and wringing wet.

They lay clasped together for a time, Tess on top of him. She heard his breath whistling in and out of his lungs, and his heart beat under her ear. "Jesus," he finally said.

She smiled.

"Was it...did you?" he tried. "I mean, I never felt..."

"Don't lie," she said mildly.

"I'm not lying, Tess."

She reached a hand up and pushed his hair off his forehead. His skin was slick with sweat. She laughed softly against him.

"What?"

"Nothing."

"Don't lie," he said, repeating her words.

"Just, oh, I don't know. Us. Who would have thought…?"

"Yeah."

She raised her head and looked at him. "This meant something to me, Dan."

"I know. It did to me, too."

She wanted suddenly to say *I love you, Dan Hadley*, but it was far too soon. And perhaps it wasn't true.

She slid off him, cuddled against his side, a hand on his chest. He had practically no hair on his chest, she noted, surprised. There was so much she had to learn about this man. So much.

They lay together, and a faint breeze from the open window touched them.

"Are you cold?" Dan whispered.

"A little."

He pulled the quilt over them. "Better?"

"Mm."

She felt herself sinking toward sleep. "Dan?"

"Uh-huh."

"We didn't finish the dishes."

"Screw the dishes."

She smiled in the dark, and felt his arms encircle her. So strong, so good, so safe.

"Dan?" she murmured again.

"Yeah?"

"You're not alone anymore." She snuggled closer.

"Go to sleep, Tess," he said softly.

TWENTY

Finding Frank Ferrara was not easy. Dan had located Pearl in Seattle in a day, but Frank had truly gone to ground.

Dan had flown to Florida from San Francisco the morning after...the morning after the interlude with Tess. He couldn't allow himself to think about it in any other terms. It had happened between them. Unplanned. And he'd never experienced anything quite like their lovemaking. And that was what it had been, lovemaking. Every time he thought about it, whether on the plane or in the rental car he'd gotten in Tampa or on the drive south to Sarasota, he marveled. He couldn't lie to himself. With Susan, as with others before her, it had been sex. Good sex. But with Tess it had been different. He remembered that night, when she'd said in a sleepy, sated voice that he wasn't alone anymore. He hadn't realized until then, lying there holding Tess, just how alone he'd been. And it must have scared the hell out of him.

The next morning Dan had screwed it all up. He stood in front of the mirror in the Sarasota motel, shaving. Thinking back, he grimaced. He must have done it deliberately, he thought, some sick subconscious urge, a shrink would say. He didn't know about that, but he did know how Tess had reacted.

She'd been cooking breakfast. He recalled with stark clarity how soft and lovely she'd looked, shy. Smiling for no reason, a beautiful, heart-melting smile.

He'd sat at the counter, drinking a cup of coffee, and somehow the words had come out of his mouth. "You can tell me now, you know."

She'd turned to him, her hair tousled, the smile still on her lips. She'd come over to him and run a hand across his bare chest, making him go all liquid inside. "What?" she'd murmured.

"You can tell me," he'd managed to get out. "About the gun."

He should have known by her reaction. He should have realized and shut up, but he'd apparently been bent on self-destruction.

"What?" she'd repeated, but in quite a different tone of voice, and she'd stepped back from him.

"Tess, hey, you don't have to worry anymore. You trust me now, don't you? You know..."

"Oh, my God," she said, and she leaned back against the counter, staring at him.

"What? What's the matter?" he asked, not seeing it. Stupid.

"You did it so I'd tell you," Tess whispered, her voice full of agony.

It took him a moment. "Hey, no, Tess..." he stammered.

"You don't care about me, do you? You lied, Dan. You don't even know what the truth is!"

"Please, Tess, you've got it all wrong."

"No, I don't. You used me, you bastard." Then she turned away from him, put her face in her hands, and he saw her back shaking.

He went over to her and touched her shoulder. "Tess, look, I have to go to Florida today. I have to leave. I don't want you to think… I wouldn't do that to you."

She whirled on him. "So, does that mean you love me, then? You really and truly love me and you want a relationship? You want to commit?"

"Tess," he said, nonplussed. Love, commitment?

"Either you slept with me to find out about the gun or you really care. Goddamn it, Dan, which is it?" she cried.

His silence had been all the answer she needed.

He'd left on that note. Now he knew she'd never tell him, and he still couldn't understand exactly how everything had gotten so twisted. He hadn't, he honest to God hadn't slept with Tess to get the information from her. But love? He knew it had been very special between them. But love?

Dan spent his second day in Florida searching for Ferrara with no luck. There were a bunch of Ferraras on his list, but none checked out. He was beginning to think Frank's family was listed under a different name. A sister or mother with a new last name?

The third day he concentrated on the trailer parks from Bradenton south to Venice, knocking on doors in an intense autumn heat wave, asking managers about Frank, showing his picture from the news clipping at the Childress murder trial. Dan, of course, knew Ferrara, having interviewed him for the Childress trial and then seeing him testify in court about how Robbie had threatened his life. Dan had also learned Frank had been in Aspen for the wine festival. Frank would never miss a ritzy event. At least a hundred people in Aspen had told Dan that. Whether or not Frank had been in the tent when Robbie had been shot, no one recalled. He hadn't been on the vol-

unteer list. And he hadn't been a paid participant. But
people still managed to get in even with the tight security. And that was what Dan needed to drag out of
him: Had he been there? And if he hadn't, what was
his alibi?

Dan checked at the local motor vehicles department to see if there was a car registered to a Frank
Ferrara in Florida. He checked at the driver's license
bureau, flipping his ID badge quickly. It was no go.
Dan knew Ferrara had a current Colorado driver's license, but apparently not one in Florida. And he was
beginning to wonder if the info Tess had gotten was
all wrong.

Knowing Frank's expensive tastes and habits led
Dan to the fancy nightspots out on palm-tree-lined
Lido Beach and Longboat Key. He drove up and
down the strip of fancy hotels and tropical resorts,
stopping at bars and restaurants, showing Frank's
picture, asking questions. Then, finally, on the fourth
night there, he stopped at the Chart House on Longboat Key. It overlooked Sarasota Bay, pelicans nesting
on pilings, palm fronds clicking in a hot wind, mil-
lion-dollar yachts cruising in the bay, the sunset turning the sky orange and magenta. Two very pretty
young girls dressed in Hawaiian-style sarongs
opened the doors and greeted him. Nice touch. And
he was immensely glad for the blast of air-conditioning—Florida in September was a visit to hell, as far as
Dan was concerned. He showed the two girls Frank's
picture.

"I wonder if you've ever seen this man..." he began.

"Oh, Frank, sure," one of them said. "He should be
here in, say, about an hour. If not tonight, then tomorrow."

"Is that a fact," Dan said, and he grinned.

* * *

Cody was as delighted as a kid in a candy store when he hung up the phone after a long chat with Maggie Pedersen. He walked to the window and watched the leaves swirling below in the Little Nell courtyard, piling up in the corners as an autumn storm threatened, and he wondered just when would be the most strategic moment to leak this information to the voracious press.

He envisioned the headlines in the tabloids: Aspen District Attorney in Love Nest with Married Man. Can Barbara McCleary Still Run the Bergen Trial?

It was going to crush Barbara.

Cody felt bad about that. He truly liked McCleary. Hell, she made his old heart do somersaults. But she was a sharp lady, and she'd get over the blow. The question was, would she even be allowed to stay on the case?

Cody would have to think about it. He didn't mind dirtying her—everybody in this business got dirty eventually. But to possibly destroy her career? Cody really wanted to mull that over.

Bob Winthrop dragged his ponderous body out of his car and eyed the pawnshop. He'd been to so goddamn many in the past two weeks, from Monterey to Carmel and over the coastal range. He was running out of sporting-goods stores and pawnshops and beginning to believe Bergen had bought the gun off some street dude. If Bergen had bought it at all; he might have owned it his whole life, despite his protestations that he'd never owned a gun. That had been Bergen's story, anyway, the one he'd told before Cody Morris had arrived in Aspen to shut him up.

Bob entered the pawnshop in Salinas and scrunched up his small nose. He hated the dank, dusty smell of these places. It reminded him of people on the skids, people who sold all their worldly possessions with every intent of buying them back. They never did. There were power tools and tool chests and guitars, sets of golf clubs and tennis rackets. There were bicycles and skateboards, skis and stereo systems. Some old TVs. There were cases of pins and jewelry and rare coins. Guns, knives and rifles. Junk everywhere. It flat-out stank of losers.

Bob flipped his California P.I. identification at the shop owner, who was just doling out twenty bucks to a kid for a boom box. Then he told the guy what he was looking for, and he showed him a photo of Lawrence Bergen.

The guy looked nervous.

And Bob got a familiar itch under his skin.

"You sure you never sold this man a handgun?" Bob repeated.

The proprietor shook his head and wouldn't meet Bob's eyes. "Nah, never seen him before. Well, I seen him on TV. I know who he is—guy who shot Childress."

"That's right," Bob said. "And we think he bought a gun from you."

"Hey," the man said, "no way. It would have to be registered."

So that was the problem, Bob realized. The man hadn't come forward because he was afraid he'd get his business license yanked for selling an unregistered handgun.

Bob leaned over the counter and lowered his voice. "It's a shame you didn't sell a gun to Bergen, man. There'd be a lot of reward money. And, hey, I'm sure if you had sold one, you would have registered it. It's not your fault if the goddamn bureaucrats lost the paperwork. Happens all the time."

"Really?" The man's eyes slid to meet Bob's.

"Oh, sure, buddy. Say you filled out the required forms and sent them in. Is it your fault no one can find them?"

The man pondered that. Then he said, "You mentioned reward money. What would a guy have to do to get it?"

"Well, now," Bob said, "it would help to have some sort of a sales receipt with Bergen's name on it. And then this person would have to testify at the trial in Aspen in January. All expenses paid. And on top of the reward money...might be a sweet deal."

The shop owner rubbed his chin.

"Of course, there'd be magazines and newspapers clamoring for the story, and they pay great. Then there're book and movie deals. You get the picture?" Bob smiled, friendly.

"Uh-huh," the man said. Then, "Tell you what, Mr...."

"Bob. Bob Winthrop. And you are?"

"Nate Huff, Nathan," the man said. "Tell you what. I'll see what I maybe got in my files. Okay?"

"Fine by me," Bob said.

"You come back tomorrow."

"I'll do that."

"How much did you say that reward was?"

"We'll discuss it when I see what you have."

"Okay," the guy said. "That's fair. I gotta think this whole thing over."

But when Bob returned at 10:00 a.m. sharp the next day, the wind had gone out of Nate Huff's sails. "It was there. It was right in the file cabinet," he kept saying. "Bergen came in here last February and wanted a handgun. I mean, I recognized him right away, seen him at that Childress trial and all that. I told him it would be a two-week wait on a handgun and he got pissed off, said he needed it like now. He peeled off some big bills, you know. What was I to do? Anyhow, there honest to God was a receipt in my files, man. It said L. Bergen on it. I recognized him right away the day Childress was killed, and I went and looked in my files and it was there. I didn't call the cops or nobody, see, because it wasn't... You know, the paperwork got lost and all. But it was there!"

Bob thought fast. "Was the receipt a numbered one?"

"Yeah, they all are. Consecutive."

Shit, Bob thought. Then they couldn't fudge a new one. Cody Morris would subpoena his records and catch it in a minute.

"What if I just testify that it happened?" the shop owner was asking. "I can do that. But would I still get a reward?"

"Uh, yeah, I'm sure you would," Bob said absently. His testimony wouldn't carry the weight it would with the sales receipt, but it was something. And a couple of jurors would believe it, especially if this guy took a polygraph. McCleary could slip the results into the court records somehow, which would connect Bergen to a .22-caliber handgun. It wasn't like having the gun in her hands to show the jury. But it would do.

"How much will I get paid?" the shop owner was asking.

"I'm going to find out," Bob said. "I'll be back this afternoon. You just keep looking for that paperwork, buddy."

"I spent half the goddamn night looking," Huff growled. "It's like one day it was in my records and the next day it was gone. I just don't get it."

But Bob did get it. Dan Hadley. He'd bet a year's income that Hadley had beat him here. Son of a bitch.

* * *

Frank Ferrara strolled into the Chart House restaurant on Longboat Key two nights after the greeters had told Dan he frequented the place. He strolled past the pretty girls, gave a high sign to the head waiter and walked into the bar area, nodding at the bartender, taking a stool.

Frank liked the Chart House. It was where the younger and wealthier Sarasotans hung out. A good place to make contacts. If he was in on a Friday night, he was usually invited out on a fishing trip in the gulf on Saturday, on one of those nice fifty-foot sportfisherman boats. Or parties. Frank was always asked to the local get-togethers from Clearwater all the way down to ritzy Naples. It was funny. Everyone assumed he had a modest trust fund or something and that he only took bartending jobs as a lark. Not a soul knew he lived with his married sister in a trailer park between Sarasota and Bradenton. He talked the talk. Skiing in Aspen, partying in Beverly Hills, golfing in Palm Springs. He made it a point to know the right places.

"Do you live out here on the Key?" someone would ask, and Frank would evade the question by saying he was visiting relatives, and his residence was really in Aspen.

Women adored him. For the most part he was outgoing and charming and handsome, his dark eyes twinkling, his smile white and boyishly crooked. He'd never left a woman unsatisfied in bed. It was his trademark. He also rarely dated married women, preferring the divorcées. Andie Childress had been an exception. He'd really dug that chick.

He ordered a gin and tonic—back shelf only for Frank—and struck up a conversation with the bartender. There were five or six people sitting on stools, four or five more groups sitting at tables, awaiting dinner reservations. And it wasn't until Frank glanced up through the candlelit dimness that he recognized the single man at the far end of the bar, a beer tilted to his lips. The man smiled thinly and made an almost imperceptible nod in Frank's direction, and Frank's limbs turned to rubber.

Dan Hadley. He'd found him.

I could run, raced through Frank's brain, but before he could move, Hadley had picked up his beer and was sauntering toward him. Too late, too late.

The first words out of Frank's mouth when the P.I. slid onto the stool next to his were "I don't have to say a thing, Hadley. Not one word. You're wasting your time."

"That's not a very nice way to greet an old pal," Hadley said. "You had to figure I'd track you down eventually."

"Yeah, I thought about it."

"And from the looks of it, Frank, you sure didn't want to be found."

"Bullshit, Hadley. I'm visiting my sister is all."

"Uh-huh," Hadley said. "So let's cut to the chase. What do you say?"

Frank clamped his mouth shut. He knew what was coming.

"Where were you when Childress was shot?"

Frank swore. "Man, this is not fair. You'd think I was the only one who'd had a run-in with the creep."

"A run-in? Oh, Frank, I think it was a little more than that. You were screwing Robbie's wife. He threatened to kill you."

Frank shrugged. "Like the whole world doesn't already know that, thanks to you."

"Hey, you were the one with Andie, not me. Now, how about an answer, Frank? Where were you?"

"At home."

"At home in Aspen?"

"You already know I was in Aspen or you wouldn't be here."

"Very good, Frank. And is there anyone who can alibi you?"

"I don't need an alibi. If I did, the cops would be asking and not some half-rate P.I."

"Oh, you got me with that one, Frank. So, how about that alibi? Or maybe you were alone. Home alone."

"I'll tell you who I was with, but then that's it. Leave me alone. Deal?"

"No deals, Frank. Let's have the name. You want to clear yourself, don't you?"

"Her name's Janet. Janet Frietas. But I doubt you'll find her. She's an Aussie and her visa ran out."

"Swell," Hadley said. "You know that's as good as no alibi, Frank. And with the way you felt about Robbie—"

"Hey, Bergen did it. Everyone knows that. There's not a chance in a million he'll get off. And you know the funny thing? I'm happy as hell Childress got it. Me and about a million others. Bergen should get a Nobel Prize for doing Childress."

"Mm," Hadley said. He took a long draw of his beer, set it down and then turned to Frank again. "You own a gun?"

"Oh, come on."

"Do you? It'd be better to tell me now than to have it come out on the witness stand."

"The...? You can't be serious. Why should I testify? Jesus H. Christ, Hadley, why?"

"Do you own a gun?" the P.I. repeated.

"No."

"You wouldn't lie to me?"

"I don't own a gun. Why don't you talk to Andie's sister about the gun? Everyone on the planet knows the chick took it."

"Is that a fact," Hadley said.

"Hey, you can call me to testify, waste your time and mine. It won't mean a thing this round, Hadley. You helped get Childress off after he murdered Andie, but the public isn't going to fall for these tactics again. Not this time. And not in Aspen. You're dealing with a different mentality and you know it. Man, you are desperate. And by the way," Frank said, "how come you're working on Bergen's team now? I mean, after what you did to them?"

Hadley didn't answer.

"Christ," Frank said, "don't tell me you grew a conscience."

Hadley only shrugged, and then he got up, peeled a few dollars off a wad from his pocket and tossed them on the bar. "If I were you," he said, "I wouldn't leave Sarasota. You will be subpoenaed. If you take off, Frank, it's going to look real bad. Know what I mean?"

"Go to hell," Frank muttered, and Hadley turned on his heel and left. When he was gone Frank let out the breath he'd been holding the whole time. There wasn't a chance he was going to testify. Not one damn chance. First, Janet the Aussie hadn't been with him, and second, he hadn't been at home. He'd been in the tent. And if Hadley found that out...

Shit, Frank thought, he was really in for it now.

Tess left the law office in downtown Monterey feeling totally drained. She'd just finished the deposition, which had been conducted by McCleary's assistant, Paul Howard. Patrick had been there with her as Cody's representative, and he'd been diligently tough with some of Howard's questions—in truth, she hadn't had to answer much more than she had during the June interview she'd given to McCleary. Still, the preparation, the whole ordeal, had exhausted her.

Patrick stayed in the guest room that night and he was very sweet and considerate, disappearing into Carmel for dinner, keeping out of her hair when he got back. The next morning he flew out of San Jose, heading for Aspen to report to Cody.

Tess was alone again. She watered the houseplants, fed the cat and telephoned Paula, desperately needing a friend. But Paula was at a conference in L.A. and wouldn't be back for a few days.

She sat on the living-room couch, still in her bathrobe, and curled her feet beneath her. Today would be a good day to call the UCLA Medical Center and talk to the director again. Maybe she could start a residency in February, after the trial. No matter what happened with her father, her life had to go on.

Sure, she thought. The truth was that no matter the outcome of the trial, her career was over before it had begun. No one was going to admit her into a residency with the shadow of doubt that was always going to accompany her. No one. Not even in one of those hospitals in the Caribbean. Never.

She put her head down on a cushion and gripped it, overcome by loneliness and doubts. And there was no one to comfort her. Not a living soul. There had been someone, though, if only for a night.

She gripped the cushion more fiercely and fought the sob welling up from deep inside. And it was as if he was there with her, touching her hair and her cheek and her arms, stroking her. She could feel his phantom touch. The ache swelled in her, a wave ready to crest. And then it broke.

"Goddamn you, Hadley," she moaned, and she lay and cried until there were no tears left.

TWENTY-ONE

It was snowing hard the December afternoon Dennis Wilson rushed into Ken Hatchett's office waving the subpoena he'd just been served. But his lawyer was on the phone and Dennis had to wait, bursting with fear and impatience, until Ken finished his conversation.

"Look," Dennis said, "look what I just got!"

"Well, we knew you would, didn't we?"

"I know, but—"

"Relax, you don't have anything to worry about. They've got the murderer."

"But Morris will drag me through the coals, you know that. He'll crucify me!"

"It won't be pleasant, but always remember, Dennis, you're only a distraction."

"Christ, this is awful. Some Christmas present," Dennis moaned. "Can I leave town? Can I get out of it some way?"

"I wouldn't advise that," Ken said. "Just hang in there. It'll all be over soon. And I'll prep you. I know exactly what Morris is going to ask you."

"Do you?" Dennis asked mournfully.

* * *

All through October, November and half of December, Tess had put off returning to Aspen. She studied her textbooks and logged extra hours at the nursing home, trying, but failing, to forget the upcoming trial and Dan's betrayal. Finally, her mother had asked Cody to call her and tell her it was time, and she couldn't procrastinate anymore.

She landed in Denver, switched planes to take the short express hop to Aspen and looked out the window at the snow-covered mountains, reliving the anger and hurt she'd felt when she'd realized what Dan had done to her. And now she had to face him again, all the way up to the trial, which was three weeks away, and through the whole awful ordeal. Months, perhaps. They'd be in close proximity, unable to avoid each other. She'd braced herself for the meeting, for the pain of his constant presence, but it made her so damn mad that she had to go through that, an added anxiety, on top of her father's murder trial. On top of her having to testify at that trial.

She'd gotten her subpoena, and it had caused her several sleepless nights. She didn't want to talk about it or think about it, but Cody would force her to, so she couldn't escape that, either.

Escape. God, she wished she could just run away.

Everyone else on the plane was on vacation, carrying their ski-boot bags, dressed for the slopes, talking excitedly of where they'd ski and how the snow conditions were and whether a storm was expected.

Tess had one consolation and one only, but it was a precious one she carried close to her heart: she hadn't told Dan about the gun. No one knew. No one had found it. It was three weeks before the trial, and no other living soul knew where it was. Snow buried the gun now, deep snow, and it wouldn't melt till spring, when the trial would be long over.

Cody was certain there wouldn't be a conviction without it, and Tess knew there was no other connection to the gun—Dan had seen to that. So her father might very well get off.

Of course, there was the D.A.'s case, and McCleary had bragged often enough to the media that it was airtight.

Both sides were overwhelmingly confident, but only one would prevail. Which one?

The plane landed at Sardy Field, and her parents were there to pick her up. She kissed her mother, managed to embrace her father. The display of affection with Lawrence wasn't so bad; she could do it, she'd told herself. She could stand it.

Winter had transformed the valley. Instead of green it was white, the mountains covered with snow, piles of it along the highway, soft white cushions on every roof and tree branch. The sun was out that day, but her dad told her a storm was approaching and pointed out the streamers of snow blowing off the high peaks, foretelling the cold front.

"You look thin," Carole said. "Tess, honey, have you been eating?"

"Yes, Mom."

"Leave her alone, Carole," her father said. "She just got here."

"I have a turkey and lots of good stuff," Carole went on, "and Cody's having a Christmas dinner for all of us in his suite, and…"

Tess didn't hear the rest. A dinner, she thought. Dan would be there. Could she get out of it?

"And we considered getting reservations at the Renaissance for New Year's Eve, unless…" Carole paused. "Tess? Is that okay?"

"Yes, Mom, it's fine. I'll get fat."

"It's so good to have you here," Carole said. "It's been so long."

"Carole, we've spoken to her every day, for Lord's sake," Lawrence said.

"It's not the same as having her here."

Lawrence said nothing more; apparently he didn't concur.

"How's the residency coming along?" he finally asked as they turned off Main Street toward the Gant condos.

"Stalled," Tess said. "I think they're all waiting to see what happens at the trial."

"Tess," her mother said sharply.

"Sorry, I only meant—"

"It's okay," Lawrence said. "I know what you mean."

The usual strategy session was going to be held in the Bergens' condo that afternoon. Everyone would be there, Carole had told Tess, and they were all looking forward to seeing her again.

I'll bet, Tess thought. She wondered how Dan would react, wondered how he felt about her, how he could have pretended so well, so damn convincingly, that she'd swallowed his act hook, line and sinker. That orphan story—she bet it was a lie, too, along with everything else about him.

Tess had barely finished unpacking when the troops arrived for the session. From her bedroom she heard her parents welcoming them; she recognized the voices: Cody, Patrick, Brad and Steve. She listened for Dan's voice, her chest tight, but she didn't hear it. Thank God. Maybe he was off on one of his investigatory junkets.

Cody made a fuss, embarrassing her. Brad, Patrick and Steve shook her hand. "Glad you're back. Good to see you again."

"This girl is one brave kid," Cody said, beaming. "She did great at the deposition. Just great. We're all proud of you, gal."

Then they got down to business, and Tess learned a lot about the case, things she hadn't been privy to when she'd been in Monterey for these past few months.

"Okay," Cody said, looking at his notes, "we've found a gun registered to Dennis Wilson. Dan traced it. Yup, a .22-caliber. Wilson lied. That's good news. He had motive, opportunity and means. He'll be easy pickings on the stand."

"What about Pearl?" Brad asked. "Has he been served with the subpoena yet? Anyone have feedback on his reaction?"

"Dan's got that stuff." Cody looked at his watch. "He should be here any minute."

Tess felt her heart squeeze. He was coming. He'd be here soon. She'd have to be in the same room, talk to him, pretend nothing had happened. She shut her eyes for a moment, preparing herself.

Cody was looking around. "Anyone have questions about the witness list McCleary submitted?"

"Uh-huh," Patrick said. "What's with this guy, Nathan Huff?"

"The pawnshop owner. He'll testify that Lawrence bought a .22-caliber from him." Cody smiled. "But there's no corroboration, no paperwork. It's only his word. I'll make sure the jury knows that, don't worry."

The door to the condo opened then, and they all turned their heads. Dan strode into the room, taking off his coat as he came in. "Sorry I'm late," he said. "I was waiting for a call."

Tess looked down, afraid to meet his eyes. He'd see her, though, and he'd have to say something.

"Hello, Tess" came his voice. "Glad you're back."

She glanced up, and their eyes met for a moment, met and locked, and she tore hers away, feeling sick. "Hello," she said, and she knew everyone must be able to hear the pain in her voice.

"Have a good trip?" Dan asked. He sounded so casual, so unconcerned, as if nothing had happened between them. She hated him even as she envied his cool composure.

"Yes, fine, thanks."

Cody asked Dan about his latest information.

"Yeah, Pearl got the subpoena, and the server said he was upset," Dan replied, seating himself on a chair that had been left unoccupied for him. He crossed an ankle over his knee and ran a hand through his wind-tousled hair. "And Ferrara got his. Same thing. Pissed off and worried."

"Excellent," Cody said. "I like my witnesses rattled."

Tess listened to the conversation: Pearl, Wilson and Ferrara, who would hold up best on the stand, who would crumble, how the jury would perceive each one. But all she could see was Dan: the sandy blond hair, the strong nose and jaw, the flat planes of his cheeks and the deep-set blue eyes. His mouth and his hands. His mouth on hers, moving, probing her, that surprisingly soft mouth…

Stop it, her mind cried, and she tore her thoughts from him and forced herself to pay attention to the lawyers. Her father's future was on the line.

"So, Dan, who looks like our best bet?" Cody was asking. "Who looks most guilty to a layman?"

Dan shrugged. "Hard to say. Wilson may be too sympathetic—the wife and kids. Ferrara's kind of slimy, though. I like him."

They discussed that for a while, then they talked

about the order in which Cody would call his witnesses. "It depends on what order Barbara uses, too," he said. "I may have to call someone to rebut testimony she's brought out. But, honestly, she doesn't have any surprises. Unless she comes up with something we don't know about. New evidence."

Tess ducked her head, aware they were all thinking about her, her and the gun.

No one could ask her directly, she knew. No one but Dan, and he wouldn't, not anymore, not after what he'd done to her. But they were all thinking about it, wondering how she'd hold up under intense interrogation from Barbara McCleary. Wondering if she could take it. If she'd break down and confess. It was unspoken, but it was there, a nagging worry—how would Tess do on the stand?

They finally left, and Tess took a breath, the first real one she'd taken for hours. She'd made it through, been in the same room with him. She'd done it, and she could do it again.

Over the following weeks, there were endless meetings, briefings and phone conferences, the scripts Patrick and Brad worked on for Tess, preparing her for hypothetical situations on the stand, questions Barbara and Paul Howard were sure to ask. It was the questions they couldn't foresee that panicked Tess, kept her tossing and turning at night, unable to enjoy Carole's endless cornucopia of culinary delights.

Christmas approached. Aspen filled with skiers, working up to the holiday frenzy. The streets were crowded, the restaurants and shops full; the beautiful people landed their private jets at Sardy Field and walked the streets wrapped in elegant furs. The *Silver Queen* gondola ran endlessly up the mountain, delivering skiers to the groomed runs. The bars couldn't pour drinks fast enough.

But in the Bergens' condo and in Cody's suite, it was all work. The trial date loomed, feared but awaited impatiently at the same time.

And still the prosecution didn't have the murder weapon.

Tess decided it was worse than Robbie's trial, because then she and her family had been the wronged ones. Now they were the accused, on the defensive.

And the press never let up.

Carole rarely went out anymore; she couldn't handle it. They had groceries delivered, take-out food delivered. Tess tried to go for walks or cross-country skiing, but they followed her, no matter how she disguised herself, sticking microphones in her face, chasing her with video cameras.

That was awful, but maybe Dan Hadley was the worst. He was always there at the meetings, blond and unflappable. Even when Tess stayed in her room, she knew when he came into the condo. She could feel it in her belly; his presence crawled on her skin. She knew when he was there.

God, how she detested it all.

Her father kept her at arm's length. He was always pleasant, always in control, but there was that coolness between them. It hurt Tess, because they'd been so close. She wanted it to be the same as it had once been; like a child whose parents divorced, she wanted to ignore reality and have things back to the way they used to be. When Lawrence talked to her—always small talk, inconsequential chatter—the questions stood between them like a ticking bomb: Can the gun still be found? Will you break on the stand?

She couldn't live like this for long, she knew. Something had to give.

If only she could talk to someone about her secret. Ask someone directly what she should say when Barbara questioned her about the gun on the witness stand. Maybe try to get the gun out of its hiding place and destroy it. No, she didn't dare do that. But if she could talk to someone about it, voice her fears and her dilemma, her sadness, the awful feeling of being trapped by duty and family and a situation she'd never asked for. And the press, always the hungry press. But there was no one she could talk to, nowhere she could run to, nowhere to hide.

Cody was giving his dinner on Christmas Eve. Everyone on the team was invited to his suite, everyone was supposed to buy an inexpensive gift to swap, and everyone was supposed to forget the trial for one evening.

"But you have to go," Carole told Tess when Tess stated her intention to stay at the condo. "Cody will be upset. It'd be rude."

"Tell him I'm sick," Tess said.

"Tess, honey, he just saw you this afternoon. He'll know you're not sick."

"Mom, I don't want to go."

"Whyever not?"

"I just don't want to. I'm not in the mood."

"Theresa Bergen," her mother said, "you simply have to go."

So Tess took a shower, did her hair, brushed color on her cheeks and put on lipstick. She wore a knee-length black skirt and a blue silk-knit top, black boots, and Carole smiled and touched her and told her she looked beautiful.

It was a perfect starlit night, the mountains silver against the black sky. Cold and clear. Their breaths froze as they walked to the Little Nell Hotel, the snow crunching underfoot.

The town was packed, people everywhere, crowding the sidewalks, buying last minute gifts, window-shopping, indulging themselves in cashmere or jewelry or paintings or gourmet chocolate or snakeskin cowboy boots. Or ski boots or new skis or one-piece designer ski suits or snowboards.

Cody was the perfect host, charming and avuncular, pressing eggnog and champagne on everyone. There were appetizers of every type, and the dinner was delivered by the best caterer in town. There was even a Christmas tree.

"How lovely," Carole said.

"Wonderful," Lawrence added.

Steve Sutton and his wife were there. Brad and Patrick were there, too, and their wives, who'd joined them for the holiday. At Cody's expense. And Cody's secretary, who'd done a lot of work for him both in Aspen and back home in Idaho. And Dan. Of course Dan was there.

He looked incredibly handsome, Tess registered, despising herself, in a blue shirt and sport coat. He always wore blue shirts—did he do it out of carelessness or did he know that blue matched his eyes?

Everyone acted as if this was a normal holiday party; no one spoke of the trial. It was all social and light and utterly artificial.

Tess tried to smile, holding a glass of eggnog, taking occasional sips of the rich stuff. She met the newly arrived wives, she spoke, she smiled and answered questions.

Cody hugged her and kissed her under the mistletoe. She ate a canapé, took a sip of her drink. But all the time she was acutely aware of Dan doing the same thing she was—being social.

She tried to stay away from him, but it was difficult in the crowded living room of the suite. Occasionally they came close or were included in the same conversation.

Didn't anyone notice how distasteful this was to her? Didn't anyone see how matters stood between Dan and her?

The dinner was set up as a buffet, and it was sumptuous. A holiday feast. Everyone ate and complimented Cody and groaned at how full they were.

The evening was torture for Tess.

Finally, finally, Carole said she was getting tired. Lawrence, always solicitous, got up and went for their coats.

"You can stay," Carole suggested to her daughter. "It's still early."

"Oh, no," Tess hastened to say, "I'm tired, too. I'm ready to go."

They left after prolonged, endless thanks and holiday wishes, and when they stepped outside of the hotel into the clear, frigid air, Tess felt an enormous sense of relief.

They began walking back to the Gant, Lawrence's arm around Carole.

"What a nice party," Carole was saying, when someone called out Tess's name from behind.

They all stopped. Tess turned and her insides froze. It was Dan.

"Hold on there," he called, striding toward them. "I thought I'd see you home."

"Oh, Dan, how nice," Carole said.

"There's no need, really," Lawrence added.

Dan had reached them by then, his breath pluming in the cold. "Well, I was leaving, anyway, and my hotel is in this direction."

Tess said nothing.

He walked next to her, following her parents. "I've been wanting to talk to you," he said in an undertone, and he put a hand on her arm, slowing her, letting Carole and Lawrence pull ahead.

Tess could barely stand his touch. She tried to edge away, but he kept his hold on her arm, then he stopped and pulled her around to face him.

"Let me go," she said.

"Wait a minute, Tess. Just give me a second."

She subsided, not wanting her folks to notice anything, not wanting anyone to know her shame. He stood there, so close, his features shadowed, his expression unrevealing. But she knew he could read *her* face; it was an open book, and pain was written on every page.

"What?" she asked, trying desperately to hold on to the tatters of her pride.

"I know you think I acted like a bastard," he said.

"Forget it."

"Tess, I didn't mean for it to happen. It wasn't what you think."

"Okay, fine, Dan. Can I go now?"

"Hang on. I'm trying to tell you I did not sleep with you so you'd tell me about the gun. You have to believe me."

"Sure. Whatever you say."

"Tess, don't be like this. I'm not your enemy. Jesus, we've been through this before. You know I'm on your side."

"You're on my *father's* side." Her heart beat furiously, and she was hot all over; she prayed he didn't notice.

"I'm on *your* side." He hesitated. "And when the trial's over, Tess, maybe then—"

"What, Dan? Maybe what?"

He searched her face in the darkness. "Don't act dumb. You know what I mean."

"I haven't got the faintest idea."

"Look." He seemed ill at ease. "Can we go somewhere? A bar or something. Can we talk?"

"No," she said.

"Dammit, Tess."

How could she still love him, yearn for him, shiver with delight at his presence? And how could she hate him so much at the same time?

He touched her cheek with his fingers, and she drew back as if stung.

"Tess," he said.

"Go to hell, Dan." And she turned from him and walked away as fast as she could.

Barbara McCleary felt like a school kid summoned into the principal's office. Judge DeCarlo had called her that morning and ordered her to be at his house that afternoon. He had something to discuss with her, and Barbara knew what it was.

She drove to his house, feeling nervous and put-out. God, she hated being on the defensive. She hated being wrong.

DeCarlo was livid. He stood in his living room, the lights on his Christmas tree blinking cheerfully behind him, and reamed her out.

"What the hell is this I'm hearing?" he asked. "You and Eric Pedersen?"

"I don't see that it's anybody's business but ours," Barbara tried.

"You take on a high-profile case like this and you don't think who you're screwing is public property? Wrong again, Barbara."

"It has nothing to do with the case, Your Honor."

"It compromises what goes on in my courtroom, and I won't stand for it," he said angrily.

The aroma of baked ham wafted in from the kitchen, and wood smoke from the fireplace scented the air. So Christmasy, Barbara thought illogically. "I'm sorry it had to come out like this," she replied.

"You realize who it came from?" DeCarlo asked.

"Cody Morris."

"Who else? That bastard is relentless." The judge glared at her. "And you fell into his trap, you fool."

"You're supposed to be impartial," Barbara said carefully.

"Listen, I don't care who you screw. It's what everyone else thinks. The jury, for instance, god-dammit."

"Do you want me to resign?" No one would ever know what the words cost her.

"I don't know. Let me think about it."

Oh, God, Barbara thought. All these months, all her work...

"I'll let you know. Now, my kids are coming over."

"Merry Christmas," Barbara said dryly, preparing to leave.

"Right," DeCarlo said. "Merry Christmas."

Barbara drove home to an empty house. Eric was with his family. She hadn't seen him in a while, what with his kids home from school. Or was Maggie keeping a tight rein on him?

She wanted to see him badly; she was lonely and worried to death about whether she'd be allowed to stay on the Bergen case. She needed company. It was Christmas, for God's sake. She needed comforting, cheering up. She needed Eric's arms around her.

She put a turkey TV dinner in the oven and looked outside at the snow-covered landscape. She hadn't even put up a Christmas tree or hung a wreath on her door. Too busy, too focused on the trial.

She ate her Christmas dinner alone and watched *A*

Christmas Carol on TV for the twentieth time, and she felt just like Scrooge, a man she'd always admired, poor, misunderstood Ebenezer Scrooge.

Merry fucking Christmas.

TWENTY-TWO

It was January. New Year's celebrations in Aspen, which, in the end, the Bergens had avoided completely, were well over. Now Tess, Carole and Aunt Sis sat one row behind the defendant's table in the courtroom, where they could see and hear everything, and where they could lend support to Lawrence. That was, Tess often thought, both a blessing and a curse.

How ironic that she should be sitting in a courtroom again, listening to a murder trial, how similar in so many ways, yet how different in the most profound way, for this time Tess was on the side of the accused. There were no cameras in this courtroom, either; Judge DeCarlo ruled his domain with an iron fist.

Tess found some sort of stoic center deep inside and sat through the proceedings without expression, afraid one of the sketch artists would capture her for the evening news. She refused to turn and look at the people who jammed the room, because she knew Dan was there. She was only too aware of him sitting somewhere behind her.

Barbara McCleary had been allowed to stay on as

lead prosecutor, it was noted by the media. Probably because no one else could be found to take over quickly enough, the pundits agreed, and, after all, an Aspen jury would be a pretty tolerant and sophisticated bunch of folks.

So Tess sat through the jury selection: seven women and five men, a mix of young and middle-aged. She sat through the opening statements, masterly expositions by Barbara and Cody. One promising to prove how Lawrence Bergen had the opportunity, the means and the motive to murder Robbie Childress; the other promising that there were serious flaws in the prosecution's case and much more than reasonable doubt that a man of such impeccable character as Lawrence Bergen had murdered anyone. The show had begun.

Barbara taped "The Judge's Advocate" the day the jury was seated, so she could hear what Craig and Gail thought of it. They might have some insight that Fran Rose lacked. She watched it in her office, alone, eating a bag of potato chips.

"So," Gail was saying, "after three long days, the plaintiff got seven women seated. I think in a case like this, women will have a lot of sympathy for Lawrence Bergen. That's what Cody Morris was aiming for."

"Oh, but that cowboy, juror number thirty, don't you think he'd also be sympathetic toward a man who took justice into his own hands?" Craig asked.

"Maybe," Gail said, "but jurors can surprise you. Frankly, I thought Cody would use one of his peremptory challenges to get rid of the plastic surgeon, number fifty-three. He seemed to be a real law-and-order sort of guy."

"The ski instructor struck me as a bad choice for both sides. He asked to be excused for cause. He apparently makes all his money in the winter, and he was very upset at being chosen."

"Yes, but which side will he take his bad humor out on?"

Craig shook his head, long suffering. "It's always a crapshoot, Gail, isn't it?"

Barbara munched on a potato chip and concurred; still, she felt confident. Fran Rose had been an enormous asset. For instance, she'd found out which of the prospective jurors were card-carrying NRA members, gun enthusiasts, and Barbara had used up three of her peremptory challenges to ax them.

Gail changed to a more general subject. "Overall, Craig, how would you describe this jury?"

Barbara leaned forward, intent on his answer. They were right about the women, she thought, but the men she'd had to choose from were squirrelly, too. She and Fran didn't trust many of them—they could be shoot-'em-up types and ardent backers of Lawrence Bergen.

"Well," Craig replied, "I'd say it's a pretty well-balanced jury. Blue-collar workers, some professionals. A good jury."

Barbara and Fran thought so, too. Except, as Craig had noted, for the cowboy, who was probably still in favor of lynching. But she'd used up all her strikes getting rid of the softhearted sentimentalists who saw Lawrence as a hero.

"We can't forget the mythical sophistication of Aspen juries, though," Gail was saying. "They're supposedly sharp and see through to the truth of things."

"And what about pretrial publicity?" Craig reminded the audience.

Yeah, what about it? Barbara thought.

"Well, I think all the pretrial furor in this case cut both ways, for the defendant and against him. It's a

tough call on which way it could prejudice people,"
Gail said. Then she pivoted to another camera. "The
fact is, we don't want people prejudiced. Our system
requires a fair and impartial jury."

"Right," Barbara said caustically to the empty
room. "Fair and impartial." Then she scrunched up
the empty chip bag and made a perfect overhead shot
into the wastebasket clear on the other side of the
room.

"Keep your edge, McCleary,"she muttered to herself. "Just keep the edge sharp."

The days rolled by, each one an exercise in detach-
ment for Tess. At night she and Sis and Carole con-
soled one another. Lawrence was staying with Cody
for the trial's duration. It was Cody's habit to do this,
provided, of course, his client was not in jail at the
time.

The press was an ever-present irritation, like nagging mosquitoes. The Aspen police and sheriff's deputies did their best to keep Tess and her mother and
aunt away from the worst of the bloodsuckers, but
there were always a few who got through.

"No comment" became Tess's mantra.

The first prosecution witness was the medical examiner, who testified as to the cause of death, condition of the body and caliber of the bullet. Routine
stuff, setting the stage. Then Barbara McCleary
changed gears dramatically and put Ali Barnes, Robbie's fiancée, on the stand.

Ali was adequately weepy the entire time she was
on the witness stand. She'd been carefully prepped, it
was obvious, because she stopped to think before answering Barbara's questions and often looked to the
D.A. as if for confirmation of her answers.

"You were to be married to Robbie Childress, weren't you, Ms. Barnes?" Barbara asked.

"Yes, last July. We were very much in love."

Cody Morris shifted his position and groaned out loud. Someone in the packed courtroom snickered and garnered DeCarlo's glowering displeasure.

"And you were in the tent that afternoon of June 20 of last year?"

"Yes, I was right next to Robbie." Ali paused, then remembered. "The whole time."

Barbara took her through the scene, then, step by step. "So you saw, with your own eyes, Lawrence Bergen shoot Robbie?"

"Yes."

A buzz in the courtroom.

"You saw the gun in Lawrence Bergen's hand, you saw him pull the trigger, you heard the shot...."

"Leading the witness," Cody interrupted, bored.

"Sustained. Tell the story in your own words, Ms. Barnes," Judge DeCarlo said.

Ali looked startled. "In my own words? Okay, well, I saw Mr. Bergen with a gun. I heard a shot. Robbie fell down, then everyone started screaming and running."

"Thank you, Ms. Barnes. Oh, one more thing," Barbara said. "Can you point out the man who shot your fiancée?"

Ali pointed, her hand shaking, tears overflowing her eyes, but somehow not smudging her mascara. "There he is, that's him." And everyone in the room looked at Lawrence Bergen.

When it was time for cross-examination, Cody stood up and shot his cuffs. He beamed in a fatherly way at Ali Barnes, then his expression sobered, and he said, "All of us here are very sorry for your great loss, Ms. Barnes."

"Thank you." Ali's spiky lashes lowered demurely.

Then he began to question her in minute detail about the moments before and after Robbie's murder.

"You saw the gun, Ms. Barnes?"

"Yes."

"Describe it."

"Well, it was, you know, a gun."

"Big, small, silver, steel, black, semiautomatic, single-action?"

"Objection, badgering," Barbara said.

"Please describe the gun, Ms. Barnes."

"Well, sort of small, but well, not too small. And sort of silver-colored. Maybe steel...metal, anyway."

"And you saw it in Mr. Bergen's hand?" Cody smiled. "Which hand?"

"Which hand?" Ali looked at Barbara. "I don't know. It all happened so fast."

"You saw it, though."

"Yes."

"And you saw him pull the trigger?"

"Yes."

"Well, Ms. Barnes, if you saw the gun so clearly, I wonder why you didn't warn Robbie? Or yell?"

"There wasn't time. Like I said, it all happened so fast."

"But not so fast that you couldn't see the gun in Mr. Bergen's hand? You're under oath, Ms. Barnes."

"Yes, no, I mean I saw it, I did."

"And then what happened to the gun?"

"He must have given it to his daughter," Ali said, pointing to Tess. "To her."

"You saw this happen?"

"Everyone knows that," Ali said emphatically.

Cody looked at Barbara and grinned. "Move to strike the witness's last statement, Your Honor. Hearsay."

"So noted."

"Now, Ms. Barnes, on to another subject. Is it true you've signed a three-million-dollar contract with a major publisher to write a book about Robbie Childress's murder?" Cody asked.

"Well, yes…"

"And isn't it also true, Ms. Barnes, that if, indeed, you did not witness the actual shooting, your contract wouldn't be worth much?"

"Move to strike, Your Honor," Barbara called out.

"Overruled, Ms. McCleary. It's pertinent."

"I did see it, I did," Ali said.

"And isn't it also true, Ms. Barnes, that you are now engaged to marry Lloyd Hicks, the director of last year's action thriller *The Beast*?"

"Yes," Ali whispered.

"That is, by the way, a very lovely diamond, Ms. Barnes," Cody said pointedly.

"Objection, irrelevant," Barbara snapped.

"Sustained," the judge agreed.

But everyone had heard: Ali Barnes was engaged again, only seven months after Robbie's death.

"No further questions," Cody said with such carefully honed contempt in his voice that no one could mistake what he thought of Ali Barnes's story.

Tess wondered what everyone else thought of it. Hard to judge that, but she was beginning to appreciate Cody's talents.

Barbara had more witnesses, of course, in the following days. The police chief who'd held Lawrence for questioning and the detective who'd taken down his story before Steve Sutton had arrived. They were both good witnesses, straightforward and professional.

"Tell us in your own words what Lawrence Bergen

said when you had him in the station, please," Barbara said to the detective.

"He was very calm. He told us he had not shot Childress, that someone next to him had done it and stuck the gun in his hand, and he wasn't sure, but he had subsequently either dropped or thrown the gun away in shock and confusion."

"Did you ask Mr. Bergen if he'd ever owned a gun?"

"Yes. He said no, he had never owned one."

"And was Mr. Bergen able to identify the shooter?"

"No."

"Even though the man was so close to him he could put the gun in his hand?" Barbara asked.

"That's what he said," the detective insisted.

Barbara shook her head, then she looked at the jury and held her hands out, palms up, exuding utter disbelief.

"Your Honor," Cody protested.

"Enough of the Stanislavsky method, Ms. McCleary. Get on with it," the judge said.

There was still time that day for Cody to cross-examine the police chief and the detective, getting them to admit that Lawrence's story, although unlikely in their experience, could be true. It was all Cody could do, and Tess knew it.

Barbara began calling the first of the festival participants the next day, those who'd been in the tent near Robbie Childress. All their stories were similar: they saw Lawrence talking to Robbie, it was crowded and noisy, they heard a pop. Some had seen Robbie fall, most hadn't.

On cross-examination, Cody got every one of them to admit that no one had heard what the two men were talking about, no one actually saw the shooting itself, and no one saw what Lawrence Bergen did with the gun.

Tess, listening intently, cringed inwardly.

Dan went out for Mexican food that night, sick to death of pizza and sub sandwiches in his room. It was relaxing to walk the cold streets among the masses, the red-cheeked, enthusiastic vacationers. The streets of Aspen were strung with holiday lights, the bare-branched aspen trees on the mall entwined with tiny white ones. Pretty. Artificial but pretty.

The bar of the Mexican place was jammed, its affable host telling everyone, "Ten minutes, only ten minutes' wait," an outright lie; but he did it so nicely no one complained. Dan sat at the bar and had a Dos Equis beer, and he listened to the conversations around him. Mostly they were about skiing. The trial was secondary to the tourists.

He wasn't there for long, munching chips with hot sauce, when he saw Bob Winthrop push his way through the crowd. Winthrop spotted him instantly, and his small features screwed up into a sneer. He pressed forward, his bulk opening a path to Dan.

"Well, well," Winthrop said, "look who's out on the town."

"How're you doing, Bob?"

"Okay, okay."

"That's good."

"You picked the losing side this time, buddy."

"Really."

"Sure did. But I gotta admit, that trick you pulled at the pawnshop was cute."

"What trick, Bob?" Dan asked innocently.

"Cut the crap, Hadley. You got the receipt, cleaned up after your client. Totally illegal, by the way."

"You must be on some weird drug, Bob. I haven't got a clue what you're talking about."

"Right."

"Want a beer? I'd be glad to buy you one."

"No thanks, Hadley. I'm watching my weight."

And they both laughed.

The next morning Dan was at the courthouse at nine, as usual. He didn't have to attend the trial, but he was there every day, nevertheless, listening to testimony, looking for any hint—no matter how small—that a prosecution witness was lying, embellishing, concealing something. If he could prove it, Cody could often destroy the witness's credibility on the stand, making it appear to the jurors that every word out of the person's mouth had been false. It was Dan's job.

And there was Tess. He'd been keeping an eye on her, worried about her state of mind, worried about how she'd do on the stand. He'd sat there day after day watching her up there in the front of the courtroom, her shoulders square, her back straight, and he could only guess what she was going through.

Regret clawed at him; if he'd handled the situation better, if he'd been more sensitive, he could have gotten her to confess and helped her with her burden. But no, he'd been a goddamned caveman, and he knew it now. Now, when it was too late.

That morning he waited outside the courtroom with the usual crowd. The doors weren't open yet, and everyone milled about impatiently. He saw Cody and Lawrence approach the stairs then, and behind them, Carole and Sis and Tess.

It was the first time since Christmas Eve he'd seen her face-to-face. She looked pale, tired but composed. Her hair was pulled back and clasped in a large clip, and she looked beautiful to him. Ethereal. A tired angel, so pale and thin she might float away.

"Tess," he said, moving to her side.

She looked at him, then switched her gaze away and tried to move on. He put a restraining hand on her arm. "Tess."

"What do you want?"

"How are you doing?" he asked.

"I'm fine."

"Good," he said.

"Excuse me, I've got to go," she said, and she swept by him.

Dan listened to the testimony all that day, but his gaze stayed on Tess. He wished he could do something to help her, but he knew she'd never allow that. The enmity she felt for him was final and deadly. He'd seen to that.

There were more Bon Vin Festival attendees that day. Barbara asked the same questions, and Cody asked his. They had all seen Lawrence and Robbie talking, and no one had seen the actual shooting. Routine, boring.

But Barbara McCleary had an ace in the hole for the end of the day. Melodramatic but effective. She showed a videotape of a CNN talk show from last year, before the Childress trial, in which Lawrence was interviewed by a well-known host who covered timely but controversial topics.

Shit, Dan thought, knowing what was coming. Point for the prosecution.

Carole Bergen sat in the courtroom and watched her husband in the CNN interview. When she'd watched its original airing, she'd been proud of him. Proud of his dignity and his clarity and his beliefs.

But now Carole was seized with fear. It made

Lawrence look like a man who wanted vengeance, a man who'd stop at nothing to achieve it.

"You're confident of the outcome of this trial, then," the talk-show host asked soberly.

"Absolutely. I have great faith in the D.A.'s ability. The case is so obvious. There's no doubt in my mind that Robbie Childress will be found guilty," Lawrence stated.

"And if he is found guilty, Mr. Bergen, what do you feel is the proper sentence?"

"Well, of course, that's up to the jury to decide in the penalty phase, but I'm hoping he gets the death penalty."

"You believe in the death penalty, Mr. Bergen?"

"Oh, yes, for certain heinous crimes—and my daughter's murder is one of these—I believe death is the only proper punishment. I believe Robbie Childress deserves to die for what he did to Andie."

Carole could see how bad it looked. She sat there in the artificially darkened courtroom and tried to control her nerves. Cody had warned her there would be bad moments, but she was to remain strong throughout, he'd said, because he'd get his licks in. God, she was trying.

Carole, Sis and Tess left the courthouse that day in a somber mood. Their police escort hustled them through the crowd; they never even saw Lawrence or Cody or the team. It was cold out, and Carole was glad she could pull her coat collar up to hide her face.

As they headed for the police car that would drive them home, Tess had hold of one arm and Sis on the other as they hurried out through the door, down the back steps of the courthouse. But the press and the gawkers were there, too, knowing their route by now. Running the gauntlet, Sis called it. And they had to do it twice a day, every day.

But today was worse than usual, because that tape had looked so bad for Lawrence. Everyone would think about it now, the jurors, the press, the spectators in the courtroom.

Carole kept her eyes lowered until they reached the police car. She felt like vomiting.

Barbara held an impromptu celebration in her office after court that day. The whole team was high on adrenaline and success, and they all knew they'd scored big with the tape.

"A confession before the fact!" Paul Howard crowed, pouring himself a glass of wine. "I love it!"

"Masterful," Barbara said, and then, loving the sound of the word, she repeated it. "Masterful."

Melanie, the secretary, giggled. "Do I get a raise?" she asked.

"We all do," Barbara said, grinning.

"And we have more," Paul said. "Lots more. We're going to win this one, Barbara."

"You bet your ass," she agreed.

"Don't count your chickens," Bob Winthrop said, the voice of reason. "This trial isn't over yet."

"It doesn't matter. We've got it under control," Paul replied.

"Masterful," Barbara said again, drinking her glass of wine in one long swallow. And the best of it was that the jurors would play the tape over and over in their minds all weekend, Lawrence's voice ringing in their brains: "I believe Robbie Childress deserves to die for what he did to Andie."

Masterful, Barbara thought again.

Her joyous mood lasted until she stopped at a red light on the way out of town that evening.

In the opposite lane a familiar car was also halted at the light—Eric's Cherokee. Barbara sat there in her car for what seemed hours, looking straight at Eric, his wife next to him, and their two kids in the back seat.

Maggie, the vicious bitch, was talking to Eric, chattering away, and he was answering. Smiling, nodding his head, his eyes on the red light. He never saw Barbara, never even noticed her. And when the signal changed, he drove past her, not recognizing her familiar car or her sitting in it.

A horn honked, and Barbara realized the light was green and she was still sitting there. She stepped on the accelerator and shot ahead, and by the time she got home, she was miserable. She turned on the TV, switched back and forth to news accounts of the day in court. Everyone agreed how damning the CNN tape had been.

"Masterful," she whispered dully.

TWENTY-THREE

The time passed spasmodically for Tess—the minutes listening to testimony dragged, but the days flew by. It all began to run together in her mind, and she couldn't judge anymore how her father's case was unfolding. The only thing, really, that she could remain focused on was her impending testimony; each day it loomed closer, and it colored her every thought. What would she be asked? What would she answer? Oh, she'd studied the script, but it couldn't cover every eventuality, and she had to wonder if she could lie under oath. For that was what it boiled down to, lying. The moment of truth. How ironic.

The question tortured her night and day. She'd look at her father, sitting at the defense table, so proud, so untroubled, his serenity undisturbed, and she envied him. She wished with all her being that she was as sure of her choice of action as he was.

The witnesses appeared, were sworn in, answered questions. Barbara McCleary was direct and sometimes strident, but she made her points. Cody Morris was always dressed in his Western-style jacket and silver-and-turquoise bola tie, and he, too, made his points, although it was still the prosecution's case. Cody was keeping his ammunition dry.

An expert from the Colorado Bureau of Investigation lab in Montrose testified for half a day on the matter of powder burns and gunshot residue.

"There was residue on Mr. Bergen's jacket consistent with his shooting a .22. The right side of his jacket had more residue, hence we deducted the shooter was right-handed. The swabs from Mr. Bergen taken at the police station that afternoon also showed residue, although his hands were free of residue," the man said.

"I'd like it to go on the record," Barbara said, "that Lawrence Bergen is right-handed."

Tess saw several of the jurors eye her father appraisingly.

"Is it reasonable to conclude that Mr. Bergen got his residue on him from a shooter standing next to him?"

"Well, not really. You see, a small handgun like a .22 only spreads residue six to eight inches, so a person would have to be very close indeed," the man said.

"Thank you, Mr. Franklin. No more questions, Your Honor."

Cody sauntered up to the witness stand. "Mr. Franklin," he said in a gentle tone, "can you explain why there was no gunshot residue on Mr. Bergen's hands?"

"He wore latex gloves."

"Ah, I see. So if he had worn gloves, one would expect them to have residue on them, correct?"

"Yes."

"But the gloves you examined did not contain residue, isn't that so?"

"Well, yes, but they'd been subjected to a lot of

abuse—wine, mud. We couldn't find much of anything on them unfortunately."

"Hm, that's interesting. And how did you know these gloves had been worn by Mr. Bergen, sir?"

"My lab was given them as evidence. I took the police's word for it. My job is not to—"

"Yes, yes. So you tested a pair of gloves labeled as belonging to my client?"

"Yes."

"I see," Cody said with heavy sarcasm. Then he changed his line of questioning. "Mr. Franklin, I saw in your forensic report that the amount of gunshot residue on Mr. Bergen's jacket was less than is usually the case."

"Yes, but still within the parameters of a gunshot from a .22."

"Would you say it was possible that the residue came from a shooter standing very close to Mr. Bergen?"

"Very unlikely."

"But it is within the realm of scientific possibility?" Cody pressed.

"Well, I don't—"

"Is it possible, Mr. Franklin?"

"I suppose so."

"Yes or no, Mr. Franklin."

Reluctantly. "Yes."

"In fact," Cody said, "you've never testified in a case where so little residue was found on the shooter, have you?"

"No, I have not," Mr. Franklin admitted.

"Objection!" Barbara barked. "Your Honor, Mr. Morris is quibbling about vague possibilities. The forensic report states clearly—"

"Sustained."

But the jury had heard.

The forensic psychologist testified. His name was Dick Lambert, and he was a skinny, studious-looking man with thick glasses that were too big for his face. Barbara skillfully directed his testimony to show that Lawrence Bergen was a man fully capable of planning and executing a murder to avenge his beloved daughter's death.

Tess listened and felt defeat settle on her like a heavy weight. Mr. Lambert was a very good witness. Because he was right, Tess had to admit.

Cody had a rough time with the man, unable to make him back down from his assessment of Lawrence. At last he scored one point, however.

"So, Mr. Lambert," Cody asked, "how many trials have you testified at?"

"Oh, about forty, I guess. I haven't kept count."

"Mm, I see. Forty trials. That's impressive. Tell me, Mr. Lambert, have you ever testified on the side of the defense?"

"Well, actually, the prosecution usually requires my services."

"So, you've never, not once in your forty-odd trials, ever testified for the defense?"

"No."

Cody's face fell into lugubrious folds and he shook his head. "Is everyone guilty in your eyes?" he asked in a concerned voice. Then, quickly, before Barbara could object, he said, "Sorry, I withdraw the question, Your Honor."

Barbara sat at her table, fuming.

The day approached relentlessly, the day Tess would have to testify. She studied the jury and wondered what they thought, what they would think of her. She studied her father and marveled at his self-possession.

Carole and Sis did not talk about the trial in the evenings. It was an unspoken rule. They spoke of everything else, the weather, the way the town filled with people, the beautiful fireworks set off on the Saturday night of the January Winterskol celebration. They kept their spirits up as well as they could, and listened eagerly to Cody's nightly pep talks.

Lawrence remained unruffled. Somewhat removed but pleasant to everyone. Impossibly pleasant.

The prosecution's case rolled along, hitting snags whenever Cody stood up to cross-examine a witness. The pawnshop owner was next on Barbara's witness list, and Cody was looking forward to doing the man in. "Don't miss the show tomorrow," he told everyone.

Nate Huff had come from Salinas for the trial. He was a small man, muscular, with lank hair slicked back and a new suit that was too small for him.

Barbara established who he was, what his business was, and asked him to point out the man who'd entered his shop in February of last year to buy a handgun.

"He's over there," Huff said, pointing.

"Let the record show Mr. Huff has indicated Lawrence Bergen," Barbara said smugly. "And can you recall what kind of gun you sold Mr. Bergen?"

"A .22-caliber pistol. In very good condition."

"Let it be noted," Barbara said, "that the bullet recovered from Robbie Childress's body, as already testified to by the CBI lab and the medical examiner, was a .22-caliber bullet." Then she smiled and said, "Thank you very much, Mr. Huff, no more questions."

Cody started right in on the fact that the gun was unregistered. "You do know, Mr. Huff, that the law requires you to register every gun you sell?"

"Yes, sir."

"Then why is this gun you allegedly sold my client not registered?"

Huff shrugged. "I did the paperwork. I can't help it if some bureaucrat somewhere lost the stuff."

"How convenient," Cody mused. "The government lost your paperwork. My goodness, how careless of them." He paused, then went on, looking down at one of his shirt cuffs, adjusting the silver-and-turquoise cuff link. "But you do, naturally, have a sales receipt for the gun."

"Uh, I had one, but—"

Barbara stood up abruptly. "Mr. Huff has testified that Mr. Bergen bought a gun from him. I don't see—"

"Your Honor, I really do have to establish whether there is proof beyond a reasonable doubt that my client did indeed purchase a gun," Cody said.

"I'll allow it," DeCarlo replied.

"You don't have a sales slip, then?" Cody asked.

"Well, I did, but it was taken out of my office."

"It was taken out of your office, Mr. Huff? Oh, dear, did you have a break-in, then, a burglary? Was anything else stolen?"

"Well, no, but—"

"Nothing. A pawnshop, all those valuable items for the taking, and nothing was removed but a single sales slip?"

"That's right."

Cody turned to the jury. "No registration, no sales slip, but Mr. Huff contends that Lawrence Bergen bought a gun from him. Of course, Mr. Bergen has been in the news, on television a lot, and his plight is well-known, so I wonder—"

"Objection! Pure conjecture!"

"Sustained."

"Why didn't you come forward with this information in June, Mr. Huff?" Cody asked. "Certainly you knew the police were trying to locate the murder weapon."

"I didn't know," Huff muttered. "I didn't watch TV."

"Even though there's one on all day long in your pawnshop?" Cody asked.

"I don't watch it," he muttered. "But I'm telling the truth about him buying that gun from me. I even took a polygraph, one of those lie-detector tests and—"

Cody held a hand up, stopping him. "The results are not admissible as evidence, Mr. Huff, so we really don't need to hear about it."

"Yeah, well, the D.A. lady told me to tell you that, so you'd believe me."

"Well, well," Cody said, glowering at Barbara, who was smiling triumphantly. "How Machiavellian of you, Ms. McCleary."

"No personal remarks, please," the judge said. "The record will record that Mr. Huff took a polygraph test, although its results are not admissible. Go on, Mr. Morris."

Cody turned back to Nate Huff, studying the man for a minute before asking, "Is it true, Mr. Huff, that you contacted several tabloids trying to sell your story?"

"No, not at all."

"I can get three editors to come here and testify that you called them," Cody said. "Should I do that?"

Huff paled. He said nothing.

"Should I get them, Mr. Huff, or do you wish to retract your denial?"

Still no answer from Huff.

"Is it true, then, that you have a vested interest in making us believe you sold the murder weapon to

Mr. Bergen when indeed there is no proof you actually did so?"

"Mr. Morris," the judge warned.

"Withdrawn, Your Honor. I'm done with Mr. Huff."

On redirect, Barbara made sure the jury heard all about the polygraph Huff had taken.

"Tell us about the test," Barbara said.

And even while Cody was leaping to his feet to object, Huff said, "I passed it. I was telling the truth."

"Your Honor," Cody protested.

"Yes, yes, Mr. Morris, we'll strike it from the record. Enough of that, Barbara."

"No more questions," she said, unable to hide her glee.

The final day of the prosecution's case dawned— the day Tess was scheduled to testify. She hadn't slept well, and she couldn't eat breakfast.

"Honey, eat something. You'll get sick," Carole said.

"I will later. When it's over." She couldn't bear her mother's solicitations or her aunt's grave expression.

She dressed in a navy blue wool suit approved by Cody, one that made her look suitably respectable. And believable, she assumed.

She tried to put on makeup, but her hand shook, so she had to settle for lipstick alone.

The worst, she kept thinking, would be taking the oath: "I swear to tell the truth, the whole truth and nothing but the truth." And after she'd said those words, her right hand raised, her left hand on a Bible, would she then do what she'd sworn? Would she? Could she?

She'd heard Cody explaining it to the boys at one of their sessions. "Look, everybody lies in trials. The witnesses lie, the lawyers lie, the accused lies, the police lie. It's the name of the game. You assume it."

But that didn't provide Tess with an answer, either; she wasn't one of those people who took the truth lightly. It was precious to her, necessary.

But protecting her father and obtaining justice for Andie were just as precious and necessary, and therein lay the conundrum.

They were driven to the courthouse by a policeman, as usual. She worried incessantly about her mother's reaction should Carole learn the truth about her husband and her daughter, but Carole wouldn't stay home.

The media was waiting at the back door of the courthouse. The police rushed her through. It was a bitingly cold, sunny January day, and Tess shivered uncontrollably even in her coat.

Inside, there was more room, and Tess stopped and took a deep breath.

"You holding up okay?" came a voice next to her. Dan.

"No," she said.

"Can I do anything? Coffee? A glass of water?"

"No," she said, "you can't do anything."

He stood there looking at her, a frown drawing his sandy brows together. "Listen, Tess, hang in there. Do what you have to do. Not what you think your dad wants you to do or Cody or anybody else. What you can live with."

She searched his face. "Why are you telling me this?"

He shrugged. "Somebody needs to say it."

"Thanks," she said softly. God how she wished she could reach inside and tear out her feelings for this man, tear them out of her body and hurl them from her forever.

She was allowed to go up to the front of the courtroom to talk to her father and Cody for a minute before she had to wait out in the hall to be called to the stand.

Cody gave her a confident smile. "Just go with the script," he said. Lawrence looked at her, just looked, and she couldn't help hearing Dan's words in her head as she went out back into the corridor. *Do what you can live with.*

The day began.

"Please call your first witness, Ms. McCleary," DeCarlo said.

"I call Theresa Bergen to the stand," Barbara said in a clear voice. She looked stunning in a black suit, short enough to show off her long legs. She stood tall and straight, her cropped hair accentuating the bones in her face.

The bailiff called Tess. She rose. Her knees were weak. She took a deep, shuddering breath and began the walk to the witness chair. She felt dizzy, as if she might faint. Cody whispered as she moved past, "Don't worry, I'll protest until they all throw in the towel."

But could Cody really protect her?

She finally reached the chair. The courtroom was breathlessly quiet as the clerk swore her in. She repeated the words of the oath, the fateful words, and her voice was small. Dots swam in front of her eyes. Was she swearing away her family's survival with these words? Was she swearing away her father's freedom, the meaning of Andie's life and death?

She felt the urgent and fearful weight of final justice, and it was too heavy for her to bear.

Barbara met her eyes as she sat in the witness chair; there was a slight smile on the D.A.'s face, and Tess could hear her unspoken thought: *You're all mine now, Tess Bergen.*

Barbara reminded the court that Tess was a hostile witness, and they were to take that into account. Then she began her questions.

She led Tess through her walk to the tent that June day—they'd all been over this before.

"It was very crowded," Tess explained, "and I got there late so I could avoid the worst of it."

"What time was that, Ms. Bergen?"

"Around one-twenty."

"And then what did you do?"

"I went into the tent, and I tried to get over to where my dad's tables were. It took me a few minutes because I could hardly move."

"And did you finally reach your father?"

"Yes, I did."

"What was he doing?"

"I could only see his back. He was talking to someone."

"Did you see the person he was talking to?"

"No, it was too crowded."

"And then, Ms. Bergen, tell us what happened."

"I...I've never been quite sure what order things happened. It was so crowded and noisy. I guess I heard a noise, a pop, and then people started screaming."

"Did you see your father then, Ms. Bergen?"

The words came from far away, as if meant for someone else. Did you see your father then? Yes, she saw him, saw him whirl around, recognize her, his daughter, saw the shock in his face. She saw herself, as in a speeded-up film, snatch the gun from his hand and turn to run. She saw herself swept up in the panic, pushed along, falling, getting up, running, stumbling, outside in bright sunlight, running, run-

ning. Away from the tent, along the street, past the
Gant condo. She heard sirens split the air, but she
raced up Ute Avenue, up the bike path. Hot, sweating, the gun banging against her side in her bag. Past
the few houses. The cemetery. The cool, shaded,
abandoned old cemetery. She stopped suddenly,
panting, then rushed into the peaceful aspen groves,
past rusted iron grilles and crumbling, overgrown
tombstones. No one had been buried there in a century. She saw herself drop to her knees in front of a
small white marble tombstone—and its engraving
etched itself forever on her brain: Lettie Nevitt, Aged
Thirty-three Years, Gone But Not Forgotten. The
same age as Andie was, she thought, and she grabbed
a sharp rock from the ground, gasping for breath,
sweating, and she began to dig.

"Ms. Bergen, please answer the question," Barbara
was saying.

"What? Excuse me, what was the question again?"
Tess asked, her pulse pounding in her ears.

"Did you see your father after you heard the shot?"

"Well, yes, I guess I did, for a minute, but everyone
was screaming and running."

"Ms. Bergen, did your father give you the gun
then?"

"Objection," Cody said calmly. "It has not been established there was a gun."

"I beg your pardon," Barbara said. "All right, Ms.
Bergen, did you see a gun in your father's hand?"

"Objection," Cody said. "Ms. Bergen's deposition
states clearly that she did not see what happened between her father and Robbie Childress."

"Your Honor," Barbara said, "this is the trial, not
the deposition, and I—"

"I'll allow the line of questioning," DeCarlo said.

Barbara shot Cody a triumphant look.

"Did your father give you the gun, Ms. Bergen?"

"Objection, badgering the witness."

"Mr. Morris, enough," the judge said.

Barbara asked again. "Was there a gun in your father's hand?"

"I…I couldn't see very well. It was crowded."

"Please answer the question, Ms. Bergen."

"I'm not sure. It was such a huge crowd."

The judge stopped Barbara and said to Tess in a kindly but firm voice, "You must answer the questions, Ms. Bergen. Yes or no. Proceed, counsel."

"Did your father give you the gun?" Barbara repeated.

The courtroom was deathly silent. Everyone there, everyone massed outside, every news program in the country, they all awaited her reply. Everything hung on her answer. She remembered Dan's words again: *Do what you can live with.*

"No," Tess said in a strong voice, "my father did not give me anything."

There was a murmur in the courtroom that built into a cacophony of voices. Judge DeCarlo banged his gavel and called out for order. The uproar continued, though, and Tess could see Cody grinning and her father staring at her.

Tess sagged in the witness chair, her job done. She hadn't lied, she hadn't. She was the one who'd pried the gun from her father's fingers. I can live with it, she thought, realizing that truth for the first time.

Barbara McCleary glared at Tess, hands on her hips. "No further questions," she snapped. "The prosecution rests, Your Honor."

Cody watched "The Judge's Advocate" that night. He was dying to know what they thought of Tess's testimony. He himself had been thrilled with the way she'd come through. Like a trouper. And believable as heck. That was one tough gal, and he was proud of her.

"Are you insinuating that Tess Bergen was not being entirely truthful?" Craig was saying.

"I think I am," Gail replied.

"Oh, come now, that woman was as honest a witness as I've ever seen. You're too suspicious, Gail."

"I see Cody Morris's hand behind her testimony."

"You think he told her what to say?"

"I have no idea, Craig."

I did not, you smart-mouthed female, Cody thought. She knew what she had to do without a lick of coaching.

"If a lawyer knows a witness is going to lie on the stand, he can't put that witness up there, Gail. It's enough to get a lawyer disbarred, for goodness' sake."

"Ah, but if he gets away with it and it works, Craig, he's won the case. A disreputable attorney could easily do it, it's done every day in courts all over the country."

You bet it is, Cody thought. But not by me, missy. I have a more subtle touch. And I still win my cases.

"You don't mean to imply that Cody Morris is disreputable, do you?" Craig raised a brow.

"Certainly not. He is a respected and successful member of the bar," Gail intoned.

Lying bitch, Cody thought, then he chuckled to himself. This was turning into a street brawl. And he'd been in his share of those. Always won, too.

Tess spent the weekend recovering from her ordeal, like a climber who'd made it back down from Mount Everest, depleted, exhausted.

She hadn't lied.

She slept a lot. Twelve hours on Friday night, ten on Saturday. And when she wasn't asleep she was curled up in bed, thinking, praying that Cody would turn the trial around in her father's favor. She asked herself a hundred times over the weekend: Had her testimony helped? Had anyone believed her?

On Sunday morning she decided she had to get out and go for a walk. Alone.

"Are you sure?" Aunt Sis said. "You know how the media is. Someone will recognize you."

But Tess was insistent. She put on a big black parka, a black knit hat, a long black scarf, which she wrapped around her nose and mouth, and she headed out.

It was a bitterly cold morning, but clear as a bell. On the mountain the skiers would already be carving turns in the fresh powdery snow that had fallen yesterday. She would have liked to have been up there, skiing. Now there was a novel concept. There were actually people on that mountain oblivious to her troubles.

She started down Durant Avenue, her boots crunching in the new snow. She'd just passed the Little Nell Hotel, when she paused and thought, What the heck, her father and Cody would be up, putting the finishing touches on the defense strategy.

When she knocked and Steve Sutton let her in, the whole team was already gathered. She looked around, greeting everyone, taking off her coat, mouthing thank-yous to the unanimous congratulations over her testimony. One person was conspicuously absent, though. Dan. She'd expected to see him, had been prepared when she'd entered the hotel lobby. Well, good, she thought. This was easier.

Lawrence kissed her on the cheek and smiled, saying, "God, Tess, I'm glad you're done with that." She longed for her father to hold her and tell her how grateful he was, how he knew they were in this together, how he no longer felt guilty about her actions. But it wasn't going to happen. Her heart ached.

After a time she began to feel awkward. Her testimony was over and she was in the way now. And her father...he was in a friendly mode, chatting with everyone, his true feelings buried so deeply that no one was going to uncover them. Least of all her.

Barely noticed, Tess stood and put on her coat. She wondered why she'd stopped here in the first place. To see her father? To get a few pats on the back for her performance on the stand? Or was it something else, someone else. Someone who wasn't even here.

"I'm going for a walk," she announced, trying not to break into the conversation.

"Alone?" Patrick asked, looking up.

"I'm incognito," Tess said, returning a smile, giving everyone a wave. "See you later."

But at the elevator Cody was suddenly there. "He's in Florida," Cody said, putting a hand on her coat sleeve.

"What?"

"Dan. Dan's in Florida. He left late Friday."

"Cody, I really—" she began.

"Ferrara took off."

"Oh. You mean Frank ran?"

"Looks like it. So Dan went after him."

"Well, I hope he finds him," Tess said, punching the elevator button. "I really do."

"Don't be too hard on him," Cody said then, his hand still on her arm.

"Excuse me?" she said.

"On Dan, honey. The pain he suffered as a child is kinda like an old pair of boots that still hurt your feet. You know you've gotta get rid of the goldanged things, but somehow they're too familiar to just toss away."

The elevator came and went and Tess merely stared at Cody. Finally she nodded. "Was I that obvious?"

"Uh-huh."

"Dan, too?" she dared to ask.

"Yeah, Dan, too," Cody said.

She took her walk. And later that same day she took another walk, only this time in the opposite direction, up Ute Avenue along the snowpacked path toward the cemetery.

Walking helped her to stop thinking. And she didn't want to think. But as she moved past the old Ute cemetery and the light of day dimmed, she paused, considering, then she moved on, the cold embracing her, the moon casting chiaroscuro shadows on her path.

Dan leafed through an in-flight copy of *Time* but had no idea what he was reading. His thoughts were elsewhere.

"Man, this sucks," Frank Ferrara said from the seat next to Dan's. "You're determined to ruin my life, Hadley."

"Shut up," Dan muttered.

"I don't know what you think's gonna happen when Cody Morris puts me on the stand. I've got nothing to say."

"Shut up," Dan repeated, and he turned another page.

"Everyone knows what the verdict's going to be. People are on to your tactics. This really sucks."

Dan looked out the window and locked his jaw. He couldn't get Tess out of his head. It was as if he was diseased. He saw the torment and anguish on her face

as she'd entered the courtroom the morning she'd testified. He saw her trying to make eye contact with her
father and failing, and that hurt him. The Bergens had
always stood together. A real family. But ever since
Tess had taken the gun from her father, a rift in the
love and trust had opened. And now it was a chasm.

Yeah, it hurt. It always would, and he'd always feel
guilty. If he hadn't helped get Childress off... But that
was beating a dead horse.

"I don't suppose you found my friend, the Austra-
lian chick," Ferrara was saying in Dan's ear. "Nah,
you wouldn't even try. Why would you want to alibi
me? You wanna make it look like I did Robbie. Why
would you help me?"

Dan said nothing.

Tess. She'd done pretty damn well on the stand,
held up to McCleary. And Tess had barely flinched
when she'd told the court—told the whole world—
that her father hadn't given her the gun. Hell, even
knowing Tess, Dan almost had to believe it. But
would anyone else? It was hard for him to judge, because he was so close to the case. He'd been studying
the jury, though, and he was very hopeful.

Dan wondered how the verdict—innocent or
guilty—would affect the Bergens. He hoped they
could handle it; he'd hate to see them destroyed. That
would be the worst, because there weren't many families as close, as solid, as the Bergens. Well, not in
Dan's experience, anyway.

And to think that he'd been instrumental in their
demise just about killed him.

If he had a family, he'd never let anything tear it
apart. Never. No matter what.

But then, what the hell did he know about families?

He could, of course, still have one of his own. He
wasn't that old. But the only person he could imagine

fitting into his life was Tess. And he'd blown it. He'd had his chance. He could have told her his darkest secrets—that he was scared right down to his socks of love and commitment. Scared he'd be left high and dry. And that "something good" he'd been awaiting all his life was just a fairy tale. It wasn't waiting around any bend in the road.

Yeah, sure, he could really see himself telling all that to Tess. Right. Like he was one of those guys who could bare his soul and then burst into tears. No way. Maybe it worked for some, but he'd feel like an idiot. So, yeah, he'd screwed it all up because he was a chicken. Too damn bad.

"My face'll be all over the tabloids again...." Ferrara was rattling on.

Dan turned toward him. "So write a book. Sell your story. You know the drill."

"Maybe I don't want to."

"Sure," Dan sneered.

"I can't believe you came after me, Hadley. You're a real prick, man."

"And you're a rocket scientist," Dan shot back. "You made it so easy I laughed out loud." Dan thought about that. He'd flown into Florida, staked out the sister's trailer, and sure enough, Frank had shown. Why? Because he'd been staying at a friend's in Fort Myers, been invited to a black-tie affair, and he'd needed his tux, which had been at his sister's. What a joke.

"Yeah, you sure know how to make yourself scarce," Dan said.

"Fuck you, Hadley."

Dan grinned. "Yeah," he went on, "I called Cody and told him I had you. And you know what? Cody just chuckled. He's loving it."

"I don't know why."

"Because you ran. Because now Cody can bring that out on the witness stand. You know how that's going to sound?"

"No. How?"

"Like you're guilty of something."

"Bullshit."

"Whatever," Dan said, and he turned back to the window.

TWENTY-FOUR

Cody started small, constructing his case like a composer building to a symphonic crescendo. He put several festival participants on the stand, with their unvaried answers that they hadn't seen Lawrence shoot Robbie. Then he added a couple of experts on bullets and gunshot residue, who stated that residue from a .22 could easily spread to someone next to the shooter. All repetitive stuff. Nice tunes but only background. Then he began to pull out the stops, one at a time, and the music became louder and multilayered, both more direct and more subtle.

Sandy Martinez, the defense psychiatrist, looked like the college professor he was, careless curly hair, sagging tweed jacket, even a lopsided bow tie. But his testimony was unequivocal and convincing.

"A man like Lawrence Bergen, imbued with all of society's rules, taught all his life not to lie, cheat, steal, commit adultery or to kill, could never, in my opinion, raise a hand to anyone in violence," Martinez said. "He has no history of violence, no childhood trauma to induce antisocial behavior, no feelings of inadequacy or a need to hurt others. He is simply incapable of murder."

"Thank you, Dr. Martinez," Cody said fervently.

Barbara attacked the psychiatrist from every direction, but he refused to budge in his opinion. Finally she gave up. "No more questions," she said, and with a baleful eye she watched Martinez make his way out of the courtroom.

The next day saw Dennis Wilson called to the stand. He was very nervous, and even from the rear of the courtroom everyone could see the sheen of sweat glistening on his face. His voice was so weak he had to repeat his answers.

"You lived in Robbie Childress's caretaker unit, Mr. Wilson?" Cody asked.

"Yes."

"And you had a quarrel, is that correct? He terminated your employment, and you had to move out in the middle of the winter?"

"Yes."

"Speak up, Mr. Wilson."

"Yes."

"And, at the time, your wife was pregnant?"

"Yes."

"Was it a hardship for you?"

"Yes."

"And, Mr. Wilson, did you threaten, in front of friends, to kill Robbie Childress?"

"No."

Cody held up papers. "But I have right here depositions—"

"I was just mad. It didn't mean anything."

"Oh, I see." Cody raised his eyebrows and appeared to consult some notes at his table, then he returned to Wilson. "Shortly thereafter, that is, after your threats, the windshield of Mr. Childress's Range Rover was smashed by a rock, and the police questioned you about it, is that correct?"

"Yes, but I didn't do it."

"Well, surely, Mr. Wilson, you had reason to greatly resent Mr. Childress."

No answer.

"Didn't you?" Cody pressed.

"I guess so."

"Where were you at 1:20 p.m. on Friday, June 20, of last year?"

"In the tent."

"Thank you, Mr. Wilson."

Barbara questioned the man gently, reasserting that while he was angry at Robbie, he didn't shoot him.

On redirect, Cody dropped the bomb.

"Do you own a handgun, Mr. Wilson?"

The man seemed to shrink in his skin.

"Well, Mr. Wilson?"

"No." He licked his lips.

"But I have here a copy of a registration for a .22. How could that be, Mr. Wilson?" Cody held the piece of paper up in his fingertips.

"I...I lost it years ago."

"That's interesting. Well, I'm sorry for your loss, Mr. Wilson," Cody said sarcastically.

"Your Honor—" Barbara began.

"Withdrawn," Cody said.

"You may step down, Mr. Wilson."

Roger Pearl was the next witness. Cody established that he was the man who had written many letters to Lawrence Bergen during and after the Childress trial.

Pearl was composed on the stand until Cody asked if Roger was familiar with antigay statements Robbie Childress had made. "Are any of these documented statements made by the deceased familiar to you, Mr. Pearl?"

"Ah...ah, no, I, ah...no."

"Really." Cody moved to the defense table and picked up a handful of letters, then turned to the judge. "I would like to place into evidence these five letters written by the witness and mailed to Mr. Lawrence Bergen, the defendant."

Roger Pearl turned the color of putty.

After the letters were placed into evidence, Cody walked to the witness stand. "Did you write these letters, Mr. Pearl?"

"I...ah..."

"I can have a handwriting analyst brought in to—"

"Yes."

"We can't hear you, Mr. Pearl."

"I wrote them, yes."

"Now," Cody said, "I'd like you to read these aloud for the jury." He handed them to Pearl, who was now slumping in his seat.

"Please," Pearl breathed, "I...I don't really..."

"Your Honor," Cody said. "Mr. Pearl wrote them. He can read them."

"Mr. Pearl, read the letters," Judge DeCarlo said.

Roger Pearl read haltingly. The ugly phrases fell from his lips like a damning confession. "Robbie Childress must be killed...make sure it's a heart shot...everyone wants him dead." On and on and on. The venom dripped from the pages. When he finished, he kept his head down, staring at the last letter in his hand, and he didn't look up until Cody asked him another question.

"Why did you lie to my investigator, Dan Hadley, about your whereabouts the day Robbie Childress was shot?"

"I didn't lie."

"But, Mr. Pearl, you told him you were in the Cascades fishing, when in reality you'd flown to Salt Lake City to visit...a friend."

"I forgot."

"You forgot. You were actually driving your... friend's car that day, that Friday, June 20, weren't you?"

"Yes." Faintly.

"You left early Friday morning and returned Saturday, correct?"

"Yes."

"I'd like it to go on the record, Your Honor, that Mr. Pearl could easily have driven to Aspen in time to be at the festival tent at one-twenty in the afternoon."

"Objection," Barbara said. "Pure conjecture. There's absolutely not a shred of evidence that Mr. Pearl did anything like that!"

"Overruled. I'll let this line of questioning continue for now."

"Did you drive to Aspen that day, Mr. Pearl? Did you?"

"No, I went to Canyonlands."

"And we have your word on that?"

"Yes."

"But we had your word that you were in the Cascades fishing, Mr. Pearl, and that wasn't true, was it?"

"No."

"Why should we believe you now?"

"Objection!"

"Sustained."

"All right. Well, Mr. Pearl, do you own a .22 pistol?"

"No."

"But you instructed your friend, Teddy Delaney, to purchase a handgun."

"I... He didn't do it, though. And it was only for his protection."

Cody shot Pearl a skeptical look, then he moved on to a new subject. "You took Mr. Delaney's car early that Friday morning, didn't you, and you took a gun, too, didn't you, Mr. Pearl, and you drove to Aspen, got into the tent and shot Robbie Childress, isn't that correct?"

"No, no, no," Roger Pearl wailed.

"Are we really to believe you, Mr. Pearl?" Cody asked softly.

"Move to strike, Your Honor! This is prejudicial and inflammatory."

"So noted. Careful, Mr. Morris," the judge growled.

"I'm finished, Your Honor. No more questions."

Barbara tried her best to repair the damage. She asked Pearl about his mother and his job at Boeing. She tried to present him to the jury as a thoughtful, caring son and responsible citizen.

She brought out the fact that there wasn't an iota of proof that he'd gone to Aspen, no proof that he'd been in the tent, no record of him buying a pass to get in. Pearl answered her questions forthrightly and gratefully.

But it may have been too little too late.

It was the usual gathering at the Little Nell: Cody, Lawrence and Carole, Patrick and Brad and Steve, Tess and Dan.

Oh, Tess was aware of Dan as she sat in the suite munching a piece of pizza and drinking a Coke. She couldn't stop sneaking surreptitious glances in his direction. He was wearing the same shirt he'd worn that night in Monterey, only this time under a heavy wool sweater. And his jeans...were they the same, too? His hands were the same, hands that had tenderly stroked her collarbone and the hollow at the small of her back, her thighs, her breasts. The mouth was the same. The thin lips, the slight tilt at one corner, as if he were amused by life's riddles. The eyes. So blue and deep-set, the gaze penetrating but giving nothing away, a bottomless blue abyss to which everything was drawn in, nothing returned. Oh, how well he'd cultivated that knack of keeping his feelings concealed from the world. He'd slipped and let her in once. But that had been only temporary.

Tess took another bite of pizza and then put the remains of the slice on a plate, wiping her hands on a linen napkin. Typical of Cody. He'd ordered pizza from the local delivery service, then had the hotel bring up china and linen.

She half listened to the lawyers as they brainstormed tomorrow's witness list. "I'd like to see you get Ferrara shaking on the stand," Brad said to Cody. And Steve. "Do you think the judge will allow testimony on his affair with Andie?" Then Steve caught himself and pivoted to Lawrence and Carole. "God, I'm sorry. That was totally insensitive."

Lawrence waved it aside and Carole nodded, then said, "Cody, you were wonderful with that horrible man today. I just know the jury took in every word of those letters. And the business about Canyonpark—"

"Canyonlands," Lawrence corrected her.

"Yes, well," she said, smiling prettily, "that business was certainly food for thought. Where was he, really, do you suppose?"

Tess still watched Dan. The way he listened intently and rarely spoke. The pitch of his head, the thrust of his jaw and how sometimes his nostrils flared ever so slightly before he'd nod or shake his head. She hung like a lovesick puppy on every move he made, every utterance, the way his hair flopped onto one side of his forehead. She hated herself for her weakness. He'd used her in the worst way a man could use a woman. And she'd let him. Yet the truth was she still wanted him.

It began snowing around nine. Tess walked to the window and stared at the snowflakes that swirled down out of the blackness. It was mesmerizing, soothing, even though her head was still swimming with the trial and her father. And with Dan.

The meeting broke up shortly before ten, and those who were leaving the hotel put on coats and hats and gloves.

"I'll walk you home," Lawrence told Tess and Carole, and he followed them out into the hall.

The Bergens and Steve Sutton rode the elevator down together, then said good-night in the lobby. Dan came down a minute later, and Tess made a snap decision. "You go on ahead," she said to her parents. "I'll catch up." Then she turned to Dan. "Can we walk together for a minute?" she asked.

"Sure," he said.

They walked along Durant Avenue, then crossed the street and went down Galena to the brick mall in the heart of downtown. There were hordes of people milling around the streets, peeking in closed shop windows, coming and going from restaurants and bars and nightclubs, snow on their heads and shoulders. The talk was all skiing.

"Can you imagine," Dan said at her side. "A vacation. I'll never think of Aspen like that."

Tess smiled sadly. "Neither will I." Then she looked up at him, blinking as snowflakes settled on her eyelashes. "You're wondering why I'm talking to you."

"No, Tess, I—"

"We could be friends," she said. "Well, a little more than acquaintances."

He gave a short laugh.

"I just wanted you to know I'm not, well, I understand about you...about... Oh, God, I'm embarrassing myself."

"Tess—"

"You've done your best for my father. I'm grateful."

"Jesus, Tess, will you stop? I don't want thanks from you. I took this job for selfish reasons."

"That's okay."

"Is it?"

"Dan, I'm not going to lie to you. Or to myself. I didn't take you...us...that night lightly. You hurt me a lot."

He turned away, shoulders hunched, hands in pockets. "I know, Tess. I didn't mean to, but..."

"But people do what they have to do. I understand that. I'm trying to understand, anyway."

"Ah, Tess..." he said hoarsely. "You never should have gotten near me."

"I couldn't help it," she whispered.

He stopped and faced her and took his hands out of his pockets. A street lamp nearby made a halo of light in which snowflakes spun dizzily. He put his hands on her arms and studied her face. "You'll never know how sorry I was," he said.

Her face was upturned, wet with melting snow, and he bent down. His lips touched hers, warm against her cold skin. She leaned into him, and he put his arms around her, around the bulk of her winter coat, and they stood like that for a long time, enfolded in the darkness and the falling snow and a small measure of peace.

Dan raised his head and let out a long breath. It plumed in the air and drifted away into the darkness. "We shouldn't have done that."

"Why not?"

"It makes it harder."

"Oh. So you're leaving."

"No, I didn't mean..." He hesitated.

"What did you mean?"

"I don't know. I need to do some soul-searching, Tess. I can't give you any answers now."

"You'll never be able to answer me," she said, and she could feel a fist of pain tighten in her chest.

He tried to put a hand on her cheek then, but she turned away. "Tess..." he said.

She couldn't listen to his denials any longer. "Good night," she said, and she started off without him.

"Hey, at least let me walk you home," Dan called after her, but she was rounding a corner, and his words drifted off into the storm.

Dan arrived at the courthouse the next morning, hoping to see Tess. He wasn't sure what he'd say to her if he did see her, but he craved her nearness, craved the sight of her, the sound of her voice, the slightest wisp of her scent. Like a junkie, he was addicted, and he couldn't stop himself from the wanting.

She was already seated in the front, however, and he couldn't get to her. Maybe at the morning recess, he thought.

Today was Frank Ferrara's turn. He'd been under guard since Dan had brought him back to Aspen. They all knew he'd bolt if he could.

But now it was too late for escape; Ferrara was waiting in the hallway outside the courtroom, watched over by a court bailiff and a policeman until he was called.

The clerk spoke, everyone rose, and Judge DeCarlo stalked in. Cody asked for the court's indulgence for a moment before he called his next witness.

"Go ahead," the judge said.

Cody spoke directly to the jury. "Ladies and gentlemen of the jury, my next witness is a hostile one, very hostile." There was a titter of laughter. "And I wish you to take that into consideration. My investigator, Mr. Hadley, had to go to Florida, locate him and fly him back. I think you'll see that this man had the motive, the opportunity and the means, much more than my client did, to shoot Robbie Childress—"

"Your Honor," Barbara said angrily, "this goes beyond indulgence. Mr. Morris is giving his summation! I object strongly."

"Sustained. Call your witness, counselor."

Ferrara slouched in, looking rumpled and belligerent. He got sworn in and sat in the chair.

"Now, Mr. Ferrara, we'd all like to thank you for your appearance at this trial," Cody said. "And I'd like to ask you a few questions now."

"Right," Ferrara said dryly.

"Did you know Andrea Childress?"

"Yes." Sullenly.

"Did you have an affair with her?"

"Yes."

"And you testified to all this at Robbie Childress's murder trial?"

"Yes."

"You also testified that you had a fight with Mr. Childress over his wife, and that he made a threat against you, is that right?"

"Yes." Bored.

"What was Robbie's threat?"

"He said he'd tear my heart out if I got near Andie again."

"He'd kill you?"

"Yes."

"And what was your reaction to this threat?"

"I got the hell out of Dodge. I went back to Florida. Robbie could be a mean son of a bitch."

"You were afraid of Robbie?"

"Yeah, so? Anyone who crossed Robbie had reason to be afraid of him."

"But you did return to Aspen upon occasion, Mr. Ferrara?"

"Sure, I had friends here."

"Were you in Aspen the weekend of June 20 through the 23rd, at the Bon Vin Festival?"

Ferrara hesitated. The courtroom was silent. "Yes," he finally said reluctantly.

"Were you, Mr. Ferrara, in the tent that Friday afternoon for the grand tasting?"

"No."

"You're under oath, may I remind you?"

"I wasn't in the tent."

Cody switched direction. "Do you own a handgun, Mr. Ferrara?"

"No."

"Have you ever owned one?"

"Maybe, I can't remember."

"But, Mr. Ferrara, witnesses confirm that you said you were going to buy a gun to protect yourself from Childress."

"I didn't, though. I left town."

"I see." Cody put a finger to his lips and concentrated for a minute, then he said, "So, Mr. Ferrara, you had an affair with a man's wife, he found out and threatened you, and you even had a fight, but this left you with no animosity whatsoever against this man, only fear of him. Am I stating your case correctly?"

"Yes."

"So, Mr. Ferrara, why did you run last week?"

There was a pregnant hush in the courtroom.

"I...I don't know."

"You don't know?" Cody shook his head. "You don't *know?*"

"I didn't want to testify."

"Why not, Mr. Ferrara? After all, we're engaged in a search for the truth here. My client, Lawrence Bergen, is on trial for his life, and if you can help shed some light on the case, I'd think you'd want to cooperate."

"I can't help Mr. Bergen. I don't know anything about who shot Childress."

"Oh, really? You don't know anything? But you ran and you admit you didn't want to testify. What are you hiding, Mr. Ferrara?"

"Nothing. Nothing!"

"Were you in the tent that Friday afternoon, Mr. Ferrara?" Cody thundered.

"No!"

"Did you go there and get in with your .22 pistol and shoot Robbie Childress?"

"No!"

"Did you—"

"Objection, badgering the witness," Barbara called out. "Mr. Ferrara answered the questions."

"I apologize, Your Honor. No more questions," Cody said contritely.

In cross-examination, Barbara immediately got to the validity of Ferrara's alibi on the Friday in question.

"So you were with your girlfriend, Janet Frietas, at the time Robbie was shot?"

"Yes."

"Where is Miss Frietas now?"

"She's in Australia. She went home."

"Unfortunately we couldn't get Miss Frietas to return to testify, but I do have a letter from her, saying she was with Mr. Ferrara that day." Barbara held up the letter. "I'd like to enter this in evidence as exhibit number fifty-two."

"So entered," the judge said.

On redirect Cody had only one question. "Mr. Ferrara, did anyone else, anyone at all, see you the afternoon of June 21 of last year?"

"No," Frank Ferrara said. "Janet and I...we spent the afternoon alone."

"Mm," Cody said as if in total disbelief, and then he dismissed the witness. The jurors watched Ferrara all the way out of the courtroom, and juror number nine shook her head in disgust.

The next witness was a security guard on duty at the festival tent the day of the murder. He was an elderly man with a shock of white hair. Retired, he told the court, but he volunteered for a lot of community events.

"Yes, I was on duty that day. Right at the main entrance."

"Let me ask you, sir, is it possible for people to beat the security system and get into the tent without buying a pass?" Cody asked.

"It sure is. We try our darnedest, but there's always someone who sneaks in, especially if they know the ropes. It's usually locals who are too cheap to pay for a pass."

Someone stifled a laugh.

"Could Frank Ferrara have gotten in like that?"

"Objection, Your Honor. Conjecture."

"All right. Let's take a hypothetical local resident who wanted to get in the tent. Could he do so?"

The guard, whom Cody knew to have a daughter the same age as Andie Childress, looked at Lawrence Bergen with obvious sympathy, then said to Cody, "Damn right he could, and with a gun, too."

The courtroom erupted into a cacophony of sound, and Judge DeCarlo pounded his gavel, calling for order. Dan smiled, watching Barbara's futile efforts to shake the security man's position.

The defense case was complete, every witness a note in Cody's symphony, each leading to the final climax, and ending with a bang.

Oh, yeah, Dan thought, Cody was good. But just how good remained to be seen.

TWENTY-FIVE

Tess never watched TV anymore, especially the news. She couldn't bear the images of her father, her mother, herself, up there on the ubiquitous screen for everyone to see. The pictures bludgeoned her every time, no matter how she prepared herself. But even worse, old footage of Andie, of Robbie, their wedding pictures, for God's sake, were paraded across the screen reminding everyone of the whole endless, sordid mess.

But she couldn't resist tuning in to "The Judge's Advocate" for their hour-long special that night.

"I don't care about reasonable doubt," Gail was saying, "or all the hostile witnesses Cody Morris parades through that courtroom who had motives to murder Robbie Childress. This is a smart jury. And they aren't one bit fooled, Craig. They believe Lawrence Bergen did it."

"Gail, Gail, Gail," Craig sighed. "You simply refuse to get it. There's not a person in that entire courtroom who gives one hoot whether Bergen pulled the trigger. To a man, and of course a woman, each and every one of them considers it justifiable homicide."

Was he right? Tess thought. Oh, my God, did peo-

ple really believe that? Would the jury see it that way?
She'd been so cut off from public opinion for so long,
she couldn't judge whether Craig Kramer was right
or not. She hoped, though. Oh, did she hope.

"Justifiable homicide," Gail said, her voice drip-
ping with scorn, "occurs when a person believes himself or his loved ones to be in immediate physical
peril. It does not apply to revenge killings."

"The Bergen family, an innocent family, was in immediate moral peril, if you will, Gail. You shouldn't
read the law so rigidly. It's meant to be pliable. I believe, and I think the majority of the populace believes, that Lawrence Bergen was in an untenable position, as serious, as dangerous to him, as if a gun
were literally held to his head. Justifiable homicide,
yes."

"Fancy semantics, Craig. Even Cody Morris
wouldn't argue that sort of murky law."

"Probably not. He assumes everyone believes it already. In the gut. It's what's right, Gail."

"Well, I suppose you're allowed to spout that kind
of foolishness, but it's not the law. The law needs
stricter parameters and more stringent applications."

"We'll see, won't we, Gail? Tomorrow, when the
case rests."

Tess watched the remainder of the show, then tip-
toed to her bedroom, not wanting to awaken her
mother or Aunt Sis. She was glad she'd watched the
special, praying Craig was right in saying everyone in
the courtroom considered Robbie's death justifiable
homicide. If that was true, then tomorrow, when
Cody rested the case for the defense, the jurors would
find her father innocent. If Craig was right.

She dreamed that night about the gun and Andie,
and even Dan was in it somewhere, standing off to
the side, watching the dream as if he wasn't really a

part of it. It was a strange dream, flitting in all directions. And the strangest thing of all was that Andie was so alive in it.

Tess was awakened the following morning by the voices of her mother, father and aunt in the hall. She blinked at the clock. It was seven-forty-five. She jumped out of bed—court resumed at nine.

As she pulled on her robe, she heard Carole saying, "Oh, God, Lawrence. What if…? I'm so afraid—"

"Shh," Lawrence said. "Cody will rest the case today and everything will turn out okay."

"I just know it will," Aunt Sis said.

"But—" Carole began.

"No buts," Lawrence said. "It doesn't matter what the verdict is, darling, don't you see that? I'm at peace with it. Andie's at peace. Can you understand?"

Tess opened her bedroom door and looked straight at her father. "Are you really at peace, Dad? Are you?" she demanded.

He returned her stare for an agonizingly long moment, and then she saw the most amazing thing: there were tears in his eyes.

"Oh, Dad," Tess said. "Why didn't you talk to me?"

"I couldn't. After what you did… I didn't mean for you to… You know that, don't you?"

"Yes," she said. "Of course I know that."

Lawrence looked at her, met her eyes for the first time in a long time. "Are you okay with it, Tess?"

She held his gaze squarely. "Yes."

"Thank God," Lawrence said.

"And you, Dad, did you mean what you said? You're okay with it, too?"

"I am." He took Tess into his arms and she laid her head on his chest. "Now I'm okay with everything. I wasn't before, but I am now."

"You should have told me right away." Carole suddenly spoke up. "I know you were both trying to protect me from the anguish of knowing, and I let you. I needed to tell you...that it was all right. We should have gone through all this together. Andie would have wanted us to."

And then Lawrence pulled Carole into the circle and Carole cried. Tess did, too.

Sis cleared her throat. "Can I get in on this?" she said, and they all laughed, relief and love enveloping them, and held their arms out to her.

Barbara McCleary was a dark flame, slender and tall, wearing her black suit, her dark eyes flashing ferociously. She paced in front of the jury and ticked off her points. Tess watched, intimidated by the woman's certitude and utter confidence, as the D.A. made her summation speech.

But then, Barbara represented the truth, didn't she?

Her points were clear: motive, opportunity and means.

"Of all the people on this earth, Lawrence Bergen had the most obvious motive to kill Robbie Childress. Despite, no, because of Robbie's not-guilty verdict, Lawrence Bergen took justice into his own hands.

"His opportunity is as obvious. He was the last person seen talking to Robbie. By dozens of people. You've heard the testimony from many of them.

"Means. He bought a .22-caliber pistol from Nate's Pawn. You've heard Nate Huff testify to the sale and identify Mr. Bergen as the man who bought the gun.

"It's a clear case. And while you may have sympathy for Lawrence Bergen, that in itself is not enough to preclude a guilty verdict. Your job is to rule on this case, not on a nebulous idea of justice. You must send the message to every citizen of this country that we cannot, as a society, abide the cold-blooded murder of someone you wish vengeance on. Lawrence Bergen is guilty of the premeditated murder of Robert John Childress and must be punished, or our entire system of law is in danger. Thank you, ladies and gentlemen of the jury. I have confidence that you will do the job for which you are gathered here."

Tess watched the jurors, trying to decipher their expressions, their body language, but they gave nothing away, their faces impassive.

Then Cody stood, a solid middle-aged man with a shock of white hair and a distinctive Western-style jacket over a crisp shirt. He spoke to the jury as a friend, as a neighbor, a buddy, his cowboy twang just evident enough, but not overdone.

"Well, now, ladies and gentlemen of the jury, you've just heard a fiery speech, and I know you've taken it to heart. But, folks, believe me, this case is not about the rise and fall of civilization as we know it. Whatever your verdict, men will not run amok on the streets of our fair land murdering people. Hell, no.

"This case is about one man, Lawrence Bergen, a fellow like you and me. An ordinary guy, a businessman, a good father, a good husband, a good citizen. He suffered a tragedy in his life, a terrible one. Losing a child is, no doubt about it, the worst thing that can happen to anyone.

"And Lawrence suffered, as any of us would in the same circumstances. But, by God, he didn't murder anyone because of it, just as none of you would murder because of the same kind of tragedy.

"He is innocent. Despite Nate Huff's questionable testimony, there is no proof whatsoever that Mr. Bergen ever owned a gun. No one has found a shred of evidence that he bought one or owned one. No one—" Cody paused dramatically "—has ever found the murder weapon. It disappeared—magically, it would seem. Unless you believe the district attorney's theory that Mr. Bergen's daughter somehow conspired with her father and spirited away the murder weapon. Ridiculous. Silliest thing I ever heard." Cody smiled warmly at the jurors. "Now, I'd sure like to believe in magic, but isn't it a heck of a lot more believable Robbie Childress's murderer ran out of that tent in the godawful panic and took the gun with him? I ask you.

"Yes, Lawrence Bergen was there, talking to Robbie just before the gunshot was heard, but no one, not one of the witnesses, could attest to the fact that he saw the shooting. As for Ms. Ali Barnes...well, I leave the credibility of her testimony up to you, folks. And we have brought to this courtroom, ladies and gentlemen, three other men who had equal, no, much better means, motive and opportunity to murder Childress that day.

"Now, if that doesn't constitute reasonable doubt, I don't know what does." Cody looked each of the jury members in the eye, then said in a somber voice, "The prosecution has not survived its burden of proving my client's guilt beyond a reasonable doubt. The district attorney's office has not done its job. Therefore you cannot, in conscience, return a guilty verdict. My case rests, folks, in your hands." He paused. "And in your hearts."

The trial was over.

The jury filed out, and Tess studied them, every one of them, each face familiar to her by now. But she couldn't read anything in the carefully neutral expressions. Oh, God, what did they think?

It was only noon when the jury started deliberations, and Cody had made arrangements for the entire defense team and the Bergens to have lunch in a private dining room at the Little Nell Hotel.

It was a good idea, Tess thought, because they all needed some kind of ritual to come down from the immense tension of the trial.

Tess sat between her father and mother and felt the comfort of Lawrence's strength. She knew that he really didn't care so much about the verdict. He would take what came, because he felt he'd done the right thing. Now that Carole knew and accepted it, now that he'd released Tess from her guilt, Tess could go on no matter what happened.

"They'll return a not-guilty verdict," Brad was saying. "I know it. I could tell by the jury foreman's eyebrows."

"His eyebrows," Steve Sutton said.

"They went together, like this." Brad demonstrated. "He was deciding right then."

"You were wonderful, Cody," Aunt Sis said. "They'll believe you. I would."

"Well, thank you, ma'am." Cody beamed. "I'm very optimistic."

"How long do you think they'll deliberate?" Lawrence asked.

"Till tomorrow, maybe," Cody said. "I don't think it'll take too long. It's not a complicated case."

"I'd like it to be over," Lawrence said simply. "For my family."

Carole put her hand in his and held on tight.

Dan sat across the table from Tess. He was quiet, his face unreadable. He joined in the conversation from time to time, but it was as if he wasn't really there.

"So," Patrick asked him, "what's on your agenda now?"

"I'll go home to San Francisco," Dan said. "Probably return to the old firm." He pushed back the hair from his forehead and smiled. "Although I might work for Cody again if he ever wants me."

"Of course I want you," Cody said. "You did a superb job, son. I have your phone number, don't worry."

Tess thought about that night, the snow falling, settling on Dan's shoulders. She felt his lips on hers, the sweet ecstasy of his kiss. And now he sat across from her, without expression, and she couldn't tell whether he was hiding his feelings from the rest of the team, from her—or from himself.

He'd said he had soul-searching to do. What soul-searching? Either he loved her or he didn't. But no, for Dan things weren't so simple. He came with baggage. He didn't trust his feelings, or hers, she supposed.

She looked at him across the table and wondered what he would decide. She met his eyes, held them for a minute, and he didn't look away. He reached across the table and touched her hand briefly. Tess's heart ached with love for him, with fear, with anxiety about the verdict.

"It'll be okay," Dan said softly, and Tess wondered whether he referred to the verdict or to them.

"A toast," Steve Sutton was saying, "to Cody, the Miracle Worker," and he raised his water glass.

Everyone clinked glasses then, and for a moment they were all united in optimism.

"Well, son," Cody said self-deprecatingly, "the miracle isn't done yet."

The telephone rang in the Bergen condo at three the next afternoon. Everyone froze for a heartbeat, then Lawrence went and picked it up.

"Okay," he said into the receiver. "Yes, we're all ready. We'll be waiting for the car."

He hung up and turned to them, his face grave. "They're back. We have to go."

Carole sobbed once, then straightened her shoulders. Sis hugged her brother. Tess stood slowly, feeling empty, a hollow torso with a madly beating heart inside.

"They're sending the police car," Lawrence said. "It'll be here right away."

The police escort had to clear a path for the Bergens. Microphones on extension poles were stuck into their faces, video cameras abounded, cameras were held high in photographers' hands, flashing photographs over the crowd.

They met with Cody, his assistants, Steve and Dan in the hall outside the courtroom.

"Only a day," Cody was saying. "It looks good. A quick verdict is usually a not-guilty one."

"I hope so," Lawrence said tightly. He was pale but composed, always in control. He'd never break down, Tess knew. Every bit of emotional anguish had gone into his act of vengeance, and he had little left over for self-pity.

They sat in their usual seats. The courtroom was packed and abuzz with speculation. Dan sat behind Tess, and he put a hand on her shoulder. She gave him a grateful glance, then looked forward again, but his hand remained, strong and heavy and comforting. Hope crept into her, a tiny, warm flame. She tried to douse it, but it burned on.

Carole reached for her hand as the jury filed in. No one smiled or looked at Lawrence. They all had identical solemn expressions; their responsibility obviously weighed heavily on them.

The clerk intoned his speech, and Judge DeCarlo

strode in, black robe flapping. Routine, but not the least bit routine today. This day, this February afternoon, snow threatening outside, clouds obscuring the peaks, was different. It was the beginning of the Bergens' future.

"Have you reached a decision?" DeCarlo asked the jury.

"Yes, we have," the foreman replied.

"Let's have it," the judge said, and the clerk, in the infuriatingly slow tradition, took the paper from the foreman's hand, walked to the judge and handed it to him. The judge read it, giving nothing away, handed it back.

"Will the defendant please rise" came the words.

Lawrence stood, Cody beside him.

The verdict was read to the hushed courtroom. "In the case of the State of Colorado versus Lawrence Bergen, for the first-degree murder of Robert John Childress, we the jury find the defendant not guilty."

Tess gasped and felt faint. There was a moment of the most absolute, unnatural silence, and then a burst of applause and cheers, while Judge DeCarlo banged his gavel.

He finally got the crowd quiet and polled the jurors, asked each one if he or she concurred with the verdict. Each and every one gave a firm yes. Their answers were delivered in monotone. "Yes," "Yes," "Yes," came the unanimous verdict, one after the other, from the ski instructor to the plastic surgeon.

"Thank you very much, ladies and gentlemen," DeCarlo said. "You are dismissed."

Tess fell back in her seat. Carole was sobbing next to her, face in her hands. Sis was patting her sister-in-law on the back. Lawrence had sat down again next to Cody, and his head was lowered, his shoulders heaving. Patrick and Brad and Steve slapped one another on the back. Cody grinned, his hand on Lawrence's arm.

It turned into a madhouse then. Lawrence rose and they all held on to each other, laughing and crying, and somehow they were outside, microphones thrust into their faces, cameras clicking and whirring, the crowd swirling around them, people shouting.

For once Tess didn't mind the media. She answered their rapid-fire questions, unabashedly wiping away tears. "I'm thrilled that justice was done. We owe everlasting thanks to the men and women of the jury. We're all very happy and relieved."

"What are your plans now, Ms. Bergen?"

"Oh, I don't know. I'll go home to Monterey, and I guess I'll work on getting my residency. I still plan to be a doctor."

When they left her alone for a minute, she looked for Dan, but she didn't see him anywhere. And it occurred to her that he hadn't been part of the wild celebration in the courtroom. He must have slipped out. An abrupt uneasiness tempered her happiness. She wanted so desperately to share her joy with him. Thank him. Tell him what she felt. Everything. But Dan Hadley was gone.

Barbara McCleary had never been so disappointed in her life. Frustrated, furious, hurt, baffled—she was all those things. She'd made a good case. She'd done everything right. She'd brought the truth to light, goddamn it, the truth. And she'd lost.

She remained in the courtroom after it emptied, alone, shuffling papers, pretending she needed to be there. Not one newsperson approached her for an interview, no one congratulated her for a job well-done or thanked her for her agonizing months of work on behalf of the public she protected.

No one gave a shit about her.

She sank down on the chair, leaned an elbow on the table and rested her forehead on her hand. What hadn't she done? Where had she failed?

The missing gun. She'd underestimated its significance. Or had it been the jury's reluctance to see Bergen punished? They hadn't given any credence to the evidence at all; they'd merely righted some perceived wrong. Or perhaps the jurors, all locals, had in some way punished her for the scandal of her affair.

She would never know.

She stood, gathered her papers and stuck them in her briefcase, and finally left the courtroom. In the broad hallway outside she paused, tempted to escape down the back stairs.

She could hear the crowd out front on the steps of the courthouse, questions yelled, clapping, shouts.

No, she decided, she wouldn't slink away like a scared rabbit. She'd face the world. She'd done her best. For the rest of her life she'd know, deep down inside, that she'd proved Lawrence Bergen murdered Robbie Childress.

A figure emerged from the shadows at the end of the hallway. Barbara drew in her breath. It was Eric.

"Hey, you did your best," he said.

"It wasn't good enough, was it?"

"You never had a chance," Eric said. "I told you." He was studying her, a sad smile on his face. "You going to be okay?"

"Sure, I'm fine. You win some, you lose some. Goes with the territory." She shrugged.

"Good."

"Eric—"

"I have to go," he said hastily.

"Sure. See you."

"Goodbye, Barbara."

Shit, she thought. That was that. There was no mistaking the finality of his farewell. Pile it on, Barbara thought wryly. Dump on me some more.

Oh, well, maybe after the hullabaloo died down, someone would remember her. Maybe someone would still want a book. Why not? Barbara could give them the whole story now, no need for courtroom propriety. She walked out into the cold February afternoon, to the top of the courthouse steps, and drew in a breath.

God, what a zoo.

Cody Morris came out of the mass of people, the crowd parting as if he were Moses, and stood beside Barbara, taking her hand.

Cameras flashed, video operators turned their glass-lensed eyes on them. She straightened and put a gracious smile on her face. A good sport, that's what she wanted to look like. It's not winning, it's how you play the game, she told herself silently.

Bullshit.

It was at that moment Cody leaned close and whispered something in her ear, then he said to the gathered reporters, "This pretty lady is one helluva good lawyer, gentlemen. She scared my pants off more than once in that courtroom. She deserves a whole bunch of respect. She's got a great career ahead of her."

Barbara said, "Thank you," and nodded to everyone, keeping the smile on her face. Cody squeezed her hand, then let go and departed to join his exonerated client. Barbara was left there on the steps of the courthouse facing the media Cody had bequeathed to her.

"How do you feel, Ms. McCleary? What's your next case? Do you think justice was done? Where did you lose the case, Ms. McCleary, on Tess Bergen's testimony or Nate Huff's?" A hundred questions, yelled from a hundred avid reporters.

She gave a few answers, nothing touchy, and asked that they all phone her office for appointments.

"All I can say is, I'm of course disappointed in the outcome of this trial, but I have to defer to the jury's decision. That's our system, and I'm sworn to uphold it. Thank you very much, ladies and gentlemen."

"Ms. McCleary! Ms. McCleary! What did Cody Morris whisper in your ear?"

Calmly she replied, "He congratulated me for a good fight. Now, if you'd let me through... Thank you so much," she said, but as she made her way through the crowd, along the sidewalk to the courthouse annex, she had to hold in hysterical laughter. And when she reached her office and dropped her briefcase on the floor, the laughter finally erupted. What Cody had really said in her ear was that he'd like her to come up to his ranch in Idaho for a little R and R. And "I would sure like the company of one fine-looking, damn intelligent female such as you, Barb."

Barb.

She laughed until her sides were splitting. But when she was finally done, sitting alone in her empty office, she thought, well, maybe I will. Maybe old Barb here will do just that.

Dan leaned against a lamppost across the street from the courthouse and watched the wild charade. There was Lawrence again, giving ten interviews at once, and Cody on the wide stone steps holding forth. Carole and Sis were near the bare-branched apple trees lining Main Street, reporters gathered around them, too. And Tess...he couldn't spot her. Probably over by the entrance to the police department in yet another throng.

He'd done his job. But this time he felt better about doing it. He had to ask himself if he felt bad about Pearl and Wilson and Ferrara, but he guessed he didn't. Hell, they'd probably sell their stories to tabloids and make out like bandits.

He'd go home now and return to investigating cases for hotshot lawyers. It was what he did. But from now on, Dan decided, he'd be more careful about which ones he took. If he didn't believe he was on the right side, he'd turn the case down.

He let out a breath in the cold air, glanced up at a spear of sunlight parting the thick clouds over the mountains, and he wondered if justice had truly been served. He shrugged mentally. He guessed it depended on a person's point of view. For the Bergens the answer was yes. Apparently for the public at large, too. And Dan was making no apologies for himself or his own beliefs. He did have one regret, though: Tess.

He watched from his place by the lamppost, an invisible man. It occurred to him that in the old days he would have retired to the nearest bar. Had a stiff drink.

He had no hankering to do so now. He no longer needed one.

TWENTY-SIX

Cody, of course, threw the victory party at the Little Nell. The whole nine yards: champagne, caviar, pâté, stuffed shrimp, trays of cheeses and meats and vegetables on every available surface.

It was not the victory celebration an outsider would have expected. The atmosphere was rather subdued. Everyone smiled and chatted and talked about their future plans, but present in the suite was the shadow of the verdict—not guilty—when everyone there knew the truth. Tess realized there was always going to be that shadow. She believed there should be. Just as Andie's death was an ever-present shadow on all their lives. And that was the way it should be.

Lawrence and Carole stayed close together, his arm either around her shoulder or her waist, and Carole smiled more often than she had in years. Lawrence rarely smiled. He spoke pleasantly to everyone, accepted the congratulations graciously and talked about his plans for the magazine—he was considering selling it, traveling with Carole.

"She's always wanted to see Africa," he told everyone. "Haven't you, dear?"

Sis nudged Tess more than once. "Look at those two, would you?" she said fondly.

And everyone wanted to know Tess's plans. That was easy. "Residency or die trying," she told them.

Everyone was there, Tess noted, everyone but Dan. She even asked Cody if he knew where Dan was, but all Cody said was that he was sure he'd be right along.

The party went on, and dusk fell and a storm blew in, but Dan never showed up. He'd gone home, she was positive. Packed up and got on the road to California. Her heart fell as if it had been torn in two.

Carole came over to Tess and announced that they were going to pack and leave as early as possible in the morning, and Tess felt a spear of anxiety pierce her belly. She hadn't thought they'd leave so soon. A day. Two, she'd counted on. Enough time to get the gun and somehow destroy it.

"Tomorrow morning?" she repeated.

"Your father wants to go as soon as possible. My Lord, honey, neither of us have been out of this valley since June. June of last year."

"Tomorrow," Tess repeated, and she gave her mother a weak smile. "I better, uh, get on back to the condo and organize my stuff."

"There's time in the morning." Then Carole turned to her husband. "Tell your daughter not to go running off."

"I have things to do," Tess said, and she met his eyes and knew he was reading her mind.

"Are you sure?" Lawrence said carefully.

Tess only hesitated a fraction of a second. "I'm absolutely positive," she said, and her gaze slid away. This was something her mother did not need to know.

But before Tess said all her goodbyes at the door,

Lawrence put his arms around her and hugged her tightly. "I can do this for you," he whispered in her ear. "Maybe I should—"

"No," Tess said against his chest. "You'd never find it. I only hope I can. The snow…"

"So it's outside?"

"Oh, yes," she breathed. "I'll tell you all about it. But not here."

"I love you, Tess," he said.

"And I love you, Dad."

"You'll be okay?"

Tess gave a shaky laugh. "Don't worry. I'll be fine."

"Yes, I know," he said, and he let her go.

She stopped by the condo, changed into jeans and put on a big sweater to wear beneath her heavy parka. Then she found the warmest pair of gloves, the warmest hat, and tugged on her tallest boots. God only knew how high the snow was going to be or if she could even find the spot. So many old tombstones. And now there was a blizzard outside.

She got the big utility flashlight from the trunk of her father's car and a long screwdriver—the only thing she could find that would even begin to work as a digging tool. She needed a shovel. But there wasn't one. And even if there had been, she could just imagine what someone would say if she was spotted carrying a shovel over her shoulder.

"Oh, there's Tess Bergen. Must being going to dig up the gun."

She wanted to laugh. Instead, she tucked the flashlight and screwdriver into the front of her parka, zipped it back up, put her head down against the driving snow and began to make her way up Ute Avenue along the bike path, which had several inches of fresh snow on it.

There wasn't a living soul on the route, and almost

no light, just the faintest illumination from the few houses she passed. And then she was at the cemetery, a rising slope of snow-covered humps and snow-covered trees.

She needed her flashlight but was afraid to turn it on yet. Best to wait until she was deeper into the stand of aspen trees.

She floundered in the snow as soon as she left the path. Crotch deep in many places, it sucked Tess in like quicksand. She sank down and had to crawl her way up to a standing position again.

She went slowly then, testing the snow with her weight. And she wasn't sure where she was. Even after switching on the flashlight, she couldn't tell a thing. First, it was dark, but in the winter it was unfamiliar. And the driving snow, swirling sideways, and the wind howling in the treetops, almost as if the dead were screaming their rage at her intrusion.

Dear God, Tess thought, that was a comforting image.

About halfway up a steep slope she stopped and tried to read the old inscriptions on some stones, but the rock was so pitted and worn she couldn't tell a thing, and the snow was in her eyes. This was close, but not the spot. It had been more level after she'd negotiated the slope. Yes. Somewhere on top.

She moved on, carefully, testing the snow with a boot before putting her full weight down. Step by slow step. Up the slope. The flashlight pierced the eddies of snowflakes that seemed to rush at her out of the blackness. The wind screeched through the branches.

She checked two more half-buried stones, then shone her light on a tall monument. Unfamiliar. She swung the light. Over there. That half-fallen iron frame. She'd seen that before. Yes. Now, where was

Lettie Nevitt, aged thirty-three years, gone but not forgotten?

Tess turned and swung her light to the left and the right. Where was it? Over there? Down in that swale? By those trees? It had been small, still very white. Marble, she guessed. Where was it?

"Dammit," she said, and the storm answered her.

"Tess."

Fright exploded inside her.

"Tess?"

The voice was familiar. She saw him moving toward her from out of the darkness.

"Goddamn, woman," he said, "couldn't you have hidden it closer to the path?"

"Dan," she breathed. "Oh, Dan, how did you...?"

Then he was there. Right next to her, gently pushing the flashlight aside so it wasn't blinding him. "Your father," he said.

"My...?"

"Yes, Tess, he told me the minute I got to the Little Nell."

"But I thought you'd gone."

"I was considering it."

"How did you find me?"

"Followed your tracks," he said. "Now, do you mind if we finish up here before someone else figures it out?"

"You mean...?"

"Yeah, like the D.A. or the cops. I don't know what they could do with the damn thing at this point, but let's not push it. Okay?"

"Okay, Dan," she said, overwhelmingly grateful for his presence.

With both of them looking, they located the little white stone in short order. Digging the gun out was not quite as easy. And the storm, if anything, was worse, really slashing at them now, icy fingers of cold and wet tearing at their noses and cheeks as they both dug at frozen ground that desperately wanted to keep its secrets.

And then Dan had it in his gloved hand. A small metal gun, like a child's toy. Tess stared at it, trying to recall that hot summer day, how it had felt and smelled and banged against her hip. How surprisingly heavy it had been. How dangerous.

"Well, I'll be," Dan said, and he stuffed it in his parka pocket and pulled Tess up by the arm. "Let's get outta here."

"What're you going to do with it?" she asked, taking his hand, following, her head bent to the driving snow.

"Take a boat trip out on San Francisco Bay, I guess."

"No one will find it?" She was practically yelling into the wind to make herself heard.

"Out there? Get real."

They seemed to reach the snow-covered bike trail much faster than it had taken to hike in. And then they were moving quickly down Ute Avenue, toward the condos, which were lit up in the distance. Tess's gloved hand was still in his, and he was practically pulling her along, head bent, shoulders hunched.

"Goddamn, I hate this place," Dan muttered once.

Then they were at her door, the alcove sheltering them from the storm. Tess opened her mouth to say something, to thank him, but Dan spoke first.

"Look," he said, still holding her, but with both hands now, "why don't you drive to California with me in the morning?"

"Dan, I—"

He cut her off. "Let me get this said," he went on.

"If I stop now, it'll take me ten years to get up the nerve to start again. But I don't want to blow this."

Tess held her breath and felt the heat rush into her cheeks.

"I want you to get your residency at a San Francisco hospital."

"You do?"

"And I want you to move in with me. Well, with me and Cleopatra."

"Who's—"

"Never mind that now. Just say yes. I feel like a goddamn fool standing here confessing all this."

"You haven't confessed anything, Dan Hadley."

"I haven't?"

"Do you love me?"

"Of course I do," he said.

"Okay then." She couldn't believe it. She couldn't even think. She only knew how crazy in love she was and how happy. Blissfully happy. "I love you, too, Dan. And I'll never leave you."

"Then it's yes? You will?"

"Of course," Tess said, and she put her arms around his neck and smiled.

He lowered his head. "Tess," he whispered, "if you'd said no..."

"Dan," she whispered back, "don't you think you better tell me who Cleopatra is?"

And then he grinned. That rare, beloved grin of his. "You'll meet her," he said. "But I guess I better warn you. Last time I saw the lady she was pregnant."

Then Dan kissed her soundly.

From the critically acclaimed author of
Iron Lace and *Rising Tides*

EMILIE RICHARDS

Comes an unforgettable novel about two families ruled for generations by a flawless but deadly treasure.

Beautiful Lies

It's a pearl so flawless, it has no price, but those who possess it pay dearly. For generations it has cursed the Robeson and Llewellyn families, unleashing a legacy of rivalry, greed and murder.

Now Liana Robeson and Cullen Llewellyn embark on a heart-pounding odyssey to find their son and the missing pearl. Swept into the wild beauty of Australia, they are plunged into a deadly game with a rival who will go to any lengths to possess a treasure as fatal as it is flawless.

On sale mid-March 1999 where paperbacks are sold!

Look us up on-line at: http://www.romance.net

MER492

One spring morning,
Summer Shepherd disappeared...

THE
DISAPPEARANCE
JASMINE
CRESSWELL

Ordinarily the FBI refuses to negotiate with terrorists. But
Summer is the daughter of the U.S. Secretary of State—so
they clearly have to make an exception.

Why Duncan Ryder received the ransom demands
remains a mystery. Yet it is Duncan who orchestrates
Summer's release, helps her convince the authorities she
didn't stage her own kidnapping and helps rescue her
friend from the same captors. And, in the end, it is only
Duncan who can help her expose the shocking truth
behind her disappearance.

On sale mid-March 1999 wherever paperbacks are sold!

Look us up on-line at: http://www.mirabooks.com   MJC486

Looking For More Romance?

Visit Romance.net

Look us up on-line at: http://www.romance.net

Check in daily for these and other exciting features:

Hot off the press

View all current titles, and purchase them on-line.

What do the stars have in store for you?

Horoscope

Hot deals

Exclusive offers available only at Romance.net

Plus, don't miss our interactive quizzes, contests and bonus gifts.

PWEB

"Stella Cameron is sensational!"
—Jayne Ann Krentz

STELLA CAMERON

UNDERCURRENTS

Mike Kinnear thought Susan Ackroyd was the pushiest woman he'd ever met. She thought he was irresponsible. And yet, Susan's beginning to admit that he's good to have around—especially now.

First her boat was sabotaged. Then the threatening phone calls began. The final straw: a car bomb.

If danger hadn't threatened, Mike never would have guessed that Susan had such hidden strength. And Susan would never have realized Mike knew so much about love. Danger has brought them together. But can they both get out alive?

"Her narrative is rich, her style distinct, and her characters wonderfully wicked."
—Publishers Weekly

On sale mid-March 1999 wherever paperbacks are sold!

Look us up on-line at: http://www.mirabooks.com   MSC495

Let award-winning author

Susan Wiggs

sweep you away to romance and adventure on the high seas!

When an awkward socialite and a fiery, temperamental sea captain embark on the voyage of a lifetime, the result is an unforgettable adventure. En route to exotic Rio de Janeiro, Isadora Peabody discovers a wondrous new world, an unexpected charm school in a motley crew of sailors and a passionate new love for a man she's terrified to believe in...but sure she can't live without.

The Charm School

"...Susan Wiggs at her best. Jump right in and enjoy yourself—I did." —Catherine Coulter

On sale mid-April 1999 wherever paperbacks are sold!

Look us up on-line at: http://www.romance.net

MSW491

Two weeks ago, the only adventures
Lorraine Dancy experienced were
in the movies.

DEBBIE MACOMBER

Now Lorraine's starring in her own version of
Romancing the Stone—except that this is her *life*.
A trip to Mexico's Yucatán coast ends her search
for her father, but it also lands her in trouble—
framed for theft and pursued by both the police
and a local crime boss.

Enter Jack Keller—a renegade who makes
his own rules. As a favor to Lorraine's father he
reluctantly helps her escape. In his boat. Just like
The African Queen.

But with ruthless pursuers...and an attraction to
Jack that's as risky as it is intense, there are
troubled waters ahead....

MOON OVER WATER

**Available beginning April 1999
wherever paperbacks are sold!**

MIRA

Look us up on-line at: http://www.romance.net   MDM533

If you enjoyed this
suspenseful tale by bestselling author

LYNN ERICKSON

Don't miss the opportunity to pick up her previous
titles by MIRA® Books:

#66426	THE ELEVENTH HOUR	$5.99 U.S.☐	$6.99 CAN.☐
#66054	ASPEN	$4.99 U.S.☐	$5.50 CAN.☐
#66178	NIGHT WHISPERS	$5.99 U.S.☐	$6.99 CAN.☐

(limited quantities available)

TOTAL AMOUNT	$
POSTAGE & HANDLING	$
($1.00 for one book, 50¢ for each additional)	
APPLICABLE TAXES*	$ _____
TOTAL PAYABLE	$ _____
(check or money order—please do not send cash)	

To order, complete this form and send it, along with a check or money order for the
total above, payable to MIRA Books, to: **In the U.S.:** 3010 Walden Avenue, P.O. Box
9077, Buffalo, NY 14269-9077; **In Canada:** P.O. Box 636, Fort Erie, Ontario L2A 5X3.

Name: _____

Address: _____ City: _____

State/Prov.: _____ Zip/Postal Code: _____

*New York residents remit applicable sales taxes.
Canadian residents remit applicable GST and provincial taxes.

MIRA®

Look us up on-line at: http://www.mirabooks.com   MLEBL0499